Dry
Spells

Dry Spells

ARCHANA
MANIAR

LAKE UNION
PUBLISHING

Text copyright © 2024 by Archana Maniar
All rights reserved.

Published by Lake Union Publishing, Seattle

www.apub.com

Amazon, the Amazon logo, and Lake Union Publishing are trademarks of Amazon.com, Inc., or its affiliates.

ISBN-13: 9781662519512
eISBN: 9781662519505

Cover design by Liron Gilenberg
Cover image: © E.Hanazaki Photography © Hiraman © Darren Robb / Getty Images; © Brent McTavish / Arcangel; © 3DMI / Shutterstock

Printed in the United States of America

To Bakula and Harshad

Chapter 1

Los Angeles, April 2006

I always thought my fate was decided the day my father got kicked off the bus from Opera House to Breach Candy. As he tells the story, he was a dashing young bachelor back then, his mind swirling with the ideas and optimism of youth. He had fallen asleep on the bus shortly after boarding and missed his stop. When it was discovered that he hadn't paid the proper fare, the conductor tossed him out of the bus while it was still moving. Bombay in the summer of 1970, my father explained, was a different world. Still rousing himself awake as he dusted his clothes off, he noticed a long line of people congregating near the American Embassy. Curious, he decided to inquire. And that is how, five months later, he found himself in possession of an American visa. Three months after that, he stood shivering in the bitter cold at a Greyhound bus stop in New York City, a world away from home, on his way to some place called Buffalo. Such was the way of destiny, he said. One ill-timed doze can change your life.

I came along less than three years later. Born in Buffalo, I was raised in the suburban sprawl of Los Angeles, in the heart of "The Valley". The San Fernando Valley to be specific. My parents gave me the name Shyamala. Shyamala Mehta. Though it's pronounced exactly how it's spelled, my name has inspired angst even among the least tongue-tied of my fellow Americans. Whenever it is read aloud, I prepare myself to have it mispronounced several times and wait for an analysis of its origin. *Is that Indian or Pakistani or something? I'll never remember that name.* And though I have tried and tried, there is simply no good way to anglicize it.

So, when my co-worker Patrick Welch unexpectedly resigned his position at our office in Mumbai, I shouldn't have been surprised when someone came up with the idea of sending me in his place. That someone came in the form of my new boss Joe Westfall. As fresh-faced and fashion-forward as Joe was, he belonged to a different era, and not in a good way. How a guy like him could work his way up the ranks of corporate America in the twenty-first century was a mystery. Since his hiring, he'd initiated several conversations about topics of questionable relevance to my work—inquiring about my "country of origin", marveling at how I had no accent, and professing how much he enjoyed chicken *tikka masala*. Boss or not, I had little patience for him.

"Do you have a second, Shy?"

"I'd really prefer if you called me Shyam-ala," I reminded him from my desk.

"Sure, sure. Will do." Joe took the chair opposite mine. He stroked his chin as if he had a beard. I wondered if he could grow one yet.

"Anyway, you probably heard that Patrick Welch left us in a real lurch when he resigned?"

"I heard something of the sort."

"He was right in the middle of the software conversion so we need someone to fill his position asap." Joe placed special emphasis on the acronym, smiling a toothpaste-commercial smile. "*You* would be a perfect fit."

Our company, JTM, was a Los Angeles-based architectural firm with international ambitions. Over several years, it had expanded into Europe and East Asia and now was trying to penetrate the market in India. Patrick Welch was a software engineer who oversaw the company's transition to a new software system. He'd been continent-hopping under JTM for some time, and most recently had found himself in Mumbai. I was many years his junior and had trained with him, but so had others with far more experience than me.

"Oh?" I shuffled the papers on my desk, my brow furrowed at the suggestion. "A perfect fit? Why exactly?"

Joe seemed exasperated at having to state the obvious. "You *are* Indian, aren't you?"

My eyes widened. As the only Indian American in the office, I had often found myself thrust into the untenable position of resident expert on all things pertaining to the South Asian subcontinent and its billion and a half people. Contrary to Joe's impression, my heritage didn't make me any more suited to work and live there than he was.

"You're going to blend in a hell of a lot better than anyone else."

"Why doesn't it sound like I have a choice here, Joe?"

"You always have a choice. Only one choice means a fast-track future at JTM, however."

Move abroad? With JTM's expansion, it had always been a possibility. But I wasn't ready to move. And I definitely wasn't ready to move to Mumbai. Then again, I didn't want to find myself out of a job opportunity either. Something about Joe's demeanor suggested there would be repercussions to turning down the offer. Maybe there wouldn't be another chance at a promotion.

"How long is the assignment?"

"Six months, maybe a year?" Joe continued to smile his perfect smile as I glowered at him, my jaw slack.

"Shy, don't be mad. This wasn't my idea. Upper management asked me to put a name forward. I recognized an opportunity for *you*. You're good at what you do. And come on, you *are* Indian."

I stood up, signaling that the conversation was over. "It's Shyamala."

"That's what I like about you Shya-ma-la! You're not one to mince words! Listen, think about it and get back to me tomorrow." He winked at me before turning and walking out of my office, leaving my door wide open.

I shook my head. If there was anything redeeming about Joe, it was that he didn't take my insubordination personally.

I stood at my window and peered down at the street. Afternoon traffic was picking up but the flow was orderly. I closed my eyes and tried to remember Mumbai, the city formerly known as Bombay. I was thirteen when I last visited. While my friends were spending their summer break at sleepovers and pool parties, I was half a world away, in a place as familiar to me as the dark side of the moon. Twenty years later, I only had fragmented recollections of India—screeching car horns, incessant rain, rationed toilet paper. India lived on mostly as a vague sensation best described as discomfort. There was one thing that I recalled in vivid detail, however: in India the people were mostly small and the vermin were mostly big.

I thought of my little ranch house with its quaint front porch and freshly trimmed topiaries, its warmth welcoming on those foggy LA mornings. Los Angeles was home, I didn't want to leave, and I certainly didn't want to move to India. On the face of it, there was no good reason for me to go.

But then again, there was no good reason for me to stay either.

◆ ◆ ◆

4

That night, in desperate need of advice, I called my best friend Claire who insisted on stopping by after her shift in the hospital so she could get the lowdown face to face. Claire and I had been friends since we met in second grade. That was when my family had moved to a new neighborhood and I was forced to change schools. I was placed in Mrs. Alston's "English-as-a-second-language" class. It was a well-intentioned class, created to ease the transition of Spanish-speaking students into English-only lessons. There was one problem though. Despite the amber color of my skin, I didn't speak Spanish.

On the first day I sat perplexed, not understanding a single word that was being spoken. I knew there had been some mistake but was too shy to point it out. During recess, Claire asked if we could play handball together. As the only Chinese-American kid in the school, she must have seen a potential friend in the only Indian-American kid—must have sensed a sort of kinship of the other. We immediately hit it off. When I told her that I was in Mrs. Alston's ESL class, Claire was outraged. After recess, she walked up to Mrs. Alston and told her that I spoke English just like her. For kids like us, English was the language in which we teased each other when we hung out at pizza joints and ice-cream shops. It was the language in which our dreams of blue-eyed movie stars played out. It was the language in which our thoughts were forged. And though our parents spoke to us in our native tongues at home, when it came to expressing ourselves, English was the only language that we ever truly knew.

After dinner, I changed into old cut-off jean shorts and a T-shirt and waited on the front porch taking in the scent of orange blossoms in the air. Claire eased her car into a tight spot in front of my house and made her way toward me.

"Oh my God, that beer looks terrific!" She grabbed the bottle out of my hands, fell into a beaten-up Adirondack chair, popped off the cap and took a swig in one swift motion.

"Hi Claire, have a beer, will ya?" I laughed.

"So did you decide what you're going to do?" She peered at me as I took the other chair.

I shook my head. "I've got to give them an answer tomorrow though."

"You could think of it as a career opportunity?" she said, a bit too brightly. Claire had always been lousy at hiding ambivalence.

"Well, unfortunately, the alternative to this 'career opportunity' is a professional dead end, or worse. That's all I need. Without this job, what else do I have?"

Claire shot me a sympathetic look as she took another sip.

"But then I think about starting anew, working in India, where I barely speak the language and I think I'd be crazy to even consider it."

"It won't be LA, that's for sure."

"I could definitely use some time away from all the marriage talk, though. Mom brings up the ticking of my biological clock in every conversation. Like I somehow missed the fact that everyone around me is getting married and having children and I am still alone. Like I've forgotten that I planned to settle down and start a family. Oh and to top it all off, Dad actually wants to take out an ad for me in the matrimonial section of *India Abroad*. He even brought me a copy." I nodded to the newspaper which was open at the section in question.

Claire picked it up and read:

"'*Highly educated Gujarati boy seeks fair, beautiful, slim, never-married, family-oriented, US-born girl with East/West values,*'" she read. "These ads are from another century!"

I smiled. "Well, now there's an online version too."

"The girls are all 'fair and family oriented' and boys are all 'tall and well educated'. Why bother with the euphemisms? They might as well say 'light skinned and chaste' or 'taller than your daughter and not poor'." Claire snickered.

"The problem is that I am not fair, nor can I be described as 'family oriented'." Smirking, I took a swig from my bottle. "My parents are trying so hard to find someone for me. They don't hear me when I say that I'm not ready to put myself out there again, much less get married. I can't take it, Claire."

Claire was silent, listening intently.

I scanned the porch and the garden beyond. "I always imagined I'd live here with Neil. I haven't been myself since we broke up. I can't seem to move on."

"Listen Shyamala, it's going to take time. You'll get through this." She reached out and laid her hand over mine.

I nodded even as I wondered how, exactly. "I just feel adrift— like I'm just going where the current takes me. And now, I've got this huge decision to make and no time to think it over. I'd never considered leaving LA, much less moving to the other side of the world!"

Claire glanced pensively toward the fading sky. "It's a huge decision, I know. But you can't just sit here in your perfect little LA ranch house thinking about the past. I'll miss you, but maybe this is exactly what you need right now? Just imagine it—you have an opportunity to leave it all behind and go on the adventure of a lifetime."

I followed her gaze to the horizon. She was right. It wasn't really about the job—this was a chance to escape the past.

I glanced at her, grateful as ever to have her friendship.

Claire raised a brow and smiled. "Plus there are other potential benefits. Maybe you'll run into Hrithik Roshan! I never understood a word of those Hindi movies your mom used to watch but Hrithik is freakin' hot!"

I couldn't help but laugh. "You, Claire Chang, are hopeless!"

We chatted for the better part of three hours until finally Claire had to go. I walked her to her perfectly parallel-parked car.

As I walked back up the path to my little house, I glanced at my garden. The petals of my gardenias glowed a magical blue-white in the moonlight. From the angled edges of my boxwood hedges to the aroma of the roses that floated about the garden, everything was as it should have been.

No, not quite. Neil was gone.

And all of it was weighted with memories of him.

There is an amorphous place between sleep and waking where the dream world lingers as if it is reality. A transient place—at the moment of its acknowledgment, it evaporates, leaving the real world in its stead. Morning after morning, month after month, I had found myself holding on to that place, relishing the comfort that resided there. For those fleeting moments, I experienced the contentment of the life I once led.

Neil and I had met through mutual college friends. Usually cautious with my first impressions, I fell for him during our very first conversation and I fell for him more with each date. He was outgoing and funny and didn't accept the excuse that I couldn't go out with friends late in the evening because I was already in my PJs. He wasn't particularly serious or observant, but he added a dash of irreverence to my somewhat regimented life and I reveled in his spontaneity. My parents, for their part, were over the moon when they met him. He checked all the required compatibility boxes. His family hailed from the state of Gujarat in India just like ours did. They practiced the Jain religion like we did. And I didn't let his good Indian boy qualifications get in the way of our relationship, as I had done before. We were together for six months before he proposed in front of all his friends. Our engagement was spent imagining how we were going to create the perfect life together.

The night before our wedding was the *garba raas* celebration, when family and friends gather for what is traditionally an evening of raucous celebration and folk dancing—imagine four hundred people packed into a community center, North Indian songs blaring through the speaker system, women clad in ornate half saris with heavily pleated skirts twirling about in harmony to the music while the men in their elaborate *kurta* suits perform a much wilder, uproarious version of the dance steps. *That* was the night Neil chose to leave me.

Dancing in the innermost circle, at first I didn't even notice that Neil's arrival was delayed. A half hour after he was supposed to arrive, there was no sign of him. I didn't give it much thought. He was coming with his parents and they often ran late, in what was affectionately known among many South Asians as IST, Indian Standard Time.

Finally, one hour into the *garba raas*, I began to worry. Something was wrong. This was no ordinary event; this was a celebration of our union. *Where was he?*

I was suddenly stricken by the fear that he had been injured in a car accident. Over and over again I called him on my cell with no answer. Then, to my relief, his parents entered the hall. I sought out Neil's familiar form nearby, but he was nowhere to be found. His parents regarded me with an expression I will never forget—a mixture of pity and regret. He wasn't hurt, they told me. He just wasn't coming. In an instant, my relief ebbed like a wave receding, leaving me to gaze at the truth that had always been etched in the sands below. It was a truth I should have seen before. *He never loved me.*

Word of my humiliation filtered through the crowd. One by one, as the guests found out, they shook their heads and glanced toward me. I withered with each sympathetic stare. My parents cradled me between them and nudged me gently out of the hall and into Claire's car. That night, she sat with me as I cried myself to sleep.

I was with Neil when a warm shaft of sunlight struck my face early the next morning. Then, the dream world lifted and the freight train carrying nearly three decades' worth of my hopes for the future crashed before me with unimaginable momentum.

Since that first morning, three years ago, I dreaded those first few moments after awakening. I still had not finished picking up the pieces.

Claire was right—maybe it was time to try and leave it all behind.

Chapter 2

Los Angeles, May 2006

The day before I left for India was one of the most picturesque days of the season in my hilly enclave not far from Los Angeles. I ate a quiet dinner on my patio amid the sycamore trees and gardenias, thinking about my upcoming move to Mumbai.

When I had told my mother about my decision to take the job, she had warned me that Mumbai was struck by drought. She immediately rang her sister Vini to check how the city was faring. Before long, my mother and Aunt Vini were urging me to stay with her in Mumbai. I tried to convince them that I'd be just fine in the JTM corporate apartment but neither woman would have it. Finally, I relented, hoping to avoid any further discord with my mother before my trip. And just like that, I wound up committing to living with my aunt whom I had seen just a handful of times in the past twenty years.

Having spent days trying to figure out what to pack, I wound up laying out the bare essentials—work clothes, old *kurta* tops, toiletries, sandals, and running shoes just in case I was able to find a good place to jog. After dinner, I went to my room and tossed everything into two suitcases. In my carry-on, I packed an oversized sweatshirt, a toothbrush, my iPod, and a weathered old copy of *The Good Earth* that I borrowed from my father's bookshelf so I had something to read on the journey. I would have to find whatever else I needed in India.

On the morning of my departure, fog had inched in from the ocean like a giant serpent, sending tentacles over hills and reaching feelers into the valley floor below. The moon was obscured and the stars invisible behind the thick shroud of clouds. Lower-lying mists reflected the light from the streetlamps and bathed the street in an eerie orange glow. A pre-dawn silence imbued my street. Weary after a night of poor sleep, I slunk about my house reluctant to shatter the stillness. After a quick shower, I threw on some jeans and a T-shirt, and braided my long, unruly black hair into a practical, plane-friendly plait.

It was still dark when my father knocked at the front door. As he loaded up the suitcases, I turned off the lights and locked the door, giving the knob one last reverent jiggle. I walked down the footpath toward my parents' sedan, grateful that my father would keep an eye on the house while I was gone.

"Morning Mom," I said as I let myself into the back seat.

"Good morning *beta*. So today is the big day, *na*?"

"Yep." I tried to still the edge of anxiety in my voice.

It had been well over a decade since I had lived with my parents. Even so, like wagon wheels stuck in deep ruts, we fell into age-old patterns when we were together. When it came to traveling in the car, Dad always drove, Mom always took the passenger seat, and I always sat in the middle of the back seat with my legs perched upon that annoying central bump that divides the floor of the car in two. From that vantage point, I felt like I could read exactly what my mother was thinking.

We were two clocks, never set for the same time. Always out of synchrony. I never understood why. Perhaps it was because Mom was always worried. When I was little, on warm spring days when Californian mothers dressed their children in shorts and T-shirts, my mother put me in a long-sleeved shirt, a puffy black vest, and polyester pants. Even though we lived on the wrong coast, she seemed to live in constant fear that I would encounter a nor'easter. When I played soccer, Mom was convinced I would get a concussion from hitting the ball with my head. When I took gymnastics, she was worried I would fall off the balance beam in a way that might compromise my ability to reproduce. When I ate too much ice, she was certain I would catch a cold and end up with pneumonia. When Neil asked me to marry him, she suggested a longer engagement just to be certain. And when I didn't want to take him back, she was sure I had made a grave mistake. Now, she lived in perpetual fear that I would live the rest of my life alone. Perhaps finally, she and I feared the same thing.

As if on cue, my mother cleared her throat. "Shyamala, I have something I want to say. Your father and I have been worried."

Oh no, I thought. *Not again. Not now.*

"Mom, if this is about my being single and over thirty, I'm aware on both accounts." I took a deep breath.

"Shyamala, listen to your mother for a second," my father said, eyeing me in the rear-view mirror. He was usually astute enough to avoid interfering in an argument between mother and daughter. This had to be serious.

"Yes, Shyamala, it is about the fact that you are single and thirty-*three*. Time is passing. Getting married and having children—that is what you have wanted all along. My only wish is for you to have what you have always wanted."

Why was my mother always trying to tell me what it was I wanted? How could she even know? We grew up a generation and a world apart. I slowed my breath further, trying to calm down.

"I know you kids wait longer here in America but how many marriageable boys will remain when you are thirty-five or thirty-seven or for-ty?" My mother's Indian accent grew more noticeable. With her sharply enunciated 't's, she placed increased emphasis on each increasing number.

"Mom, I'm moving out of the country. Maybe we can have this discussion when I get back?"

"I want to ask Vini to introduce you to some boys while you are in India," she said with finality.

"Are you serious? Wait, I have an idea. Maybe I'll just get married and settle down there? Or better yet, maybe I'll be some guy's ticket to get into the United States?" My throat clenched around the words. Why wasn't she listening to me? As much as I didn't wish to be alone, as much as I had wanted to settle down, I just wasn't ready to put myself out there yet. I was an American, how would I ever relate to a guy from India, much less make an entire life with one? To suggest it was ridiculous! It felt as though my mother was asphyxiating me with her good intentions.

"Shyamala, we know that the past few years have been difficult—since you broke off the engagement with that boy," my father interjected.

"*I* didn't break off the engagement. He left me at the altar. *He* rejected me. Remember?"

"But that was years ago now," my mother said. "Put it in the past. You have to move on. At your age, your father and I had been married for eight years and already had a child. It has not been perfect, but we have lived a good life. The problem with you kids is you want everything to be just so. But you can't have it all. It is time to grow up." If there was sympathy in her voice, I couldn't hear it.

I stared at her, my eyes stinging as I tried to contain the hurt. How could she not know that the wounds that Neil left had scarcely scabbed over? And today of all days, she had chosen to pluck at the tender edges.

"Seriously Mom, does it really make sense to compare our lives? I'm happy for you. Taking care of Dad, being a homemaker. But you moved half a world away—to this country that is rife with possibility—and you've lived exactly the same life you would have led in India." I reveled in the harshness of the words as they left my mouth. "That may be how you define fulfillment, but it is not the life I want!"

My mother stiffened.

"*Hai, hai.* Shyamala, *chup*! How dare you speak to your mother this way!" Reflected in the rear-view mirror, Dad's eyes seared through me.

Instantly, I realized I had said too much. As quickly as the anger had overrun me, it shattered and reconstituted itself as deep regret.

The car hummed along on the freeway as my mother gathered herself. When she finally spoke, the hurt she felt was unmistakable. She turned to my father. "It is okay, Dev. She is just telling the truth—the truth of how she sees me, of how she sees my life."

From the backseat, I watched her expression settle. The truth that I had spoken was taking root in her mind and from it was sprouting a deeper realization. I scavenged my brain trying to think of ways in which I could take back what I had said. By the time we pulled into the departure area of LAX, it felt as though we might have driven the full distance to India.

I had thought that my parents might offer to walk me to the gate. Instead, my father pulled into the passenger-unloading zone. We gathered my belongings and stood near the trunk.

"She just wants you to be happy," said my father in his half-pleading, half-reasonable voice. I had never doubted that she wanted me to be happy. I loved her for it. Problem was, we just seemed to have such different ideas about what it took to get there.

My mother got out of the car and gave me a quick farewell embrace. It was an obligatory hug and more than I deserved.

"Mom—"

"It's okay Shyamala. You have a safe trip."

"I didn't mean—"

"You were just speaking what was in your heart." She turned away from me and sat down in the car, closing her door with a brisk thud. My father gave me a squeeze, walked to the driver's side, and paused before getting in. He looked at me one last time, making sure that I saw the disappointment written on his face. My heart sank as I watched their Oldsmobile pull away.

A dull ache lingered in my chest as I watched the terminal fill with little gray-haired women in saris wearing socks under sandals, mothers with stylish tunics chasing after small children, business-people preoccupied with their laptops, and twenty-somethings on a pilgrimage to a land that was not their own.

The first several hours on the plane were a blur. I napped on and off. In the seat beside me was a woman in her thirties. My father would have smugly picked her out as another ABCD like me. ABCD, or American-Born Confused *Desi* was a term of endearment and derision in equal parts, used by Indian parents to describe their American-born, identity-torn progeny. *Desi*, meaning from the homeland, was the word Indians used to describe themselves and each other.

I rubbed my cheek, suddenly conscious of the crease where my face had pressed against the edge of the seat. Not only was her face creaseless, she was flawless from head to toe. Her hair seemed untouched; each silky black lock was in its place. Her eyebrows were perfectly symmetric, thick and youthful, each remaining hair in line as if fearful of being plucked. Her designer outfit was complemented by matching heels. I had known many ABCDs like her, prayed beside them at temple and taken classes with them in college. On Monday afternoons they were prima ballerinas and on Wednesday evenings they were Olympic gymnasts. In middle school, they sailed to popularity wearing the trendiest outfits. Their first cars were brand-new luxury sedans. When they went off to college, they partied hard and so long as they maintained their grades, their parents didn't ask any questions. Girls like them had been granted everything an expatriate parent could offer. My father might have called them ABCDs, but to me, they never seemed particularly confused or *desi*.

American-Born Confused *Desi* or not, our suburban American lives must have seemed unrecognizable to our parents. Many of our fathers shared tales about leaving India with little more than a one-way ticket to the US and a semester's worth of college tuition. Many of our mothers had left everyone they loved to create lives in a foreign land with men they had known for mere weeks. Our parents were children of India, raised in tiny two-roomed apartments with families of nine or ten people and accustomed to hauling water up flights of stairs every morning for lack of plumbing. One short generation later, we lived with our small nuclear families in four-bedroom, two-and-a-half-bathroom tract homes and had never left anyone behind.

When I returned to my seat, I tried to watch an in-flight movie but found it dull. I listened to music on my iPod but grew weary of that after a while. Finally, I pulled the book I had borrowed from my father out of my backpack. *The Good Earth* had a plain green cover with a gold-gilded typeface that had faded over the years. The pages had a sweet, musty smell with hints of cardamom and cumin

17

that reminded me of India. As I thumbed through the weathered pages, I happened across paragraphs that someone had underlined and annotated. The handwriting had flourishes that were different from my father's script. I tilted the book to get a better look and a photograph fell out. On the back were inscribed the words, "Shyamala age 3 months". I turned it over. Creased at the corners and discolored, it was an image of my mother and me that I'd never seen before. Wearing a tiny red tunic top, I was propped up on a park bench surrounded by evergreens. The yellow and green baby blanket that my mother had crocheted for me was tucked into the crook of my arm. I smiled in the direction of the photographer in that vague way that babies do, my hair caught up in a breeze.

My mother stood behind me. She wore a form-fitting purple sari. The breeze had undone strands of her straight black hair which framed her lovely face. But something about the photo was not right. There was a hollowness about my mother—as if her thoughts were elsewhere and she did not share in my infant's delight at minute discoveries the way a mother might be expected to. She seemed alienated from the moment, disconnected.

As a teen, I was obsessed with old photographs. The black and white ones taken before my parents moved to the States, the ones taken before my birth, captured my imagination. I wanted to understand the history that came before me, to feel connected to a collective past. My obsession probably grew because my mother rarely spoke of her life in India. Sure, she mentioned her mother and father and she spoke fondly of her sister. I hung on to every word of those stories, but I craved to hear more. I wanted to hear stories about her dreams and disappointments, aspirations, and heartbreaks. Perhaps knowing about her past, with all its imperfections, would make my own failures seem less insurmountable.

For his part, my father was more than happy to tell stories of the past. My mother sat and listened and though her eyes mirrored my father's emotions, she never added anything to the stories. I always wondered why.

I put the photo back into the book and sighed. I studied the projection of our route on the seatback monitor. Our plane still hovered over the same nondescript section of the map as two hours before. The inches that separated North America from Asia on the screen seemed like an unbridgeable divide.

Chapter 3

Bombay, 1951

Pramila rushed down the stoop of her apartment building into a crowd of family and friends gathered for a wedding procession. She had picked her finest dress that morning. It was pale pink and hung loosely from her thin frame, the hem of the skirt ending at her bruised and knobby knees. She wore sandals that permanently bore the imprints of her older sister's feet. Woven into her two braids were two matching pale-pink ribbons.

Now in the thick of the crowd, Pramila peered between saris of green, gold, and magenta as they fluttered unpredictably in the January breeze. Voices echoed from a short distance ahead. She craned her body to see where they were coming from. Petite in stature, even for a six-year-old, she could see nothing. She pushed her way forward through the throng, finally emerging from it and into the warm sunlight.

She twirled her braid as she considered the scene. A group of unfamiliar women had blocked the gate of the apartment grounds and would not let the wedding procession pass. Her uncles, one of whom was the father of the groom, approached the women and an argument erupted. Standing with their hands on their hips, the women were unlike any Pramila had seen before. Their saris draped distinctively over their broad shoulders. Their eyes peered out from under heavy brows and their jaws closed sternly in determination in the same way her father's did. Pramila counted six women in total, though one woman did the talking. She wore a sari the color of turmeric. When she spoke to the men, she looked squarely into their eyes. Her tone was deep and demanding. Pramila had never seen a woman address a man in such a way. One of her uncles called them *hijra*.

Pramila grasped for her mother's hand, only to realize that her mother stood far behind. She began to worry. Why had these women blocked the exit? What did they want? She tried to fight the fear growing within her.

Despite the fluttering within her chest, Pramila watched, mesmerized. The woman in the turmeric-colored sari seemed to be demanding something but the men in the groom's family seemed to be withholding it. The women of the clan clapped their hands together as their leader began swaying. With exaggerated arm and hip movements, she began to dance in a manner the girl had only seen in pictures at the cinema. Near the gate, the others followed suit. The men retreated for a moment and discussed the situation. Then, the groom's father pulled a thick stack of rupees from his pocket, stepped forward and, to the delight of her friends, placed it into the hands of the woman. Pramila resented the exchange, wondering exactly how many Cadbury chocolates she could buy with such a sum.

The woman tucked the stack of money into the blouse of her sari. She walked toward the crowd. Her eyes settled upon the little girl with the pale-pink dress. As she approached, the woman smiled an unequivocally feminine smile. Pramila could see her eyes close-up now—liquid black and shimmering like the Arabian Sea on a crescent moon night. The woman came nearer and, putting her face close to Pramila's, whispered in a voice so faint it was nearly swallowed by the wind,

There are many, my child, who believe that fate befalls us regardless of how we choose to act. But long ago, a guru born in these lands taught that fate befalls us <u>unless</u> we choose to act.

The woman beamed at the girl and, as if turning word into action, slowly spun her robust frame in a full circle, her petticoat swirling gracefully beneath her. Then she gestured to her compatriots by the gate who promptly stood at attention. They did not let the party pass until they had received a second, thick stack of rupees.

For days Pramila thought about the remarkable woman and the words she had uttered. Eventually, though, they were lost to her memory like so many days walking to school along the ocean wall at Marine Lines and the sense of contentment she felt when her tiny hand was enveloped in the warmth of her father's.

But then, one day, she remembered.

Chapter 4

In transit, May 2006

After an excruciatingly long layover in Hong Kong, night followed us en route to India. It remained firmly entrenched when the plane lurched into what, I prayed, was its final descent. Once the landing gear hit the tarmac and the plane shuddered to a stop, I sighed. My journey had finally ended.

The instant the airplane doors opened, the cool air of the cabin dissolved. It was replaced by air that was so thick that it sank like molasses into the lungs. I gasped, only to be overcome by an odor so noxious that I could practically taste it. Even though decades had passed since I had last smelled it, I recognized the scent immediately. It was Mumbai. Mumbai, a tiny curve of the world in which the weight of humanity presses down lopsidedly, a city where open sewers coexist with towering skyscrapers, a city in which the aspirations and failures of innumerable citizens can be measured in sheer sweat, a city reclaimed from the ocean constantly fighting the elements that wish to draw it back into the sea.

Emerging from customs, I rolled my suitcase into the waiting area swarming with a mass of people. Among them were taxi and rickshaw drivers and men offering to haul luggage for a fee. The crowd pushed and shoved, partly seeking business, but I suspected, mostly out of habit. I searched for a familiar face in the sea of unknown brown faces. What happened if Vini aunty forgot to pick me up? How would I find my way in this strange, chaotic, and immense city? It took me a while to realize that an unmistakably familiar voice was calling my name. I turned to it and smiled.

Even though she was several years older than my mother, Vini appeared the younger sister. Her long black hair was peppered with silver strands that twisted through her single, thick braid. Thought marks traversed the span of her forehead and gave her a stately appearance, but in phone calls and on her rare visits to the States, she was always joyful and light. And though the miles between our worlds had kept us from being close, I was fond of her. We embraced in that sideways manner characteristic of Indian aunties and uncles. It was full of sincerity but with some discernible awkwardness that I imagined must have originated from an unresolved Victorian sensibility common to that generation. Breast contact was implicitly forbidden.

"*Tu kem che beta?* How are you, my dear? I hope they did not give you trouble in customs." Her accent had the fine definition of Oxford English but with a distinct Indian lilt. She gently pulled my backpack off my shoulder and placed it over her own.

"Hi Aunty. No trouble in customs." I could feel my anxiety melting away in her presence.

"Glad you had no headaches. My God, I am seeing you here in India after such a long time. How long has it been?"

"Twenty years."

"That many? Last time you came, I was not sure you would return!"

"Me neither, Aunty." I laughed.

"What is this aunty business? 'Aunty' is such a generic term. We are in India, you must call me Maasi, isn't it? I am your mother's sister. You know this saying, '*mummy nai tau maasi*'? If not a mother, a mother's sister is the next best thing, no? I am so happy you have come!"

"Thanks, Maasi." She slung her arm over my shoulder. Her touch was comfortable and welcoming.

We pulled out of Shivaji International Airport in Vini maasi's old black Ambassador. The car had to be at least thirty years old and moved with the heavy confidence of a long-past era. Since it did not have air conditioning, my aunt drove with the windows open. The sight of her behind the steering wheel was one to behold. Her braided hair came undone in the wind. Her silver strands shone in the moonlight lending her an otherworldly appearance. In my jet-lagged, travel-weary haze, the whole picture seemed like a hallucination. I might as well have been riding in an old Ambassador through the streets of Mumbai next to one of those sword-wielding, demon- destroying Indian goddesses. She was the walking antithesis of my mother.

As we traveled through Mumbai, I felt distinctly like those times that I had gotten off the elevator on the wrong floor in my office building. At first, the place felt familiar. But then I would notice that the furniture was arranged differently. The paint was a different shade of yellow. Eventually, I would realize I wasn't in the right place. In Mumbai, the landmarks of a modern urban landscape were all present—tall buildings, cars of many makes, and enormous billboards (including one marketing condoms that said rather brazenly "Surprise her every night"). But the differences came in the subtleties: the weather-worn appearance of the apartment complexes, the three-wheeled rickshaws parked on the streets each with drivers slumbering inside, and the open trenches on either side of the road that carried the city's waste. In parts of Mumbai as many as a million people lived in one square mile, and as we drove, I wondered about the lives that played out behind upstairs apartment windows, locked storefronts, and inside taxi-cabs. My mother's gaze, as a girl and then a woman, must have settled upon these same sights. To her this was home.

Another twinge of guilt struck me as I thought about my mother. In one fell swoop, I had rejected the life she had built and accused her of living the same traditional life in the US as she might have had in India. But the truth was it never bothered me that she had chosen to be a stay-at-home mom. During my school days, she volunteered at the library, bringing back volume after volume that she read voraciously. Once I had gone off to college, she had filled her time working for any number of charities. Her days seemed full and varied, and her observations and opinions informed. Through it all, she had been there for every one of my childhood milestones. And though I had always wished to work full-time, I never thought less of her for choosing not to. No, I wasn't rejecting her life as a traditional Indian mother; I had lashed out at her because she had struck a nerve.

She was right, I didn't want to be alone. Loneliness pervaded every moment of my day. But the thought of having my parents set me up with someone "compatible" made me uneasy. I couldn't settle for an arranged marriage. Having felt it once before, I wanted to experience the undeniable force that draws two people together. Maybe she was right: maybe I was a child of the American appetite. Good enough simply was not good enough.

The Ambassador glided smoothly through the sultry Mumbai night. Beyond the road and the beach was a stretch of blackness that must have been the Arabian Sea. Maasi pointed out a few sights, visible in silhouette. Haji Ali Dargah, the mosque that sat within the sea during high tide, and Mahalakshmi, a Hindu temple constructed in homage to the Goddess Lakshmi for allowing construction of a causeway to connect two of Mumbai's seven islands back in the early nineteenth century.

We drove near the sea for a while before entering a tree-lined area with modest, rolling hills. In the early morning light, I could see tall apartment buildings interspersed between glamorous old mansions. I wondered what these mansions must have looked like during the British Empire, before years of moisture and heat had taken their toll. I imagined English gardens and afternoon tea under the shade of overgrown mango trees. Their discolored exteriors bore the patina of the many layers of civilization that had inhabited this place. As we drove by, even in the pre-dawn light I found splendor in their resilience.

Finally, my aunt turned the Ambassador into her apartment complex. A thin man in his early fifties lay asleep on the front steps. On hearing the car, he awoke and greeted us. Before I could suggest that I would carry my own suitcase, he had hoisted it atop his head. By the time Maasi and I had shuffled up the three flights of stairs to get to her apartment, he had the first suitcase lying at the entrance. He smiled shyly, his teeth permanently stained red from chewing betel nuts, as he skipped down the stairs. I glanced at him, uneasy in the realization that he was likely Vini's servant.

As Vini maasi ushered me in and I took in the sights of the main room, I realized that the inside of her apartment had hardly changed. Every wall of the flat that did not have a window on it was covered by old wooden shelves and each shelf was crammed with books. During my last visit, I had rummaged through the collection and found a copy of *Alice in Wonderland* amid poetry collections of Rabindranath Tagore, Edith Wharton's *The Age of Innocence* and John Locke's *The Rights of Man*. There were a great many more titles in Hindi and Gujarati. A small television was jammed in among the books. In the center of this fort of words was a thinly cushioned sofa. The air had the aroma of sandalwood incense and cumin.

"Do you remember my place? I can still picture you sleeping on the sofa with—which book were you reading?"

"It was *Alice in Wonderland.*"

"You must have felt as lost then as Alice when she fell down the rabbit hole. You were most out of your element last visit. Well, I want you to be comfortable this visit, isn't it?" She walked toward a short hallway and opened the door to the right. "You will be staying in this room."

I peeked inside and saw the telltale green metal cabinet. During my last stay, I had spied my aunt stashing her change purse, embroidered silk saris, and a pair of stunning paisley-shaped emerald earrings in that *cabat*, as she called it. Whenever she had stashed her valuables inside, she carefully locked the cabinet with an old brass key and tucked it into the waistband of her sari petticoat. Back then I had wondered what other treasures lay beyond the locked double doors. Now, I considered the fact that one typically doesn't store treasures in guest rooms.

"Um, Maasi, isn't this your room?"

I had a sinking feeling about what was to come. I braced myself for the single most exhausting aspect of an Indian welcome: *agraha,* a form of insistence that relies on wearing your guest down until they acquiesce to your hospitality.

"What? How do you know? You haven't been to my house for twenty years!"

Strategy one for Indians when offering a boon to someone who might refuse out of courtesy: obfuscation.

"Maasi, I know that this is your room. You sleep here. I'll sleep in the guest room."

"No, no, you sleep here. The air conditioning is here only. You will be more comfortable here," she insisted.

Strategy two for Indians when offering a boon to someone: emphasize practicality.

28

"Maasi, I'm not going to sleep in your room." I mustered as much authority as I could.

"*Arré* Shyamala, you have come from so far. How am I going to tell your mother that I made you sleep in my crowded guest room? She will never send you back to visit me again. Nobody who visits me ever sleeps in there."

Strategy three: guilt trip.

"Vini maasi, I'm not going to let you give up your room for six months."

She switched to Gujarati, a language that lends itself to insistence far more effectively than English. "*Chaal ne, tarre a room maaj re vanu che.* Come now, you are going to stay in this room no matter what."

Strategy four: do not give the appearance of choice.

Exhaustion overpowering me, I was far too tired to argue anymore. "I'll stay tonight. But starting tomorrow, I'm staying in the guest room."

"*Kal ni vath kale.* Tomorrow we will talk about tomorrow."

"Okay Maasi. But, before I do anything else, I would love a shower."

"*Hai, hai!* Oh my goodness! Water supply is very low this year. In the morning, it starts at six but it runs for two to three hours. In the night, it runs from five for another two hours only. If you wish to take a shower you will have to wait until then, *beta.* I have some buckets in the bathroom, if you'd like to take a bath."

I took my bath out of two buckets that night, distressed that I could turn the faucet and find it had run dry even here, the swanky part of Mumbai. In California, a place that was perpetually drought-stricken, rationing meant not watering the lawn on certain days; drought or no drought, the water always flowed.

When I emerged from the bathroom, Vini was sitting at the table, sorting papers.

"I thought your mother was going to join you in Bombay while you were visiting. It would have been fun, no?" Maasi peered at me.

"Did she plan to come to India with me?" Honestly, I had no idea what my mother was planning.

"She mentioned it on the phone shortly after you took the position here. She thought it might be an opportunity to spend time with you."

"Well, that would have been nice." Perhaps she thought better of the idea given the constant tension between us.

Maasi smiled knowingly as my cheeks flushed. It was painfully clear that my mother and I weren't getting along.

"Well, she knows you will be busy with work. And she is quite busy these days too, no? Is she still working with that place that helps the people without homes?"

"You mean the volunteer gig at the homeless shelter? Yeah, I think she still does that. She has been helping out more at temple as well."

My aunt squinted, trying to read me.

"How about your papa? Is he still telling his stories? As he gets older, they seem to get more imaginative. Isn't it?"

"I think the word you are looking for is 'embellished'. Or maybe 'preposterous'?"

Maasi chuckled.

"The first time I met him, he told me a crazy story about how he had almost agreed to marry some girl who lived in Borivali. But then, one night, a vision of a girl dressed in a red wedding sari with a veil covering her lovely face came to him. Only days later, he met your mother. He was convinced that she was the girl in his vision. At the time, I was thinking that he was some hopeless romantic. Then for a while I thought he was just trying to make your mother laugh. Now I realize that it is actually a bit of both, no?"

It was true, my father was a hopeless romantic. And he always tried to make my mother laugh. I nodded. A yawn escaped my lips.

"Shyamala *beta*, I can talk all night. But you should get some sleep."

She led me to her room. She paused to make sure I was settled before closing the door behind her. My head sank luxuriously into her pillow as my exhausted body dissolved into the mattress. *What a delight to be horizontal*, I thought, before drifting off to sleep.

Chapter 5

Mumbai, May 2006

The next morning, I awoke to knocking. Startled and disoriented, I rose abruptly and answered the door. It was the milkman come to make his delivery. I had scarcely made it back to the bed when the vegetable seller came knocking. Before she left, the man who had carried my luggage up the stairs earlier that morning appeared at the threshold. Maasi, emerging from the bathroom, freshly showered and apologetic for all the morning activity, introduced the man as Rajesh. He had stopped by to give her updates on the repairs required for the Ambassador. They went downstairs to look at the car. Surrounded by such industriousness, I abandoned any notions of going back to bed.

I wandered into the tiny kitchen and found a girl washing dishes. She couldn't have been older than fifteen. Although she was as thin as a waif, when she turned to me there was a certain gravity about her. On her nose, she wore one diminutive diamond stone that shone exquisitely against her skin. She wore a clean but faded tunic set. From my prior trip to Mumbai, I knew that many residents had school-age servants. Still, I was more than a little dismayed to see one in Vini's kitchen.

"Hallo," she said nervously. If not for the fact that I had blocked the exit, she might have tried to slip out of the kitchen.

"I am Shyamala, what's your name?"

The child said nothing.

Maybe she doesn't speak English, I thought. I didn't speak enough Hindi, Marathi, or Gujarati to scrape a sentence together. We smiled at each other uncomfortably instead.

Suddenly, she pointed to the bathroom and rushed off, closing the door behind her. Moments later, I heard the sounds of laundry being done: the drip-drip of small quantities of water, the thwack-thwack of clothes being beaten with a wooden paddle, a bucket scraping the floor, then a return of the dripping as water washed away the soap. Against this soundscape I made my way into my aunt's room in search of my belongings.

My luggage had been stowed neatly in the corner near my aunt's *cabat*. After peering out into the living room to reassure myself that there would be no witnesses, I dragged my bags into the guest room, spied a mostly empty dresser with enough space for my clothes, queued my iPod and began unpacking.

I was putting the last of my work clothes away when the girl came out of the bathroom. She stood at the door wiping her wet hands against her tunic.

I pulled out the earbuds. "Yes?"

The girl pointed at the stack of dirty clothes that I had from my trip. "*Main dhone ke liye aapke kapde le ja sakti hun?*"

"Sorry, I don't understand." I shrugged. "Are you saying you want to wash these?"

She pointed at the bathroom where she had been washing the clothes.

"No. No, that's okay. I'll wash them." I waved at the clothes as if somehow that would clarify matters. I never handwashed my clothes but there was absolutely no way I would let her wash them for me.

"*Thik hai.*" She seemed disappointed.

I was certain that I had insulted her by refusing to hand over my dirty clothes. On the other hand, neither my 8,000-mile journey to the opposite side of the Earth, nor my tepid bath out of a plastic bucket, made me feel quite so far from home as did the fact that a girl who should have been in school had offered to do my laundry for me.

She started back toward the bathroom.

It bothered me that I didn't know her name.

In the living room, local news was blaring from the little TV.

"The water situation in Mumbai is dire, states head of Brihanmumbai's Municipal Corporation," the female anchor announced with an Anglo-Indian accent.

"Yes, in fact, Lake Tulsi, one of the most famous lakes in the Mumbai area, which supplies a significant portion of the city's water supply, has nearly run dry," continued her male counterpart.

Images of a parched lake appeared on the TV screen. I didn't understand the specifics of Mumbai's auxiliary water sources, but the vision of the low water line and the cracked earth of the lake bed, combined with the limited supplies in Vini's building, alarmed me.

The camera panned back to the anchors.

"Water prices are rising rapidly and supplies are being supplemented by tankers. The situation in the slums is—"

"Even our complex has had to bring in tankers," Vini said as she approached.

Lost in my own world, I nearly jumped out of my seat.

"Sorry *beta*, didn't mean to frighten you! Just got back from the market. Did you meet Shalu?"

"Yes." I made a note of her name. "She's doing the laundry."

Maasi studied my reaction—was she uneasy about having such a young maid? "Did you give her your clothes to wash?"

"Um, no. I'll just take care of them." I wanted to say more. I wanted to say that I resented the idea of a child having to work when she should be at school. But I was a visitor in Vini's house, in Vini's country, and I didn't know if I had the right.

"Well, whenever you tire of washing your clothes, give them to Shalu. For now, let us finish making lunch."

Maasi and I sat at her tiny table to enjoy the spread. As I scooped my first bite of spiced green beans with *roti* smothered with *ghee* and moistened with her rich lentil soup, I told her that I had moved into the guest room. She tried to argue. Too late, everything has been unpacked, I told her. Score a small one for the American, I added. She laughed. After relishing the savory, I sampled the unnaturally orange mangoes that are touted as the delight of the season. The juice of the fruit ran down my arm as I sucked the nectar from the pit. I had tasted many types of mangoes before—Mexican mangoes and Philippine mangoes and Hawaiian mangoes. Hadens and Pikos and Kents. None could match the flavor and sweetness of the Indian Alphonso. I nodded to myself. The mango was meant to be an Indian fruit. The Almighty must have personally seen to that.

◆　◆　◆

I had exactly three days off to settle in Mumbai before starting my new position. Three days to adjust to the twelve-and-a-half-hour time change. I emailed my parents and Claire about my safe arrival and took naps, many naps.

Vini suggested, on several occasions, that I explore the neighborhood to get my bearings. But even though I was way overdue for a run, I found the prospect of leaving the flat beyond daunting.

I had heard tales about the treacherous Mumbai traffic and of foreigners being mugged. There was no way to blend in either—any self-respecting Indian could instantly pick me out as an American. I thought back to my last visit to Mumbai twenty years ago, when I happened across a monkey in a local garden. Not a usual occurrence in LA, so naturally I took a photograph of it. Immediately, a pan-handler, who happened to be the monkey's owner, jumped out of the bushes and demanded payment. I gave her the only dollar bill I had in my pocket. Disgusted, she threw it back at me. *Not enough money.* She and the monkey chased me across the gardens until I reached my mother who finally shooed her away. No, I thought, I didn't need an altercation over a monkey or anything else. Better to stay put until I absolutely had to go out into the city. Truth was, even back in LA, I'd become a homebody of sorts—opting for PJs and a movie alone over dinner and an evening with friends.

But Vini wasn't satisfied having me holed up in the flat. Late one afternoon, she announced, "We've had an invitation from Attaji, you know, the gentleman I told you about who lives on the fourth floor? He wants us to stop by for *chai*. I want you to meet him—you'll love him."

Despite my jet lag, I agreed to go. It seemed like a low-risk outing and it would be nice to get to know the residents in Maasi's building. My neighbors in LA were mostly career-minded professionals who never seemed to have the time for more than a passing hello, so the invite was a welcome change.

As we climbed the steps to the fourth floor, our footsteps echoed in unison. That is how it had been with my aunt. In step. It was a world apart from my experience with my own mother—we couldn't even agree on the same direction, much less the same rhythm. Maybe it was easier to live with people you didn't know well. Vini always said what she thought. With her there was no minefield of shared history to navigate through. I felt no pressure to live up to someone else's version of the perfect life. I could breathe.

Vini maasi rang the doorbell. There was some shuffling behind the door and then it squeaked open.

"Ahh, welcome, welcome Shyamala. Come, come. I am so happy you and Viniben could join for *chai.*"

A handsome man, even in his eighties, Attaji could have strolled right out of a black and white newsreel from the 1940s. His hair and beard were a stark silver and contrasted with the warmth of his earthen brown skin. He wore an Indian-spun cotton shirt and pants with a brimless white hat. He walked with a cane, though, after observing him for a while, I doubted it served any real purpose other than to add to his old-world charm.

He invited us to the couch and waited for us to take our seats before sitting.

"Ahhh, Shyamala beta," he said affectionately. "You look so much like your mother."

"You've met my mother, Uncle?" It felt natural to refer to an elder by adding a familial term.

"Ahh, yes. She stops by for tea whenever she comes to visit Viniben." He opened his arms dramatically. "So, a long-lost daughter returns to India? What is it that brings you here?"

"Work. There's a project here that it seems I was made for, at least that's what my boss says."

"I take praise where I can find it. Better not to think too much on it, no? Did you leave anyone behind in America?" he asked, so coyly I almost didn't realize he was prying. I pushed away the sudden longing for home and the thoughts of Neil that came in its wake.

"No Uncle, just my parents."

"Well, we can absolutely fix that. No problem. We have plenty of suitable men here. I am sure we can find you a worthy young candidate!" His tone was grandfatherly.

"Come now, Attaji. If you keep talking this way, Shyamala will get the impression my sister put you up to this, isn't it?"

"I am an old man. There was a time when all this matchmaking business seemed such a ridiculous time-pass only. But now I realize how much one craves for another to grow old with. It has been twenty-eight years since I lost my beloved. I miss her still." Attaji's eyes welled. He stood abruptly and made his way to the kitchen. "I have already put the tea on, it must be close to boiling now."

Twenty-eight years. I tried to imagine the depth of Attaji's loss, how he carried on for so many years without her. I hadn't known Neil for even a quarter of that time.

Attaji came back with a tray full of snacks and a pot full of *chai*. After pouring the tea, he sat beside me and barraged me with questions. Each time he asked me one, he reached for another item to put on my plate. After the pistachio roll, it was a savory puffed rice snack, then came another *mithai* made from condensed milk. Seeing how much I enjoyed them, he piled additional portions on to my plate as he recounted stories of his life with his wife. Dutifully, I ate everything, between sips of *chai*, enchanted by tales of Attaji's past and afraid he might take offense at my leaving food behind.

When I placed my hand over the plate to block the next onslaught of food, Attaji backed away for a moment. Then, when I was distracted by conversation, he lovingly dropped more snacks on to my plate. He did the same to Vini.

"*Tame to ky nathi leta.* But you aren't taking anything," my aunt said, pointing at his empty plate.

"Ahhh, Viniben, I am an old man. A little tea is all this body needs. These types of snacks don't sit well at my age. Plus, the host takes far more joy in feeding guests than in eating, no?" Attaji smiled, satisfied with himself.

Late that evening, as we left, he made me promise to come by for a visit later in the week. Entirely beguiled by the old man, I readily agreed. Next time, I'd be sure to come with an empty stomach.

"Until then." He lingered at the door and then we heard it creak shut behind us.

"Will you be ready for dinner when we get home then?" Maasi asked. I looked at her in disbelief and she burst out laughing. "He is charming, isn't it?"

"He really is." I recalled the mischief in his eyes as he kept loading up my plate.

"Some of the neighbors refuse to associate with him because he is not Hindu. Others say we are so cosmopolitan for having a Muslim in our building. Like we are doing something progressive or charitable. I think it is all nonsense. He is a fine man full stop."

I struggled with the notion that anyone could hold Attaji's faith against him. Vini was right, he was a fine man. If he had to pick an ally though, I thought, Vini would be a good choice.

Chapter 6

Mumbai, May 2006

"Shyamala, it is six-thirty! We both overslept! It's your first day of work! Between your jet lag and my getting old, we need to avoid staying up so late, isn't it? You need to get ready for the work. Get moving, *phataphat*!"

I sprang out of bed and got bathed as quickly as I could. Rushing, I put on the skirt suit that I had set out the night before. The blazer fitted like a straitjacket. I tossed the outfit aside, opting for a *salwar kameez* that made me look like an Indian aunty going to the vegetable market. That wouldn't work either. Exasperated, I settled on slacks and a blouse. I wore my straight hair in a simple, practical ponytail. I quickly applied eye liner and a subtle shade of lipstick. I shoveled down some deep-fried garbanzo flour chips, took a couple of sips of *chai* and enough bites of pickled hot-peppers to put some spring into my step, grabbed my purse and dashed out of the door to wait for my car.

I felt more than a bit on edge. It was hard enough making a good impression on the first day of work anywhere, but my first day was in a foreign country, a world away from LA. Would the staff accept me as their new lead? Would I blend in as my boss Joe expected or would I just be the foreigner—the American? On top of everything else, it was my first foray into the city by myself.

Frazzled and nervous, in my haste I ran squarely into someone on the landing outside Vini's apartment. My considerable momentum nearly propelled both of us down the flight of stairs. Fortunately, my victim managed to grab the handrail and regain his balance in time to stabilize the both of us.

"Oh my God, I am so sorry!" I cried.

"Not to worry. For a change I was looking where I was going. Otherwise, I am afraid we would be in a heap on the ground floor." He spoke in English, running his hands through his wild salt and pepper hair.

"Thank you for grabbing the handrail!" I considered the concrete landing below. I found myself breathless.

"We are not even acquaintances and already you have said 'sorry' and 'thank you'. Let me guess. *You* are the girl from America that my ma keeps talking about." He smiled, his eyes squarely meeting mine.

"Are you sure it was the 'sorry' and 'thank you' that gave me away and not my accent?" I scrambled to straighten my clothes.

"You don't seem at all impressed by my insight into American manners." He watched me with apparent amusement.

"I'm more impressed with your sense of balance." I looked down at my watch—I was going to be *so* late.

"I'm Arjun. And that is the first time anyone has told me that they were impressed with my sense of balance." He laughed, clearly feeling no haste himself. "And if you don't mind me asking, your name is—?"

"Meht—just call me Shyamala." I groped around for my keys, which had broken loose from my purse in the collision.

"I would ask you how you have found India so far but it seems you have somewhere you need to be?"

I clasped my hands together. "I'm sorry, I overslept this morning and my ride is probably waiting for me at the gate already."

"Oh of course, I completely understand. Perhaps we will cross paths another time." He picked my keys up off the floor, handed them to me, and stood aside.

"Thank you," I said, making quick eye contact. I turned and hurried downstairs, my thoughts lingering on the conversation briefly. Eager to get to work on time though, I refocused on what lay immediately ahead.

Even though I had seen it being cleaned each day since my arrival, the staircase leading to the ground floor already looked like it needed to have a broom taken to it. The sweepers of Mumbai, it seemed, were losing the battle against the constant influx of grime. No matter how many times they swept during the day, the mire of the city found its way into the building, dusted the steps, filled crevices, and gathered in corners. The dirt was an unrelenting force of nature. I took care to avoid it.

I stepped out into an early morning version of Hades. Heat rose from the pavement outside and radiated off the building. I looked at my watch. It was 8:03 a.m. JTM's driver was to pick me up at 8:00.

The white-haired milk-delivery man rode his bike through the gates. He eyed me as he passed by, his bottles clinking in his storage crate. The household help began to arrive shortly after. One, two, three, four, five people in all, I counted. The time ticked away.

At 8:40, I loosened the watchband now stuck to my sweaty skin and called JTM to figure out where my driver was. If we left now, even with traffic, we might make it to work a little after 9 a.m. The phone rang but nobody answered. Finally, at 9:15, a blue Honda City rolled through the complex's gates. The driver was a heavy-set man who looked to be in his fifties. While the hair on his head may have been receding, it was plentiful everywhere else.

It popped up in obvious tufts over the back of his neck, sprouted out of his ears, hung from his nose, and grew like an unmowed lawn from his arms.

"You are Ms. Mehta, isn't it? I am Subhash." He didn't seem the slightest bit rushed.

"Hi Subhash. I thought you were going to be here at eight. Are we going to make it to the office on time?" I slid into the seat in the back of the car.

"On the time only," he answered with a sideways head bob.

We drove down the tree-lined slopes of Walkeshwar with the windows wide open. We passed Chowpatty Beach and traveled alongside the sea on Marine Drive at a healthy pace. The hot air blew into my shirtsleeves causing them to billow. As we moved along the bay, there was a distinct quality to each breath—one fishy—one fresh—one salty—one sweet.

The road curved luxuriously around the bay and just ahead, seemed to disappear into the sea. The buildings grew taller and more ostentatious, announcing our arrival into the financial district. We passed a long stretch of empty land and then doubled back in the opposite direction passing that same piece of land once again. Soon we were driving back along Marine Drive headed toward Vini's house and it was clear Subhash had no idea where he was going.

"I think we are going back in the same direction we came."

"I will get you to your business. I am taking shortcut only."

"Should we ask for directions?"

Finally, when we passed the same oval field for the third time, Subhash gave in. He pulled over, hailed a young man walking down the street, and got out of the car to chat with him. I tried to follow what they were saying but could only make out a word or two. The men spoke for a while. As they shared a laugh, my panic threatened to spill over.

Finally, the young man pointed directly ahead. "*Seedha, seedha.*"

Subhash tilted his head from side to side several times as he returned to the car.

"Do you know which way to go?"

"It is just this way, you see, straight ahead. No problem."

The car proceeded, mundanely traveling through space and then seemingly traversing backward in time as the Churchgate building appeared, a nineteenth-century mirage in a modern urban desert. The building had a heavy Gothic base, tall turrets and Mughal-inspired white domes. Subhash craned his neck once again to seek out landmarks, the most obvious of which he had passed without any sign of recognizing it.

"Can you just call someone?" I begged.

"I have got no mobile."

My collar felt like a vise around my neck. I tugged at it. Here I was, stuck in the company car, nearly an hour late for my first day at work, and my driver was the only adult in Mumbai who did not have a mobile.

"Excuse me, can you just pull over? I'll hail a cab." I tapped his shoulder with one hand while I groped through my purse for my mobile.

"*Achcha.* No need for taxi, we are here only."

"What? Is this Nariman Point?" All around me were large, multistoried complexes that housed banks, consulting firms, and financial offices. Just beside us was the JTM building.

"We are here. See, no problem!" Subhash spoke with conviction. "I will be coming to pick you up tomorrow early, no?" He smiled hopefully.

I exited the car, slamming the door. I expected to hear the car pulling away from the curb. Instead, its resting grumble continued behind me. I glanced back to find Subhash idling the car, watching me dutifully. He grinned and waved. Until I entered the building, he waited on the street.

The JTM office was all straight edges and symmetry—it might have been in New York, Berlin, or Tokyo. As I wandered into the expansive reception area, my clothes clinging to me like plastic wrap on yesterday's leftovers, the receptionist was the only soul in sight. The clock on the wall read 10 a.m.

"I'm Shyamala Mehta from the LA office. I'm so sorry about the time!"

"Oh no need to apologize. Unless we have a meeting with US, most of our people come to work at ten-thirty at the earliest."

"Ten-thirty?" A slightly crazed laugh escaped me. I flattened my disheveled hair wondering why it hadn't occurred to me just to ask when the JTM's staff in Mumbai started their workday. With a nod-shake of the head, I said, "Sure. Of course, of course."

The receptionist led me to my new cubicle. Perhaps I would be able to exert a modicum of control in its 36 square feet.

Thirty minutes later, the first of my co-workers finally entered the office. She peeked her head over my cubicle. Just shy of six feet tall, she was an Amazon by Indian standards. Her demeanor was playful and warm. I liked her immediately.

"Hello! You must be Ms. Mehta. I am Natasha Shah. We spoke on the phone several weeks back. We'll be working closely while you are here." She paused, assessing my condition. "Are you okay?"

Even more aware of my unkempt state, I said: "Let's just say it's been a long morning."

"Did you have any trouble finding the office?" Her brow was furrowed in concern. "Oh no, they didn't send the new chap, did they? What is his name? Surya or Suraj or something."

"Subhash."

"Did he get lost again?"

I nodded.

"I'll have to let Ajay know. Subhash got lost picking him up from Flora Fountain just yesterday. He wound up taking Daniel to Worli instead of Parle just two days ago. I think he is newer to the city than he let on or, worse yet, he may be somewhat geographically challenged. We may need to let him go."

I thought back to the hopeful expression on Subhash's face as I entered the elevator.

"No, no. Don't worry about it. It was partly my fault. Plus, I know what it's like to be the new one in town."

"Well, be certain to tell me if he keeps getting lost. Let me take you around the office and introduce you to everyone. Actually, you and I are the only ones here so maybe I'll just take you around the office, *na*?" She smiled.

With Natasha present, the starkness of the office faded immediately. She introduced me to each of the members of our team as they arrived: Gayatri, Ajay, and the "other American", Daniel. It was apparent the group worked well together and that Natasha had earned their confidence. In the time since Patrick Welch had resigned, she had stepped up to become their acting leader. Suddenly, I questioned the wisdom of putting me in charge of the project. I may have known how to convert legacy programs into modern software systems but I had no idea how to navigate the cultural mores in a foreign land and the personal allegiances of people who knew each other but to whom I was a complete stranger. I spent much of the day feeling out of my depth.

At 8 p.m., as the office staff wrapped up for the day, Natasha announced that we were all going to dinner. Although everyone had been welcoming, the day had been exhausting and I badly wanted to head home, but I bit my tongue. If I was going to fit in, I'd better do as the team did.

Natasha had chosen a South Indian restaurant where we could eat piping-hot lentil soup, spicy condiments, and steaming *idlis* while sweltering in the Mumbai heat. I ordered *idlis*, freshly steamed patties made from a rice and lentil blend served with lentil soup, and heaps of salty-sweet-spicy coconut chutney.

To my right at the table sat Ajay. A sweet twenty-something, I had previously noticed his rail-thin physique and his too-tight-at-the-hips, tailored pants. He professed to have fallen madly in love with at least three different women just since our dinner had begun. Next to him sat Daniel, the other American, who hailed from Portland, Oregon. He was in his late twenties by my guess, just over six feet tall and strapping. Over dinner I learned Daniel had volunteered to stay for another tour in Mumbai for JTM. The reason became clear quickly. She was sitting next to him: Natasha. As opposed to Ajay, Daniel actually was in love.

On my left was Gayatri. In her mid-thirties, she had a razor-sharp sense of humor. It was already apparent that she worked hard by day and played hard by night. She made it abundantly clear that for her, falling in love would have been the worst of all fates, a hindrance to a life in which she answered to no one.

I scanned the group, suddenly self-conscious. Was I so easily gauged? Could they sense that I was the jilted lover of the bunch— the one seeking an escape from her troubles in their bustling city?

"Miss Mehta, when did you arrive in India?" Ajay asked stiffly.

"Ajay, please no need to be formal, just call me Shyamala."

Gayatri let out a moan. "See, that is your bloody problem, Ajay. You fall madly for girls from afar but the minute you speak to a woman it is like she is your aunty! You're never going to get anywhere with that approach!"

Natasha smiled. "As you can see, Shyamala, Gayatri quite enjoys egging Ajay on."

But Gayatri wasn't done with her commentary. She tapped me with her elbow and laughed. "Ajay aside, just a warning Shyamala, two stones and a lingam and every guy in this country thinks he's God's gift to women—even if he can hardly string a meaningful sentence together!"

Ajay cleared his throat, shot a dirty look at Gayatri, and glared at her while addressing me. "If we could get back on topic, Gayatri? Very well. Shyamala then, when did you arrive?"

"I got to Mumbai three days ago." The minute I spoke, Gayatri seemed as though she might burst. Ajay and Natasha snickered when Daniel came to my rescue.

"Oh no, not again, you guys! Shyamala, let me save you some grief. About this Mumbai-Bombay bit. I was just like you once, using the term Mumbai, thinking it is the non-anglicized version of the word 'Bombay', but Gayatri has apparently concluded that the term Mumbai is meaningless. Saying 'Mumbai' apparently sealed me in as a total foreigner. Just in case it wasn't obvious enough given my utter lack of pigmentation. Hey Gayatri, when do you plan to start the campaign to re-rename the city?"

"Listen Daniel, Mumbai is just the Indianized version of an anglicized version of the original Portuguese term for the city. *Bom Bahia*, meaning good bay. *Mumbai* has no actual meaning!" Gayatri argued.

"But one could argue that *Mumbai* is named after the Goddess Mumbadevi!" Daniel shot back. Gayatri rolled her eyes.

"Oh, and if you really want to get Gayatri fired up, just call Flora Fountain Hutatma Chowk! Or is it Martyrs' Square? Even the city's squares and streets have gotten a good renaming," Daniel added.

"Listen, rename all you want. Flora Fountain is always going to be Flora Fountain. Bombay is always going to be Bombay!" Gayatri shifted backward into her seat as if she had closed the case.

"They argue about this as if there was a right answer—as if anyone will ever know for sure. Shyamala, where are you staying in *Bom-bay*?" Ajay asked.

"I am staying at my aunt's place in Walkeshwar."

Gayatri's eyebrows perked up. "Walkeshwar is pretty posh. But staying with your aunt? I am guessing you live on your own back in America."

"Gayatri, don't pry. She might be living with somebody over there, maybe she does not want to talk about it to strangers," whispered Ajay. It seemed he was either protecting my dark secret or my virtue, or maybe a little of both. Was it just me or was everyone in this country obsessed with whether I was single?

"Well, just so we're clear, I don't live with anyone back in the States."

"My point exactly. You were probably used to coming and going as you pleased," Gayatri said kicking Ajay under the table. "Now you must have to answer to your aunt."

I thought about Maasi and the comfortable pattern of life in the flat. "Not really. I was a bit worried about moving in with my aunt at first. But she's really easy to live with. I don't feel I have to answer to her at all. I enjoy staying with her."

"See Gayatri, Americans don't complain the way we do." Ajay looked at Daniel.

"Shyamala, please don't set such a high bar! They'll hold me up to it as well," Daniel broke in. The four of us laughed. I felt remarkably at ease among this group and after a full day of excitement, the banter between friends made me even more comfortable. Dad always bragged about how acceptance was a pre-eminent Indian trait, how it enabled people to endure the oppressive heat, the torrential rain, the open sewer system, and the relentless crowds. Maybe, I thought, it would enable them to embrace a complete stranger like me.

◆ ◆ ◆

During the ride home, Subhash was chatty.

"Where you are coming from in USA?" The melodic sound of his Gujarati accent sang through his every English word.

"The outskirts of Los Angeles."

"I am not meaning about the clothes. I am asking where you are living."

"Outskirts is another way of saying that I live just right outside of Los Angeles. The suburbs."

"Oh, *achcha* that is very nice. Near to the American Bollywood, no?" He bobbled his head side to side in the rear-view mirror.

"Hollywood? Yes. I suppose it is. Near to the American Bollywood." I smiled.

"Well, I am from—what you said—the outskirts of the Ahmedabad. We moved to Bombay few weeks back only."

"I guess we are in the same boat then."

Subhash looked at me through the rear-view mirror and opened his mouth to ask me a question and then just as soon, he stopped.

"Ahhh yes, *achcha achcha*," he said, grinning and nodding to himself. "Same boat only."

Subhash drove the entirety of Marine Drive. The car windows were rolled down and the scent of the sea saturated the air. It was a welcome antidote to the dreamy lull into which I had fallen. I gazed out of the window taking in the coastline.

I knew that Mumbai was once a series of islands. The islands had been connected by large reclamation projects to create the city.

As I took in the view of the Arabian Sea, I tried to imagine the many conquerors of times past who had sailed the same waters and had become entangled in the web of islands and others who had sought land routes to India. Most had come here seeking power and wealth. The Mughals, the Portuguese, the Dutch, and the British—they had come and gone. Now there were new conquerors on the horizon. And though they didn't necessarily come to India on trade vessels or navy ships, these conquerors of capital were seeking the exact same thing. JTM was among them.

By the time Subhash let me out at the entrance to my aunt's apartment at midnight, I found myself wide awake.

"I will be coming to pick you up tomorrow early, no?" he had said hopefully.

I stepped out of the Honda. "Take your time. How about nine-thirty?"

He idled the car and watched as I entered the building. Once again, he lingered until he was certain I was safely at my destination.

The apartment was still when I entered. My aunt sat on the couch, engrossed in a book. The fan whirred overhead. The living room window was open, almost wistfully, to allow in even the slightest draft. Instead, what entered was the heat radiating off the asphalt street below.

At the sound of my entering, Vini startled.

"Oh, hallo Shyama!" She put the book she was reading aside. "How was your first day at the office?"

"Well, aside from getting lost on the way in, appearing as though I had been struck by a typhoon, and showing up entirely too early, I'd say the day went resoundingly well!"

She smirked. "You and your mother share a similar taste for irony, isn't it?"

"Maasi, my mom is many things, but ironic isn't one of them."

51

"Come, *beta.*" She gestured for me to sit down beside her. "If you think that, you don't know much about your mother."

I dropped on to the couch. Vini was right—I didn't know much about my mother, especially when it came to her past.

"Well, you will not believe it, but your mother was among the naughtiest of the kids in our building. And we were a naughty bunch. We lived in a *chawl*, in Bombay proper."

"*Chawl?*"

"*Chaali* means walkway. You see, all of the flats in the *chawl* complex were open to a common walkway. The *chaali* is where we played and studied. I used to write out my maths equations on the floor with chalk. It is where we kids worked on our pranks. Only at night did we come home. It was a simple time—a happy time." Vini's voice was brimming with nostalgia.

I nodded eagerly for her to go on.

"We didn't have much in the way of money back then. Our flat had one bedroom, a common room, and a kitchen. When we were very young, your mother and I lived in that tiny flat with our parents, my father's parents, and one of our father's friends who moved from the village."

I imagined seven people squeezing into a miniscule downtown flat. "Did you ever have a moment of privacy?"

"Rarely. Then again, we didn't know any differently, no? We had one common water closet for the entire floor! That was twelve apartments, all with minimum six people living in them. Imagine it! We used to think 'God have mercy, please let me use the bathroom before Kashyapbhai.' Your mom and me, we would rush to use it first thing in the morning because once he got in"—she coughed—"it was not advisable to enter for another two hours. And we didn't have those Western toilets back then either. Half the time, the plumbing was not working properly." The expression of revulsion on my aunt's face suggested that the trauma of the state of the *chawl*'s toilet still lived with her.

"There was one time, Pramila had the idea of putting a firecracker in the toilet. All the kids in the *chawl* thought this was a great idea. She had us convinced that the only way to fix the toilet was to blow it up and start all over again." Vini chuckled to herself.

"Mom hatched this plan?" I struggled to imagine my mother conspiring to plant what was essentially an explosive into a communal loo.

"Yes, of course. Anyhow, that day we all stood outside the latrine. We were so excited. I lit the firecracker and then Pramila rushed into the bathroom, threw it into the toilet hole. She never delegated the most dangerous part of the plan, you see.

"There was a loud pop-popping sound and then a huge cloud of black smoke burst from the bathroom bringing with it the unspeakable smells. The odor hung in the air for days afterwards. Nobody dared to even step foot near the toilet. What to do? We had to use the water closet upstairs. We could not escape the smell even in our flats. I could hardly eat for a week. Thank God we did not set the whole building on fire. Our mother was furious. Our father, on the other hand, scolded us a bit. But I think he took some unspoken joy in our misdeeds and *masti*."

I was grinning, impressed as much by the sisters' misdeeds as their flair for the dramatic. Still, I wrestled with the idea that the mother I knew sounded nothing like the mischievous child being described to me.

"It's hard to believe that Mom would hatch a plan like that. She always seems so by-the-book."

"I visited the old complex some time back. One of our friends from the old days still lives there. We walked around the building, you know, remembering the past. You can still see where we cut off the wooden spheres that decorated the top of the banisters in the stairwells! Climb any staircase in the building and you will not find a single one remaining. You see, your mom thought that they would make great cricket balls. She cut the first one off and next thing you know, every kid in the complex had themselves a new cricket ball! Anyhow, the only person he asked about from our old days was Pramila. Somehow, she earned the respect of every child in the building."

"I can see why." Having been raised in a world of seatbelt laws and bicycle helmets, there was something delightfully liberating about hearing these stories of reckless abandon. As unbelievable as it was, the thought of my mother as the ringleader of a group of rag-tag pranksters in the *chawl* filled me with unexpected pride.

My mind was still abuzz at 2 a.m. when my aunt retired for the night. I sent my parents an email about having survived my first day of work, wanting to tell my mother about the memories Vini maasi had recounted but something held me back. I retrieved *The Good Earth*, and went back to the couch. Without reading, I flipped through the pages searching for the old photo. Once I found it, I settled on the distant look on her face. A wistfulness swept over me again. Why had my mother never seen fit to tell me the stories Vini had just shared? Within the unspoken, my mother seemed to be saying something.

Chapter 7

BOMBAY, 1959

Once again, it was Pramila's idea. Gautam thought the scheme was ingenious. Along with a third schoolmate, Akash, they had discussed which teacher was the most deserving. Without any debate, they agreed on Mrs. Lokhandwala. Having grown up in the wake of the struggle for independence, the three friends saw themselves as young Indian freedom fighters striking a blow to Mrs. Lokhandwala's British Empire. Students and teachers alike would speak about this day like it was legend.

The lesson started as usual. Mrs. Lokhandwala sat at her desk, presiding over her classroom the way Pramila imagined the Queen of England might preside over her court. Mrs. Lokhandwala was a heavy-set woman with beady eyes that children found to be unnervingly close together. What she may have lacked in peripheral vision, however, she made up for with an exquisite sense of hearing. She seemed able to detect the smallest infraction in the furthest reaches of her classroom. It was a rare day when Mrs. Lokhandwala didn't take it upon herself to mercilessly rap a child's knuckles with a yardstick.

On Mrs. Lokhandwala's command, the students opened their books to page 67 and began to recite John Keats' *The Eve of St. Agnes*. Nobody understood the verses. They had begun reading English only two years ago. Pramila tried to contort her mouth to create the words of the poem; words like "meagre" and "purgatorial". English was a ridiculous language, she thought, full of odd pronunciation rules and more exceptions than the cockroaches they had counted in the commissary that morning. She was relieved when they moved on to their writing lessons. From time to time, she checked the clock.

At 11:25, Akash raised his hand. "Madam, may I turn on the fan? It is very hot in here." Mrs. Lokhandwala's classroom tended to get hot in the late morning. Thankfully, the school had finally installed electric fans, though the one in this room only worked intermittently.

Mrs. Lokhandwala narrowed her tiny eyes. "You may."

Akash walked slowly and self-consciously to the switch at the back of the room.

He flipped the switch and returned to his seat. At first, the hum of the fan was accompanied only by the sound of pencils scratching against paper. Then, somebody snickered. Pramila resisted the temptation to look up. Shoes scraped against the floor. Then, somebody else snickered.

"Silence!" Mrs. Lokhandwala scanned the class and returned to grading papers.

The silence lasted for a minute or two. Several classmates were looking up with as much discretion as they could muster. Soon though, the subdued giggling of the classroom surpassed the acceptable level.

"Do you people not understand the meaning of the word 'silence'? I don't even want to hear you breathe!" Mrs. Lokhandwala yelled, again turning her attention back to grading papers.

A few students gestured toward the fan. With barely contained amusement they nodded to each other. It was working, Pramila thought. She nodded at Gautam, who gestured at her with two fingers.

As planned, two minutes later, Pramila raised her hand. When Mrs. Lokhandwala didn't see it, she cleared her throat. The teacher scowled at her.

"Madam, may I turn down the fan? It is too fast." Pramila hoped to draw more attention to what was hovering above the class.

"Too hot. Too cold. Too slow. Too fast. You all are very spoiled. No, Pramila, you will keep your seat. When I attended school, we had no fans. We did not even have electric lights."

Crouching at his desk, the student next to Pramila giggled.

At this point, Mrs. Lokhandwala sensed that something was amiss. She stood up and her eyes darted around the room. "I know you are up to something. This class is always up to something. I have a mind to tell the headmaster. All that hard-earned money your poor parents have spent sending you to this school. Useless. Thankless. That is how you people are. So Pramila Desai, if you have something to say, I would suggest you say it now."

"I don't have anything to say. We do have something to show you though." Pramila pointed at the fan and every pair of eyes followed toward where the heavens might be if not obscured by the ceiling.

Pramila finally succumbed to the temptation to look up. There they were, six roaches, each about an inch in size, rotating up above as if flying of their own volition. She marveled at each six-legged, gleaming creature attached to a fan blade by a piece of string, the latter made invisible by the rotation of the fan. The students had abandoned even feigning interest in their writing lessons and stared at the fan in abject wonder. Pramila took the sight in, the reanimated roaches, the glee of the children admiring their handiwork, and the expression on Mrs. Lokhandwala's face as she realized what was happening.

Standing in the middle of the classroom, the teacher focused her sights on the iridescent creatures that now took center stage in her little empire.

"*Arré baap re!* Are those cockroaches?" Mrs. Lokhandwala asked, horror written all over her face. She backed toward the chalkboard and away from the fan.

"From our lunchroom, Mrs. Lokhandwala. They were found dead just this morning," came Pramila's small voice from the back of the room. "We picked the plumpest of the winged ones, though we had a great many choices."

All eyes fell on Pramila. Then, a chorus of student voices chimed in.

"Did you see the dead rat in the lunchroom last week? That is not the first time I have seen one!" Adi said, addressing his classmates.

"The teachers would never set foot in that place. It is a filthy place, a complete embarrassment," Nalini announced. The kids nodded in agreement.

"I told my mother about the lunchroom and she has forbidden me to eat there." Gautam made a throat-slitting gesture.

"Silence!" Mrs. Lokhandwala stood near the chalkboard, her body shaking with anger. Her jowls quivered. "Don't just sit there, somebody turn that fan off!"

Her voice had taken on a deranged quality. Hearing it, the class could no longer suppress its joy. The classroom exploded with laughter, delighted as their most reviled teacher backed herself into the far corner of the room for fear of the spinning cockroaches.

The children had won, if only for a moment.

Mrs. Lokhandwala cowered in the corner of her classroom, deciding how to exact revenge on her class. She started to speak, but in her anger the words weren't forthcoming.

At length she said, "If you do not turn that off this instant, I will have all of you expelled!"

She grabbed a chalkboard eraser off its railing and wound up. With rage, she released the eraser and threw it with remarkable speed. The eraser sailed over children's heads, under the cockroaches in mid-flight, and with absolute precision struck Pramila squarely in the chest. It left a large imprint on her dark-blue uniform. Within moments, Mrs. Lokhandwala had released all the erasers—Pramila counted twelve. It was a remarkable display of accuracy, for Mrs. Lokhandwala managed to hit Pramila with each one. A cloud of dust enveloped her. When it finally dissipated, she was covered in eraser prints and chalk dust.

The teacher looked at the mayhem from the corner of the room, paralyzed by a combination of fury and fear. The veins at her temples bulged and the fibers of the muscles of her neck grew taut as if the anger might actually explode out of her.

"I will see to it that you never set foot in this school again! Now get out!" she screamed, hand shaking as she pointed at Pramila.

After the classroom bedlam, Pramila had tried to wipe the chalk dust away, but it was bound to the material of her navy-blue pinafore with preternatural tenacity. Had she given it her all, she could probably have beaten the chalk dust off, but as news of the incident in Mrs. Lokhandwala's class traveled through the school, classmate after classmate had pulled Pramila aside in the hallway to express solidarity for bringing attention to the sorry condition of the lunchroom. She found herself unwilling to wipe the chalk dust off, wearing it home with pride.

She had scarcely taken two steps into the flat when Ba walked into the main room. Her face fell on seeing her younger daughter dusted with chalk. "*Arré*, what happened to you? Why are you covered in chalk dust?"

Pramila handed Ba a note. Time stood still as Pramila watched Ba's eyes scan the paper left to right, left to right. Then Ba's expression changed from curious to furious.

"Pramila Desai, you should be ashamed of yourself! Just because you don't like something or someone, it does not mean that you can do whatever you wish! Do you know how fortunate you are that your father sends you to school? Not every girl gets to attend school at your age and most aren't lucky enough to be attending one that is so expensive!"

"But Ba, if you would only hear my side of it," Pramila countered, knowing full well it would have been best to keep her mouth shut.

"*Chup!* I don't want to hear another word from you! Mrs. Lokhandwala let you off easy just throwing chalkboard erasers at you. I would have done much worse. Go sit by the door to the *chaali*, where everybody can see you. Don't wipe one speck of that chalk dust from your clothes! Don't move until your father gets home! And don't you dare think of any more pranks!"

When Pramila sat down at the entrance, a small plume of chalk dust rose around her. She thought back to Mrs. Lokhandwala's erasers. How on earth did she develop such a precise aim? Pramila had always imagined the woman to be near-sighted! She shook her head for a moment before becoming still again. Through the open door behind her, she felt the heat of her mother's glare against her back.

The entrance of the flat opened into the *chaali*, the common walkway shared by their floor. Having heard that Pramila was being punished in plain sight, children throughout the complex made it a point to come ogle at her, making faces and smirking as they went off to play in the courtyard. With her mother watching from the kitchen, Pramila dared not utter a word.

When her father finally arrived from work, Pramila's thin buttocks were sore from sitting on the tile floor. She could see him come down the *chaali*. His silhouette was unmistakable. He was among the tallest men in the complex. He wore a charcoal-gray Gandhi cap and a light gray tunic—unwilling to adopt Western fashion the way other men his age had.

"Pramila, tu anhiya su kare che? What are you doing here? Come inside."

"Papa, Ba said not to speak to anyone," she whispered.

"Well, certainly, your mother would make an exception for me, no? Why are you covered in dust?"

Ba stepped out of the main room. She handed the note to her husband.

Pramila watched as her father read the letter.

"I will have to think about a punishment suitable for such behavior," he said. Pramila hoped it was mostly for the benefit of her mother.

It was not until after her mother had gone to bed for the night that her father made mention of the headmaster's note. Pramila was doing her grammar lessons in the *chaali*, the only place in the complex that had electrical lights. Her father joined her, reading a book by John Maynard Keynes. Intermittently, he took a puff or two from his hand-rolled *bidi* cigarette.

When she had completed her lessons, Pramila stood up.

"Papa, can I dust my uniform off now?"

"Yes, I am surprised your mother let you eat your dinner like that—I am surprised she let you eat at all! She was very angry!"

Pramila finally dusted herself off. She sat down next to her father.

"Cockroaches, ha? You always said the lunchroom is infested with them." He looked down at her.

"Papa, you should have seen them fly!"

"Mrs. Lokhandwala?" he guessed, his tone playfully conspiratorial.

"Yes, Papa, she is horrid."

"I know she is. You realize there will have to be some sort of punishment, no? You cannot do such things at school. Or at home either, for that matter." He took a drag from the *bidi*.

"I know, Papa." She wrung her hands.

"I have one question for you though, Pramila."

"What is it, Papa?" She turned to him.

"Why did you not wipe the chalk off your clothes before you came home?" He puffed again on his *bidi*.

She thought back to when she had proposed the whole roach-reanimation plan to Gautam and Akash. What had inspired her to suggest the idea? It was something someone had told her long ago—something about fate and how it befell those who failed to act when the time was right. "Somebody had to do something Papa. And I am not ashamed that Gautam, Akash and I were the ones to do it. So why should I wipe the chalk dust away?" She shrugged her shoulders.

He held her gaze for a moment and swallowed hard. Pramila recognized the gesture. She did the same when trying to quell an unexpected surge of emotion. Her father set aside his book and put out his *bidi*. She gathered her grammar books, conscious that Papa was observing her, knobbly kneed and still dusted in chalk as she was. Just as she had felt the heat of her mother's glare in the afternoon, it was her father's pride she felt at her back tonight.

Chapter 8

Mumbai, May 2006

One thing had become clear the moment I arrived in Bombay: this city could not be shut out. It surged and seethed and seeped beyond any barrier and found its way into every sense. Each breath was an effort, as if my very diaphragm were resisting it. The mattress upon which I lay, the fresh clothes that I put on every day after my bath—everything felt damp against the skin. Everywhere I went my eyes were treated to a feast of colors. Saris and tunic sets of inconceivable combinations: magenta with mustard, emerald with violet, crimson with azure. My nose too, lived in a constant state of shock—never sure whether it would be met by a scent that was nasty or sublime. And the noises! I have never encountered an absolute absence of silence except in Bombay. Walk into the apartment complex, climb to the top floor, close the doors and windows behind you and still the racket of the city finds its way in.

Bombay even managed to trickle into the JTM building for all its apparent hermetically sealed, modern office building insularity. In between project management meetings, *chaiwalas* off the street swarmed in to deliver hot tea. And, each day, after I had concluded the first round of international calls, like clockwork, tiffin*walas* delivered warm home-made Indian lunches to office workers in stacked stainless-steel containers.

Between the hired staff who were expected and the neighbors that dropped in without notice, Vini maasi's apartment often felt like the bustling Churchgate Station. It wasn't long before I had met nearly every neighbor in my aunt's building. They were quick to ask me where I lived in the States, and, in the next breath, to tell me about their relative who lived abroad. There were Purnima aunty and Kaushik uncle who lived on the third floor and had a son working in Australia. There were Amish and Shruti who lived with Amish's parents on the second floor. Shruti's brother was studying in England. I met Jagdish uncle and Deena aunty who had just moved back to India after fifteen years in New Jersey. Every one of them had visited Disneyland. Most had seen the White House. When I had last visited India in middle school, I was the worldly one, the one who had insights into another land and another way of life. I wowed everyone I met with my Walkman and Converse sneakers. This time, my hosts seemed far more worldly than I. There was nothing I owned that they were in want of.

As I met the neighbors, I was surprised at how quickly I came into their confidence and how candidly they spoke to me. I learned things that they would never admit to each other for fear of judgment and rumor. Within my first couple of months in Bombay, I became privy to the drinking habits of more than one resident, a neighborhood gambling ring, an inter-caste affair, and an out-of-wedlock pregnancy. It was apparent that, as an American, my neighbors assumed that my moral compass was intrinsically askew. They thought I had no standing to judge them.

But nobody was as smugly superior as Vini's next-door neighbor. One night, when we were heading back to the flat, we ran into her.

"You must be Shyamala! *Ay-la*! You are a carbon copy of your mother. I heard from the other neighbors that you were visiting. Your aunt never tells me such things," she said with a wink in my direction.

With her henna-colored hair, she looked to be in her late fifties. Under thin eyebrows her eyes flitted about, taking in what we were wearing.

"Shyamala, this is my next-door neighbor Champaben Trivedi," Vini said wearily. Turning to her neighbor, Maasi added, "Champa, we both know that you are very good at finding out exactly what you want to know."

"I *do* have my ways. It is good you have come, Shyamala. It is about time someone came to keep an eye on your maasi. Listen, you must come to my flat for dinner. We can watch *Sa Re Ga Ma Pa* on our new television. That is a very famous TV show here. We must teach you the way we do things in India, you will not learn such things from your aunt." She winked again.

What the first wink did not accomplish, the second did. I was entirely put off.

Maasi *glared at her*.

"*Ha, ha. Amme josu.* Yes, yes. We will see." The words were more than noncommittal, suggesting Vini's firm conviction to just the opposite.

Champa, for her part, seemed completely oblivious.

"*Chalo*, okay so it is fixed. You will come for a visit. We will set a day," she said with a single sideways head tilt as she disappeared into the flat right next door to Vini's.

"Listen, be careful around that woman, *beta*," Vini warned, her voice hardly a whisper. "She walks about like she is the prime minister of this complex. She wants to know who is doing what with whom. She loves spreading rumors about everybody in this place including Attaji. She even tried to get him kicked out of the building once. Who would do such a thing to that man?"

Her tirade continued as we entered the flat.

"She is *al-vays* talking about that television. Like we have never seen one before! It is ridiculous! 'We must teach you how we do things in India, you will not learn such things from your aunt,'" Maasi mimicked. "She is something else. She is *al-vays* telling everyone that she fasts on Wednesdays for religious reasons. But I have seen her eating at the *bhelpuriwala*'s cart at the corner on more than one Wednesday. It is shameful."

I had never seen Maasi utter a harsh word about anyone. I took note to beware of my next-door neighbor.

Still fuming, Vini muttered to herself, "It is truly a miracle that her son has turned out to be such a good boy."

◆　◆　◆

If I initially feared that Mumbai's JTM team would not accept me as their new lead, that fear proved to be unfounded. The team made a great effort to guide me through the workings of the Mumbai office and, despite the long hours, my transition was relatively seamless. In fact, if anything, JTM Mumbai felt far more cohesive than JTM LA. Natasha, in particular, was beyond welcoming. Within my first week, she had invited me to dinner at her parents' house, drinks at her favorite bar, and her sister's wedding. If there was one thing that I had learned in Mumbai so far it was that Mumbai-ites love to play host, and Natasha was no exception.

Born far from the subcontinent and living mostly among Americans, I had never been properly versed on how to successfully refuse an invitation from an Indian. Declining an invitation is an art form acquired only through years of experience in dealing with other Indians. I stood no chance. No matter how tactfully I turned down an offer, it seemed that those extending the invitation simply would not accept "no" as an answer. This is how I wound up attending Natasha's sister's wedding without ever having met her.

I was thrilled to be asked but demurred, concerned that I might be barging in on a family occasion. Natasha wouldn't have it. And so, dressed in an ill-fitting yet spectacularly bejeweled art silk sari that she insisted I borrow, I ventured out into the grueling heat and oppressive humidity of late May. As much as my skin chafed against the netted fabric that lined the inside of my blouse, I was excited to witness a wedding on Indian soil and relieved that Natasha had invited the rest of the JTM team as well.

The festivities began when the groom's family, led on horseback by the bridegroom, descended upon the wedding hall like a small army, complete with a band. Undeterred by temperatures that could melt the asphalt under their feet, they danced right outside the building, with the groom, now dismounted from his horse, at the center. The bride's family greeted them at the entryway of the wedding hall and was soon drawn into the celebration. Natasha stood out among her family, luminous in an amethyst and gold sari. I spied Daniel from afar, gazing at her intently.

Gayatri found me and grabbed me by the crook of the arm. We entered the wedding hall together, stopping at an enormous ice sculpture at the entrance.

"Well, I guess this serves to remind us that thoughts of drought should be left at the door," I observed.

We watched as the intricately carved swan slowly melted away into a puddle. Most guests hardly noticed its presence as they moved on to the festivities.

"I wonder just how many water tankers are needed to make sure the rich can show off their ice swans and leave their water glasses undrunk?" Gayatri seethed.

We made our way to the wedding hall which would have been grand enough to hold *durbar* for the Mughal emperor Akbar when he received dignitaries. At the center was the *mandap*, an elevated wedding enclosure that stood about ten feet high. It had intricate wooden carvings that gleamed with gold paint. Sashes of red organza were wrapped around the pillars. Two ornamented, oversized wooden chairs stood under the enclosure. Placed directly in front of the chairs was a raised metal vessel that would contain the sacred fire. Turmeric-colored carnations and sweetly perfumed jasmine were strung up in leis that hung off the outer edges of the structure.

Natasha sought me out from the crowd. "You'll love this Shyamala! If you see his shoes, grab them and do not let go."

"What? Whose shoes?"

"The groom's! Among Gujaratis like us it's tradition for the bride's side of the family to steal them!"

Then, just as the groom approached the *mandap*, havoc broke out. Five young men and Natasha rushed him, snatching at his shoes. At the same time, several young men from the groom's side of the family boosted him into the air, his legs akimbo in front of him. His turban, which was not so much a wrap as a hat, tilted forward to cover both his eyes. The only thing about his outfit that seemed undisturbed were his shoes. The scuffle attracted people from both sides of the aisle, the audience laughing and cheering.

"*Arré bhai ne chalwa do ne!* Come on now, let the brother pass! It is his big day," a gray-haired man pleaded.

The response from the bride's side was action. Now they grabbed the groom's feet, shoes and all. The whole mob toppled forward. After this, it was difficult to see much of anything. There was just a tangle of arms and legs. Among them was the barefooted groom, still peering out from under a tilted turban. Natasha, who appeared untouched, was holding his shoes. She grinned trium-phantly at her future brother-in-law.

"This is too good. Your wallet better be filled with five-hundred-rupee bills. Otherwise, you don't stand a chance of leaving this place," she gloated. "I'll catch up with you later to collect my payment!"

Then, as if the melee had never happened, everyone took their seats. The shoeless groom and his parents climbed on to the *mandap* and the priest began the ceremony with a prayer to Lord Ganesha.

Natasha's sister entered the hall dressed in a traditional red and white bridal sari. Her hands were decorated with henna which formed sinuous floral and paisley patterns on her hands and up her arms. Nearly all of her visible body was adorned, from the diamond tikka pendant that hung in her hair, to the anklets that jangled around her feet.

Sitting by myself in the audience, I observed Natasha. Gilded and graceful, she anticipated every step in the wedding ceremony. She had the leis ready when it was time for the bride and groom to place one around the other's neck. When they circled the fire, she held her sister's sari out of the way. How seamlessly she fitted into the scene! She was meant to be here. There was an inevitability in her presence. I, on the other hand, was extraneous. I had none of her knowledge of the right thing to do in the moment. I did not belong.

This inevitable extraneous dichotomy was driven by one choice: my father's now fabled decision to join the line at the American Embassy the day he got kicked off the bus in 1970. That single decision led to his move to the United States and every-thing after. What would've happened if he had just walked by the embassy instead of stopping to ask questions? Who would I have been if he and my mother had stayed in India—if I had been born here? Would I have been able to shift languages without thought, between English, Gujarati, and Hindi? Would I have ever doubted that I belonged in the country of my birth or questioned whether my birthplace was my birthright the way I did in America? Would I too know, by instinct, the next step of the marriage ceremony? The neck of my sari blouse rubbed against my collarbone. I adjusted it.

"It's crazy isn't it—this place?" Daniel took the empty seat beside me.

"It is."

"I have been dying to speak to someone who isn't Indian about this! I can never talk about this at work because there are always so many Indians around."

"Daniel, this is India, there are bound to be lots of Indians here." I glanced around me to make my point, only to find that there wasn't a single Indian, or anyone else for that matter, in earshot. "And believe it or not, I *am* Indian."

"You know what I mean, you're a fellow American. Someone who won't dismiss me as a high-maintenance tourist type. You have to admit that this city stinks! I have never smelled a stench quite so obscene as the stenches I have smelled here. And the toilets . . . don't even get me started. Do you know that I map out my route each day so that I can find a restroom with some semblance of sanitation? It's totally ironic. Every Indian that I have met is so meticulous about cleanliness inside their household and yet there is an utter lack of sanitation in public restrooms."

I couldn't argue with any of this.

"You know what though? I have never loved a place that I hated so much. No day is the same as the one before. One day you may not have water, the next day you may not have electricity. Even the trip to work is an adventure. You never know if your rickshaw will veer into opposing traffic or your driver will take you to Worli instead of to the office!"

Daniel's speech seemed to gain speed at this thought.

"Last week I took the train to work during rush hour. It was insane! This guy makes it to the station as the train is leaving the platform. Just when you think he has no chance of catching the train, ten pairs of arms appear from the compartment, sweep down, and lift him into the train even though it is already busting at the seams. It's exhilarating. I've been taking the train to work ever since," he said, his breath running out.

Before I could respond, he continued. "It is hotter than hell here. I don't think I have stopped sweating once since I got off the plane. There are people at every turn. And to get anything done, you have to know somebody or be willing to pay them off. This city, this country, it just devours you. It makes you feel alive. I am not sure I will be able to leave this place," he concluded.

We watched as Natasha assisted the bride with her finely beaded sari.

Daniel nodded to Natasha. "Or her. I'm in love with her."

"I know." Watching the wedding festivities and hearing Daniel profess his feelings for Natasha, I couldn't help but feel a twinge of envy.

"Now if I can only convince her that she's in love with me."

"Is she? In love with you?"

"I think so—as much as any one of us could know what lives in another person's heart."

"Well, it doesn't seem easy—for all the obvious reasons."

"What, because I'm a white guy visiting Mumbai temporarily and she is Indian, because her parents are uber-conservative, and mine haven't even met her?"

I was no stranger to the desperation I heard in Daniel's voice. Neil and I didn't have the cards stacked against us in the same way that Daniel and Natasha did, and even then, we didn't make it.

"If the two of you want to be together and I can do anything to help, I am happy to try."

71

Daniel turned to me and grinned. "Well, there might be something you could do. Natasha plans to invite me over to dinner to meet her parents. Join us, please!" he begged.

At first I hesitated, sensing the potential for melodrama, but then I saw the hopefulness written in his face. "Well, I suppose she was going to invite me to her parents' place anyway. If Natasha thinks it is a good idea for me to join, I'm game."

The ceremony, which had gone on for the better part of two hours, seemed to be reaching its conclusion and the audience began reassembling. The couple made their way slowly, bowing before and touching the feet of the elders until they finally reached the bride's parents. As the bride reached down to touch her parents' feet, the entire family began to weep. I stifled a few of my own tears, caught up in the groundswell of emotion. It was as if this bittersweet moment was tethered to a distant yet collective memory. I knew this much about an Indian marriage: a daughter marrying and leaving her parents' home was an irrevocable separation, an admission that she now belonged to someone else's family. In another era, she might have been bidding her family farewell forever—rarely to be seen or heard from again. It was this eternal fragmentation that the mothers and fathers and daughters and sons in the audience recalled as they wiped the tears from their eyes. Times may have changed, but in India, the past is seldom far behind.

After tears had been shed, the family composed itself. Natasha blocked her new brother-in-law's exit and lightheartedly demanded ransom for his shoes. The groom pulled out his wallet, acquiescing to tradition. Having made her point, Natasha smiled at him sweetly and refused the ransom. She stepped out of the way, handed the shoes back and embraced her sister once again.

While the wedding guests regrouped for the reception, I spotted Ajay and Gayatri from afar and crossed the hallway to meet them. Gayatri was addressing a group of people. "Why on earth do brides always look so scandalized when people start clanking glasses for them to kiss their grooms? It's absolutely prudish! Indians would have you believe that we were all conceived immaculately, *yaar*. One billion bloody immaculate conceptions!" Ajay delivered a nudge of the elbow to Gayatri, as a few passers-by gave her dirty looks. Just as I approached, a voice called out.

"Shyamala?"

I turned.

"Arjun here! You know, from the collision on the landing? Thankfully, no staircase here for you to knock me down!" He ran his hand through his disheveled salt-and-pepper hair, beaming.

"Oh, hey Arjun! No staircase, aren't you lucky!" I laughed. "What are you doing here?"

"I guess it's a small world even in this megacity. The groom is my maasi's husband's cousin's son. You know these Indian weddings; the *entire* family is invited! Even people the couple hasn't met before!"

I took the chance to look at Arjun more closely. He wore a fitted taupe *kurta* suit with an art silk indigo vest. I figured he had to be about my age, maybe thirty-four or thirty-five. His skin was several shades lighter than my own and he seemed about two days unshaven despite the formality of the occasion. His stubble, too, was salt and pepper in color.

"How do you know the couple?" he asked.

"The bride is my co-worker's sister. And you're right, I've never met either the bride or the groom! By the way, I am so sorry about rushing off the other day."

"Well, you *can* make up for it. Maybe you could take me out for coffee?"

I tried to read him. His gaze was intent, discerning, yet somewhat unrevealing. Was he merely curious about the new American girl in the complex? Or was he actually asking me out because he

73

was drawn to my blunt, more-than-slightly frazzled, collision-prone nature?

Either way, it was another invitation I didn't know how to refuse. "Sure, coffee sounds good."

But before we could continue our conversation, Natasha appeared at my side. "Shyamala, come and meet my sister."

"*Achcha* then. I'll call you to fix a day!" Arjun announced. As Natasha ushered me away, his smile was resplendent.

◆ ◆ ◆

The next morning, I decided to go to temple with Vini. I was heading to the shower when Maasi's landline rang. I was closest, but my aunt rushed to pick it up, pulling the receiver into her room. She eyed me as she listened for a moment, then hung up.

Must have been a wrong number, I thought. Realizing I had forgotten my new sandalwood soap, I walked to my room and grabbed it off my dresser.

The phone rang again. My aunt picked it up before the first ring finished. She closed the door as far as she could with the cord passing through. A thin shard of morning light made it into the hallway. I tried to ignore Maasi's hushed tones behind the door. The more I tried not to listen in, the more I found myself drawn into the one side of the conversation I could hear.

"What has happened? Is it okay to keep talking?" Vini maasi asked.

She listened attentively to the response.

"I am by myself now. I have time."

It was quiet again as she listened.

"Has somebody said something to you? Somebody becoming suspicious, isn't it?" My usually carefree aunt sounded increasingly concerned.

Another pause.

"I don't intend to say anything about the matter. If you keep quiet too, who will discover it?" My aunt's tone was clandestine.

Silence again.

"All right then. I will phone you later." Vini hung up abruptly and returned the phone to the hall table, then went back to her room. I made my way to the bathroom with utmost stealth. Through the cracked door, I could see her breathing rapidly as she unlocked her metal *cabat* and looked for something inside.

Chapter 9

Mumbai, June 2006

Vini maasi commented once that people have a sort of seasonal amnesia. Monsoons of today are always rainier than monsoons of yesterday. Summers present are always hotter than summers past.

But really, she said, this summer *was* the worst she could ever remember. The heat was unprecedented.

I couldn't comment on summers past, but for a Californian spoiled by arid heat, it was hard to fathom a hotter summer that this sweltering one in Mumbai.

Nobody mourned the passing of May.

With the arrival of June, the promise of the monsoons became a shared preoccupation. Anticipation for the rains seemed to enter every conversation. Articles about water scarcity appeared in *The Times of India* nearly every day.

According to Vini, in posh Walkeshwar, the residents went from having running water around the clock to having running water for just a few hours each day. The extra supplies hauled in by tanker trucks came at a steep price. The desperate demanded water out of an Earth that had little more to offer them. In public-address announcements celebrities pleaded with the public to reduce consumption. In a city that lived in perpetual fear of water shortages, few could remember anything like this.

The desperation for rain was not limited to people. The whole city had taken on a languid disposition. The animals that roamed the streets of the city, dogs mostly, looked sullen. The massive centuries-old banyan trees that were a fixture of this part of the city were dusty, weather-beaten, and wilted. Even the Hanging Gardens, which stood as a verdant oasis among the tall white buildings of Malabar Hill, were peppered with dead shrubs and bushes. The Arabian Sea was placid and betrayed no sign of the storms that could renew Bombay. The drought had seeped into the consciousness of the city and it could think of one thing only: water.

Still, people carried on. Day laborers suffered the brutal heat. Rickshaw drivers and taxi drivers kept their routes. Trains continued to move the masses. At home, the milkman came to deliver early every morning. And Shalu came on weekdays to do the laundry and dishes.

Several nights of the week, by some sort of agreement to which I was not privy, Shalu slept at my aunt's flat. One moment she would be engrossed in her evening chores, the next she would retrieve the thin mattress under my aunt's bed, lay it on the kitchen floor, turn off the kitchen lights, lie down in the clothes she had worn all day, and fall fast asleep on the floor not far from the pots and pans. She was undisturbed by our conversations and the occasional late-night visitor. While she seemed to sleep without a care, I never forgot about her presence on the floor of the kitchen. I simply couldn't get used to the thought that a child worked as a servant in a house in which I was living. Week after week, I wondered about her circumstances.

My thoughts spilled, without warning, into words, one Saturday morning. "Where does she live, Maasi?"

"Who?"

"Shalu. Where does she live?"

Vini measured her words. "She and Rajesh live about a thirty-minute bus ride from here."

"Rajesh is her father?" It seemed an unlikely arrangement, father and daughter working for the same woman.

She nodded.

"And they live in a slum?"

"I have never been there, but it is a slum where they are living." My aunt didn't seem to expect the line of questioning. Fearing I might have offended her, I soaped the dishes and tried to quash the judgment that had crept into my voice.

"I just wondered how they must be faring with the drought and all."

"I expect they are having some difficulty. Those who have the least are al-vays asked to sacrifice the most, isn't it? They received far too little water to begin with but with the drought, things are much worse."

"I can't even imagine. With the situation and work and all, is she still able to go to school?"

"Yes. She comes here in the morning, works for a few hours, and then goes to school. It is not a perfect situation for a child but nothing is simple in this country."

My aunt said no more on the topic. Every time I saw Shalu though, I wondered about the providence that handed us such disparate lives.

◆ ◆ ◆

At three o'clock one day in early June, I left for Churchgate Station to meet Arjun.

On stepping into the mid-afternoon heat, I understood immediately the enduring pragmatism of the siesta. With the thermometer nearly summitting the century mark and humidity not far behind, I couldn't even imagine how it felt to be cool.

In the shaded confines of the coffee bar, Arjun was already at a table reading a newspaper. He wore a crisp black collared shirt that was not tucked into his loose-fitting jeans. His wavy graying hair looked uncombed and wild. He ran his hands through the mess of hair to keep it out of his face, though it seemed determined to obstruct his view. I watched as he turned toward the window, drifting off, it seemed, on some current of reflection.

Arjun stood up to welcome me, took my right hand in his, and gently kissed my cheek. I was taken aback by the forwardness of the gesture. During my childhood, the only kisses that I had witnessed among Indians occurred as endearments between adults and young children. I had never seen adults exchange such intimacies.

"So Shyamala Mehta, we finally get to have a proper conversation!"

"I'm sorry, Natasha whisked me off before we could finish our chat last time!"

"I suppose it would be unseemly to refuse to meet the bride at her own wedding!"

We both laughed.

"I never got to ask you, what is it that brings you to India?" Arjun's voice was smooth and silvery, with an accent that was all modern Mumbaikar. "Just visiting for a few weeks?"

"Oh no—I'm here for at least six months. I'm helping the architectural team at my firm transition to a new software system. Vini maasi has been kind enough to host me while I'm here."

He smiled warmly at the mention of my aunt. "I have known Vini aunty since my parents moved to the next-door flat almost twenty years ago. I used to find excuses to go over to her place so I could explore the books on her shelves. Your maasi is a first-class character. She is very opinionated. And viciously truthful. It is what

I like best about her. She does quite well to keep my mother in line."

Something clicked in my mind. "Wait, your mom is Champaben Trivedi?"

"The one and only—but please don't hold that against me." He shook his head and laughed.

So, Arjun was the "good boy" Vini had been referring to that night she'd ranted about Champaben on the landing. Whatever her alleged misdeeds were, it was hard to imagine holding them against him. There was such a sincerity about him.

Arjun asked about my life in Los Angeles. I asked him about the drought. He mentioned his gigs working as a freelance writer by night while managing his father's factory by day. He had apparently just applied for a position as a staff journalist in New Delhi. He asked about my first impressions of Mumbai. The conversation between the two of us was effortless, with neither ebb nor lull.

We sat in the café for the better part of an hour and then wandered about the streets near Churchgate. In the scorching mid-afternoon heat, there was hardly a soul in sight.

"Are you doing all right, Shyamala? Perhaps we should head to the water's edge. It might be cooler there. You would like to see the Gateway of India no doubt?"

I hesitated. Mere mention of the Gateway evoked memories of my last visit and the massive rats that scurried around the building with the self-assuredness of bipeds with opposable thumbs. And then there was the heat.

"You know, the Gateway of India? It was built to honor the arrival of King George V and Queen Mary in 1911? Elephanta Island can be seen from there. Would you like to see it?"

"Um, sure." I hoped I sounded braver than I felt. "You certainly sound like the right man to show me around."

The taxi dropped us off a short walk from the Gateway of India. By my guess, the building must have been just shy of a hundred feet tall. It had a wide base, a central archway, and two smaller archways on either side. The structure seemed a fusion of Indian and Anglo architectural styles with intricate lattices, scalloped arches, an internal dome and other Indian embellishments all subsumed under a practical, authoritarian facade. There was something vaguely Gothic about it. It stood grand but aloof to the cityscape around it.

Just beyond the Gateway lay Bombay Harbor, gray-brown and murky. Arjun pointed toward Elephanta Island where, according to him, ancient Hindu ruins honoring Lord Shiva dated back to the fifth century. As we walked to the building, we were surrounded by hundreds of people; locals out for a stroll, tourists posing for pictures, loiterers doing nothing in particular, pan-handlers begging in English and French and German, and hawkers of everything from made-in-China toys to *bhelpuri* snacks.

When we entered the shadow of the massive structure there was a hollow coolness, the kind one feels when entering a cave. I tried to imagine the world in which such an ostentatious building would be built for the arrival of a single, solitary couple. Light shone through carved stone panels above the entryways.

"When King George and Queen Mary arrived in 1911, they only got to see a miniature mock-up version of the Gateway." Arjun's boyishly enthusiastic voice echoed through the building.

"Not the real thing?"

"Just a model made of cardboard. It took years to reclaim the land and the structure was only completed in 1924. The irony is that though King George V and Queen Mary never entered through the Gateway, when the last British troops left India in 1948, they left through it."

In the shadow of the Gateway, I felt swept up in the grandeur of my surroundings. I asked Arjun about the palatial structure across the street. "Is that the Taj Mahal Hotel?"

"Yes. At the Taj you can go sit in climate-controlled rooms, marvel at the opulent surroundings, and sip champagne more bloody expensive than the average Indian's annual salary. It is a way to visit India without having to set foot in India," he answered with intensity.

"Can we go in and see it?" I asked, hopefully. Despite his strong opinions, Arjun seemed like a man who would indulge my curiosity. I felt immensely comfortable in his presence.

He laughed and shook his head. "I suppose."

We stepped foot in the lobby. Immediately, the frenetic pace of the city slowed. The murmur of quiet conversation replaced honking horns and screaming hawkers. I had finally found a place where my pores could take a respite from sweating. Had it not been for Arjun's company, I would've surrendered to the 72°F perfection and laid myself prostrate on the pristine marble floor.

Beyond the reception desk, guests lounged about in supple, low-backed chairs that overlooked a garden with lush tropical plants. We passed high-end stores selling brand-name merchandise and wandered into a massive stairwell with a wide staircase. It had dark wooden handrails and elaborate wrought-iron banisters. The stairway bifurcated at the next floor, leading to open hallways on opposite sides of the massive space. I could see the stairwell continue up, floor after floor after floor. I gawked at the sight. If it existed, I thought, a stairway to heaven might look like this.

Arjun led me up one flight of stairs to the Sea Lounge restaurant. Just beyond the sunlit tables were a series of large windows from which I could see Bombay Harbor and the hubbub of the Gateway of India. A middle-aged host stood near the entry, dressed in a black suit. If my being an American was apparent, it certainly didn't impress him. The moment Arjun stepped into the establishment, however, the host's bearing changed. Arjun carried himself as if he were a regular, transforming himself from graying hipster with a social conscience to a pragmatic *desi* who knew exactly how to work the system.

"Welcome to the Taj. Boss, would you like a table?" asked the host.

"Give me a moment." Arjun lifted his index finger. Then he looked at me. "Would you like to have a bite here?"

"I don't think I can afford this place—"

"It would be on me. You are my guest. If you would like, we can get a table." His eyes were lively and kind.

Lost in the moment, I nearly said yes. I had no doubt he would have treated me to dinner. But this didn't seem to be his scene. He cared too much about the reality that lay on the other side of the luxurious walls. I didn't feel right taking him up on his offer.

"No, I'm good."

"Sure?" He was visibly relieved.

"Yes."

"I'll take her to see the view for a moment though," Arjun informed the host with a self-assured nod of the head.

"Absolutely boss, for a moment. We have several tables by the windows reserved for customers who will be arriving shortly."

We stood by the windows to take in the view of the Arabian Sea. I couldn't stop thinking about Arjun's restrained bravado with the host, his ample graciousness toward me, and the way his shoulder now rested delightfully against mine. After a few minutes, we retraced our steps to the ground floor. As we made our way down the winding staircase, I took in a breath of reality. *Be careful not to read too much into your time with Arjun*, I reminded myself. Surely, he was merely being a quintessential Indian host. In any case, after all I had been through, the last thing I needed was complications.

On the way out, I stopped in the opulent restroom. An attendant watched as I washed my hands, standing at the ready to hand me a washcloth. I observed her reflection in the mirror by the sink. Her graying hair was swept up into a bun. She waited on me, patiently, as I suspected she did with all the women who used the facilities. She could have been a grandmother, an elder who might have expected to be cared for by an extended family as Indian tradition typically dictated. But she was here, handing out washcloths to tourists, expats, and wealthy locals. Why? What was her story? She reached forward to hand me a cloth hand towel.

"Thank you," I said. The sound of the phrase bounced off the marble walls and echoed back to us again and again. With each reverberation, the words lost their force.

I dried my hands on the soft cloth, disquieted. If only for my own reasons and only in this moment, how did I express that I saw her as more than a purveyor of linens for the wealthy?

"*Na-ma-ste.*" I took care to pronounce it the way Indians do, acutely aware of how my yoga teacher in LA always put the accent on the wrong syllable. I put my hands to my chest in the prayer position and dipped my head forward, the gesture that went with the greeting, fully expecting her to laugh at me.

"*Na-ma-ste,*" she responded kindly, without a trace of amusement on her weathered features.

I reached to my wallet to offer her a tip.

She shook her head, refusing to take what I had yet to offer.

I turned away from her, unsettled. In my small gesture of offering money, the urban do-gooder in me thought I was helping. I was only helping myself really, helping myself feel better about my own generosity in a world of haves and have-nots.

◆　◆　◆

On our way home, we hit the peak of central Bombay traffic.

We drove slowly past colonial-era buildings made from English-style bricks and mortar but with distinctly Indian flourishes—balconies with carved wooden walls and round towers topped with domes. Though worn by time, lack of maintenance, and a ubiquitous black mold that covered their surfaces, these buildings had tremendous character and stood the test of time. Other buildings were not so fortunate. They were decaying with wide cracks spanning their walls and visible water damage from years of monsoon rains.

"It's hard to believe people live and work in these buildings," I said.

"Hundreds of thousands of people move to Bombay every day but nobody moves out. Every square inch of this city that is habitable is inhabited. People live and work in buildings that should be condemned. But they live in these places because they have no choice. And, of course, our people are believers that when it is your time to go, it is your time to go." Arjun sighed.

I nodded, my eyes still fixed on the scenes outside. How many times had I heard my father say those words? When he lost his job as an aerospace engineer, it was fate that was to blame. When he and my mother bought their first brand-new car, it was their good karma (not their hard work) that was given credit. And when it was time for the end, well, even that day was preordained. Yet, as often as we ABCDs heard these beliefs uttered, we had been seduced by the American legacy of self-determination. We witnessed our parents weather hardship through guile, frugality, and perseverance. We watched them sublimate the thrill that comes with success with one eye always on the rough times that might lie ahead. The proof of self-determination stood before us in the tangible form of our mothers and fathers. A serene acceptance of destiny made no sense to me.

Suddenly, our car rolled to a standstill. A group of young men ran past our taxi.

"This doesn't look good," Arjun said to me. "*Idher roko*. Pull over here." He motioned to the driver to turn into an alley on our left. As we came slowly upon the street, it was clear that it was jammed with cars as well.

Voices rose from the rear, growing louder as they approached. We craned our heads behind us to stare out of the back window. Within seconds, a large group of people, mostly men, had rushed toward us. A young woman carried a sign that read '*For corporations, water flows; to poor Mumbaikars hardly a drop goes*'. Several men banged the hood of the taxi and the cars that were around us. I was alarmed. A mix of curiosity and apprehension filled Arjun's face. Our driver got out of the car and began shouting curses at the people as they ran by. Waves of protestors passed us.

Once it became clear that the crowd had no inclination to interfere with us, the driver got back into the car.

"More protests. I have never seen so many. Every year thousands of people in this city become sick from drinking the water that comes from the taps. Even then they demand it because contaminated water is better than no water at all."

I shook my head. "The situation really sounds dire."

"Civilizations have fallen for lack of water," Arjun agreed.

"And here I was, worrying about being alone for the rest of my life." The thought had barely formed itself in my mind before it escaped censorship at my lips. I restrained the immense urge to kick myself. What had made me divulge that particular truth and on our very first outing together? There was just something about Arjun—something that inspired candor.

Arjun smiled. In his eyes was, it seemed, an awareness that I had revealed too much.

His voice became hushed. "Do think of me when you find yourself alone in this city. It seems hard to believe in a place as jammed with people as this, but quite often I find myself in the same predicament."

I stared wordlessly at Arjun as, finally, with a start, the car began to move again.

Later that night I thought about our conversation. *Alone.* Arjun must have picked up on how I had used the word—to know what I meant when I spoke it. I wasn't referring to occasional solitude when one craved company. I wasn't speaking of a Friday night without plans to go out with friends. I was speaking of loneliness; the type that silently pervaded my suburban house every evening as I ate at a table set for one. It was loneliness that accompanied me to bed every night and greeted me every morning without leaving an impression on my sheets.

Chapter 10

BOMBAY, 1962

Pramila disappeared from the flat before her mother could remind her that she was much too old to be playing games with boys. She erupted out of the landing and into the alley to join a game of *gilli danda*. Just beyond the line of parked Lambretta scooters, Gautam had scratched a large circle into the dirt, and was now fielding alongside Manu from the fifth floor, Rakesh from the ground floor, Pradeep from the complex next door, Arun from the building across the street, and Harsh who lived next door to Gautam. Vivek had taken the position at bat in the center of the circle, which was roughly four meters in diameter, holding the long wooden *danda* bat in his hand. He was poised over two heavily vetted rocks that were the group's prized possessions. The rocks provided the ideal surface upon which to balance the much smaller stick, the *gilli*.

Vivek looked up from the *gilli*. "Pramila! How long it took you! Come be on my team!"

The makeshift playground was little more than a narrow alley between two apartment buildings. Pramila lined up behind the batters, Vasant who lived on the same floor as her, Jagu from the third floor, Sam from Arun's building, and Pinku, who was a bit of a mystery since nobody knew his real name or where he lived exactly.

Without any official warning that the game had begun, Vivek swung the *danda* downwards toward the end of the tiny *gilli*, causing it to fly into the air. He swung the *danda* when the *gilli* was chest high and with a "WHAP!" hit the *gilli*. He placed the *danda* on the circle in the sand.

"*Arré baap re!* That is a long one!" yelled Pinku. "Good luck catching that—you'll not be able to get Vivek out this time!"

Manu slid to catch the *gilli* but couldn't reach it. He cursed. Everyone in the crowd knew that Manu and Vivek had an unwritten rivalry. Whether the rivalry was for the title of best *gilli-danda* player or for Pramila's affections was a bit of a debate.

Pinku approximated how many *danda* lengths the *gilli* had traveled. "Six!" he announced. "Six points our team!"

Manu kicked the ground in disappointment.

Vasant was up for bat next. He positioned the *gilli* with great patience.

"*Eh, Vasant, jaldi kar!* Hurry up! We do not have all day," Manu yelled.

Vasant adjusted the *gilli* twice before hitting it into the air and swinging as it came down. The only sound was the sound of air being sliced. This happened once, twice, and three times.

"You are out!" Manu announced smugly while looking at Vivek. Then, as usual, Vasant put the *danda* down and, with slumped shoulders, made his way to the end of the batters' line.

Jagu was up next and scored three points. Sam struck out when Harsh managed to catch the *gilli*. And Pinku wowed everyone when he managed to hit a double by hitting the *gilli* twice while it was in mid-air.

Finally, it was Pramila's turn.

She hit the *gilli* gently so that it sailed upward. This was her favorite moment of the game, watching the *gilli* come back down and waiting to hit it at just the right moment. She swung the *danda* and hit the *gilli* with such force that it took a second to find the *gilli* in the air.

"*Arré? Shabash!* What? Well done! That is a harder hit than even Vivek's. How do you do that?" Vasant asked.

Rakesh initially ran to catch the *gilli* but realized it was out of reach. He stood back and watched as it hit the ground far behind him.

"Strong arms, what else? You all try carrying water buckets upstairs to the flat every morning instead of making your sisters do it! That is how you get this kind of swing. Strong arms," Pramila said.

The two teams lost track of time but not the score. By the time mothers began to call for their children, the score was 30-31 with Manu's team in the lead. They held a short celebration.

"Shall we play tomorrow?" Vivek asked his team, his eyes directed at Pramila.

"I will be here," Pramila said, hoping to escape her chores once again.

"Us too," said Pinku for Sam, Pradeep, and Vasant.

Manu approached Pramila and said quietly, "Remember there is always room on our team for you!"

"I won't forget." Pramila wondered if any of the other boys had noticed Manu's comment. Before Manu could say anything else, she made her way to the building.

As she entered, her schoolmates Mira and Deena were talking on the steps.

"Why do you always play with those boys only?" Mira asked, her attention on the remaining stragglers in the alley.

Mira was a chubby girl who carried her girth in her center section and had a very prominent chin, the opposite of Deena, who was unnaturally tall with a rather high forehead. Whenever the two girls were together, Mira did most of the talking.

"It is fun, why else? Also, I am the best hitter on the team. They need me."

"You are a very strange girl, Pramila. Playing with those boys all day, coming home with dirt all over yourself," Mira chided.

"Better than sitting on the steps gossiping!" Pramila bristled at the criticism.

"Have you noticed the way Vivek looks at you, *yaar*? And Manu too. It is no wonder only that those two are fighting all the time," Mira whispered.

"Oh Mira, stop dreaming of him. Vivek belongs to Pramila, isn't it?" Deena said finally.

"He does *not* belong to me!" Pramila retorted. Heat rose in her cheeks.

"He could be yours though. You would be a good match, caste and all. And he looks like Raj Kapoor in that film *Aashiq*!" Mira raised her eyebrows. "Vivek is more than suitable, isn't he Deena?"

Deena nodded.

Pramila's patience was wearing thin. "Look Mira, I am not interested in Vivek so consider him yours. I have no time for such nonsense."

"Of course not! Do you think you are going to be prime minister someday?" Mira laughed at the absurdity of the idea. "You are too busy with your head buried in those English books and your mind thinking weird ideas to notice how lucky you are! What a loss! Come on Deena, let's go."

Mira and Deena did synchronized about-faces and climbed the stairs, round one on the left and tall one on the right. From behind, Pramila thought, their contrast was even more striking.

Later that night, after dinner was eaten and the dishes washed, Ba took out a burlap bag of rice. She spilled the grains on to two large plates. One for Pramila and one for herself. Pramila wanted so badly to slip out of the kitchen and lay her weary body down on her mattress. But Ba pushed one plate toward her. A large heap of rice with countless grains still to be sifted through stood between her and that mattress.

Ba took the other plate and began removing dirty or misshapen grains. Pramila grudgingly pulled the other plate toward her. She swiped at a trail of the fragrant basmati rice until she could see nearly every grain in it. Again and again she did this, sorting just as Ba did.

Then, her mother began to hum. Ba rarely sang but, when she did, it was something to behold. The melody was heavy with longing. Pramila had heard it before and though she could not recall the exact words, the song evoked the memory and mood of a rain shower at twilight. Before she knew it, lost in the sweet sound of her mother's voice, Pramila had sorted through each and every grain on the plate.

She thought about the rice grains as they made their way across the plate. Maybe that was how life was too. At fourteen, Pramila had countless moments yet to be experienced stacked before her like that heap of rice. At one instant, that heap seemed unending. But those moments would pass just as the rice grains she had sorted through and someday she would look back wondering how quickly she had swept through those times. How did she want to live them? There were a million ways and yet for a girl there were but a few. And which way sung to her? There was one thing for certain, she did not want to live the way Mira had suggested. Not with Vivek or Manu. She thought about that for a while. Not with Vivek or Manu or anyone else she knew either. Then how? What did she want? Had she the right to want anything at all?

◆ ◆ ◆

Sometime later, Pramila found herself sitting on the train with her father. He was busy reliving his favorite scenes from the English movie that they had just seen at the Eros Cinema. "That Gregory Peck chap made a most wonderful Atticus Finch. The book was too good, I was worried the movie would not do it justice."

Even mention of Mr. Peck's name made Pramila blush. He was a handsome man.

"*Tane movie gamuthu?* Did you like the movie?" Papa asked.

"*Bahu gamyu mane.* I really liked it. But they were speaking a different type of English."

"American English is quite distinct from the British style, the type we are used to speaking in India. From now on, I am going to speak to you in English only."

"*Kem*, Papa? Why?"

"It may be useful to you someday. I don't know whether it is a good thing or not only but it seems that English is the language of the future."

"Papa, are you going to marry me off to some boy in America?" Pramila asked with a half-smile.

"That is your mother's business, no? I just wish for you to see the world. Maybe someday you can take me also."

"See the world?"

"Yes, Paris, Nairobi, Kuala Lumpur, Cairo. Maybe you could become a hostess on Air India or some such thing. Is that so crazy?"

Papa had such ideas! She expected him to laugh along with her, but his expression was hopeful. He was not joking.

Of the women Pramila knew, none worked outside the house. None had traveled outside the country. Every woman she knew was either a mother, a grandmother, or a spinster who had been unable to marry due to what was considered an unhappy accident of fate.

It was unusual enough that her father planned to send his daughters to college. Mira and Deena and countless other girls were never even expected to finish secondary school. But for her father to suggest that she travel abroad, educated, unmarried, and unbetrothed, as part of some sort of profession—that was unprecedented.

When the train finally rolled to a start, Papa began to speak of the film again. Something about the greatness of ordinary people and how children often saw the truth more clearly than their elders. She listened to him, somewhat distracted, imagining herself as an air hostess serving Gregory Peck on a flight bound for Cairo.

Chapter 11

MUMBAI, JUNE 2006

Living with Vini maasi allowed me to glimpse traits in her that I might never otherwise have noticed. My aunt had taken the cliché of the sad old spinster and gutted it entirely. She spent much time in her living room surrounded by magazines and books, gathering from them the same comfort that others derive from husbands and daughters and sons.

Vini rose out of bed without any predictability. Regardless of when she awoke, she started her morning on the balcony, her abundance of hair falling behind, silvery strands catching the golden morning light, her arms splayed out in front of her, with the balcony door open behind her. Then, she noisily pulled out her newspaper and read the pages sometimes over coffee, other times over *chai*. She asked for my opinion on a number of topics and was disappointed when we were in agreement. She sought every opportunity to have her mind changed. Not that changing her mind was necessarily easy.

For all their similarities in looks, I could hardly believe my aunt and my mother were so very different. Neither fear nor expectation burdened my relationship with my aunt. With my mother they animated our relationship. When I was a child, my mom had feared my every action would result in self-annihilation. When I grew to be an adult, she constantly reminded me of my own aspirations until they felt as heavy as expectations. After my breakup with Neil, her fears for my future and the weight of those expectations had grown unbearable.

My aunt seemed to fear nothing—not the prying eyes of rumor-prone neighbors, not a late-night drive through Mumbai in the Ambassador, not living alone in her Walkeshwar flat far away from family. Though she did appear to have a peculiar obsession with the telephone. I noticed it after I started getting calls of my own on her line. Vini was at the phone by the second ring. Whenever I got to the phone before she did, she hovered about to find out who I was speaking to. She seemed edgy. It was the only situation in which I felt I may have overstepped her hospitality. Eventually, I directed people to call my mobile.

Late one afternoon, Vini had just walked in from an errand when the phone rang. I let her answer it. She spoke in Hindi but I could hear the dismay in her words. She mentioned Shalu's name. After a short conversation, my aunt hung up.

"Did something happen to Shalu?"

"That was Rajesh. Shalu has typhoid. He is at the hospital with her right now," Maasi said gravely.

"Oh no! Is she going to be okay?"

"Last time I saw Shalu, she did not look well. I told her to stay home for a few days, to get some rest. Rajesh says she had high fever and pain in the stomach starting yesterday. He took her to the public hospital. He said that the infection was in her blood and her BP was very low. She is getting medicine and fluids."

"Typhoid. That's serious."

"He sounded worried. I hope they are treating her properly." Vini was distraught. "I know three people who had typhoid last year. They lived in fine flats in this part of Mumbai. Even they are not safe. But things are very, very bad in the slums. It was bad before, but now with the drought. What to do? If a man is thirsty enough, he will drink even dirty water, isn't it?"

I bit my lip. How many times had I left the water on while brushing my teeth back in LA—clean water running down the drain—without giving a thought to how many people in the world might fight for a chance to drink a drop of it. "There must be something we can do," I urged, even though I couldn't name it.

"This problem—it seems like it is beyond any of us."

"Can Rajesh afford the hospital?"

"I offered help with hospital bills, but Rajesh said no only."

We both sat at our usual spots on the couch and looked silently in different directions. Vini seemed at a loss for what to do.

I proposed the first option that came to mind. "I should go visit her in the hospital."

"You want to go to the public hospital to see her? I don't think that is a good idea."

"Why not?"

Vini maasi paused. It probably wasn't commonplace for a woman from the swanky slopes of Walkeshwar to visit her servant in the public hospital.

"I am just not sure—it's just not something that is done . . ."

It didn't seem like Vini to let convention stand in the way. It felt as though something else was going on—something that I didn't understand.

"Maasi, Shalu is in the hospital, we've got to do something! I'll go."

Vini's brow remained furrowed. "Well, you have no idea where to go, so I had better come too."

◆ ◆ ◆

The hospital was a ramshackle old building in a rundown old neighborhood. The taxi driver pulled over at the side of the road in a barrage of honking horns.

As soon as we entered the hospital, I had the immediate desire to walk right back out of its double doors and away from the sickness. The air on the ward was heavy with the smell of bleach and sweat. As we walked down the corridor, I peeked into several of the hospital rooms. Each one was packed with cots. Family members sat at the bedsides of loved ones, feeding them from tiffins or covering them with shawls that seemed to be from home. We checked in at the nurses' station. As we made our way to Shalu's room, I was aware that several staff were watching us.

"It's like they know that she is a servant and you are her boss. How do they know we are not her family or her friends?" I whispered.

"People just know." Vini stopped at the doorway of the room.

Shalu's room was tiny, though it was furnished to accommodate three patients. Two of the beds were empty and sat unmade. A fluorescent lightbulb illuminated the center of the room, casting an unnaturally white light there while leaving the corners in relative darkness. It was the type of light in which everyone, patients and visitors alike, looked sickly. The aqua-blue paint on the walls was peeling and seemed an unnaturally garish color in which to house the ill.

Rajesh sat in a chair next to Shalu's bed, his back to the door, staring out of the small window next to an even smaller wall mirror. He rested his hand next to his daughter's, his little finger just touching hers. When he heard us enter the room, he slowly turned toward the door. It took a moment for him to register us in his sights. Once he had, he stood up with a start. He seemed a different man from the one who had bounded up the staircase carrying my luggage to Vini's apartment. His back was hunched and his clothes unkempt. His bloodshot eyes darted back and forth between my aunt and me as if he were deciding what to say to us. Then he slumped back down into his hard-backed chair and his expression transformed from surprised to resigned. He turned to his daughter.

Shalu lay on a small metal-framed bed. She was sleeping fitfully. Her hair had come undone from the thick black ribbons that had held it in place. The tiny diamond that studded her nose, which usually sparkled brilliantly against her dark skin, was dulled in the unnaturally white light. Sweat beaded at her lip. Her cheeks were sallow. She had an intravenous line in her arm with fluid running through it. She looked so tiny and frail in the hospital bed that my heart sank at the sight of her.

"How is she?" my aunt asked in Gujarati.

Rajesh looked at his daughter. Tears gathered at the verge of his lower lids.

"*Bo beemaar che.* She is extremely sick." Rajesh delicately ran his index finger along Shalu's colorless cheek. "She is hardly able to recognize me. I cannot lose her."

"Try not to worry. The doctors must be giving her strong medicines. Shalu will get better. But we just must be patient, no?" Vini seemed to be trying to calm herself as much as Rajesh.

"They have taken good care of her here. With all that has happened in past—I just—I do not have the strength to do this again."

My aunt considered Rajesh intently. Some sort of understanding seemed to pass between them.

"You must not compare to the past. This is not the same situation. Shalu will be okay." Vini's voice cracked with emotion.

Rajesh sighed. He didn't respond to my aunt; instead, his gaze settled on Shalu. He seemed to find reassurance only in the ebb and flow of his daughter's breath.

After my aunt had spoken to the doctors, we sat with Rajesh and Shalu for some time. I wondered about what tragedy had befallen Rajesh in the past and how my aunt came to know of it. I looked at Shalu in her hospital bed, then her father in his hard-backed chair, then the reflection of the scene in the small wall mirror with the unexpected image of me within it all. I felt helpless, unable to do anything to change her situation.

Shalu's condition remained tenuous for several days. Between fevers, she had paroxysms of chills. Her body was limp, her skin ashy. At first, the antibiotics the doctors gave her were not working. Eventually, with Vini's dogged inquiries about why Shalu was not getting better, the doctors changed her regimen.

◆ ◆ ◆

Two days later, on the commute to work, Arjun texted. "How is Shalu?"

My heart was heavy as I recalled her sickly appearance. I texted him back. "She's terribly ill. Going to hospital later today with Maasi, will let you know more once I do."

Subhash had picked me up earlier than usual that morning so I could get to JTM before our meetings began. The first part of the software conversion was behind schedule and we'd had to accelerate our timelines to stay on target. The entire team had been pulling long hours for weeks now. I needed the extra time to catch up on my work. But my thoughts were with Shalu. Thankfully, Natasha was kind enough to offer to lead the afternoon meetings so I could visit her with Maasi.

During most of our visits to the hospital, it made sense to let Vini do the talking. It almost seemed like she was reluctant to leave me alone with Shalu and Rajesh. Perhaps she was trying to bridge the language barrier between us? I didn't protest. I was more than slightly self-conscious about my Hindi. But having witnessed Rajesh's heartache for days, at our fourth visit I couldn't remain silent. It didn't feel right to express my concern for Shalu in English, so while Maasi stayed back at the nurses' station to make some inquiries, I headed to Shalu's room, rehearsing what I was going to say in Hindi.

As I entered, I greeted Rajesh and attempted to inquire about her condition. "*Aap ni Shalu kaisu hee?*" The words were awkward in my mouth.

"Huh?" Rajesh replied. It was obvious that my first attempt at Hindi had missed its mark.

"*Shalu kem cho?*" I tried in Gujarati.

I heard a slight squeaking sound come from Rajesh's direction, which quickly turned into a chuckle and escalated into frenzied laughter. I hadn't realized my Gujarati was that bad.

"It has been a first-class day," he said in Gujarati. "First class! The fever has broken. Shalu has awoken—she opened her eyes and recognized me. She even said, 'Papa'!"

"That is wonderful!" I settled into my broken Gujarati.

Rajesh glanced at his daughter and swallowed hard. His eyes grew misty again.

"It is not so common for someone like you—like your maasi— to come to this kind of place. Those first days, I didn't know what was going to happen only. Did I need to prepare for the worst? Shalu is all that I have. As I thought this, you and Viniben walked into the room. You cannot know how much that has helped me. Your family has done too much."

Rajesh's gratitude made me uneasy. "It is nothing, really."

"This is not the first timing that you people have been helping me and my Shalu."

I was entirely focused on his words—hoping to understand what was going on between the lines—to understand Vini's initial hesitancy to visit Shalu in the hospital and Rajesh's comment about what my family had done for his.

Just then, Shalu muttered something unintelligible. She tossed her head about and began arguing with someone who existed in some far-off realm of her imagination.

Rajesh rushed to her bedside and grabbed her hand. "*Beti, tu phir jag gayi*. My sweet girl, you are awake again."

Shalu raised her head and turned to her father. She struggled to keep her eyes open, the fatigue quickly overwhelming her. She dropped her head back on to her dented pillow. Her fingers twitched as she tried, weakly, to grasp his hand.

Vini walked into the room saying something about how there wasn't a nurse to be found on the floor. She saw Shalu grasping Rajesh's hand and stopped mid-sentence. Relief washed over her irate expression.

"Maasi, Shalu woke up and her fever has broken!"

"*Shabash!* That is great news!" A wide grin appeared on her face.

Rajesh turned to Vini. "Thank you, Viniben. Thank you for everything."

"What is this thank-you business again? I've told you before, all that matters is Shalu—that she is feeling better, no?" my aunt scolded warmly.

Rajesh tilted his head from side to side in agreement.

"Let us give them some time," Vini said with a nod to me, though I had the distinct impression she wished to stay.

We made our way to the door, both of us glancing at father and daughter before leaving. We hailed a taxi to take us home. My aunt was quiet for most of the route. She seemed to be mulling something over.

We were about halfway home when she said, "Can you imagine that half of Bombay's population lives in the *jhopadpatti*? You know, the slum? That is like eight million people, maybe more. Eight million people," she said, thinking out loud. "No rain, not enough water, too many people, more and more coming into the city every day, buildings coming up like bamboo shoots in fertile ground."

I shook my head.

"People with the means, you know they have their ways to get what they need and more. Why fix the system when you can pay off this tanker chap or that municipal bugger to get more than your fair share? Maybe the system is beyond a fix. Who was that famous *gora* fellow in England?"

"Hmmm, famous white guys in England, let me think about this," I said, scratching my head in jest.

"You know, the one who stole from the rich and gave to the poor?"

"Robin Hood?"

"Yes, yes, Robin Hood. I guess he is more legend than man. Legend or no, Bombay needs someone like that—someone who bends the rules for the right reasons."

I nodded. That was a creative way to address the problem—not that I was any expert.

"Shyamala, our lives here, they must seem odd to you, isn't it?" she asked at length.

"How do you mean?"

"Well, you must see the dirt and the poverty and the desperation of so many people packed into this city, no? This place is not like America."

I thought about Shalu drinking contaminated water and contracting typhoid—that was something I had never dreamed possible in the US. On the other hand, America-the-dream was different from America-the-reality. "Yes, there is a difference here. All of it, the dirt and the poverty and the desperation, they're not hidden here. They cannot be ignored. It's all just out there for you to see. In America, though, the same conditions are present—they're just not always so obvious—and the scale is different."

Vini wasn't going to be distracted by generic musings about the state of the human condition. "I won't deny or defend. But is that what you'll tell your friends about us when you go back home? Will that be what you remember?" My aunt turned to me, awaiting an answer.

"Of course not, Maasi, there is so much more to this city."

"When injustice is everywhere, people stop seeing it anywhere, no? It becomes like a—like a billboard on the roadside that you see every day but you cannot remember what the advertisement says. You stop noticing. But there are a few who remember each line in the advertisement. Some who recall per-fect-ly every time the advertisement is changed. Just as there are some here who never stop seeing the injustice."

"Maasi, you mustn't feel like you have to explain anything to me."

"No, Shyama, I don't want you to think that the situation is al-right with me."

Though I suspected this particular train of thought had originated in Shalu's hospital room, I knew she was speaking about something much broader. I was moved by her candor.

Something about the way she spoke—the conviction with which she expressed herself—reminded me of my mother.

Chapter 12

Mumbai, June 2006

Two days after her discharge from the hospital, Shalu was back at Vini's flat. My aunt urged her to stay home and recover, but Rajesh insisted that she return to work. Shalu, he said, was anxious to get back to her routine. I knew that money was tight for Rajesh's family. Perhaps there was no choice.

I wanted to continue the conversation that Rajesh had begun in the hospital. It was apparent that something tragic had befallen Rajesh, something that my aunt had known about, something she had helped him through. I wanted to know more. Once Shalu came home, however, Rajesh reverted to his formal ways. Now that the boundary had reappeared, I wasn't sure I would have the chance to finish the conversation.

On her return, Shalu refused to be coddled. If the laundry loads were too light (Vini had begun to hand wash them just like me), she asked why she didn't have the usual amount of clothes. When we told her to skip washing dishes for the day, she snuck into the kitchen and did them anyway. On another level, though, Shalu became more relaxed. When I spoke to her in my broken Gujarati or my unique rendition of Hindi, she answered in long sentences. It took me a while to catch on that she was testing me. She repressed her smile, mostly, but occasionally broke into laughter when I accidentally said something vulgar.

Several days after Shalu's return home, Kaushik uncle from the third floor stopped by asking for my aunt, who was on her daily trip to the market.

"Is everrrything okay?" he asked, his "r"s prone to intermittent rolling. "We heard that your girl has been in hospital."

"Our girl?" I resented that he didn't use her name. "The only person who has been in the hospital is Shalu."

"Ah yes, Shalu. We heard that she had some type of issues."

"Issues?" I thought of how sick she had appeared that first day I went to the hospital and how scared I was for her.

"Fee-males of her age these days—" Kaushik uncle said, shaking his head dramatically.

"Excuse me?" All I needed was for a middle-aged man to tell me about what was wrong with *females* in the modern world.

"Things are changing you know. The fe-males—"

"Wait," I said, annoyance flaring. "What are you implying?"

"Must I say it?" He leaned in toward the door and whispered. "She is prrregnant, no? That is why she had to go in hospital."

"Pregnant? Who said this?" I was enraged. Who would start such a rumor?

Kaushik uncle would have been a dreadful poker player. His eyes rested upon the door of our next-door neighbor.

I tried to compose myself. "Kaushik uncle, with all due respect, Shalu isn't *pregnant*. She had *typhoid*. Whoever's spreading these types of rumors needs to be taught to—*to mind their own business.*"

"Typhoid? She had the typhoid? There must be some mix-up isn't it? Not to worry. Tell your maasi that we were just inquiring to find out how she was doing without the help."

Kaushik uncle took the stairs in twos as if fleeing the scene of a crime.

Without the help? How about asking how Shalu was doing? How about an ounce of empathy for the human being who was on her deathbed just a few days ago? I was in a rage. I went over and knocked on Champa's door.

There was no answer.

I heard footsteps coming up the staircase. I was prepared to ambush Champa as she turned the corner.

"Maasi?"

"Shyamala, what on earth are you doing?" she asked, her eyes round and unblinking. The sight of me knocking on Champa's door had apparently inspired terror in her.

"I need to speak to Champa."

"Get back from there! Have you lost your mind? Why would you wish to speak to her?" Vini firmly removed my hand from the door.

"She's despicable that's why." I was so angry I could barely formulate the sentence.

"This is true no doubt, but even if she opens the door, and you inform her of such things, I don't think you will convince her."

"She's spreading rumors. She's been telling people that the reason Shalu was sick and needed hospitalization was that she was pregnant!"

"Pregnant?"

I nodded.

Maasi clenched her jaw, the vein in her temple bulging.

"The nerve of that woman! She is beyond despicable. She just loves to create scandal where there isn't any. She has no idea what Shalu was going through! Shyamala, get out of my way!"

My aunt nudged me away from the door and rapped on it again and again. But her knocking was no more effective than mine. After several minutes, we admitted to ourselves that Champa wasn't going to answer. We had nothing to show for our fury other than chafed knuckles.

◆ ◆ ◆

I stood on my aunt's balcony peering down at the street. The scene below, which had become familiar to me over the past several weeks, felt strange to me again. I watched as a plastic bag and a piece of paper swirled around each other, caught up in a breeze. Why, in a country with so much trash, could one never find a trash can? I looked over at the wrought-iron gate. Were they fixing the water pipe yet again? How many times was it going to take?

What was I doing here? I was miles from home, in a place I didn't understand, alone as ever. How would I survive for another five months in Bombay—or Mumbai—or whatever the hell it was called?

Craving a familiar voice, I checked the time difference and dialed Claire who let me vent for a while before she had to go back on shift. I hung up reluctantly. My thoughts took a predictable turn at times like this. I tried to resist but quickly lost my footing. The past was drawing me back in.

A few months after our breakup, Neil had stopped by at my house, unannounced. My mother, who had been visiting, answered the door. She invited him in and offered to make *chai*. I came inside from my backyard, only to find the two of them sitting at the kitchen table, exchanging pleasantries over teacups and snacks.

My mother excused herself and I found myself alone with Neil. He apologized for leaving me at the altar. He told me that his parents thought he had made a mistake and wanted us to try again. But when he stood in front of me and told me he still loved me, I knew it was a lie. I had waited so long to hear those words!

But in the months since he left me at the altar, something within me had changed; I was finally seeing clearly. Could it be that he wasn't just lying to me but lying to himself as well? I reacted before my thoughts had fully coalesced. His *chai* unfinished, I practically pulled his chair out from under him and nearly pushed him out of the door, slamming it behind him. I collapsed against the door and slid down it as it closed. I couldn't even muster the strength to cry.

After all that happened, I had still been in love with him. As I heard him turn the car's ignition, I imagined, for an instant, the feel of his hand against the nape of my neck and the tenderness of his fingers as he swept the hair from my face. I wanted so much to chase after him and feel those things again. If I had opened that door again, I would have given in to him entirely.

I had wanted Neil to come back to me, had wanted to settle down with him, but now sitting slumped at the front door, it became painfully apparent to me that the cost was far too high. Maybe it was just the idea of him, the idea of the life we had planned to make together that had held sway over me all those months since he left me at the altar? But none of that mattered if he didn't truly want me.

When my mom came back, she glanced around. "Shyamala, where is Neil?"

"Gone."

"Where?" she inquired, the finality of the word "gone" taking a moment to sink in.

"I told him to leave. I told him never to come back."

"What? Why? He had come to ask your forgiveness. Did you even give him a chance?"

"He just didn't get it Mom."

"Get what? What was he not getting?"

"I'm not sure he understands what he did to me. He told me that his parents thought he had made a mistake."

"So? He did make a mistake, no? Isn't that what you have been saying for months now?" My mom's accent was becoming thicker. "For months you cried for just this thing."

"Not once did he admit that *he thought* he made a mistake. He just doesn't get it, Mom."

"I do not get it myself, Shyamala. He was offering you exactly what you wanted, no?"

"There is no going back, Mom." I didn't tell her that Neil had said he loved me because I knew it wasn't the truth.

"I do not understand you kids. You make every-thing so complicated. You think life fits into the little boxes. Mid-twenties: time to have fun. Late-twenties: work on career and have fun. Early thirties: finally time to get serious about finding someone especially if you want kids. The someone has to be smart, and handsome, and just so and so. And if things don't work out, if things are not perfect, you just give up. Just like that."

"If things don't work out? You make it sound like I made the decision on a whim! This is my future that we are talking about. Shouldn't I be able to decide what is best?"

Mom looked out of the window. Somehow, this infuriated me.

"Why are you second-guessing me? Actually, never mind. Why am I surprised? You always second-guess me."

"I am not second-guessing you. I am just expressing the facts. Not everyone gets a second chance to have what they have wished for. Here you are getting a second chance—and you are just giving it away—just because Neil did not say, 'I made a mistake Shyamala' exactly the way you wanted him to."

"It is too late."

Mom opened her mouth as if to say something. I focused on it, waiting for her to speak. All manner of righteous indignation was poised at the tip of my tongue.

Instead, she bit her lip. At length she said, "It is not for me to decide. That much is true."

"That's it? That's all you have to say?"

"Yes. Shyamala, I did not come here to fight with you."

"But you are not going to support my decision either? Right?"

"You have so many choices nowadays. I think sometimes it makes life harder."

Another humorless laugh escaped me. "That's just another way of saying you don't believe I am making the right one, isn't it? Listen, Mom. I'm tired. I'm going to lie down."

This argument had occurred many months ago. But now, from Vini's flat, thinking back to that day, I remembered something that had previously slipped from my memory. I recalled awakening from my nap to the scent of Indian cooking. Mom had fixed an entire Indian meal: *rotis*, *sabji*, *dal*, and rice and had set the table for dinner. On the plate, she had left a note saying, "Call me if you want company."

Despite everything that had happened, she had taken the time to make sure my belly wouldn't be empty. If I could only see her concern for my love life as just another kindness—like the one waiting on the dining table for me that day.

For several days after my conversation with Kaushik uncle, Vini maasi and I held a sort of vigil outside of Champa's door. Maasi was sure to keep an eye on her place during the day when I was at work and I did the same when she went on an outing or to temple. If we heard footsteps on the staircase, one of us was sure to barge out of the front door to see if they belonged to Champa. If she was going out of her way to avoid us, it was working.

One Sunday morning, dressed in threadbare pajama bottoms and a camisole, I cracked open the front door to get the newspaper. I heard someone rounding the corner up the stairs. I stood straight up and opened the door completely. One way or another, I was going to confront Champa about the rumors she was spreading.

"Did I catch you by surprise?" Arjun smiled.

"I was expecting—"

"My mother?" he asked. "I can tell by the look on your face. She and my father have gone away to stay in Devlali for a few weeks. What has she done this time?"

"Um. No need to worry about it, I'll chat with her when she returns." It should have been no surprise to see Arjun in front of his parents' flat. Still, I found his presence slightly disarming.

"By the way, thanks for sending all those updates on Shalu's condition. I am so relieved she is better!" In the wake of her illness, we hadn't seen each other since our visit to the Gateway of India but Arjun had continued to keep in touch by phone.

"It was scary. She was so sick! Thank goodness she seems to be back to her usual self."

Arjun nodded and smiled. "That is good news, *yaar*. Listen, I have an idea. Why don't you come with me tonight for a walk at Chowpatty?"

He observed me and I felt conscious of the bareness of my shoulders and the sheerness of my cotton pajama bottoms. Why did a part of me hope that he might be taking note as well?

"I'd really like that," I said. A walk at the beach with Arjun would be a welcome escape from all those thoughts of Neil.

By the time we reached Chowpatty that evening, the sky was painted with the pallet of dusk—pink, orange, red, and lavender. Though the sea itself was calm, the beach was abuzz with activity. It was Sunday, Bombay's collective day of rest. Young lovers, unable to find a moment of seclusion in this city, took to the beach in droves. At least there, among the masses, they could enjoy a bit of anonymity.

I was conscious of being surrounded by couples as they held hands and exchanged intimacies. I wondered if Arjun was aware as well. We slipped off our sandals and walked along the shore together in easy conversation. The tide was low and the sea tame.

We stopped at a beachside vendor where Arjun bought me the most vilified Indian confectionery: the *gola*. Of all the foods my mother warned me about eating in India, shaved ice was foremost. "It could be made of gutter water for all you know," she had said. But nothing sounded quite as satisfying as a heap of flavored ice after a grueling day of heat, and Arjun assured me that this one used ice made from bottled water. As we walked along the water's edge, the feel of the sweet-and-sour ice melting on my tongue, the tepid ocean breeze against my sweat-speckled skin, the dampness of the sand as it oozed between my toes, made me feel more comfortable than I had in days.

"Still don't want to tell me about my mother's misdeeds?" Arjun asked as he walked in the shallows.

"And ruin this evening? Absolutely. I'm sure."

"Then, I'll have to insist that you tell me about something else. What do you think of this place?" Arjun's eyes met mine.

"Chowpatty is lovely."

"*Kya?* What are you talking about? I don't mean here." He pointed at the sand. "I mean here." He opened his arms toward the sky. "India. Now that you've had some time to settle in, tell me what you think of India."

It hardly felt like a fair question. But here, in proximity to Arjun, once again I found myself disarmed—as if truth serum flowed through my veins.

"It's like no other place I've been to. I feel like I could spend the rest of my life here and not understand it—I might not even scratch the surface."

"Incomprehensible. Even I find this place incomprehensible," he said, glancing at the sea. "And I have lived here my whole life!"

"I mean, a fifteen-year-old girl comes to our flat every day to wash our clothes when she should be free to read books and gossip with her classmates. I see her and I wonder exactly how many children are in her situation. I just can't wrap my head around it." It was a relief to say what I'd been thinking since the day I first met Shalu.

Arjun nodded. "The thing is that the haves and have-nots have been preordained. On some level, this is probably true everywhere. Only here, in India, there are ancient rules that make it so and to some, they transcend any modern ones. She is a have-not, what choice does she have but to work?"

"By ancient rules, you mean caste?"

"Yes. Shalu was born a have-not, and like have-nots everywhere else in the world, she must do whatever it takes to survive."

"Certainly, there must be many who clamor to change things? After all, this is the world's largest democracy . . ." I wavered. "Listen to me. I sound like an American politician. Democracy. The West proselytizes democracy like it's some sort of religion, and in the same breath unabashedly supports tyrants."

"While the East makes a first-class mockery of it with a load of scoundrels, *goondas*, thugs and the bloody baksheesh system," Arjun added.

We turned to each other.

"I think that the problem is that in modern democracy, money speaks with a much louder voice than the people. Those who have the money have the voice, the power. And they have no reason to fix the flaws in the system. That is why Shalu remains stuck in her station in life. It is not right, not by any means, but it is absolutely true." Arjun's expression grew intense, as if by debating history we could change its very course.

"We need to be real about the West too. What is the immigrant experience—or the experience of native peoples in my country? What was the experience of Africans brought on the Middle Passage? Is it not a type of caste system?"

"*Harijans* to your *brahmins*—" Arjun stopped abruptly and considered me. I stopped as well, my feet sinking slightly in the wet sand.

After a moment he announced, "Well, I think we've done it."

"Done what?"

"We've got it all figured out. Give us a few more minutes and we'll have worked out how to fix modern democracy—and the rest of it. You and me, right here on Chowpatty Beach!" Arjun beamed. Even in the indigo night, I could feel Arjun's eyes searching mine for something more. "All that is good and fine, but how do you *feel* being in India?"

"There are days when I feel I might find my liberation here." I knew the comment was bound to get a rise out of Arjun. But it was the truth.

"Liberation? You sound like one of those *goras* from the Anglo and American movies, coming to India to 'find themselves'." He shook his head, feigning disappointment.

"Ah professor, that assumes I was looking for myself."

"You're not on some grand spiritual quest to find your true self?"

"Not really. I just wanted to loosen the grip that the past has on me." I kicked myself for revealing so much again when I knew I should tread lightly.

"Thank God," Arjun said with relief.

I laughed. "Thank God? Thank God I am not on some grand spiritual quest? That's an interesting choice of words."

Arjun furrowed his brow, unable to understand at first what I had found so amusing. A light breeze rose from the ocean. Arjun's hair blew. He took a deep breath and turned to me. Just as quickly as the intensity had overtaken him, it disappeared. He smiled. When Arjun smiled, he did so generously. His whole face transformed, and his eyes shone as if from some internal source of light.

Arjun touched the crook of my arm. He stopped at a stall where a man was selling jasmine garlands and bought one. He stepped behind me and, without a word, tied the garland into my hair. His elbow brushed my shoulder. His fingers skimmed my neck. His breath was close to my ear. The intoxicating scent of the petals lingered around us. With Arjun's touch like lightning upon my skin, I wanted to know what was possible.

Chapter 13

BOMBAY, 1969

Pramila and Ba left their shoes outside the entrance of the Jain temple. Mother and daughter each stepped over the threshold, each touching the step with her fingers and folding her hands into prayer pose. Marble pillars, each one carved with its own unique motifs and themes, extended in every direction, creating between them symmetry within symmetry within symmetry. Voluptuous celestials etched from stone appeared to float from the ceiling above. Below, the beige marble floor was cold against Pramila's feet. Sandalwood incense scented the air. Two women sat silently on the floor, their legs folded into the lotus position, eyes closed and mouths moving in prayer in front of a marble statue of Lord Mahavira.

Pramila made a note to come to temple in the morning more often. In her younger days she used to count the moments until the *pujas* and prayers were done so she could play outside the temple with her friends. But now, at twenty-four, the temple had become a place of solace. She felt at ease here.

Ba, who had always been a devout practitioner of the Jain religion, had become even more so in the past year. Pramila suspected that this had something to do with her sister, Vini. Pramila could no longer ignore the whispered conversations between her parents nor the concerned glances exchanged between her grandparents.

Vini had been eager when her parents suggested that she start meeting suitable boys for marriage. She had met one after another. None of the boys had agreed to a second meeting. Nobody in the family understood why. Vini came from a good family. Though she was no film star Vini was not unattractive nor was she dark in color. In the world of arranged marriages, Pramila knew that such things mattered.

As the rejections piled up, Ba grew increasingly worried. A boy who had been rejected a few times still stood a chance of finding a match, but a girl? That was a different story. Even Papa had expressed concern. Vini, who had the top score in the city on her high-school exit exams. Vini, who could quote William Blake before she could entirely understand English. Vini, who taught herself how to do calculus by chalking equations on the concrete hallway floor. Vini, to whom all talents seemed to come naturally, was unable to achieve a match.

Pramila knew her future was intertwined with her sister's. Whichever way fate tugged at her sister, Pramila would get pulled along too. She knew what would happen if Vini did not find a match: the eyes of all the elders, her mother and father, aunts and uncles, neighbors and acquaintances, would fall upon her. Having given up on Vini, people would inquire about Pramila's situation. Never mind what Vini wanted. Never mind what Pramila wanted. No family could bear the possibility of two unwed daughters. Neighbors would shake their heads and speculate about what had gone wrong. What fate could be worse for a girl than to remain unmarried? What those people could scarcely imagine was that Pramila wanted something else. She did not know what it was exactly, for though it lived in her mind as something distinct, it had yet to acquire exact form. It existed in her thoughts only as a negative. She knew she did not wish to live the life of a married woman.

Pramila jumped when she felt a hand against her back. She turned to find her friend Kalpana standing behind her.

When they were five, she and Kalpana were both enrolled in religious school. Kalpana came from a strict Jain family. By three she could list all the *Tirthankaras*, from Lord Rishabhdev to Lord Mahavira, Jain spiritual teachers who had reached nirvana. She fasted during auspicious holidays, consuming nothing except water for days at a time. Pramila was more of a belly-full Jain believer.

"Did you hear about the lecture this evening?" Kalpana asked.

"What lecture?"

"One of the nuns is speaking."

Pramila had attended her fair share of lectures about theology at religious school. She knew about karma philosophy and how one attains nirvana. She followed the path the way the others in the flock did, by trying to live a life of non-violence. She had done what was expected of her with a sense of duty and tempered belief. The thought of a quiet evening reading with her father sounded far more appealing than another lecture about religion.

Kalpana inched closer to Pramila. "She has been to America, you know. Word has it that she had gotten in trouble for what she has been teaching."

"In trouble? With whom?" Pramila was intrigued.

"I don't know, maybe her guru? Maybe the monks? She is having some different ideas it seems. I'm going. You should come too."

Pramila imagined herself reading under the incandescent bulb in the hallway just outside her flat. It would be a comfortable way to spend the evening. But she was curious to find out about the renegade nun and what it was exactly that had landed her in trouble.

"*Achcha*. Where is it and what time shall we meet?"

◆ ◆ ◆

The friends met outside a local college building and entered together. They followed the murmur of voices to a small room. Inside, she saw a group of about twenty people. A woman, in her early thirties, sat on the floor at the front. She wore an unembellished long-sleeved white gown with a tunic over the top and her shaved head was covered with a white cloth. Pramila scanned the audience. There were so many white faces. She had never seen so many *goras* in one place.

She and Kalpana entered the room, made their way to the rear, and sat down on the floor. They stared at the backs of the strangers with blond hair and Western clothes. The *goras* sat cross-legged, their knees floating high above the floor. Pramila marveled at the paleness of their bare feet. Kalpana pointed to her own knees which, in the same cross-legged position, rested comfortably on the floor.

"They must be sitting in chairs mostly," Pramila whispered.

A young white man turned as if he had heard Pramila's comment. He smiled.

She had no choice but to smile back.

A young Indian man stepped to the front of the room. He cleared his throat. "Welcome to all. I have the honor of introducing *Shramaniji* Pratibha." He looked at the Westerners. "I see we have some people here from far-off places. For those of you not knowing the term *shramaniji*, the term is similar to your English term 'nun'."

Kalpana and Pramila turned to one another. They knew a *shramaniji* was not the strictest form of nun in the Jain tradition. A *shramaniji* had fewer restrictions on her movements and was allowed to travel abroad.

"*Shramaniji* has recently come back from America and we have asked her to speak to us about her experiences there."

The young nun nodded her head shyly.

Pramila marveled at how striking the young woman was in her white attire, the way her bright eyes were accentuated by her clean-shaven head. Before speaking, *Shramaniji* Pratibha lifted her hand and placed a kerchief over her mouth. Did the *goras* understand that she was trying to minimize the harm that her breath might cause to the invisible living beings around her?

"Please excuse my English. It is my fourth language and not my most eloquent."

Pramila looked at Kalpana, hoping to gather the meaning of the word "eloquent". Kalpana shrugged her shoulders.

"This year, I had the pleasure of traveling to America. Over the past years, many of our Jain people have moved there. It is a vast land. I cannot explain it exactly, but the soil there feels different beneath one's feet from our Indian soil, as if fewer people have trodden upon it. There is a newness to the place and with it, have come new ideas. Well, perhaps not so very new."

The nun scanned the room. With the slightest of nods, she acknowledged a white woman sitting in front to her right. It seemed to Pramila that the Westerners in the audience had a better sense of what the *shramaniji* was referring to than her Indian brethren.

"*Achcha*. By the looks on your faces, I can see many of you do not know what I am talking about. Much is happening in America—protests against war—marches against bigotry against black people. These fights reminded me of India's own fight for freedom. I do not have to tell you how the teachings of our own Mahatma Gandhi have influenced people like Dr. Martin Luther King Jr. Let us state that the violent deaths of those two men, who for all of their imperfections, tried to forge a path of non-violence, were indeed a tragedy."

121

The whites in front of Pramila and Kalpana nodded their heads.

"I must have been quite a sight walking through the streets of America with my bald head and white clothes. Everywhere I went, people would stop to ask questions. Why have you shaven your hair? Why are you only wearing white? Many asked about the Jain belief in *ahimsa*—non-violence. I would say, yes, it is true that we believe in non-violence. But you, in America, also have such a tradition. I would speak of Thoreau and the Quakers—who believed much as we do. But you will not believe the question people asked us the most. They asked why we Jain nuns clean the area around us before sitting."

Kalpana and Pramila weren't the only ones who laughed. The whites in the audience understood as well. Jainism's tenet to do no harm applied to all living things.

"Why should we be so concerned about the invisible lives that might be around us, under us?" She paused.

"I said to them, we must look from above, no? That is to say, if a person were to fly to the moon, like this Neil Armstrong did just months ago, and was to look down upon our planet floating in the vast, lifeless space beyond—what would he perceive? Would he not be struck by a certain kinship among Earth's creatures? Of one living thing with the next—human, cow, rat, lizard, ant, plant, bacteria—all hurtling through space together? What lies beyond is merely insensate emptiness. Why should we not, then, take the care not to harm another life? When each living thing is, in its own way, a miracle in the nothingness beyond our atmosphere."

Pramila sat with her back erect and her demeanor calm. Her mind, on the other hand, was swimming. She felt as though she had been reading a familiar book, a book that she could recite by the paragraph, a book with an ending that had been etched into her mind, only to find a hidden chapter that completely altered its meaning. After all those years going to temple, reciting prayers, going through the motions of a person of faith—for the first time in a long time she was hearing a compelling new argument. Certainly, the 'Earthrise' image taken from the moon had given a brand-new perspective of the fragility of the world and the beings on it. But what truly moved Pramila was the forthrightness and freedom with which the young woman spoke. *Shramaniji* Pratibha's station as a nun had allowed her the time to consider such notions.

"Many people asked about our god. This is something even many of our own following do not understand. They have fallen into notions that are not our own. So, when Americans asked me such questions, I said most simply, 'We are a religion that requires no god. We need no creator. We need no higher power to decide our fates. It is only our past actions and reactions that determine our destinies. Yes, we venerate those who have achieved perfection, Lord Mahavira for instance, He was once human too. You see, the divine resides in each of us. It resides in all living things." The Indians around Pramila and Kalpana tilted their heads from side to side in agreement.

A religion without the need for a creator? All those years going to temple, participating in rites and rituals, learning about the spiritual feats of the *tirthankaras*, Pramila had never heard such ideas stated in this particular way. She began to question her own understanding of her faith. The young nun smiled again. Gone was her shyness. In its stead came the boldness of conviction.

"There are similarities in all the faiths. But I have learned that there are also many differences. For one, we Jains do not seek to convert others. We do not claim that a Christian must give up his faith in Jesus to believe as we Jains do. We revere Jesus as well, for the message that he teaches us. We admire all who seek spiritual truth regardless of their religion. We do not deny them the validity of their spiritual paths. In my travels, however, I have learned that some faiths are not so accepting of others. Some would not allow us entrance into their places of worship and others dismissed us outright as heathens." The *goras* in the room shook their heads.

"Others were most welcoming. Pastors taught me about the importance of quest for redemption to the Christian faith. I taught them that for Hindus and Jains the quest is slightly different. We do not simply seek redemption for sins. We Jains and Hindus, we seek liberation. We seek to cast off the desires that lead to sin—desires for possession, for power, for sex. We seek to liberate our souls from those things that keep us tied to this imperfect world."

A hush fell over the room again.

"Liberation is an honorable thing. We detach ourselves from the worldly. We fast to detach ourselves from the needs of our bodies. We remain silent to detach ourselves from society. These sacrifices bring us closer to complete liberation—to nirvana. Yes, liberation is a most noble thing."

Shramaniji Pratibha paused and scanned the room. She had scarcely changed her position. Her thin, once hunched frame, was now bamboo-shoot straight. Her eyes slowly panned across the room until they met those of every member of the audience. When her eyes met Pramila's, her gaze felt like a magnetic field drawing Pramila in.

"Yes, indeed, liberation is a most noble thing. But we must be careful. When one detaches from the worldly, from conflict, from the plight of injustice, from other beings, human or otherwise, one becomes only involved in the self at the exclusion of all else. We Jains do not eat meat, yet what do we do for the emaciated dog or starving horse? We give money to our temples, but do we give money to those in need? How can one attain the freedom from all suffering when others among us suffer? I ask you this, can one attain purity of the soul at the exclusion of the consideration of all other souls?"

The nun's words were swept up into the air and rained down on Pramila like a revelation. She looked to her left and then to her right, measuring the reactions of those around her. Kalpana's mouth was agape. Pramila knew why. The young nun was challenging the path to liberation as they had been raised to know it. No wonder she was in trouble with the monks.

"There is nothing radical about what I am saying to you. Our motivations must not be God or our own souls. It must not be simply redemption or simply liberation. Our motivation must be right."

The nun stopped speaking. The audience remained silent for a moment, waiting for her to continue. Then, several people broke into applause. She raised her arm and shook her head humbly as if to ward off any fanfare.

Pramila sat still. If only she could condense the nun's words into some physical form that could be stored in a bottle to be consumed later. She imagined one of those grainy pictures of Earth taken from space, suddenly aware of the nothingness that surrounded her world. Could there be religion without a creator? Pramila didn't know. *Shramaniji* Pratibha's answer to the question was compelling. But it wasn't the answer itself that moved her, it was simply being able to ask the question.

It was then that she realized she had found her calling.

Chapter 14

Mumbai, July 2006

Since my outing with Arjun, I felt more confident traversing the city on my own. Maasi was going to a friend's house in Parle and I was headed for dinner a short drive away in Santa Cruz, at the flat where Natasha lived with her family. Vini initially insisted that she would drop me off, but after some convincing, I got her to agree to let me take a rickshaw by myself.

To discover the sound of Bombay's suburbs, you'd only have to take the usual racket of squeaking brakes, screaming vendors, honking horns, and barking dogs and add the squeal of the auto-rickshaw. As a class of vehicle, the auto-rickshaw is an utter nuisance. It swerves in and out of traffic, squeezes into tight spaces, and blasts a horn that sounds just like the Road Runner from those old cartoons. But as the passenger, I found that the auto-rickshaw was unparalleled as a mode of transport. This black motorized tricycle with its yellow roof and open side walls offered a perfect vantage into the city. Seated in the bench seat behind the driver and gazing through those open side walls, I felt the exhilaration of weaving past buses and trucks and marveled as women in saris deftly navigated the streets, maneuvering through traffic and past piles of refuse as if doing so required no effort at all. It was in the rickshaw that I felt most in tune with the city.

It was just before sunset when the rickshaw slowed to a halt. I paid the driver, entered the open gate, and headed to Natasha's fifth-floor flat. After my offer at her sister's wedding, I had been recruited by Natasha and Daniel to join a dinner party at her house—this was going to be the first time Daniel was meeting her parents and Natasha felt she needed backup. Her grandparents, who lived with them in a joint family arrangement, were gone to a party at a neighbor's place and would not be in attendance. When I arrived, it was Natasha's mother who answered the door.

"*Namaste.* You are Shyamala, isn't it? *Avvo, avvo!* Come in, come in! I am the Ashmi," she welcomed me in, introducing herself by her first name. Her English was marginally less awkward than my Hindi.

"Thank you, Aunty." I took my shoes off and walked into the living room.

The apartment was tidy. The focal point of the room was a flat vinyl couch with several weathered old cushions on it. On the opposite wall, a makeshift temple had been constructed on a buffet table. At its center was a picture of blue-hued Shiva seated in front of a snow-capped mountain, a third eye on his forehead, a snake wrapped around his neck, a trident in one arm, and the River Ganges flowing from the top of his long locks of hair.

Behind the couch was a large window that overlooked a huge flyover. You could throw a rock from Ashmi aunty's window and hit a car driving on the overpass.

I scanned the room for Natasha.

"Come-come, sit," Ashmi aunty urged.

I sat on the sofa. Ashmi aunty took a chair opposite the sofa and watched me expectantly.

I smiled at her and glanced around the room self-consciously.

The doorbell rang and Ashmi aunty went to answer it.

"Oh hallo!" she said with surprise. "Very please, come in. I am the Ashmi. You are taking off your shoes. That is very nice!"

Daniel walked in, wild-eyed, with a clenched jaw and a forced smile. When he saw me, he relaxed ever so slightly. He scanned the room, wondering, I am sure, where Natasha was.

"Thank God you're here," he mouthed to me as Ashmi followed him into the living room.

He took a seat beside me on the couch.

Ashmi aunty considered Daniel and then me and then Daniel again. He shifted somewhat in his seat.

"Can I get you cold drink? I am having some *limbu* or rose water or the Coca-Cola." Ashmi aunty's speech was pressured in the wake of the two Americans sitting in her suburban Santa Cruz living room.

"No thanks, Aunty. Please sit and visit with us. Where is Natasha?" I asked. A large mosquito cast an even larger shadow as it buzzed between the fluorescent tube light and the wall.

"Not to worry, she must be coming soon. But you must have some cold drink." Ashmi aunty rushed into the kitchen.

Daniel's blue eyes followed Ashmi aunty into the kitchen, then turned to me. "Thanks so much for coming tonight. You're an absolute lifesaver."

I was about to answer when Ashmi aunty re-entered the room carrying a tray of tall, perspiring glasses. She silently handed a glass to each of us and took her seat.

"Drink. Drink," she insisted.

Daniel and I sipped our drinks in unison. The cool water tasted like liquid roses. The room was nearly pin-drop silent—even the noise of traffic abated unexpectedly as we drank. I focused my sights at the ceiling but the mosquito had disappeared behind the tube light. Ashmi aunty patiently watched us, intently assessing our reaction to the beverage. Desperate to break the uncomfortable silence, I racked my brain for topics for small talk, landing predictably on the weather. With only a sip or two remaining in my glass, I cleared my throat to speak. Thankfully, the doorknob wiggled, the door opened with force, and in came Natasha at last. Daniel sprang to his feet.

"Hallo everyone. Sorry, sorry. I'm very late. The traffic today was solid and by the time I got to the sweet shop, the line was out of the door. Not to worry though, this place has absolutely the best carrot halwa and I got the last box," she said as she flipped off her sandals and handed the pink box of Indian sweets to her mother. She walked over to the couch and threw her arm around me, turning her back toward Daniel.

"You mustn't get filled up on the rose water. Much more is to come," Natasha announced. It was apparent to me that she was speaking to Daniel though she was focused on me.

"Yes, yes. I should know by now that I need to pace myself. It's just so hot out there that the ice-cold rose water is hard to resist." Daniel seemed invigorated in Natasha's presence.

"You must be excusing me, I am going to prepare the appetizers," Ashmi aunty interjected.

"May I come along? Perhaps I can help? I hear you are quite a cook," Daniel said, rousing himself from his awkwardness to deploy a strategy that would win over any American mother. Natasha's mother, on the other hand, seemed astonished at the offer. Daniel might as well have been in his underwear proclaiming that the flyover outside was on fire.

"No, no. You are a guest at our house. I cannot ask you to be working, no?"

"No. I mean, yes. Of course, you can put me to work. Natasha puts me to work all the time," Daniel responded, his tone light even as his gaze intently held Natasha's.

Natasha's brows lifted in a gesture of warning. Ashmi aunty alternated her sights between Natasha and Daniel as if to gauge their relationship. Then she hesitated before returning to the kitchen, alone.

"What are you doing?" Natasha snapped at Daniel, her brows furled. They were standing next to the couch—finally face to face. Daniel had this way of looking at Natasha, unburdened by an Indian tradition that denied the impulses of consenting adults.

"What do you mean?"

"You're suggesting something," Natasha hissed.

"What am I suggesting, exactly?"

"That we know each other."

"We *do* know each other. Isn't that how I got invited here?" he asked with a smirk.

"Of course, we know each other, but the way you are saying it suggests that we *know* each other."

"What, like sexually?" he said, barely whispering.

"Shhh. Don't use that word! If either one of my parents heard it—I am not sure what they would do. Just don't make it so obvious!"

The doorknob jiggled. The three of us looked at each other. Natasha's eyes widened in warning. Her father bounded through the door.

A heavy-set man with a thick mustache, between breaths he said, "Welcome. Welcome. Natasha, come, introduce me to your friends." He scrutinized Daniel.

"Papa, this is Shyamala. She is my boss from LA." Natasha's voice was almost girlish.

"Yes, yes. Shyamala. I remember her from your sister's wedding. I am Ashok. *Namaste*." He raised his hands in front of his chest in prayer position and bowed his head slightly.

"Nice to meet you, Uncle."

"Now where is this other girl? What is her name? Danielle or something of the sort?"

"Actually Papa, it's Daniel. As you can see, Daniel is a—a man. He was at the wedding also," Natasha said, with a swallow.

"*Arré?* I thought this name Dan-ielle was for a fe-male!" Ashok uncle enunciated each syllable of each word, his voice deep and resonant.

"Don't worry, I get that a lot here." Daniel laughed.

Ashok uncle did not smile.

The mosquito reappeared from behind the tube light.

"You see, Danielle is a woman's name. Daniel is a man's name . . ." The last word barely made it out of Daniel's mouth. His fair-skinned face turned red hot. I felt for him.

"It is all sounding the same to me. Please, Danielle, sit down," Ashok uncle said. "You must be quite tired after a long day in the office."

"Papa, it is pronounced 'Daniel'."

"That is what I said! Danielle. Come, come, please sit down." Ashok uncle sat in the chair across from the couch.

We all followed suit and took our seats. The room was stifling. Daniel loosened his collar to let in some air.

"So Shyamala, you live in LA is it? Let's see. Do you know this Dr Hemantbhai Doshi? Top-notch cardiologist, top notch. He lives in LA only. He is my mother's sister's son's wife's cousin's cousin."

"Mother's sister's son's wife's cousin's cousin. I'd almost have to draw a picture to understand the relation," Daniel said with a chuckle.

Ashok uncle immediately stiffened. Daniel froze, clearly regretting his attempt at a joke.

"Papa! How is she to know Hemant uncle? Do you know how many Indians live in California?" Natasha tried to break the

131

tension. I was relieved that the attention was drawn away from Daniel—he needed a moment to recover.

"*Arré?* What harm is it to ask? She might have met him at some *desi* function or through a mutual friend. They both live in Los Angelees, no?"

"Sorry, Uncle, I don't know him. Los Angeles is quite a big city." Growing up, the Americans around me used to assume that all the Indians in town knew each other. It drove me crazy. Turns out Indians did the same thing.

For a moment, we nodded our heads at each other, the way people do when they have either too much or too little to say to one another. Daniel stole glances at Natasha. Natasha peered at her father. I watched for the mosquito near the tube light, waiting for it to reappear.

When dinner was ready, we squeezed in at the small table that Ashmi aunty had pulled out from the kitchen wall to eat a traditional Gujarati meal of *dal*, rice, spiced vegetables, *puri*, and a plethora of Indian sweets, including my favorites *rasmalai* and *halwa*.

"Are you liking the food?" asked Ashmi aunty, directing her question at Daniel.

"This is delicious. It'll be a struggle not to eat all of it!"

"Why should you worry? You are much too skinny. Natasha, Danielle's plate is empty, go get him some more *puris*!" Ashok uncle ordered. "Ashmi, bring him some *papad* too."

Natasha dropped the deep-fried *puris* on to our plates. First her father's, then Daniel's, then mine, then her mother's, and finally her own.

"So, what I don't understand is why you Americans are fighting all these wars under the name 'freedom' when really everyone is knowing that you are just in it for the oil?"

Daniel nearly choked on the *puri* he had just bitten. Ashmi aunty busied herself roasting *papad*, perhaps to stay out of the fray.

"Oh Papa, can we please talk of something else?" Natasha pleaded sweetly.

"I am only asking a question. Danielle, you are not feeling offensive are you?"

"No, no, I am not offended. Not at all." Daniel took a sip of water.

"We may be American, but not all of us agree with American policy." I tried to defuse the situation for my American friend. Meeting the parents was never easy, but this was near impossible. Daniel wasn't kidding, his feelings weren't mere infatuation.

"That is an understatement, no? Many of America's policies have been a great mistake," Ashok uncle declared.

"Would you like some carrot *halwa*?" inquired Ashmi aunty, who seemed like she would rather have been in any one of a thousand other places.

"Come, Papa. All this politics nonsense is *bilkul* boring me," Natasha implored, still trying to steer the conversation away from danger.

"*Arré beta*, I am just asking a few questions only," Ashok uncle continued.

"Might I make anyone some of the *chai*?" Ashmi aunty asked.

"*Halwa, chai*, what is this? Let the bugger answer a question. How does Danielle feel about American foreign policy?"

"Well, Ashok uncle, the only thing I understand less than the actions of nations," Daniel paused for dramatic effect and smiled slowly, "are the actions of women." While the comment was for Ashok uncle's benefit, Daniel made sure to glance pointedly at Natasha.

The murmurings of mealtime halted abruptly at Daniel's comment. Ashok uncle considered the young, white American for a moment. He took a deep breath in.

"Yes! Yes, good man," Ashok uncle guffawed, "now that is the absolute truth!" His laughter boomed through the diminutive kitchen. "*Arré*, Ashmi, get this chap some of that *rasmalai*!"

Natasha rolled her eyes and I shook my head at Daniel. For their part, Ashok uncle, Ashmi aunty, and Daniel seemed to settle into conversation. Daniel actually seemed to be doing quite well to win them over. Even Natasha, who was a bit put out at first, seemed to relax slightly. I took heart in the notion that they might not have needed me after all.

After dinner was complete and the delicious desserts were stuffed into our already bursting bellies, Daniel insisted on helping to clean up. By now Ashmi aunty appeared unable to resist the charm of the all-American boy who had materialized in her home.

Eventually the men retired to the living room with the flyover as the backdrop. Natasha, her mother, and I finished cleaning up and followed shortly after.

"So, Danielle, do you have a wife or girlfriend back in America?" asked Ashmi aunty.

"Um, no. No wife or girlfriend in America."

"I keep telling Natasha, you must not be waiting too long, you know—?"

"Papa, I'm sure that Daniel does not want to talk about these things with us," Natasha interrupted.

"A good-looking chap like you shouldn't have any sort of problems, *yaar*!"

"Papa! Seriously!"

Usually, Natasha was cool, collected, and confident. But here, with her mother and her father, she was nervous and self-conscious. As if her deepest, darkest secret might be revealed leaving her vulnerable to whatever punishment her parents saw fit.

"Shyamala, what do you think?" Ashok uncle asked.

"He is rather easy on the eyes, if that's what you mean. But who knows what lurks beneath?" I laughed.

"What lurks beneath is a hard-working, sincere, intelligent, and caring young man. Ashok uncle, isn't that what you want for your daughter?" Daniel said with sincerity.

Natasha looked as if she were about to fall over. What was Daniel doing? This was the first time he was meeting her parents! Had he forgotten that despite his Greek statue good looks, he might not be considered well-suited for a girl living in the suburbs of Bombay? Just moments before he had Natasha's parents wrapped around his fingers, but now I wondered if he had crossed the line.

"This is true! What is it you Americans say? You are a catch!" exclaimed Ashok uncle.

I couldn't help but think that he was living vicariously through the strapping young man who graced his couch.

"Maybe Natasha will be finding someone like you someday," Ashmi aunty said.

"Yes, maybe a handsome Gujarati boy down the road from us in Santa Cruz or Ghatkopar?" Ashok uncle added.

My eyes turned to Daniel, who managed, somehow, to retain the remnants of a smile on his face. But his dejection was undeniable. He had glimpsed himself through Ashok and Ashmi's eyes. He wasn't the type of man they could picture as their son-in-law. He wasn't the type of man who they could imagine as the father of their grandchildren. He was nothing more than a handsome young foreigner. Earlier, the evening seemed to have been so full of promise. But now, I only wished I could've done something more to help.

Chapter 15

Mumbai, July 2006

It happened at two o'clock the next morning. The thing I dreaded most.

I awoke to a disconcerting reverberation of the intestines, a sound reminiscent of the percussion section of an orchestra. My stomach felt like a towel when it is wrung out. My brain seemed to seek escape from the confines of my skull.

I lay in bed, in a torpor. Vini checked on me many times, offering me drink and food. I refused both.

I eventually succumbed to exhaustion, falling asleep in the early morning. When I finally came to, light and shadow were swaying and rippling across my face. With great effort, I opened one eye to see the sun illuminating my room, scattered into a million separate beams of light by the leaves of the wilted mango tree just outside my window. The sight was dizzying. My skin felt hot and cold at once. Slowly, I opened the other eye and turned my face to the nightstand. Someone had placed a glass of water on it. The surface of the glass was wet with condensation. In my sickly haze, I marveled at how the cold water within the glass could call on its peers to manifest on the outside of the glass. It seemed like a kind of alchemy.

A single drop of water coalesced and slid slowly down the glass. My thoughts followed suit, a slow parade of waking dreams, of quasi-hallucinations.

How many times had I drunk a drop of water, never once having considered its path to my glass? How many had consumed it before me? Not just humans but other beings. It had been sweated out, drunk in, urinated out, bathed in, cried out, and returned to the Earth over and over and over again. Eyes closed, I could feel myself following it into corners of the planet that I could scarcely imagine. I was swimming in the darkness of subterranean aquifers, hovering weightless in the outermost layers of the atmosphere, wedged into the deepest crevices of glaciers, and twisting through the infinitely ramifying veins of trees.

I awoke several hours later, gazing at the glass of water. Here it was, sitting unassumingly on my nightstand after all those travels. I felt a presence near me. Shalu was sitting on a chair by the window, flipping through the pages of a book. I watched her quietly.

Her face was in that ever so brief transition between childhood and womanhood, yet the child remained triumphant. Though I had known her for months, the observation only struck me as I watched her, seated in the chair. There was no trace of conceit about her knowledge of the world around her and no reticence about what role she should have in it. She just carried on, secure in the belief that somehow everything would work out.

Shalu sat comfortably in the chair, oblivious to being observed. She was engrossed in the book, mouth moving slightly as she read the words.

Wait, what?

I focused my weary eyes.

"Shalu, are you reading that?" I realized it was my father's copy of *The Good Earth* which I had brought with me from LA.

"Huh?" she said, startled.

"*Tu a chopdi vancheche?* Are you reading the book?" I asked, surprised that the Gujarati sounded correct.

A childish look spread across her face, as if she had been caught with her hand in the Gluco biscuit jar.

"Shalu, I'd love to hear you read it."

She opened the book to a random page and read.

"Here I am speaking broken Gujarati, making a total fool of myself and all along we could have been speaking in English!" Whatever dismay I felt at not realizing she spoke English was washed away by my relief at finally being able to fully communicate with her. "When, where have you been learning English?"

"I have been learning the English at school only, for few years now. It is compulsory. With Auntyji's help I am attending the school. She has been paying the tu-tions since I was small. Sorry, I am not speaking it proper. Tui-tion, she has been paying the tui-tion."

"That's good, Shalu, that's really good." Vini had never mentioned her role in paying for Shalu's tuition. "Why have you not spoken to me in English?"

"When I speak the English, it sounds full of dread. Not like the American movies."

"Dreadful? Have you heard my Gujarati? And my Hindi, it's *so much* worse!"

Shalu's posture relaxed and she smiled. "*Eh vaat saatchi che.* That's true. This way you are learning the Gujarati, no?" Suddenly, she seemed grown-up.

I kicked myself for making assumptions. Assume Shalu doesn't speak English. Assume that, as the outsider, you are the only one to empathize with her struggles. Assume that, as the Westerner, you are the one with all the answers.

Shalu seemed to take pity on me. She moved her chair closer.

"Let me go at the *dava khanu* and get you some of the medicine for the stomach. How you are to say *dava khanu* in the English?"

"*Dava* means medicine in English. *Khanu* means drawer. So literally it would mean medicine drawer. But we actually call it a pharmacy."

Shalu couldn't suppress her laughter. "But I thought the drawers means one type of the underwear."

"Yes, well, sometimes 'drawers' does mean underwear and sometimes it means one of those," I said, pointing to my dresser drawers and not bothering to stifle a laugh. I was happy to see the girl re-emerge again.

She hesitated for a moment but then cleared her throat. "I know the things Champaben has been saying about me to the other people in the building. Some of the peoples in the building must believe it, you know. The way they are giving me this kind of look, like I have done something wrong, like my father is not teaching me what is right."

"I'm sorry Shalu. It's so wrong. Since the minute I found out, I've been trying to confront Champa about it."

"It is Papa that I am worrying about. He takes this type of words to the heart. He feels these things happen because I have no mother. People think I am not having anyone to teach me the right way for the girl."

"I'm not sure why people start such rumors," I said, wondering what had happened to her mother and if any of us really knew what the right way for a girl was.

"Ma died in auto-mo-bile accident when I was a baby only."

"Oh, Shalu, I'm sorry to hear that." I was still lying in bed, my torso propped up against the headboard. I reached out to grasp her hand.

"I cannot remember her—Chandrika was her name. I see her pictures and I am making up a story of how she was. Papa says that I am looking like her." Shalu spoke with a sort of detached emotion, having lost someone that she never really knew but aware that the loss had altered the course of her life.

She continued to hold her arm out so that I wouldn't let go of her hand. My heart went out to the girl. I glanced at *The Good Earth* lying on my nightstand, my mother's picture tucked between its pages. Like stars and black holes bending space-time within the universe, seen or unseen, mothers exerted an invisible force on the course of our lives.

"Let me speak to Champa."

"Please. Let us leave it be. We know what really did happen. The rest, we cannot be helping. The more we say such things are not the truth, the more people like Champaben and the others will be believing that they are. This much I know."

"But maybe if I said—"

"She cannot harm me if you are all believing in me."

I wanted what Shalu said to be true—that the innuendo couldn't harm her if we believed in her. She was probably right, in any case, that the more we denied the rumor, the more it would convince some of its truth.

"Okay, then." I sighed. "Let's not bother with all of that. Tell me what other books you have read in English."

Shalu looked relieved to discuss something else.

"*Alice in Wonderland* is my favorite. Auntyji let me read it from her shelf. That queen character is too good," she said, with a sideways head bob.

"You know what? I read that same exact book. Vini maasi let me borrow it once too."

◆　◆　◆

A week later, I was washing dishes with the tap turned down to a dribble as my aunt cleared the table.

"Arjun seems to be calling quite a bit lately?" Vini asked as she entered the kitchen, her arms full of dishes. She seemed to suppress a smile. "He's quite a young man, no?"

"Oh yeah, he's quite a guy," I responded, as though there was nothing to tell. Though I would never admit it, ever since our trip to Chowpatty, when Arjun called my heart raced like I was seventeen. Since that walk on the shores of the Arabian Sea, we'd been on several other outings around Mumbai. And even when we weren't together, I found that he was infiltrating more and more of my idle thoughts.

"Something going on between you two, isn't it?" She dumped another round of dishes by the sink. Her face was eager with curiosity, and I felt my cheeks warm.

"We're just getting to know each other. He just got an interview offer for some journalism job in New Delhi." Arjun had mentioned it a few days after our walk on Chowpatty Beach.

"He finally applied? Impressive! I've read his stories. For the life of me, I still don't understand how someone with such curiosity and kindness came from a woman like Champa! It is truly a mystery!"

"Maasi, would you mind not mentioning it to Mom? I don't know where things are going with him and I don't want anyone to get ahead of themselves." *Including myself*, I thought. Given how things had turned out with Neil and witnessing the cross-cultural troubles between Natasha and Daniel, I knew I should take it slow with Arjun. In any case, I hadn't come to India for a relationship. At best, Arjun would be a pleasant diversion on my adventure abroad.

"Don't worry, between your broken engagement and mine, your mother knows better than to try to make predictions about such things!"

Though I had heard about Vini's broken engagement long ago, I didn't know the details. Nor she did she divulge any more information now.

"If you prefer, we'll just keep it to ourselves. Until you are ready."

The water that had been coming from the tap gurgled and spurted to a halt. I turned the faucet in both directions hoping to get it to flow again.

Distressed, I turned to Vini. "Maasi, the water has run out!"

"I am surprised it has lasted this long," she said.

"But I thought we had more tankers bringing in water now, enough to last through the evening."

"Perhaps the building's use is still too high. I'll inquire in the morning."

Vini retrieved a full bucket of water from the bathroom that she heaved upon the counter. She walked into her room and closed the door behind her. Still, I could hear the clanging of keys as she unlocked her *cabat* and the squeaking as she opened its tall doors.

Mindful that I would have to make it through the entire pile of dishes with the single bucket of water, I ladled small amounts and washed the remaining dishes, listening for the gushes and trickles as the water made its way down the drain.

Chapter 16

Bombay, 1970

Vini had found a match. The boy was an engineer from a good family. Both Atul and Vini had consented to the marriage. Tomorrow Ba and Papa would meet with the astrologer to find a favorable date for the wedding. The mood in the flat was festive.

With the news of Vini's engagement, Pramila found herself daydreaming about her future. She had buried her aspirations for a long time. She inhaled deeply knowing that she was a breath closer to the life she wanted.

Pramila headed to the market to pick up ingredients for dinner, pleased to step into the temperate December air, alone with her thoughts. Though the route to the street market was second nature to her, she realized she could have found it by her nose alone—following the earthy-sweet-tangy scent of the produce.

At the market, on the pavement, stacked upon large sheets of burlap, were masses of produce: crimson pyramids of tomatoes, heaps of yellow squashes, orderly stacks of long beans, and piles upon piles of potatoes and onions and oranges and pomegranates. She marveled at the display—the absolute splendor of the ordinary.

She found the ingredient for her sister's favorite dish in a small mountain on the far corner of the market. The light-green shade of the pea pods was the color of renewal. She cracked one pod open and examined the velvety green peas inside. She looked forward to sitting with Ba and peeling the peas from their pods. There was that moment of anticipation as one opened the pod to reveal the individual peas, the sense of gratification when each little specimen was of the right size and shape, the sound of the tiny orbs as they hit the bowl, the comfort of spending an afternoon with Ba discussing this and that. Once all the pods where shed, Ba would add shredded coconut and spices to the peas and stuff the mixture into homemade pastry rounds. Then Pramila would fry the stuffed pastries until they were crisp and brown. Pramila imagined the look on her sister's face as she devoured the first sample.

Pramila gathered the produce into her canvas bag. The weight of the bag on her shoulder and the cadence of its swing were reassuring.

The time was right. Maybe she would tell everyone what was on her mind after dinner when the family would all be seated on the floor, bellies full, the mood light and hopeful. After all, Vini was going to be married, move in with her husband and in-laws and have children. She would be settled. She would do what everyone thought a good daughter did for her parents. The family would be satisfied. Then perhaps, Ba and Papa could abide by Pramila's decision.

But still, how would she say it exactly? *Ba and Papa, I've decided not to get married so I can pursue the study of the Jain dharma as a nun.* Vini would most certainly laugh at the idea. In fact, even without saying them out loud, the words seemed ridiculous. If Vini's reaction would be to laugh, what would her parents think? Would they think she had lost her mind? Would they view her decision as a rejection of their upbringing? There might be disappointment—heartbreak even.

Then again, the prospect of domestic life filled her with abject terror. Wife—mother—she could not envision herself in either one of those words.

For as long as she could remember, Pramila had worn her sister's secondhand sandals, but this time she would not follow in her footsteps. Vini had set her free. Perhaps now there would be space for Pramila to remain unmarried, to be free to have a life of the mind, to be who she truly was. What she wanted more than anything else was to learn at the feet of the nun she had met that fateful day not so long ago.

Pramila had written to the young nun, announcing her intentions. The nun had written back. *You must come here and see what our lives are like before you make any decisions*, she had suggested. Pramila tried to contain her excitement. All this time, she had felt out of place. Perhaps, at the monastery, she would finally be among kindred spirits and learn true dharma.

So today, she would change her future. Today, she would announce her intentions.

She ascended the steps to her flat as she had done thousands of times before. But as she walked the long corridor of the *chaali*, she knew something was awry. The door to the flat was closed. It was never closed at this time of day. After removing her sandals, she opened the door slowly, unsure what might await her on the other side.

The living area was deserted. She placed the canvas bag full of vegetables on the kitchen floor, and nearly leapt out of her skin when her mother called her. The canvas bag fell on its side, the carefully chosen pea pods spilling out.

"Ba, *shu theyu?* What happened?" Pramila called, as she entered the bedroom, her heart pounding.

Her father lay on a mattress on the floor, half asleep. The color of his face was hardly a shade darker than the white tile floor. He looked sick. Terribly sick. Ba was distraught. Vini sat in the corner, her head in her hands, crying quietly.

"Your father collapsed just a few minutes ago."

Pramila dropped to her knees beside her father. "Papa? Papa? What is going on?"

He glanced at Pramila, his skin ashen and damp to the touch. "*Arré!* It is nothing. I am only having a bit of stomach pain."

"Papa you rest here. I am going downstairs to call the doctor." As Pramila left the flat, Ba reached for her arm. Ba's hand was cold.

"It all happened so fast. One moment he was fine, the next he was holding his chest."

"I'll ring Dr. Shah to tell him what has happened. I have never seen Papa like this."

Pramila rushed down the stairs. She made her way to the one phone in the building, called Dr. Shah's office, and asked that he be dispatched to their flat immediately.

Her sister was pacing when Pramila re-entered the flat. Vini could hardly suppress her tears. "Oh Pramila, this is all my fault. The engagement is off. Atul backed out. We had just received the news. I don't know—I don't know what happened. Ba, Papa and I, we were just trying to make sense of it all. That is when Papa said he was not feeling well and he grabbed his chest."

The blood rushed to Pramila's face. "What? How can the engagement be off? Just like that? What kind of people agree to marry off their son only to change their mind within the hour?"

Vini began to weep.

"Vini, you must stop this crying. We must think of Papa only now." Pramila guided her sister to join their mother by his side. The only sound was the occasional sob that escaped her sister's control.

The front door creaked as Dr. Shah saw himself in. He was a boyhood friend of her father's and the only doctor he trusted.

The three women moved into the kitchen while the doctor completed his assessment. Pramila glanced at her mother. Her expression was disconsolate, but she had not shed a tear. Ba picked up the pea pods strewn on the floor, placing them back into the canvas bag. Then she grabbed the bag, placed a stainless-steel bowl on the floor, sat down, and began to open the pods. Her daughters joined her. The familiar "tink" of the peas hitting the bowl was the only thing that separated the women from the reality that awaited them in the other room.

When he walked out of the room and into the kitchen, Dr. Shah's expression was less than reassuring.

Pramila jumped to her feet.

Dr. Shah shook his head. "This is not simple indigestion. I am afraid he has suffered a heart attack. He should be seen in hospital but he is refusing. I have known your papa for some time and he is very, very stubborn. I have given him some medicine but we will not know anything until a few days."

"What can we do?" Vini asked, stifling a sob.

"Try to convince him to go to hospital. Most importantly, do not make him excited or upset. Let him rest. He is to take this medicine twice a day," Dr. Shah said bleakly.

He gave Pramila a handful of wax-paper packets full of white powder.

"Even in the hospital, I am not sure how much we could be offering." His eyes were bloodshot and clothing rumpled. He looked like a man who had given his fair share of bad news that day.

There was nothing more to be said.

The doctor shook his head again. "*Bahu saro manus che.* He is such a good man. Among the best I know." It was not common for a man to touch another man's wife, but Dr. Shah tapped his hand

147

lightly on Ba's arm, a consoling gesture. Then he made his way to the front door, head hanging low.

That evening, Pramila could not be still. She wandered the hallway of the *chaali*, trying to lose herself in the sounds of normal existence. They sounded at once familiar and strange. The clanking of dinner being made, the mutter of adults analyzing the day's affairs heard through open doors, the laughter shared by families. There was an assumption made in the course of these activities—it was an assumption she herself had made every day of her own life—that the next minute or hour or day was a certainty. As if life were eternal. Now its very transience was painfully apparent and the absurdity of all those fixations clear.

She felt as though the walls and ceiling of the hallway were pushing in toward her. She gently opened the door to her father's room and sat by his side while he slept. She admired his thick head of hair. In his late forties, there was still no evidence of graying. His skin was supple, his features so young. He had always been strong. Until now. She simply could not believe that it was his time.

Overcome again, she averted her eyes from Papa. Even at such a time, he had a book by his side. They had bought it from New and Secondhand Bookstore just the week before on a trip to Fort. *The Good Earth* lay open and was propped upside down on the floor. She picked up the book and thumbed through it. From the looks of it, Papa had just started the book. He had dog-eared the page he was on. Pramila smiled; leave it to Papa to keep reading despite the day's events.

Papa shifted and roused. "Pramila, it's late, why are you not sleeping?" He reached his pale hand toward her cheek.

"Why will you not go to hospital? They will give you medicine to make your heart stronger."

"Pramila, you know this is not the case. My time is coming."

"Papa, please! Please do not say such things," she begged.

He grasped her hand in the firm but comforting way that he had since she was a child.

"I have never shied from telling you the truth, have I? This time—it will be very difficult for you, Vini and Ba. You and your sister don't always fit in with the others, isn't it? I suppose we have raised you this way. I sometimes wonder if—if I should have done so. Look at Vini. She is so smart and capable. She knows more than every boy in this building. She could do so many things. And yet she will be measured by one event—her marriage day." Papa grasped his chest.

"Papa, please. We must not speak about these things until you are better. It will just make you upset."

"No, no, I must say this. I know that you will worry about Ba and Vini only. But I have made arrangements for you all to be quite comfortable when I leave this earth. You shall not want for anything. Jayant uncle will see to it that everything is done according to my wishes. Your mother and I have been acquiring properties in Bombay over many years. Jayant uncle will assure that several properties are sold. This way you three can move to a better flat and the rent from the remaining properties will give you a stable income. You should want for nothing. I know that no matter what is to happen, Jayant uncle will look after the three of you."

Pramila was crying now even as her father continued his matter-of-fact tone. It was as if they were having two different conversations.

Her father's voice became raspy. Even the use of his breath was becoming taxing to him. Though it pained her immensely to hear him, Pramila did not try to stop him.

"It is my fault about your sister. For you it has always been a question, but for your sister, there was no question she wished to marry. After she met with so many boys and did not get a marriage offer, I could hardly console her. She begged me, she wanted to

149

stop looking. I said, 'Please meet just one more boy and if it doesn't work, we will stop looking.' When we met Atul and his family and they said yes, we were so relieved—so happy. Look what happened." He held his right palm up and raised his shoulders. His hand trembled ever so slightly.

"Papa, we cannot predict the future. This is not your fault. You must not be blaming yourself just as Vini should not be blaming herself that you have fallen sick, no?"

"A daughter does not take responsibility for her father. It is the father that must protect his daughter." He reached for Pramila's cheek. "*Mari vahali dikri*. My sweet daughter. The whole weight of the world is on your shoulders, no? Even when you were young it was that way. Do you remember the cockroaches?" His words were slow and rife with nostalgia. He seemed to lapse into some pleasant dream.

Pramila lifted her head and sniffed. "Yes, Papa."

"I was so proud of you that day." He laughed weakly and his eyes welled up. "Pramila *dikra*, you are destined for things I could never have imagined. I realized the day you came back with chalk marks all over your frock."

Pramila grasped Papa's hand. He attempted to squeeze hers but his grip faltered.

There were so many things she wanted to say to her father about her aspirations and her dreams. She felt a searing twinge of guilt for not having come to her father earlier, when there was time. She could no longer comprehend why she had kept the truth to herself for so long. Papa would have wanted to know what resided in her heart, no matter the consequences. Even though it was just hours before, the trip to the vegetable market seemed a distant dream. How she had breathed in freely the air of possibility! Now, there was just the excruciating weight of inevitability.

Dawn began to filter through the window. Pramila cursed the start of morning. Soon her mother or Vini or Jayant uncle would come into the room and she would have to give them her father's time. Instead, it was Dr. Shah who appeared in the doorway ready to examine her father. Papa said "*Dikra*, let me finish with this chap and we will have our morning together only."

Those were the last words she heard her father utter. Even he, who sensed the depth of his illness, had taken the morning for granted.

When she saw him next, his physical form was totally unfamiliar, the light within it gone. But the sound of his voice resonated deep within her for days afterwards, the way the clang of a bell is perceptible long after the loudest notes dissipate.

She lingered in the room beside Papa after he had left the world. She held his hand. She hovered over his body. She straightened his clothes. She took his copy of *The Good Earth*, flipped to the last page Papa had dog-eared and carefully folded the page over in half, lengthwise so that the crease would never be mistaken for any other. She kept the book in her hands so it would not be misplaced. And when his handsome form was taken away, she wept. Afterwards, she held vigil there, day after day after day—until the day she could no longer feel his essence within the room.

Chapter 17

Mumbai, August 2006

It always struck me as particularly cruel that a land that meets the sea should suffer drought. The fear of imminent thirst when a vast body of water lies just within sight is enough to drive people mad. Indeed, Bombay that summer was on the verge of becoming unhinged. In wealthy enclaves, taps were running dry. Those with influence responded swiftly: they demanded the end of water siphoning by the poor. In response, police began staging raids against slums, destroying illegal water connections in some cases and, in others, mowing down entire settlements. Fueled by desperation, short tempers, and the never-ending heat, protests all over the city quickly turned to riots. Throughout the city, there was a sense of lawlessness brewing. Subhash took to driving me to work with a cricket bat on the front seat.

The drought had consumed most of northern India and beyond, threatening cities, agricultural areas, and the food supply of the entire nation. In a matter of weeks, the luster of luxuries like televisions, cars, and mobile phones began to dull in comparison to a nondescript bucket of clean, drinkable water. Storefront windows were bashed in and stores looted. The grocer downstairs from Vini's flat had an entire shipment of bottled water stolen right out of the store even while the cash drawer was untouched.

Vini remarked that, much like in times of plenty, in a time of crisis only a few hearty souls sought to understand what had brought the city to this point. People were concerned about survival in the moment, not the series of forces, both man- and nature-made, that had led them to this fork in the road. To plan for the distant future—a future in which droughts were a constant threat—was unthinkable when planning for tomorrow was already difficult. It seemed, Maasi observed, that mankind was stuck living in a state of either total complacency or abject hysteria, and rarely anywhere in the middle. It was hard to disagree with her.

One morning, before work, I headed to the store down the block. I stepped out of the building into the knee-buckling heat, passing the leaky pipe. The water scarcely hit the pavement before it evaporated.

I heard Arjun's voice behind me: "Can you believe that bloody pipe is still leaking? I thought they might have fixed it by now."

My heart leapt at the sound. Once again, I was taken aback by the effect he had on me. *Play it cool, Shyamala.*

I turned slowly toward him. "No such luck I'm afraid!"

He wore his trademark carpenter jeans and a linen shirt with a Nehru collar. His sleeves were rolled up to his forearms. He smiled.

"Hey, did you hear about your interview?"

"They had to reschedule—waiting for a call back. Honestly, I am sure I stand no chance at getting the job," he said, ever sincere and self-deprecating.

"Come on. Vini told me about your stories. She's not one to give false praise."

"I haven't wanted to bore you with all of the details and it all seems so pie-in-the-sky—as you Americans say."

"Listen, I sit in a cubicle all day talking about software with other IT geeks so freelance journalism sounds downright fascinating, I'd love to hear more about what you do." We were standing in the courtyard of the building, and though I needed to head to work, I found myself stalling to hear more. I didn't want our chat to end. Arjun wasn't in a hurry either.

"Honestly, it's hard to believe a nobody like me could even get a shot. During the day I go to the factory with my father. When I have the opportunity, mostly at night, I write. A couple of websites published my scribbles and then a few newspapers, first in India, then England, and then America. My parents can't believe that someone can make a living as a journalist."

I imagined a mother like Champa faced with such a son. "From what Vini says, it seems to be working out for you. What do you write about?"

"Well, I wrote one article about infrastructure, population growth, and water in Bombay. Couldn't sell that last story to anyone until recently. But timing is everything; now, suddenly, with the drought, even people outside India have been asking about the piece. And—" He faltered.

"And?"

"Well, there was a piece on dance bars," he said reluctantly.

"Like a strip club?"

"Not exactly—the women usually keep their clothes on and the men usually keep their hands off, but it is still sex that is being sold. Desperate women dancing for men to throw a few rupees their way." Arjun shook his head solemnly. "Anyhow, the story started out about dance bars and then wound up being about the sex trade in many forms in Bombay—dance bars—red-light districts—exploitation of *hijras*. You name it. I wound up writing an entire series!"

"*Hijra*—as in the third gender?" I had heard mention of the *hijra* when my father read me the ancient Hindu epic *Ramayana*.

When Lord Rama was banished from the ancient city of Ayodhya to serve exile deep within the forest, he told the men and women of the city to wipe away their tears and part with him. The men and women left. However, a group of people, the *hijra*, remained, standing beside him. They identified as neither men nor women. They were said to have waited in that exact spot until Lord Rama returned from exile fourteen years later.

Arjun nodded. "Some of the outfits in the West wanted me to identify the *hijra* as gay. I pushed back against using Western terms because they tend to break everything down into black and white—into dichotomy."

"My father said that *hijra* held an esteemed place in society before the British colonized India."

"Hard to know I suppose—once a land is colonized, its history gets rewritten. Can't know exactly what came before."

Arjun seemed preoccupied. He gathered his thoughts before he spoke, his gaze intent upon me. "If I get the position, I might have to move to New Delhi."

I had considered this more than once. But I was trying to think of Arjun as a summer distraction. At a loss for what to say and how to feel, I continued, "Well, I hope you get the position."

"Do you? Because I was hoping you might be disappointed, maybe a little possessive even." He ran his fingers through his hair.

I let out a breath, my resistance flagging. I had planned to come to India to escape a relationship, not to start a new one—especially not one with so many potential landmines. The pipe continued to leak. A groundskeeper stepped between Arjun and me on his way to the spigot where he began to screw in a garden hose. He eyed us as he turned up the water, which came out as little more than a trickle.

Once the gardener was done, Arjun continued. "Shyamala, you know *Janmashtami* is coming up, right?" There was intimacy in the way he leaned in toward me. He smelled of a delightful mix of ayurvedic soap and aftershave. "Anyhow, I was thinking that I could take you—I know a place where they have a damn good *Janmashtami* party."

"Yes—I'd love to go," I said as casually as I could muster.

We stood facing each other, our bodies close, the hose whistling in the distance. All this time, I had been waiting for a moment like this with Arjun—maybe not with the leaky pipe in the background or the groundskeeper lurking—but now that Arjun was in such proximity I felt more than a little apprehensive. Could he sense it? The job abroad, living with Vini, meeting Arjun—I could never have imagined that this is how my story would go.

Just then, Maasi yelled at me from one of her windows.

"Shyamala, you have a call from the US!" She didn't say who.

"Coming Maasi!" I announced.

"*Janmashtami* then?" Arjun asked.

The sincerity of his expression pushed away my doubts.

"*Janmashtami*." I nodded, my elation nearly spilling over.

I made my way to the landing. I could feel a warmth at my back as Arjun watched me walk up the stairs.

Vini was holding the phone when I got to the apartment.

She grimaced and mouthed. "It's Neil. Sorry."

I slowly picked up the receiver. I hadn't spoken to him in months. "Hello?"

When Neil spoke, his voice was sheepish. "Shyamala. It's good to hear your voice. How are you, how is India?"

"Neil." My heart pounded against my chest as I tried to slow my breath. "I'm—good. India is good. Neil, look, is everything okay? What's going on?"

"I am not sure how to say this, Shyamala. I'll just come right out with it." He seemed to be talking himself into revealing whatever he had to say. "I just wanted you to know from me and not by accident through someone else. I'm . . . I'm getting married."

"You're getting married?"

"Her name is Lisa. She's really sweet." Neil seemed at a loss for what to say next. "I—I think you'd like her."

The telephone connection to the United States was a good one and my silence resonated without the mercy of white noise. I could hear Neil breathing as he waited for a response. His nose whistled over the line—inhale, exhale, inhale, exhale.

"Congratulations Neil. Be happy and make her happy," I said tersely, surprised at how he had triggered such a sudden burst of anger. "Just do her a favor. If you decide you have stopped loving her or that you never actually loved her at all, just have the decency to tell her so before the wedding."

"Shyamala—"

I could hear my name in his familiar voice growing more distant as I pulled the receiver from my face and hung up, my hand shaking. There was nothing more to say.

Through sheer force of will, I stilled my hand. All this time, I had been mired in memories of Neil and frustrated at myself for it. So much time had passed since then, yet I was still struggling to get my bearings, struggling to shake the memories of him, or envisage a different future for myself. Being dumped by him had shaken my sense of certainty that things would work themselves out. My pulse continued to bound. How was it that Neil just got to move on? Why did I still care what he did?

◆ ◆ ◆

Early the next morning the phone rang at an hour and with an urgency that suggested the caller could only be my mother. She'd probably heard the news by now.

Aside from a cursory proof-of-life call here or there, I had hardly spoken to my mother since I left the US. The reason had been simple. Though I wanted to make amends for what I had said before leaving for India, I wasn't sure how. Not calling was a bona fide strategy to avoid the topic altogether.

I picked up the phone. "Hello?"

"Shyamala *beta*, I heard the news. I thought you might call after speaking to Neil at least. Just to let us know about his engagement."

"Oh, hey Mom. Sorry I haven't called," I said, actually feeling sorry.

"I only wish—I only wish that it had worked out between you two."

From the very day that he left me at the altar, my mother had wanted me to forgive Neil. I had seen it in her face when I walked in on the two of them drinking tea in my kitchen back in LA not long after the breakup. Her face had pleaded with me, *take him back*. She didn't hide her misgivings, especially about decisions—my decisions. Now I could feel her doubt smothering me through the phone line. I had the intense urge to hang up.

I reminded myself why she was calling. She was concerned.

"Shyamala, I just want you to have what you have always wanted," she continued.

Maybe it was because I was on the phone with her and not distracted by body language and facial expressions—but I became aware of something in my mother's voice, an inflection that had been present before that I had never understood. I had always mistaken it for doubt but, today, I heard something else. My tone softened when I spoke again.

"I know, Mom."

She seemed to hesitate on the line.

"Good, Shyamala. Good. Let me give the phone to your dad."

"Mom, wait." I wanted to bridge the gap between us but was unsure how. "It's really good to hear your voice."

"You too *beta*."

What was it about that inflection? There was a vulnerability to it—as if she were bracing herself for *my* judgment. As if her own failures had been laid bare and I was given the power of absolution—not as her daughter but as someone who had no need for forbearance.

Maybe it was all merely a figment of my imagination.

There was a flurry of sound as my mom handed the receiver to my father.

"Hi Shyama! What is going on? Hardly you have called twice since you got to India. This email-bemail business is fine for friends but we actually want to *hear* your voice. Every time we call you seem to be out! It was your mother's idea to call today. I told her, '*Arré* Pramila, no way. I am through with calling her. Let her call us for a change!' But your mother is worried. She needed to hear you." My father's annoyance was partly an act. He had wanted to call as much as my mother did.

"Sorry Dad. I just haven't been great at communicating especially with Mom. I figured I could edit myself better by email."

"*Bakwas!* Total bullshit! People say things. You both will get over it. Avoiding each other is no answer to these things. Anyway, what is this about that boy?"

That boy. That is what my father had resorted to calling Neil since we broke up. As if the mere mention of Neil's name was an affront to him.

"Well—seems that Neil is getting married, Dad."

"It's no great loss really. I never really liked him."

"Thanks Dad." Truth was that he had loved Neil—in the way that fathers without sons love their sons-in-law—at least until Neil decided not to show up at the wedding festivities.

"Well, just in case, have Vini take you to that snack place in Bori Bunder. You know the one I used to eat at in college? The *bhel* there is too good. One bite and you will forget all about that boy."

"Dad, I'm pretty sure that wallowing in my sorrows while binging on food isn't a recommended approach anymore."

"Oh, don't give me all that psychoanalysis nonsense! What could it hurt? You can think of me when you go there."

"Okay Dad, I'll do it for you." I smiled to myself. "Hey Dad, is Mom still there?"

"No Shyamala, she just left for the evening. She went to some event at the temple."

"Okay. Well, when she comes home, could you tell her thanks for worrying about me?"

"Sure Shyama. I'll do that."

"Thanks Dad."

"We'll talk later Shyamala. And by later, I mean next week. Not a month from now!"

"Yes, I'll call next week."

I felt as though I had more to say and lingered on the phone.

"Was there anything else, Shyamala?"

"I guess not, Dad. I'll talk to you soon."

"*Aujo dikra.* Bye my dear."

I hung up, still thinking about my mother's words.

Chapter 18

Mumbai, August 2006

A few days later, Natasha invited me to a night out. She was taking Daniel and me to see a movie at Bombay's old Edward Theatre. This evening was really for her and Daniel; I was, for all intents and purposes, her chaperone and alibi. To avoid any suspicions that family or acquaintances might have about a white guy accompanying her, Natasha insisted that Daniel meet us directly at the theater though she planned to pick me up right outside Vini's apartment complex.

As I gathered my things, ready to head out, I heard hushed voices in the kitchen. I wandered over to find my aunt whispering to Rajesh. Vini's back was to me and Rajesh was listening to her with rapt attention, nodding in agreement. I coughed to announce my presence and they both jumped. They took a half step away from each other.

"Oh, Shyama! I didn't see you there! Rajesh and I, we were just talking about, um, Shalu's marks in school," Vini blurted. "Rajesh was telling me that she is top of her standard."

I didn't see how Shalu's success at school was something that needed to be whispered about. I had the distinct impression they had been talking about something else.

"*Han-ji.* Yes, madam. She is top in class. I am most proud. Yes, very proud. Well, I must be going to check the car." Rajesh let himself out of the front door without waiting for a response.

Vini too bolted, rushing to her bathroom. "Well, I was just heading for a shower after being out in the heat."

I was left standing alone in the kitchen.

A few minutes later, as I waited for Natasha outside Vini's building, I mulled over what I had seen in the kitchen. What was it they didn't want to share with me? One thing was certain. Rajesh and Vini hadn't been talking about Shalu's school when I walked in on them. Still, why the furtive glances and the suspicious change of topic? Did this have something to do with the mysterious phone calls my aunt had been taking? Was there something going on between the two of them?

I wiped the sweat off my upper lip and squinted at the sky as I waited for Natasha's car to appear. The sun had retreated behind a group of gray, water-laden clouds. The weather forecaster had disavowed any chance of rain. But the sky seemed contemplative, as if considering a sprinkle or shower just out of spite. I waited to feel heavy monsoon raindrops splatter on my skin.

The skies threatened, but no rain came on the drive to the theater in Kalbadevi. Edward Theatre, with its crisp angles and Greco-Roman facade, sat tucked awkwardly among taller, more modern buildings. As we approached, Daniel was standing on the sidewalk not far from the quaint entrance. His hands were in the pockets of his slacks. He leaned against a wall, one leg bent, the foot resting against it. Had someone photographed him in black and white, he might have looked as though he were on location posing for a European haute couture fashion magazine. Local theater-goers ogled him partly out of curiosity, partly out of concern that he was far from home and lost. For his part, Daniel appeared remarkably at ease in his surroundings.

"Daniel!" Natasha darted toward him but stopped short of touching him.

"Hey Natasha!" He took his hands out of his pockets, tried to figure out where he could put them on her, thought better of it and put them back. Then he nodded to me. "Oh hey Shyamala, how's it going?"

"Fine, fine. Listen, are you two sure you want me to stay?" I felt every bit the third wheel.

"Of course. We three are here to see the film together," Natasha said, her sights not straying from Daniel.

"But we shouldn't force her—" Daniel grinned at me to assure me he was joking.

"Don't listen to him, Shyama. He is full of shit, *yaar*."

"Third wheel it is! So, what blockbuster Indian melodrama are we going to see tonight anyway?" I asked.

"We are going to see a movie called *Breathless* by Jean-Luc Godard. Edward is having a *French* film festival. After the Bollywood movie we went to see with Ajay and Gayatri, Daniel complained for a week that his hearing was off because the actress sang at such a high pitch. He has some sort of moral objection to musicals."

"Her voice *was* piercing!" Daniel protested. "In fact, I don't think the actress even sang, it was all lip-synching. And anyway, name one single guy you know who would dance in the street with all his ridiculously dressed buddies while professing his love for some girl he met just seconds ago?"

Natasha and I glanced at each other and answered simultaneously, "Ajay."

She laughed. "So you see Shyamala, rather than listening to Daniel complain about Bollywood, I thought it would be easier to go see something foreign. That is why we are here to see a French movie."

If Daniel standing alone garnered attention, Daniel standing with an Indian woman nearly stopped traffic. Patrons slowed their pace as they walked toward us to get a better look and one young man even stopped to ask Natasha if she was okay. I worried that she might lose her nerve. It was probably unprecedented for her to sneak out of her house under false pretenses to meet anyone, much less a man, and even less an American man. She was in uncharted territory, anticipating the thrill of discovery within the unknown, all the while fearing that any revelation would force a rupture with the world she knew.

As we entered the old theater, I hung back. I felt like a voyeur. No, I felt one step beyond. After years of being alone, I was living the tension between Daniel and Natasha as if it were my own.

The interior of the theater was surprisingly spacious, considering its rather humble exterior. The walls were painted pale blue except for the balconies which were accented with gleaming gold trim. Toward the front, there was space for an entire orchestra. I looked at the upper tiers and box seats and imagined stylishly dressed colonial-era Indians occupying them. I felt as though, upon exiting the theater, I might walk into the India of my father.

"This is quite a theater. Hard to imagine when you are looking at it from the outside," I whispered.

"Shyamala, why are you whispering? This is India. Talking during a movie is absolutely allowed, *na*?" Natasha asked.

"Don't get me started again!' Daniel feigned irritation. 'Between the syrupy-sweet singing of the heroines, the random dances that have nothing whatsoever to do with the plot, and the guy sitting next to me in the theater having a full conversation on his mobile phone, now you know why I have sworn off all Bollywood movies!"

Someone from a row or two behind us shushed Daniel.

"Oh sure, different rules apply when the white guy talks!" Daniel glowered at the shusher. Natasha elbowed Daniel and we all chuckled over the truth in his words.

Finally, the theater lights dimmed. The darkness gave Natasha cover of anonymity and she pulled Daniel's hand on to her lap.

I made it through about two minutes of subtitles before my eyes began to drift. I awoke during the closing credits, to find Natasha and Daniel still holding hands. It was only with the brightening of the lights that she let go of Daniel's hand. For them, I wished the movie never had to end.

We wandered out of the theater into the night. We walked down Kalbadevi Road, making small talk and glancing into store windows. I stopped short when we happened past a window full of books. The storefront read 'New and Secondhand Bookstore'.

Natasha and Daniel were in their own world, arguing whether the jump cuts during the movie were too distracting.

"Hey guys, I'm just gonna check this place out. I'll be right back."

The sweet, earthy scent of aging books greeted me at the door. Stacks of books were scattered everywhere. There were texts written in Hindi, Gujarati, and Marathi, and others in English, Portuguese, and French. Some piles stood so tall that one's view beyond was entirely obscured; others allowed one to peek over the top. The effect was of a miniature skyscape constructed of books. I accidentally knocked one of the taller piles, watched it sway a bit, and imagined being trapped under a mass of forgotten volumes. Not an entirely bad way to die.

"Be careful madam. I am still working on that stack," said the bookseller from the counter at the front of the store. He peered at me over his reading glasses. "Just last month someone found a first edition of *20,000 Leagues Under the Sea* in that exact stack." As he spoke his attention returned to the pile of books on his counter.

"By Jules Verne?" I asked, surprised to find a first edition of the French writer's work in a quaint bookshop in Mumbai half a world away from where it was published.

"One and only."

"That is incredible! Any treasures you would like to point out to me?"

He glanced up at me and smiled. I imagined he would say they were all treasures to him.

"How long has this place been here?"

"Since 1905."

"More than a century, impressive." I picked up an old army-green volume with the title rubbed off the edge and opened the cover.

"That is hardly a blink of the eye in a city like Bombay. Where are you from? Wait, let me guess." He raised his index finger.

"Ok—"

"California?"

"Yeah! How did you know?" I slammed the book shut. By now, I realized that I wore my Americanness on my sleeve, but how did he know I was a Californian?

"Well, you are speaking with an accent that is American. But I am not hearing the Midwest or South in your voice. None of those long 'A' sounds or that particular drawl. You are dressing very casually, like maybe you didn't even change before coming out with your friends. The East Coast types put more of the effort in, you know."

I furrowed my brow. How could he possibly have known I hadn't changed my clothes?

"We get many tourists here. After a while, you get to know people."

"Ever visited America?"

"I have no reason to leave this place. Look at it, it's paradise." He peered at me over his glasses, raised his eyebrows, and beamed again.

I glanced around the cramped bookstore with stack upon stack of volumes and found it hard to contradict him.

"I'll leave you to explore then," he said, disappearing behind a towering pile of books.

I poked about finding a hodge-podge of stories—among them *Heat and Dust*, *The Great Gatsby* and *Untouchable* by Mulk Raj Anand—and stood at the counter to purchase the books. The bookseller reappeared, writing the prices down on a receipt and then quickly calculating the total by hand.

After I paid, I noticed a copy of *Alice in Wonderland* on top of a stack at the counter. I grabbed it for Shalu. I pulled out my wallet again.

"Not to worry. That book is on me only. Just remember my store when you go back to America." He tilted his head back and forth several times.

"How could I forget a place like this? *Shukria*. Thank you." I took in the scent of the shop.

"Ahh, a rare word these days. You are most welcome."

I hurried out of the store with the four books, wishing I had time to collect more. I searched for Natasha and Daniel who weren't where I had left them. I spotted them a little way down the street, tucked under an entrance to a building at a secluded street corner. They stood close, lips nearly touching.

"Natasha, Natasha, is that you?" A man's voice came from across the street.

I was almost upon them now and watched as Natasha startled, her head springing away from Daniel's.

"Ohhh, yes. Hi Kiranbhai and Danishaben! I was just showing Daniel and Shyamala around town—they are friends from work, visiting from America. We just finished watching a film at Edward. Shyamala just came out of the bookstore down the street." Natasha's body retreated from Daniel's. She waved at me, trying to sound casual.

"Here I am." I rushed forward—I was Natasha's alibi, her chaperone.

"I got worried when I saw the two of you in the dark." Kiranbhai's voice, which had been kind until this point, grew stern.

"We—we were just talking." Daniel's eyes glided toward Natasha and turned back to Kiranbhai.

"I am not sure it is seemly for my cousin-sister to be caught in the dark, alone with a stranger, talking or anything else. It does not look good. This is true, no?" His question was directed at Natasha. His tone was patronizing.

"I'm no stranger," Daniel retorted, still trying to sound friendly.

"That is what worries me," Kiranbhai said.

Danishaben, who must have been his wife, grabbed him by the crook of his elbow. "Come Kiran, let it be."

"Whatever you believe you saw, please Kiranbhai, don't think anything of it. You have the wrong impression."

Natasha's desperation made me uncomfortable.

"*Mane ulloo na banav.* Don't try to make a fool of me. I am knowing what I saw. Thank God, it was me only. I will keep your secret for now. But I trust, Natasha, that you know what is the proper thing to do?"

He let the words hover in the air.

I parted my lips to speak. I wanted to defend my friends against Kiranbhai's prying comments, but Natasha glared at me in warning.

"It was nice to meet you." Kiranbhai addressed none of us in particular, then did an abrupt about-face and crossed the nearly deserted street. Danishaben followed him, taking a fleeting backward once-over before vanishing into the night.

I stood silently, unsure of what to say and how to help. After tonight, it felt like Natasha and Daniel's love story might be a bit less Hollywood rom-com and a bit more Bollywood tragedy.

Chapter 19

Bombay, 1970

For weeks, all Pramila could think about was that her father died never having known exactly what she wanted most. When she was alone, she would pretend to sit before him and tell him her plans—about how she wished to be a *shramaniji*—about why she sought a life of spiritual pursuits—about why she needed to give up the world that he had given to her. She would pause between her explanations, as if to allow Papa to answer, and then try to imagine the gentle reverberations of his voice in response. She realized that those reverberations were merely figments of her imagination, but they seemed to her as real as the voices of her sister and mother. Even though he was gone, she had to tell him.

But the longing for her father was like some sort of physical ailment that fundamentally altered the function of her body. Each night was fraught with the visceral sensation of loss. Each day fraught with a going-through-the-motions numbness.

The pain became no less acute in the months to follow. Vini remained inconsolable and refused to meet any prospective grooms. She held herself responsible for the death of her father and resolved that she would not marry. End of discussion.

Now, naturally, eyes fell in Pramila's direction. She knew what she had to do. She would proceed through life like other girls. She would get married. She would continue the family line. Like it or not, such was the natural order of things.

Pramila tucked her sorrow away, as if it were a handkerchief pushed into a pocket. She was conscious of its steady pressure against her chest. On rare occasions, she had a moment in which she could not perceive its presence. But then, invariably, a corner or edge would escape its hiding place and the entirety of her grief would be exposed.

◆ ◆ ◆

It was May when Pramila met Dev. The meeting was choreographed; Dev would arrive with his parents at Jayant uncle's flat where he would meet Pramila and her mother.

Pramila stood back as introductions were made as if she were an observer in someone else's life. Dev seemed undaunted by her coolness. Some might have considered him a handsome man, she thought to herself. He had a symmetric face, a strong jaw line, a becoming mustache. Some aunties would object to the darkness of his skin. But Pramila found his tone warm and reassuring. He walked with a slight strut, as if his physical body could not contain his confidence.

"Pramila, why don't you and Dev sit down and have a chat?" Jayant uncle pointed to two chairs in the corner of the room, eight feet from the adults.

Pramila sat directly across from Dev. She peered through the window, then off toward the kitchen, and finally at Dev. As a child, she had never been at a loss for words when talking with the boys in the apartment complex. But those were different times. She found herself unable to find anything to say to the young man who sat across from her.

Ba stopped by to offer a plate of diamond-shaped cashew sweets topped with silver foil. Then Jayant uncle's wife came with a plate of sweetened shredded carrot bites. Then came the tea and the savories.

Dev found the pile of food on his plate growing even though he politely refused each offer.

"Well, I suppose that if you decide not to marry me, at least I will go home with a full belly! Perhaps the food is some sort of consolation for a broken heart," he said with a laugh after the adults had retreated to their seats.

Pramila nodded. She marveled at how Dev's speech was natural and easy.

"To be perfectly honest, I have met with several girls. Even then, I am finding it odd. All the adults are sitting around speaking about the weather as if they are not paying attention to how you and I are coming along. And we are pretending we do not notice that they are watching us actually."

"How else would we meet and come to know each other?" Pramila asked simply.

"I guess one might imagine a scene from the American movie, all this dating business and falling in love."

"Love marriage? Is that what you want? To find a girl by yourself and fall in love and marry her?"

"*Arré, na, na. Bilkul nai*, all that is nonsense. I don't want to find some stranger unknown to my family. I want to marry somebody who has gone to a good school, somebody who can move into my house and blend into my family, somebody who knows how we live."

Pramila considered this for a moment. Dev was so invested in this decision in a way that she could not understand. She was

171

resigned to her fate and passive to its whim. But for Dev, things were different. He sought to shape his future with the incorruptible faith of someone who had never suffered loss. Pramila wished she could capture that confidence again, if only for a moment.

"What about you? What are you wishing for?"

"I suppose the same thing also." Having hardly considered the question in the past, her words did not exactly sound like a ringing endorsement to get married.

"Are you certain?" Dev sounded disappointed.

Pramila felt the pressure of the handkerchief in her pocket. The question had revealed a ragged edge of her sadness. She tried to tuck it back in, but she could not contain the whole of it. Her eyes began to water. She averted them.

"I am sorry if I have asked you a wrong type of question. I am not good at these things."

"I am fine. I am fine," Pramila said, as much to convince herself as Dev. She brushed at her eyes. It took several breaths to suppress her sorrow.

"This must be a difficult time for you."

He knew. Of course, he knew. Someone must have told him about her father's death. What was the point of pretending otherwise?

"You were asking what I wished for. I wish for nothing more than another moment to be with my father."

Dev did not try to fill the silence that followed. That was what most people did when Papa's death came up, but the words were more comfort to the consoler than the one grieving. Dev left the stale expressions of sympathy unsaid. He seemed unafraid of the grief he had uncovered in her, yet moved by it. He was so calm that the others in the room did not notice what had transpired between them. It was the first intimacy they shared.

The next day, when her mother asked her if she wished to meet Dev again, to her surprise Pramila agreed without hesitation. A sense of nervousness overtook her at the prospect that he might not feel the same way. Perhaps he might have sought a different type of woman. One who did not cry at their first meeting.

But Dev did agree to another meeting. This time at the Regal Cinema in Apollo Bunder. They were allowed to go without a chaperone.

As they left the theater, Dev seemed preoccupied. Finally, he said, "Well, I am settled. I do not want to look any longer."

"How can you be so certain?"

"Are you not certain? I wish only to marry you." There was romance in the way Dev spoke to Pramila and it made her uneasy.

"Why me?"

"I want someone who is true to herself. And you strike me as this kind of girl."

"How can you know this after we've only met twice?"

"I am a good judge of character," he said with a smile so cheerful that Pramila found herself returning it in kind.

Dev seemed so certain. But how was it that she should make such a decision? It was true that their two families were compatible, Dev's parents were willing to accept her, and Dev indulged the burden she carried. It seemed unlikely she would find anyone more suitable. For all the practical reasons they were a good fit but she had to admit that there was more. Dev had this buoyancy. He seemed to float without care through the world, unburdened by doubt or sorrow. And after all that had happened, Pramila wished to dwell in such a place.

He continued, "But I must also tell you something else. A few months back, I applied for the visa to go to America. It was purely by accident because I never had given it a thought before. Anyhow, my visa was approved and something is telling me I should go."

173

"You are going to move to America?"

"I hope to—with you," he said, his eyes searching.

Pramila tried to fathom what life might be like halfway around the world.

"What do you think?" Dev asked.

"I am not sure what to think."

"It is not a minor decision. Let's meet once again and you can tell me."

Pramila knew that Dev was giving her cover—time to think—away from the prying eyes of the elders. But she did not have long; soon they would be asking for an answer.

"All right, I will let you know when we meet next."

Move to America? In a way, she was not surprised by the proposition. In sudden steps, she left so much behind. First, she had given up her father. Then, she had been forced to give up on her wish to become a *shramaniji*. Now, she was being asked to move away from everyone and everything that she knew. It seemed a natural evolution. Perhaps it was just time to give herself up to fate.

It took a fortnight for Pramila to make her final decision. It happened while she and Ba made *rotis*. Pramila rolled small pieces of dough with a rolling pin. She placed the uncooked *roti* on a skillet. Ba took it from there. She cooked one side, then the other. Then she placed the piping hot *roti* directly on the flame until it puffed up like a balloon. Finally, she placed it on a steel dish, gave it a firm "whap" with her hand to release the steam and slathered it with clarified butter. The process had a certain rhythm. The click of the rolling pin as it flattened the dough, the whoosh of the *roti* as it landed on the pan, the scrape of the metal tongs against the skillet, the "vwoomp" of the *roti* as it expanded into a perfect circular pillow.

Pramila watched her mother labor over the stove. Ba had changed since Papa's death. As was tradition for a widow, she wore only white saris. They accentuated her hollowed cheeks and fine lines. Her usually stern demeanor and strict rules had slackened under the weight of her loss. So had the tightness of her braid. In the wake of her husband's death, Ba had given up on the exactness of life.

Pramila felt a wave of emotion. It was not quite empathy and not quite love. But both were intense within her. She wished she could unburden her mother, if even for an instant.

"Ba, I think I shall marry Dev." Though the words were spoken in Gujarati, the pronunciation felt foreign. She had never said "I" and "marry" in the same sentence before.

"You have decided? Are you sure?"

Pramila nodded. "He is the right type of person. The family has a good reputation, and we are compatible."

Ba's eyes met her daughter's. The crow's feet at the corners of them returned, as she mustered a smile. "*Arré?* Are you telling me nothing more is needed?"

Pramila felt herself blush. These were hardly topics to speak about with friends, much less her mother. "Ba! It is not so proper to speak of such things!"

"Still, Dev is not a pair of shoes that you purchase from the *zapatwala*. For shoes you must consider type and make. But to choose a husband is different. There must be something else, isn't it?"

"He is handsome, if that is what you are meaning."

Ba still did not smile. Nor did she embrace her daughter. But Pramila knew Ba was satisfied because she was more generous with her spoonful of *ghee*.

"Well then, let us tell Jayant uncle today so he can speak to Dev's family."

The next several weeks of Pramila's life snapped into place like interlocking pieces. The advice of the pandit was sought to determine an auspicious date for the wedding. Dev had an offer for a job in some place called Boof-alo, New York, and would move just weeks after the wedding. Thankfully, Jayant uncle took charge of preparations for the actual event, which left Pramila to work on the slow process of pulling up the stakes that had tethered her life to her family's and to the small flat in downtown Bombay. The future she had once imagined was a memory now so distant that it might as well have belonged to someone else.

Pramila navigated through the highs and lows, knowing that her mother was relieved to have one daughter settled in the world and that her father would have been pleased just to have her see another part of it. Ba seemed to put on a brave face, allowing Pramila's good news to push away any thoughts of her eventual move overseas.

Vini attended every festivity and fulfilled every role of the sister of the bride, but was never quite able to meet Pramila's eye. Pramila took note, saddened that fate seemed determined to lead them in directions that neither had intended and hoping it would not leave a permanent chasm between them.

The wedding was modest but Pramila was radiant. She wore a red and white sari with a brushed gold border. The fabric was intricately patterned using the traditional *bandhani* tie-dye technique. Her thick hair was swept into a bun and pulled through into a braid. Fragrant white flowers were tucked into the locks. She wore a small gold and diamond pendant that dangled daintily on her forehead from the parting in her hair. As if her long neck was not adorned adequately with a matching gold choker and necklaces, a thick lei had been placed around it. She did not smile, for that would not be becoming for a bride. And though tears did not leave tracks on her cheeks, Pramila's eyes had a watery quality. She had shed many tears earlier in the day. Tears for the life she was leaving behind. Tears for the life she knew she could never have. Tears for her father. Tears for her mother. Tears for the feared unknown that lay ahead. Her sadness lent her beauty a certain gravity. Later, Dev would tell her that he never quite shook off the effect that her expression had on him that day. Decades after their wedding, he still kept an old black and white photo of Pramila from their wedding day tucked inside his wallet—though he always said he remembered the day in color.

Chapter 20

Mumbai to Aurangabad, August 2006

"There is so much to see in India outside of Mumbai, Shyamala, we should take a trip," Maasi suggested one morning. "Plus you need to take a break from work. How about we visit Ajanta?"

"Ajanta? Do you mean the caves?" I asked. I was humoring her even though my answer was obviously going to be no. It was madness to go on a road trip by bus in the middle of what seemed to be the hottest summer in Indian history.

"It is a bit of a bus ride to get there but it will be absolutely worth your while! You'll understand when we get there."

"How far is it?" I sensed that "a bit" might be an underestimation.

She did a quick calculation in her head. "It is about two hundred miles from here. About a nine-hour drive only."

Nine hours to travel two hundred miles! I was used zipping along the freeways of California and making that distance in less than half that time. I scratched my head and tried to convey my doubt. "Nine hours, in this heat?"

"Not to worry, we will be traveling by luxury-bus!" she said brightly, the term "luxury bus" sounding like one word when she said it.

I had a bad feeling about where this conversation was heading. "Maasi, did you already buy the tickets?"

Vini hesitated before a combination of contrition and eagerness washed over her face. "Yes, I did. But you absolutely cannot miss this place, Shyamala! It is a wonder of the world! How often do you come to India? It will be a fun outing for the two of us! Come, we'll be comfortable on the luxury-bus isn't it?"

I'd seen some of the air-conditioned luxury buses—behemoths lumbering through Bombay with their tinted windows and sleek exteriors. If not luxurious, I figured the trip would at least be tolerable. Against my better judgment, I agreed.

Initially, when I saw the crisply painted bus, I was quite hopeful. Sadly the illusion lasted only as long as it took to get to the door, the right panel of which was barely attached to the hinge. The driver hoisted the door up with one arm while guiding the passengers into the bus with the other. I prayed that Lord Krishna, whose statue decorated the dashboard, might usher us safely to our destination.

The air in the bus was stifling, laden with human perspiration. If there was an air conditioner, it was not working. Several people in the surrounding seats had given up on the idea of cool, recirculated air and had pried their windows open. Even a hot breeze was preferable to the air in the cabin. Unperturbed by the heat, Vini was fast asleep before we had even left the city.

I opened my copy of *The Good Earth*, hoping to distract myself. Though I had carried it nearly everywhere I went, I had only read a few chapters since arriving in India. But the constant shaking and jostling on the bus made it impossible to hold on to the book, much less read it.

Nor could I sleep. On the rare occasion that I managed to nod off, I would be jarred awake as the bus swerved or hit a pothole. Travelling on this bus was like being on a roller-coaster without a safety bar or any expectation of survival. By the time we disembarked in Aurangabad nine hours later, my hair stood up of its own dusty, sweaty accord, and my nerves were entirely frayed. My aunt, for her part, looked well-rested and unperturbed.

◆ ◆ ◆

"I have been to the Ajanta caves many times and still I am excited," my aunt said over breakfast the following morning. "What a story this place is telling!"

Even though I was sore from the bus trip and itchy from a constellation of mosquito bites acquired overnight, Maasi's enthusiasm was infectious.

"Nobody even knew these caves existed until the early 1800s," my aunt continued. "People say that some British chap was hunting tigers in the forest and happened upon one of the cave temples. They had been lost to history for over fifteen hundred years."

Clearly, the unlikely friendship between Arjun and my aunt must have been born in part from their love of history.

We boarded another bus to get from our hotel in Aurangabad to Ajanta. As we headed into the hills, I tried to imagine lush forests instead of the brown-yellow vegetation that surrounded us. The drought was taking a toll here as well. There was a wide riverbed in which only a small stream of water could be seen.

It was a hike from the bus stop to the foot path that led to Ajanta. I could see how the growth of a primordial forest would have hidden the caves from sight. First, I saw the horseshoe-shaped stone cliff overlooking a small valley. Then my eyes homed in on the entrances into the caves where raw stone had been tamed into arches, pillars, and columns. The artistry and scale were breathtaking.

But the moment we stepped foot over the threshold of the first cave, it was clear we had entered another realm. I abandoned the pretense implied by the term "modern man". There could be no doubt about the sophistication of the people who had taken hammer and chisel to this mountain face and sculpted massive rock temples as a tribute to the Buddha starting more than two millennia ago.

Despite the crowds and the summer heat, the air inside the first cave was cool and the atmosphere serene. Vini told me it was a monastery. Here the carvings were austere, reserved—as if they had been constructed for reflection and meditation. But if the monasteries were a reflection of spiritual aspiration, other caves were a stunning tribute to the physical world. Massive frescoes graced the walls, and the art was anything but austere. The curves made by the painter's brush hundreds of years ago, apparently using metal mirrors to reflect the light of the sun into the caves, were sensual—the pigments of their palettes a celebration of the essence of what makes us human. The colors on the walls were rich and inviting—red and yellow ochre, deep greens the color of malachite, and the vibrant blue of lapis lazuli. Some segments were as bright as if the paint had just dried days ago. The images were created with perspective and mood and a sense of movement.

I felt as though I was looking at a photo album from fifteen hundred years ago, viewing snapshots of everyday happenings—middle-aged men gossiping, a woman applying make-up, people gathered in a palace, children chasing a hen, a king surrounded by dancers, a woman seated on the ground listening to a sermon. The aspects of modern life that define our daily existence, mobile phones and email and fashion and politics and the relentless ticking of the clock—all of it disappeared behind the walls of those caves. I breathed freely in the prehistoric air. I thought about the indelible work of the hands that had created that art nearly two millennia before and could not help but be ashamed. What had any of us created that could withstand the test of time and be such a tribute to the better qualities of humankind?

Vini stopped in front of a fresco of a voluptuous woman leaning against a man who appeared to be her lover. The man in the painting had a sinuous quality, his very stance an invitation to the woman.

"People are always impressed by the sleeping Buddha," my aunt said, finally turning toward me. "But I have always been partial to these paintings. They remind me of what makes us human."

After hours of wandering in the caves, we came upon the sleeping Buddha. He lay in gentle repose, stretching over twenty feet long. He was sleeping on his side, a pillow underneath his head, his face serene. It was impossible to capture the entire statue in a single frame of film and hard to imagine how an artisan could have carved the entire thing in the rock face of the mountain with such an eye for proportion. As the crowds swarmed in and out of the cave, I found myself transfixed.

On the drive back to the hotel, Vini was brimming with excitement. "The sculptures and paintings seem so alive, no? Like they might walk out of the wall and have a chat or a dance with us?"

I nodded, feeling an immediacy with the past.

"Even so many hundreds of years later, these caves are a place for escape. This is why Ajanta is so appealing. Your mother loved this place! The first time we came here with our father, she was hardly twenty years old," Vini added, almost as if thinking out loud. "I wonder if she knew back then."

"Knew what?" I asked.

My aunt hesitated, biting her lip.

"Your mother once wanted a very different life."

"What do you mean, a different life?"

"Just that she didn't want the same things the rest of us did."

"I don't understand." I felt a furrow develop between my brows.

"Maybe I am saying too much, isn't it?"

"You haven't said anything at all. Please tell me what you mean."

"There was a time that she wanted to renounce her worldly existence."

My aunt's expression was unusually serious, so serious that I couldn't help but laugh. She had to be kidding. "Renounce the worldly existence? What do you mean? To become, like, a nun or something?"

"We Jains would call such a person a *sadhvi*. Though Pramila wanted to be able to teach the Jain path and so she would have become a *shramaniji*—someone who had a bit more freedom to travel." My aunt's face remained solemn. I had to hand it to her. She was good at the deadpan delivery.

"You think I am kidding?"

"Are you telling me that you're not?" My smile settled at the edges.

"I am quite serious." My aunt's eyes met mine.

"Mom doesn't really talk about the past." I grappled with the idea, feeling as though my very understanding of my mother was unraveling. "Maybe it was just a phase or something,"

"Oh, it was more than that."

"Tell me more." There was a forlorn quality to my voice, a quality that surprised me.

Vini hesitated at first, speaking slowly as if unsure how much to divulge. "You never met your grandfather, my father. He died very young. Myself and your mother, we were hardly more than girls."

Her words gradually gathered momentum. "I still remember how he read late into the night under the light in the hallway outside our flat. There was one bulb that hung there, in the *chaali*. Late at night, when he thought we were asleep, Pramila and I would

183

spy on him. He would just sit there on the floor leaning against the wall, smoking one *bidi* after the next, consuming books in the same manner. Those books filled him with so many notions, ones that nobody could even imagine at the time. We too began to have our own notions. But Pramila, she was, how do you say it? She was on a different level. She was very, very intense. Her notions—her ideas—they were not for time-pass, they were her world."

Vini was turned toward me but seemed to be looking inwards, observing tidbits of her childhood as an omniscient being might, connecting fragments of her life as if they were pieces of a puzzle, and realizing the full relevance in a way that the younger Vini probably could not.

"Funny thing was that Papa tried to find a different way for her. But she was one step beyond his comprehension even. You see, Pramila did not want to marry or have children. She had a totally different vision. Maybe she wanted to devote her life to her beliefs, her faith. But, really, I think she wanted to be left alone with her thoughts. She was not so much renouncing the world as she was holding on to something else, a type of freedom maybe. It was unheard of for anyone to do such a thing, and for a girl? *Hai-la!*"

"What happened? What changed?" I was glued to my seat.

"Well, our lives changed when our father died." Vini glanced out of the window before turning to me again. "Shyama, this is really not my story to tell. Even I don't know the whole of it."

"Why would she never mention what happened back then?"

"Sometimes the past is too painful to mention, I guess."

"But how could I not know any of this about my own mother?"

"Listen, I didn't know and I lived with her in those days! I only came to learn much, much later."

I felt as though I was staring through a kaleidoscope, turning the barrel and watching my life come into and out of focus. I had always wondered what made my mother so distant and unreachable to me. All this time, I had thought that perhaps our times and places had simply been too far apart to broach. Now the truth was before me, uncloaked, even if I did not know its relevance. Somehow, these fragments of my mother's life had to explain the rift between us.

I pictured my mother as a teenager, standing before the statue of the reclining Buddha. It was a striking piece of artwork. I had to agree with Maasi though, the paintings were more arresting. They were snapshots of an ancient, long-forgotten world. Yet there was so much that was recognizable in those paintings: the pomp and circumstance of the elite, the affection shared between lovers, the adornments decorating women, the very ripple of fabric worn by the people—it was all so familiar. I laughed to myself and shook my head. How could a world over a thousand years ago seem familiar to me and my own mother be a complete mystery?

Chapter 21

BOMBAY, 1970

After the wedding, as was the custom, Pramila moved in with her in-laws. Dev and his parents lived only three bus stops from her mother's place but Pramila felt as though she might as well have moved somewhere east of Rangoon. Dev's family did not live in a *chawl*. They lived in a three-bedroom flat with its own bathroom. Without the presence of a common hallway, neighbors mostly kept to themselves.

The Mehta household functioned differently as well. Pramila did not want a traditional relationship with her mother-in-law. Too often that relationship was mired in strife and petty rivalry. She had hoped to get to know her *sasuma*, or Ma as she requested to be called. However, Ma disappeared from the kitchen the moment Pramila arrived. At first, she thought it was a sense of seniority and superiority that drove Ma away. But soon Pramila suspected that Ma was under explicit orders not to enter the kitchen.

Overnight, Pramila became solely responsible for running a household that prepared three full meals a day. Every morning that meant a breakfast of *chai*, warmed milk, hot cereal *upma*, sweet syrupy *jalebi*, and salty, crunchy *gathia*. For lunch and for dinner that meant freshly cooked spiced vegetables, *dal, rotis, basmati rice, buttermilk and paper-thin papad.* Preparations for one meal began before the last meal was complete. There were to be no leftovers. Such was the dictate of her father-in-law. Bapuji, it became apparent, was a man of dictates.

It also became apparent that the mood of the household cycled with the moods of its patriarch. When Dev's father was unhappy, the collective attitude of the family sunk as if weighted by an enormous anchor. Ma, particularly, trod lightly during those times. When Dev's father was happy, his ebullience was like a dirigible dragging everyone along for the ride. And, with much fanfare, he would open his doors for dinner to seemingly everyone and anyone.

It was during one such day that Pramila found herself cooking for ten people. Bapuji had sealed a lucrative business deal and had invited several business associates to celebrate the occasion. He sent word to Pramila and Ma just hours before the guests were to arrive. Pramila panicked. Hastily, she pulled out the burlap bag of flour only to find that the bottom had given way. Flour came showering down on the kitchen floor.

"Arré yaar! Oh come on! Today of all days?"

Ma rushed into the kitchen and surveyed the situation. "Let us figure out what we need from the market, you go pick it up. While you are gone, I shall clean all this up."

When Pramila returned, the kitchen was spotless. Ma had already boiled the rice, blended the chutneys, sautéed the vegetables, and chopped and seasoned the tomato-cucumber salad.

"My father used to say I was a fine cook," Ma said with pride rather than nostalgia.

Pramila smiled. Soon the two women were hustling about the kitchen, tracing and retracing their steps, as they prepared the spread.

Once the guests had all arrived, dinner was served. Bapuji directed the men to their seats as Pramila and Ma circled about the table, making sure that nobody's plate was cleared of *puris* or sweets.

After dinner, the guests were quickly rounded up and led toward the living room by Bapuji. Pramila's stomach grumbled audibly. Instinctively, she grabbed it.

"We forgot to eat lunch," Ma said.

"We were too busy preparing food to actually stop to eat it!"

The women laughed. Hastily, Pramila set the table for herself and Ma, filling the plates with generous portions of food. Just then, Dev came bursting through the door, home late from the day at work.

"Dev!" she called out. Though she had yet to grow accustomed to being his wife, Shyamala found herself pleased to see him.

The elders in the adjoining room simpered.

Bapuji scoffed louder than the rest. "What a welcome! I cannot even remember when Varsha greeted me with such enthusiasm. Such is the way of young love. That *pyaar* is much more pure, no?"

Pramila bristled at his tone. Her feelings for Dev were not for public discussion. She was growing fond of Dev but love? That was certainly not a word she would use.

"Dev, why don't you sit with us for dinner?" she asked. This time she spoke more discreetly.

Dev seemed to hesitate but then continued. "I would love to, I am famished!"

Bapuji, who had been waxing poetic about young love to his guests, stopped speaking mid-sentence. He walked briskly into the dining area. "What is this I am hearing?"

"To make it easy, I will eat with Ma and Pramila only. They must be hungry."

"They should serve you quickly then, isn't it? Then they can eat. Varsha, hurry up and serve the boy!"

"Bapuji, it is no problem. I wish to eat with them."

"*Nai, nai.* Not in this house. How many years has been since we sent the British back to their forsaken island? Hardly it has been twenty-five years since we kicked those *dholias* out. We are not about to adopt their customs. We have *desi* traditions in this place. *Samjho*: Indian traditions. First you eat with the ladies, next thing you know, you will be preparing the food for them, then you will be cleaning for them. What comes next? Pramila going to factory? You staying home with the children?" This apparently was such an outrageous concept that Bapuji chortled hysterically.

The guests half-smiled at Bapuji's commentary.

He continued, addressing his guests. "If it wasn't for her ability to cook, I am not sure what I would do about this daughter-in-law of mine. She has had so much book learning and for what? To tend to the home all day? I wonder sometimes what her father was thinking."

Pramila was aghast. How dare he insult her father? She tried to swallow her resentment like a daughter-in-law was expected to, but she knew the bitterness was written all over her face.

"Bapuji—that is quite enough!" Dev warned, sitting at the table bolt upright.

His father, who was loath to back down from an argument, focused on Dev for a moment. It was apparent that he was about to utter something in retort but then, looking at the large group of guests, reconsidered. He moved on to quip about Indira Gandhi, India's female prime minister, and whether they would all soon be Pakistanis.

Once the guests had gone home, Bapuji retreated into a furious silence. The evening left Pramila more than a little dismayed. It was a reminder that she didn't belong to this household. She wondered if she would ever belong. She wondered if she even wanted to. She slipped into a reverie, imagining the life she might have led if unbound by obligation and tradition. She tried to shake the thoughts away.

Later, Dev entered the kitchen. "Sorry about Bapuji. He has no right to insult you and Papa." Pramila noticed that Dev always used the term "Papa" when referring to her father in the same way she did.

"That is the first time I have seen you raise your voice against Bapuji."

Dev shook his head. "Truth be told, I should have started long ago."

Pramila said nothing. He was right.

"I am not like him. You know this, yes? Bapuji has never understood me. We are as different as father and son can be. You will see when we move away—when we go to America."

"Do you worry what will happen to your mother?"

"This is the hardest part about going. I think about it every day."

Perhaps, at their first meeting, she had misread Dev. He too bore burdens. Maybe she was the lucky spouse of the couple. Yes, Dev still had both parents and she only one. But Ba, though she would don the white sari of a widow for the rest of her life, had a husband whom she remembered in only the fondest of ways. Papa's regard for Ba had been as firm and constant as the earth beneath her feet. Even after his death, Ba had always drawn strength from this. Ma's married life, on the other hand, had been one of measured words and relinquished pride. Dev had to bear the burden of this. Pramila wondered if this reality had been his motivation to leave India.

She wanted to tell him, *this situation is a reflection of your mother's destiny, not yours. Only your mother can pay for her past sins.* Was that not the teaching of her faith? Was that not her own belief? There was no way to deny it though. The truth was much more complicated. Everything she had seen so far suggested that the sufferings of our beloved are inherently our sufferings.

◆ ◆ ◆

A few weeks before Dev's departure for America, his parents left for a wedding in Surat, a four-hour train ride from Bombay. Dev suggested that they go for a visit to Ba and Vini's flat, head to the cinema, and catch dinner at Gymkhana afterward.

The women greeted Pramila and Dev outside the complex.

"*Chaallo.* Ba *nu radwanu sharu thaigayu.* Great. Ba has begun to cry." Vini shook her head, smiling as she caught her sister's eye.

"Ba, please stop crying. I was here just three days back," Pramila requested, grateful that Vini seemed happy to see her.

"That is why I insisted for us to come," Dev said. "I know how much you must be missing Pramila."

Once inside the flat, Vini and Pramila headed straight for the kitchen. Busy bickering with her sister about how much sugar to put in the tea, Pramila couldn't hear the conversation in the living room between Ba and Dev.

Later that evening, after the three-hour film and paper-thin dosas and *chai* at Gymkhana, Pramila walked into the warm, starry night with Dev at her side.

"What did you and Ba talk about tonight?" She had been curious all evening.

Dev turned to her as they walked. "She asked why I was moving you so far away."

Pramila was surprised that her mother had questioned her new son-in-law with such forthrightness. "Did you tell her I knew your intentions from the beginning? Did you tell her about why you wished to move away from India?"

Dev nodded. "I told her the truth, that here in Bombay, my family have been making sweets for generations. God knows even how long it has been so. Our factory is the same. Our recipes are the same. Our scope for the future is the same. Same, same, same. How do I break free? It is not so easy here, you know. Where else can someone do this?"

191

"What did she say to that?"

"She remembered the *kanya-daan*, when we bowed to her and touched her feet after the wedding ceremony. She said it was the last time you belonged to her and that it was only to say goodbye. She admitted that the decision to move to America was ours alone to make." Dev took a moment to collect himself, seemingly swept up in Ba's heartache. "I told her that she was always welcome to our home—here or in America—for however long she wished to stay."

Pramila tried to imagine her mother's anguish. She was touched by Dev's open invitation to her mother. She thought back to the way he stood up against Bapuji the other night at dinner, the way that he allowed her to express her grief about Papa the first day they had met, and this affection overcame her. Content, she felt rather like she had awoken from a full night of sleep, her awareness heightened and her senses more receptive. The *chai* must have been strong, she mused to herself, though more seemed at work than merely caffeine.

The evening was balmy. Overhead, clouds hung low, seemingly reflecting and amplifying every perception. The street was teeming with people and Pramila noted how the air carried their laughter differently tonight. She was conscious of the full range of sounds, from the booming baritones of men sharing a joke to the melodic laughter of young women free from responsibility for the night. Pramila caught the glint of a woman's grin. There were so many expressions and sensations of joy, she thought. There was one more, though, beyond either sight or sound. Something akin to electricity. It was the one she felt tonight.

The flat was still when they arrived. Trying to avoid awakening her in-laws, Pramila slid her shoes off quietly. Then it occurred to her. Ma and Bapuji were gone. It was just Dev and her. She watched as he stood by the dresser and emptied his pockets. He removed his shirt. His dark-brown skin was warm and appealing, particularly

192

against his sleeveless white undershirt. Her eyes fixed upon the contours of his arms. Once afraid of her own will, now she just gave in to it. Her bare feet hardly made a sound as she approached him.

Pramila stood behind Dev and touched his right arm. He remained still. She moved closer to him, now facing his arm—the one upon which her arm rested. He turned and tilted his head to her until both of their foreheads touched and then kissed her. It was such a peculiar gesture, Pramila thought. In all those Brontë novels she had read nobody ever mentioned the awkwardness of the kiss. In reality, there were noses to consider and the right degree of head tilt was required. As Dev brushed her forearms with the tips of his fingers, the voice within her fell silent. More pleasurable yet was the feel of his body pressed against hers. She had not known Dev to be insistent. But tonight, there was something delightfully unyielding about him.

Dev cupped Pramila's chin in his right hand. Then his hand traveled down the front of her neck to the notch at the base. His fingers lingered there and then drifted up the back of her neck. Firmly, he drew her even deeper into him. One by one, he touched her face, her neck, the small of her back as *dupatta* and chemise were dropped carelessly on the floor. Then after shedding yet another layer of Pramila's clothes, he made his way again to the small of her back and then the curve of her thigh, touching parts of her body that other hands had never traversed before. Pramila invited each exalted sensation.

Dev fell asleep shortly afterwards but Pramila remained awake. She lay in the dark beside him, once or twice running a finger along his face. She did not bother to seek out her clothes, entranced by the moonlight shining blue on the sheets. She smiled to herself the way one does when in possession of a coveted secret. Dev was hers. And for now, all the world lay outside their door.

Dev left for America six weeks later.

Chapter 22

Mumbai, August 2006

The morning after our return from Ajanta, I was up before six. The water would only run until 7 a.m. I had been initiated into an army of sorts, a brigade of residents from throughout the city. At the same time every day, we headed to our kitchens and bathrooms, gathered our buckets and assumed our positions at our faucets. We opened the taps fully, watching as the single most valuable commodity in our city flooded into every conceivable vessel. Within the next hour, we would have to collect all the water needed for drinking, washing, cooking, and toileting for the day. After that, the taps would run dry until the next morning.

Vini and her neighbors had complained to the municipal water district. We were lucky to get anything, they had said. Vini had even called the tanker company that supplemented the municipal water supplies. She was told that the prices, which had already risen by 50 percent, were likely to double.

After collecting water for the day, Maasi asked me to deliver some food to Attaji.

I was halfway up the flight of stairs to his flat when I heard Kaushik uncle's voice. He was on the landing, speaking to

Jagdishbhai, the neighbor who had moved back from New Jersey, and Pankajbhai, a fifty-something man with a rather stout frame and an ill-fitting toupee who lived in the flat across from him.

"It is very bad, absolutely rrridiculous!" Kaushik uncle said, rolling his "r"s generously. "How can a people live like this?"

"*Hai, hai!* Water for only one hour a day! Here we are sending these tech types to the rest of the world where they design computers, build bridges, and shoot people into the outer space. But here, in India, we somehow cannot even manage the water!" Jagdishbhai replied.

Kaushik uncle spied me coming up the steps. "Come, come. Shyamalaben, join us."

"I will tell you what the problem is," said Pankajbhai, between breaths. "The leaky pipes, *yaar*! How many times have you seen the main pipe to the building leak? Multiply it by a million times and then you know where all the precious water goes! You want to fix the water problem, start there!"

"Who is going to pay to fix it?" Jagdishbhai asked. "You?"

"Everybody must pay!" Pankajbhai insisted.

"I am already spending too much money *yaar*. The price of the water from the tanker just goes up-up-up. I am not spending one *paisa* more! *Bilkul nai!*" Jagdishbhai adjusted his collar.

I wished I could just continue on my way to Attaji's house but there was no way to gracefully escape the conversation.

"You know what? We are paying more and more and getting less and less. I don't think we are getting our proper allocation. Something is going on with the water and we need to find out what it is," Pankajbhai announced.

Nobody responded to his line of inquiry.

"It is all those people living in the slum! Do you have any idea how many people tap into water lines and siphon off what we are paying the good money for?" Jagdishbhai asked.

"You cannot blame a man for trying to get enough water to help his family survive," Kaushik uncle spat.

"Until it is your water they are drinking, no?" a female voice chimed in.

"*Arré?* Champaben! It has been some time since you graced our discussions." I detected sarcasm in Kaushik uncle's voice.

"Those who are stealing our water should be put in jail immediately. You are telling me they can pay for televisions and mobiles but they cannot pay for water? Bullshit, *yaar*. Those slums take our water, the water we have paid good money for!" Champa gave me a piercing once-over.

I gave her an unenthusiastic half-nod. I wondered if she knew about my many outings with Arjun.

"You know they cannot afford the water. What would you have people do, just die of thirst?" This time Pankajbhai took issue with the notion.

"Nobody is suggesting that, *bhai*. People just have to decide what is most important, *na*? Mobile phone or water." Jagdishbhai's tone was eminently reasonable.

"So what if people have the mobile phone? In India, the true luxury is clean water and a place to do the toilet. It is a false choice you are giving. What you are saying is complete madness! Madness!" Kaushik uncle shook his head in disgust.

"How are we to become a modern city like Shanghai if we have *jhopadpattis* springing up everywhere, stealing the resources from law-abiding citizens like us?" Champa peered at Jagdishbhai for support, and he nodded.

I couldn't help thinking about Shalu and Rajesh living in the slums.

Kaushik uncle could not contain his outrage. "You speak of the poor taking water from us? What about the rich taking the water from the poor? What about all those millions of gallons that filled the swimming pools and rushed down the slides in Essel World for all those years so that the rich kids could splash in the water?"

I found myself nodding.

"It is my money and it is for me to decide how to spend it!" Champa shouted.

"We are all Mumbaikars, this water belongs to all of us!" Pankajbhai raised his voice to match Champa's.

"*Achcha*. We should ask the visitor. Shyamala, what do you think about all the drought business?" Champa inquired.

My eyes went wide as I hadn't expected to be put on the spot. I knew Champa was measuring me. But I couldn't shake the thought of Shalu and Rajesh, struggling for clean water long before water woes started for this building. And I couldn't avoid the obvious either.

"Well, I'm not an expert or anything but I don't think we can ignore the fact that global warming is at least partly to blame."

Pankajbhai, Champa, and Jagdishbhai glared at me. There was resentment on their faces, the kind of resentment reserved for the naive, the outsider, or the uppity woman who has the gall to open her mouth and render a potentially contrary opinion.

"You know, climate change? Increasing carbon dioxide levels since the industrial revolution resulting in a greenhouse effect, trapping heat in and altering the climate? Where do we think the extra carbon dioxide that we create with all of our air conditioners and cars and the rest goes?" I persisted, knowing they were well aware of the science, my gaze landing squarely on Champaben.

Like other truths widely known but denied out of expedience, my words hung in the air for a second before being swatted down.

"That is just theory only," Jagdishbhai, Pankajbhai, and Champaben said in gruff unison.

Champaben shook her head in disgust. So much for making a good impression with her. Why did it matter anyway? Arjun and I were nothing serious.

I looked to Kaushik uncle hoping for backup.

He nodded and came to my defense. "*Samjho*, global warming is absolutely real and you all know it." Then he added resentfully, "But isn't America to blame for more than its fair share of the carbon dioxide pollution? And then Americans have the nerve to come to countries like India and tell us to cut back on our pollution!"

With that comment, everyone was suddenly in agreement, each person clamoring to voice an opinion about the sins of America and the misdeeds of the West.

There was a shake-up in the office. We never knew exactly what transpired after that night at Edward but our best guess was that Natasha broke things off with Daniel. Shortly after, Daniel requested and was granted a transfer back to the States.

Gayatri held an unofficial going-away party for Daniel at her brother and sister-in-law's place in Juhu. The couple were on holiday in Bali and had entrusted Gayatri with access to the luxury flat and the fully stocked bar within.

"This place is rockin'!" Ajay announced as he ran his finger along the bar. "Tell me what your brother does that he can afford this place?"

"Come *yaar*, Aditya just stands by and looks handsome. You think *he* has the money to afford a place like this? No. This is all Maya's doing." Then Gayatri leaned toward me and explained, "Maya is only the youngest person to join the board of some big Indian energy conglomerate."

"The place seems barely lived-in." I stepped out of the sliding-glass door that led from the dining room on to the balcony overlooking the Juhu oceanfront. Gayatri joined me at the railing.

"They stay mostly in their other flat in Malabar Hill. This is their second flat, I guess. You know, to escape the city." Gayatri smiled.

I turned to the coast, to where I imagined Malabar Hill to be. The city was one uninterrupted mass looming over the water's edge.

"Nothing like going to the city to escape the city," I said.

Gayatri laughed.

The doorbell rang. She went to answer it. I wandered back into the living room.

"Welcome!" Gayatri waved Daniel into the flat.

"Thanks for inviting me to the party." He gave her a sideways hug. His smile didn't reach his eyes.

"*Chalo, bhai*. You are one of us. We had to give you a proper send-off!" Ajay grabbed Daniel by the shoulder and led him into the apartment.

Daniel scanned the studio seeking Natasha. Not spotting her, he feigned interest in the decorations instead, making his way to the couch.

"Kingfisher?" I pulled two bottles of beer out of the fridge, popped off the tops, handed one to Daniel, and sat down beside him with the second.

"You must be excited to go back to America," said Ajay. "How long has it been since you saw everyone at home?"

"About six months. My mom is anxious for me to come back." His eyes drifted to the door.

"What are you looking forward to most?" Ajay asked.

"Well, other than seeing family, I'd have to say kicking back, watching a football game and sipping on a cold beer. And by cold beer, I mean *cold*!"

The Kingfisher in my right hand felt disappointingly warm.

Gayatri motioned for Ajay to help her in the kitchen, giving Daniel and me a moment to chat.

He stared at the door, unblinking.

"Do you think it would be too much to expect Natasha to come flying through that door, begging to take me back?"

"I don't know Daniel." His anguish was all too familiar. This was poor Daniel's *garba raas*, and Natasha seemed poised to stand him up just as Neil had done to me.

"Because, if she did, I would take her back. I'd take her back in an instant. I would move to Bombay or Mumbai or whatever the hell she wanted me to call it. We could stay at our jobs. We could have kids. I could win the whole family over. If she would just give me the chance."

"I know you could. Did you talk to her?"

"I tried. I called her. I emailed her. I even cornered her in the office. She won't budge. I finally stopped because I didn't want to come off like some weirdo." He watched me expectantly.

"Daniel, I don't know what to say. I invited her—told her she should at least come say goodbye." Truth was I had practically begged her. No matter how the world around them sought to keep them apart, the least he deserved after everything they had been through was a goodbye. Neil had denied me one when he walked out on me. And if Natasha didn't show, I wasn't sure that I'd be able to forgive her.

"There is nothing to say. It's over and I know it. But still, I can't help but imagine her walking through that door." Daniel sighed. His sights remained fixed on it.

Gayatri and Ajay both focused on the door as well. If collective force of will were sufficient, Natasha would have materialized that night. But she didn't come. Not during appetizers, not during dinner, and not during dessert. She didn't show up at the airport a few days later when we sent Daniel off to America, knowing full well he would never return.

Janmashtami fell on a Wednesday. The usual street cacophony was replaced by the clamor of men on a mission. Just outside my window, a man stood on a ladder between our building and the one adjacent. Other men were shouting directions at him from below. They were working to suspend a rope between the two buildings at the fifth floor. A clay pot full of flowers and decorations hung off the rope between the two buildings.

Janmashtami commemorated the date that the famous Lord Vishnu, protector of the universe, was incarnated into his fifth human avatar, an equally famous blue-hued boy named Krishna. Krishna's other name was Shyama, he was my namesake. He was born at midnight, the time at which *Janmashtami* celebrations typically started. Krishna was a bit of a rascal as far as gods go. As a man he had a way with the ladies, but even as a child, he managed to torment them. Tonight, I would be attending *Dahi Handi* with Arjun. It was a reenactment of young Krishna's favorite pastime: stealing fresh yogurt. His mother prepared the homemade *dahi* in clay pots which she hung from the rafters for safekeeping. Even then, Krishna managed to get to the yogurt, breaking the clay pot in the process. In its modern form, the clay pot usually hovered far above the aspiring Krishnas who sought to break it and claim its contents.

The drought and disruptions of the recent weeks hadn't put a damper on the spirit of celebration. Nor did the extreme heat. I couldn't help but feel swept up in it all, thrilled to experience *Dahi Handi* with Arjun.

I briefly wondered if Champaben might have told Arjun about our argument on the landing. But then, I reminded myself that I wasn't running as candidate for future daughter-in-law—I didn't need her approval. We were just going out to have a good time. If Natasha and Daniel's situation was any indication, it was best to approach my relationship with Arjun as nothing more than casual.

I poked my way through the dresser trying to find something to wear. Jesus, had I really packed so many T-shirts and jeans? Why the hell did I pack a skirt I hadn't worn since college? I tried on a sundress, but the hemline was too short. Then I put on a pink blouse with a flared skirt but the getup felt too girly. I stood by my closet, frustrated by my lack of foresight for all things fashion.

"Shyama, are you getting ready for your wedding or for *Janmashtami*?" my aunt asked just before eight.

I opened my door, still wearing the blouse and flared skirt. Vini's expression made it clear the ensemble wouldn't fly.

"Why don't you try this?" She handed me a shopping bag. "Might as well give it to you now, isn't it?"

I was grateful for another option. Inside the bag was an emerald-green tunic with an antique-gold border and detailed gold beadwork along its neckline. The fabric had the slightest sheen to it.

"This is lovely. You didn't have to." I ran my hand along the soft fabric.

"*Arré?* Why not, exactly? You come to India once every few decades—so had better take my chance to spoil you. Seems like you can use the help, no? Now go try it on. And hurry, you haven't much time."

I laughed at Maasi's untempered honesty and went to try the clothes on. The tunic fitted well through the shoulders and bodice, tapered at the waist and then flared at the hips. It felt like the outfit had been stitched just for me. As I pivoted in the mirror, it occurred to me that I might actually blend with the crowd that night.

Vini was waiting for me when I made my way back into the living room. She tugged at the sleeve of the tunic top and leaned back to assess her choice of clothing. She nodded.

"It's lovely, Maasi, thanks."

Maasi lent me burnished gold bangles and matching tear-drop-shaped earrings. "Now you are ready for the big date!"

"It's just *Janmashtami*, Maasi."

"None of this just-just business. I was not born yesterday."

As if on cue Arjun knocked at the door. He was wearing a tailored white button-down linen shirt with a Nehru collar and his signature carpenter jeans. He grinned and leaned forward as if coming in for a kiss.

"Vini aunty!" he exclaimed, jumping back the instant he saw Maasi behind me.

"Come in if you want to say hi." I opened the door wider.

Vini blocked his path to the living room and shooed us out of the flat. "No! You see me all the time, isn't it? Go start your evening immediately, *na*? *Chalo, chalo*, out with you. And don't come home too soon!"

"Man, she sure is in a hurry to get rid of us," I said, as Vini shut the door.

We chuckled, our laughter resonating through the stairwell, making it seem as if unseen others were sharing in the joke. This only made us laugh harder. Then Arjun stopped, stepping back on the landing, away from me. I wasn't self-conscious as he took me in. He looked at me in a way different from other men, even Neil—there was no scanning from top to bottom, no brutal dissection of feminine geometry. I didn't feel his gaze on the arc of my breast or the line of my thighs. He looked at me as if he were taking all of me in, all at once.

"The *salwar kameez* suits you, Shyama."

"I know." In actuality, I was surprised at how right it felt to wear it with Arjun by my side. I hooked his arm in mine and nudged him toward the stairs.

Arjun had reserved a table at his favorite restaurant for dinner. Music played in the background but I could not discern the song over the clanking of dishes and the bustle of waiters. Our high-backed booth lent a certain seclusion to the space that was delightfully encroached upon by the scent of Chindian food—Chinese-themed fare with Indian flavor and heat. We ordered our meal and settled back, sipping wine and chatting.

The waiter brought our appetizer. Gobi Manchurian—cauliflower florets covered in a spicy batter and deep fried, then served in a sauce made of garlic, ginger, red chili, soy sauce, and tomato paste. It was so spicy I drank an entire glass of water with the first bite. Even then, I was compelled to eat another and another until the plate was nearly empty.

Maybe it was the luster of our wine glasses or the warm radiance of the chandelier overhead as it reflected in the window, but everything was alight that night. Arjun's eyes shone brightly beneath his heavy brows. He looked at me with such intensity that it seemed to have a physical effect. It was as if rather than falling, I was filling, expanding beyond my outer bounds. The flavors, aromas, sights, filled me up, as if I might spill over. I had an urge to touch his face, to feel the contrast between its shallow contours and deep contours, its smooth and rough surfaces.

"Have you heard anything about the job?" I asked, partly to distract myself from the notions in my mind.

"Not yet. The first round of interviews went well, now I'm waiting to see if I get invited to a second round in New Delhi. I imagine the competition is steep. It is a totally pie-in-the-sky notion anyway."

Thankfully, the next course arrived before I felt compelled to say something encouraging about Arjun's prospects on the job.

"This is the American chop suey," Arjun pointed with flare at the dish with Hakka noodles and mixed vegetables. "This one is veggie fried rice and this is the Sichuan *paneer*."

The scent of Indian spices—*garam masala* and coriander and chili powder—intermingled with green onions and black bean paste and rose out of the plates carried on twirling ribbons of steam. Despite the burn of the gobi Manchurian in my belly, I could not resist the aroma.

I watched patiently as Arjun spooned the American chop suey on to his plate.

"I am guessing that American-Chinese food tastes different from Indian-Chinese food? I wonder what the hell actual Chinese food tastes like," Arjun contemplated.

"At this point Arjun, all I know is that I might have to move this franchise to America."

"Listen, what makes you think that we will allow our Indian secrets out?" He laughed. "Speaking of secrets, what was it that you wanted to say to my mother? You know, that day when I met you on the stairs before we walked on the beach at Chowpatty? She mentioned she ran into you while chatting with some of the neighbors just the other day. Did you sort it out?" Arjun ran his index finger along the edge of his glass.

My first instinct might have been to tell Arjun about what Champa had done, about the rumors she had been spreading about Shalu. But Shalu had implored me to leave the issue alone and I had to respect her request. And bringing up the drought-related squabble in the stairwell didn't seem to serve any real purpose. Perhaps a bit selfishly, I didn't want anything to ruin the mood of the evening.

"Ask something else, anything else."

"Anything?" Arjun withdrew his hand from the glass, placed it next to mine, and leaned in slightly.

I nodded. Our fingers nearly touched. I kept my hand still, my attention fixed on my fingertips.

"That day, when we were standing near the leaky pipe, and Vini told you that there was a phone call for you," he paused, "who was that on the phone?"

I had practically dared him to ask me something personal, quite conscious I was doing so. But I never would've figured he'd ask me about that. I had to give it to him, Arjun had quite an intuition.

I paused for an instant. "A guy I loved. Once."

"I knew it!" Arjun ran his hands through his hair.

"How did you even think to ask?"

He shrugged. "If it was a friend or family, Vini would have said so."

Arjun grabbed his fork and took a bite of Sichuan *paneer*. He chewed it slowly.

"So?" I asked, not sure what to expect. Would he be envious? Would he be angry I hadn't told him myself?

"Is it over between the two of you?"

"Yes . . ." We were in territory I hadn't planned to explore with Arjun—after all, it was our first proper dinner together—but my guard was down and the truth came spilling out. "We were going to build this perfect life together and then he realized he didn't love me."

Arjun considered me. He stopped chewing and seemed to brace himself. With a furrowed brow he asked, "Do *you* still love him?"

"No." It was the truth. I didn't love Neil anymore. Even then, I didn't mention my reaction about the news of his engagement. Instead, I held my breath and waited for Arjun's hand to return to the table.

He sipped from his glass and then placed his hand on mine. I glanced at our hands, trying to understand what was happening.

"Well, that is all I wanted to know. I—I appreciate your honesty, Shyamala." His hazel eyes were trained on mine. "Shit *yaar*, I hope I don't come across as a jealous or possessive bugger! How could I expect that there hadn't been someone, or someones before? Shyama, all those things that have happened to you, your past, even your lovers—in a way they brought us to this moment—sitting in this restaurant eating American chop suey. Why should I be anything other than bloody grateful for that?"

At once I felt silly, relieved, startled, and elated. Maybe I *had* expected, secretly even hoped for, some display of jealousy. Instead, Arjun had spoken with unexpected candor and kindness. For the second time that night, it was as if Arjun could see all of me. On Vini's landing earlier that evening, it was my physical self. Now it was the rest of me—a simple acknowledgment of my past and everything that made me who I was. He didn't pretend to know the details—the memories that awoke me at night, the successes I celebrated, the failures I had mourned, or the joys that I sought, but he recognized that those things were the metal from which I was made. Neil could never have seen me that way—to him history was history and though he never denied me my past he never embraced it in the way Arjun just had.

Sitting across the table from Arjun, I felt like I was seeing him anew. Wild hair and discerning gaze aside, I was struck by his immense generosity. With Arjun, I felt like I could be myself, unapologetically—scars, insecurities, doubts, and all.

I was relieved when it was time to leave the restaurant. Arjun's touch and his words had left me in need of fresh air. But the tepid heat and the heavy atmosphere that greeted us outside only accentuated this longing within me.

Arjun hailed a taxi and the driver let us out on a street corner in old Bombay. The high-pitched wail of a harmonium pierced the air, its origin unseen. Arjun took my hand and guided me through throngs of people that had congregated at the late hour for the *Dahi Handi*. Jostled by the crowd of fellow spectators, we followed the sound down a narrow alley that ended in an unexpectedly ample courtyard tucked between several buildings. As we approached, the rapid rhythm of tabla drums resonated between the buildings. On one side of the courtyard, a stage had been set up with an immense sound system and several musicians.

"Cool, seems like they have live music again this year. You know, there must be thousands of *Dahi Handis* throughout the city. Of all the places in Bombay that I have celebrated though, this is my absolute favorite. Tonight is going to be damn good." Arjun bobbed his head from side to side. I found his enthusiasm impossible to resist.

Groups of young men wore matching T-shirts of orange, red, purple, and green. They milled about in the crowd that now filled the courtyard entirely, bursting out into the alley.

"Those men in the matching shirts are the different teams," Arjun yelled over the music and the crowd. I surveyed the space between the buildings. About four stories up was a large terracotta pot overflowing with flowers.

"They're going to try to break that?" I yelled back, eyeing the rope that suspended the clay pot.

Arjun nodded. "Krishna had to reach high into the rafters because that is where his mother had to store it to keep it safe! This is the story we celebrate with the *Dahi Handi*!"

"Naturally. By hanging a clay pot full of yogurt forty feet in the air and trying to get a pile of people to stand on top of each other to break it." I didn't hide my foreigner's incredulity. I glanced at the clay pot again. It was very high up.

"Oh, come now, admit it, you can't resist this!" Arjun elbowed me, laughing at my expression. I couldn't help but smile. The energy and excitement in the crowd was infectious.

"Okay, so there is something refreshing about a god who has a mischievous side. I'll give you that. But honestly, do people have to honor Lord Krishna's shenanigans by thrusting mortals four stories in the air?"

"What could mark one's devotion better? And remember there is the glory to God part and then there is the prize."

"Money?" I shouted over the music and mayhem.

"No less a god these days," Arjun replied.

The music came to a crescendo and then an abrupt halt. I scanned the courtyard. Hundreds had gathered there. There wasn't a nook or recess or balcony that was unoccupied.

Then, out of the throng, at least twenty men with orange shirts rose simultaneously as if they had levitated. Standing on the tips of my toes, I could see that the men stood on the shoulders of a much larger group of orange T-shirt-clad men. Using hips, thighs, and shoulders as if they were steps on a ladder, a still smaller group of orange shirts rose and took their positions forming the third layer of the assembly. The team members ascended barefoot, scrambling up the formation with the ease of spiders and with the same herky-jerky motion. There was method in the movement. Some of the men squatted, allowing others to clamber upon their shoulders. Then the men who were squatting rose from their haunches, elevating the men on their shoulders. Layer after layer was built this way, and the structure grew both taller and wider until it resembled a giant human pyramid—no—a layer cake composed of humans standing five man-lengths high. Now several younger men climbed atop, deftly rising to the top of the structure. I was riveted by the scene.

"Oh my God, is that a boy?"

"Yes, of course! It was the boy Krishna that stole the *dahi* from the *handi*."

The child was dressed like the boy Krishna, face painted blue and a peacock feather in his hair. He moved with a cautious confidence.

"Please tell me that's a harness he is wearing!" I shouted. Revelers nearby considered me dubiously.

"It is. But he looks to be the only one, *na*?" Arjun answered, sounding unsurprised.

The harness was tethered to a crane. Still, I held my breath as the boy made his way to the top. A previously unseen layer of men emerged, elevating the boy with care. The structure swayed. I gasped. If they failed, the boy could plummet on to a mass of men.

The layer cake now stood seven human-lengths high, each layer with fewer and fewer men until there was just one very young man upon whose shoulders the little Krishna stood. The boy raised his hand and reached tentatively for the clay pot. It was inches from his reach. He shifted his weight slightly, stretching his arm and wiggling his fingers to bring them into contact with the pot. Now the crowd gasped with me—he was nearly there.

Suddenly, the pyramid below him imploded. Even the fall was a choreographed event, each of the orange shirts tumbling to inflict the least damage to himself and his teammates. Meanwhile, the boy hung like a pendulum from the crane, swinging from side to side, smiling and waving to the crowd.

"Oh, my God! Are they okay?" I blurted as I gawked at the scene. Arjun put his fingers in his mouth, belting out a whistle of appreciation for the orange team.

"Not to worry Shyama. These buggers are absolute experts at falling. This is all quite practiced."

I inspected the crowd, seeking proof that none of the men had been injured in the fall. The ones that I could see were milling about without concern. The boy was being lowered from the crane amid a cheering audience. There were no calls for help. The spectators called for the next team to make its ascent. The thrill of anticipation ran through me.

Arjun and I stood shoulder to shoulder as people swarmed about in every direction. His eyes locked on mine, his smile incandescent. He placed his arm against my hip, drawing me closer to him. There was something about the way he touched me—it was perceptive, knowing. My breath went still. With an unexplained urgency, I turned from Arjun and took in the cityscape that had absorbed me. I felt a need to check myself, to plant myself firmly in the moment. How could I feel such intimacy standing in the midst of droves of people? I faced Arjun again as the scene, the crowd, and the chaos fell away from us. This time, he did not look at me. His arm rested against the small of my back. And now his hand tightened against my hip. My breath left me, its slow escape at once measured and immeasurable. I surrendered to the night.

With much fanfare the red and green teams tried their hands at breaking the clay pot but fell short, to the great disappointment of the swelling audience. The din in the courtyard grew louder. It was the blue team's turn. The blue-shirts were flawless in their execution and within minutes, the young man who clambered to the very top of the formation was straightening his legs, just an arm's length away from the *Dahi Handi*. A chant rippled through the audience, "*Govinda ala re ala!*"

Standing atop the pyramid, the boy grabbed at the pot and though it buckled, it ultimately held. He seized it. This time, the terracotta gave way. Flowers cascaded down on the crowd. Yogurt splattered everywhere, on the men in the pyramid and the people directly below. The crowd erupted into celebration singing. "*Govinda ala re ala . . .*" I joined in the chorus of voices.

"I think some of that yogurt may have hit me." Arjun wiped his cheek.

"Me too." I dabbed my forehead. I felt something drop against my hand. As I wiped it away, I noticed a thin mist of water was falling, each miniscule drop illuminated by the bright floodlights behind me. In a matter of seconds, the drops grew larger and larger until they were round and heavy and full of renewal. Now the splatter of rainfall joined the noise of the horde.

Arjun grabbed my hand. He yelled, "I have never seen anything like this. Practically no rain all monsoon season and now we have rain on *Janmashtami*? This is absolutely perfect."

Riveted by the spectacle of the *Dahi Handi* and captivated by the glittering mist, all I could do was smile and nod at Arjun.

At first, the people in the courtyard didn't flee from the raindrops. Staring high into the night sky, they allowed the water to bathe their faces, as if they had been wandering in the desert for decades dreaming only of water. The drops were so heavy that when they hit the ground, small plumes of dust arose around each one. The musicians, who had been playing under the cover of a ledge, continued, undeterred by either the chaos in the crowd or the falling water.

The drops came down harder and harder. Many revelers began to make their way out of the courtyard. A few of us remained behind. My clothes were drenched. My shoes made a squelching sound every time I took a step. The water fell so fast that the soil could not absorb it. Puddles accumulated. Water was everywhere. There was no escaping it. There was nothing to do but get wet.

Water was dripping off Arjun's perfectly pointed nose. His face glistened in the rain. His white linen shirt was glued to his chest. He remained still, battered by the water, apparently shocked into inaction by the droves of rain.

I was laughing now, almost maniacally. Laughing at the utter insanity of the night, laughing out of delight at being so close to Arjun, laughing because rain was inundating us and there was nothing left to do.

Arjun faced me and ran his hand gently along the angle of my cheek. I felt people running past us. I could hear them yelling excitedly. I felt myself not caring what they said.

Arjun placed his hand against the small of my back again and pulled me gently toward him. I grasped him with both hands, my fingers intertwined at the nape of his neck. Rain dripped down my legs, along my arms, down my face, and between Arjun and me. Closing my eyes, I tilted my head back, taking in the smell of wet earth. Arjun's lips glanced mine, his kiss distinguishable from the raindrops only in its warmth. With it, everything gave way. All I felt was Arjun—his mouth and his hands and his hair which had fallen against my face.

I wasn't sure how long we stood there in the rain. When we finally looked up the courtyard was nearly empty.

◆　◆　◆

By the time we got back to the complex, the late evening had stumbled into early morning. The lights on the ground floor were dimmed at this time of night, blurring the hard angles and blunt margins of the stairwell, softening the edges of the world around us. Holding on to the railing, Arjun climbed the stairs in reverse as he described those first few drops of rain. "Did you see how the drops shimmered as they fell around us?"

"I've never seen anything like it! Tonight was—I've never felt— I've never experienced anything like that before."

Arjun grinned victoriously. "I knew you would love *Janmashtami!*" He continued to ascend the staircase backward. Suddenly, he missed a step and landed unceremoniously on his backside.

I exploded into laughter. He glared at me, accusingly.

"Don't blame me, this time it wasn't my fault!"

He burst into laughter himself. "You didn't push me down the staircase this time—you distracted me. Still your fault," Arjun announced loudly, forgetting himself.

"Shhh! We'll wake everybody up!" Truth was, I wanted the last moments of the night to remain free of interruptions. I gave him my hand and helped him up.

Arjun allowed me to pass. "Good point. God forbid we wake my mother."

He was at my heels as we made our way up the stairs, his body disarmingly close to mine. Every inch of my skin, every nerve fiber and follicle waited for his touch. The cadence of our footsteps slowed and each footfall lingered on the stairwell. The last traces of our evening could be counted by the number of steps left to Vini's apartment. Despite myself, I counted each one in my mind. *Six-five-four*-I didn't want the night to end-*three-two-one*-what would happen next?

We were on the landing now, turning the corner to the apartment. I struggled to contain myself. I spun to face Arjun behind me and was about to grasp his hand when I collided with someone.

My heart leapt. I turned back to find Rajesh as shocked to see me as I was to see him. He stood in front of Vini's doorway, at the very same spot where Arjun and I were meant to kiss again.

"Rajesh?" He appeared disheveled, his shirt rumpled and untucked.

"Shyamalaben, I was just leaving." Rajesh rushed to the stairwell seeking a quick escape.

It was then I realized that Vini stood behind him, by the door to her flat, in her nightgown.

"Maasi?"

Rajesh glanced once at Vini before he shuffled down the steps.

Arjun and I watched him leave. Then we looked at each other. It was a strange hour for Rajesh to be visiting Vini.

"I'm sorry, I hope we didn't interrupt anything." I knew we most certainly had.

"Interrupt? What, at this hour?" Vini was incredulous but something seemed off. What had they been doing this late in the night?

I peeked at Arjun again, who seemed as confused about the situation as I was.

"How was your evening?" she asked, watching as Rajesh slipped out of sight.

"Fine, it was fine." *Even though it was cut tragically short*, I thought to myself, as I glanced at Arjun beseechingly.

"Well, listen, you can tell me all about it in the morning. I am going to bed," Vini said with finality. She closed her bedroom door behind her.

There was a long pause before I spoke.

"What was that all about? It's a little late for Rajesh to be hanging out at Vini's, don't you think?" I asked.

"I guess it is a little odd. But right now, Shyama, I don't really care. Let's pretend the last twenty seconds didn't happen."

We were face to face at the threshold, our clothes still wet and chilled from the deluge. I pulled Arjun toward me, my right hand at his waist. His right hand cradled my neck. Our lips met for the second time that night, the kiss just as insistent as it had been in the rain.

Chapter 23

Mumbai, August 2006

The next morning, as I filled the buckets, I remembered my strange run-in with Vini and Rajesh on the landing the night before. What was he doing with her after midnight? Surely any issues with the car could have waited until morning. And why on earth did he look so disheveled? Was he concerned about Shalu's recovery? But she seemed to have fully recovered from her bout of typhoid. I jumped through the possible explanations, but I was unable to move past the most obvious one. Could there actually be something going on between them, an affair? The idea of an older woman, or a woman of any age for that matter, having a—I struggled to put a name to it—relationship with a servant or any man out of wedlock, seemed to break every rule in Indian society.

I shook my head. Who wrote those rules anyway? So what if there was something between them? Vini was an adult. Rajesh was an adult. They deserved companionship and whatever else came along with it. I wanted every happiness for Vini—for both of them.

Rules—there were so many rules. Poor Natasha had been tangled up in them too, just like Vini and Rajesh.

Vini emerged from her room ready for the day. Her long hair was down, a wave of black and silver. Her bronze skin looked lovely against her lavender tunic set. Her *dupatta* scarf caught the air behind her, lending her a graceful authority as she strode into the kitchen.

"Good morning Shyama. I am headed to temple and then to market. Do you need anything?" She picked up containers of breakfast snacks and spooned some breakfast savories on to our plates.

"No, I'm good." I brought two cups of tea to the table and we sat down across from one another.

I took several mouthfuls of breakfast, looking at Vini expectantly. If she was curious about what had happened between me and Arjun, she didn't show it. And the confines of cultural and generational propriety prevented me from inquiring about Rajesh. She pulled out the morning edition of *The Times of India* and started reading it over *chai*.

Midway through her cup, the phone rang. Vini jerked her head up and hurried off to answer it.

"Hallo?" She eyed me and half-smiled as she took the phone from its usual spot and pulled the cord into her room, closing the door behind her.

I abandoned my *chai* and headed toward my room. Maasi's door was slightly ajar where the phone wire was pulled through. Her back was to me as she faced her open, metal Godrej *cabat*. She was studying something in her hands. It appeared to be a ledger.

I felt guilty for spying on Vini yet concerned about her secrecy. Stressful phone calls, after-hours meetings with Rajesh, the mysterious ledger in her cabinet of treasures. Was she being blackmailed?

◆ ◆ ◆

Ever since her return from the hospital, Shalu had been asking me to visit her home. I knew she lived in a *jhopadpatti*. It wasn't exactly the type of place advertised on tourist brochures and residents of squatter cities didn't usually invite their boss's niece over for brunch, so I was more than a little honored that Shalu had invited me to her house. Since Rajesh had no objections, I couldn't see a reason not to go.

Several days later, I took the afternoon off and met Shalu at Churchgate Station to catch the train to Worli. We boarded the ladies' train car. A few last-minute passengers waited until the train was in motion before jumping on to it. Since every inch of seating was taken by women squeezed in shoulder to shoulder; we stood and grasped the overhead railing as the train sped out of the station.

As the rhythmic clacking of the train against the tracks gathered speed, I glanced at the people around me. Their eyes seemed drawn to me in curiosity as well. Somehow, despite living in Bombay for the better part of three months and trying to blend in, any long-term resident of Bombay could identify me as an outsider. Even if I did not speak a word, something about my walk and bearing seemed to make it obvious I was an American. It was a funny thing, I thought, that I should finally live in a country where I bore a resemblance to the people around me and yet was still the odd woman out.

When the train began to slow for the Lower Parel stop, Shalu nodded at me to indicate it was time to disembark. When she moved through the swarm of women toward the exit, I followed. When the train had slowed sufficiently (though not completely) and she leaned forward and jumped out, I swallowed hard and did so as well. We made our way through the crowd weaving as if person and shadow. She moved with confidence through the packed station, her petite body the very vision of capability.

The slum arose before us like a city within a city—a Bombay that was a microcosm of Bombay, only denser. It was a place that had gained a type of self-possessed permanence despite being constructed of temporary building materials: corrugated tin roofs, blue plastic tarps, cardboard boxes, and scraps of burlap. The squatter city was a living statement about the capacity of human beings to recycle. All this material, sculpted into innumerable residences and industries, jammed into alleys so tight that only a single person or bicycle might be able to pass through.

Shalu continued her stride, unfazed by the trash that littered the pathways or the open gutter she walked beside. I tried not to look at the gutter, the way one tries not to look at a car accident, but finds their eyes inexorably drawn to the scene. Like a nemesis that could not be outrun, the scent of raw sewage followed us along every turn on the route to her house. I wondered why my aunt didn't pay Rajesh enough to buy himself out of this place.

The *jhopadpatti* had a somewhat different din from the city around it. It was more intimate. Off in one direction I could hear a musical number from a Bollywood movie, in another I could hear women laughing, in yet another, I could hear a child reciting multiplication tables. The soundscape changed every few steps, escaping through thin walls and open doors and revealing what was going on in each household.

It seemed that everything around us was a shade of gray—ash gray, charcoal, brown gray, dirty gray—with the exception of Shalu who wore a pink *salwar kameez* and looked as light and airy and transcendent as the Ophelia rose that I had planted in my garden last spring.

We passed a young boy bathing out of a tiny green bucket just beside the alley. I averted my eyes to afford him some privacy. On the right, a woman stood just inside her shack adjusting her sari.

Up ahead, a man was brushing his teeth. As far as my eyes could see, private acts were taking place in plain sight.

"Our place is this way only."

We turned into an even narrower covered alley. Her pink dress was briefly absorbed by the darkness.

"Here it is! Come, come!" she said.

I followed her to a structure bigger than the average gardening shed but considerably smaller than the average American two-car garage. She put her key into the padlock and turned it. The lock secured the ill-fitted door to their home. She pulled the bolt out of a hole in the door post. The door squeaked open. Shalu removed her shoes and stepped into the flat.

"Welcome, please be coming in! This is mine and Papa's house. My uncle is staying here sometimes also." Somewhere nearby a neighbor blared a Hindi newscast.

"Thanks, Shalu." I removed my shoes and placed them on the floor next to hers.

I had expected the graininess of a dirt floor under my feet. Instead, I felt the coolness of a tile. I counted twelve tiles in either direction. Opposite the entrance of the house, there was a narrow cot with sheets folded neatly off to one side and a thin mattress underneath. At the foot of the cot was ostensibly the kitchen with a flimsy shelving unit upon which rested a variety of shiny stainless-steel dishware. There was no sink and only a small portable stove on the floor. Against the wall to my right were freshly painted bright-green cabinets along with a tiny table and three chairs. A small-screen TV sat atop the cabinets. There was an old clock on the wall above the cot and a calendar with an ornate rendering of Lord Krishna. However spare, the shack was tidy by any standard.

Shalu's eyes did not stray from me, she waited for some comment.

What was one to say? This was her home. When it is all said and done, home is home.

"Just like at Vini's, I see you run a tight ship!" I said, smiling.

"Tight ship?"

"This place is spick and span."

Shalu simply shook her head.

I was realizing the hard way that English, can in fact, be two entirely different languages depending on where it is spoken.

"Sorry, that's an American saying. It means that your place is tidy and organized, that you have nothing in excess."

She still seemed uncertain of my meaning. "In other words, your place is nice Shalu," I said finally. "Where do you sleep?"

"Most of the days, of course, I am sleeping Vini auntyji's place. When I am sleeping here, I use this mat to sleep on the floor." She pointed to the thin mattress under the cot. There was a pride in her voice. As if she had never actually seen how the well-to-do of Bombay lived.

I thought about my new routine filling buckets every morning. I glanced at the kitchen which had no evidence of indoor plumbing. "Are you getting enough water here Shalu?"

She shook her head. "Before the drought even we had some problems with getting water. Now it is worse only. Sometime back, peoples came and removed our water connections. They told us they were not the legal type of connections. Then, NGO types came. They put more of the water tanks into the slum—for water storage—but the municipality will not fill the water anymore. Sometimes, we come with the buckets empty because the water has stopped before our turn in the line. Papa goes mostly. He does not like for me to do it—sometimes there is a *goonda* who makes him pay extra monies for the water."

"A *goonda*—like a thug?"

Shalu nodded.

"That's terrible!"

"Well, the *goonda* lives here also. Everyone is having to make monies, *na*?" Shalu shrugged. "Since tanks only get filled some of the times, now somebody has made connections with city water again—we will see how long that is lasting. When the municipality finds out, their people usually come back to break the lines."

I thought about all the time and effort Shalu and Rajesh spent collecting water—about washing dishes outdoors—about the unpredictability of life when you can't even be sure about your water supply. Then I thought back to LA. I thought about Claire's weekly bottled water deliveries and my perfectly green lawn with its automatic sprinklers, and how expectations define our actions.

"What to do? If you need the water, you must get it. If your plates are dirty, you must wash them." She seemed to read my mind.

Moved by her resilience, I placed an arm around her slight frame. I gave her a squeeze. "You're absolutely right Shalu, absolutely right."

Shalu opened the doors to the green cabinet and handed me a stuffed Mickey Mouse. From the looks of it, the thing had been on the brink of losing its stuffing on several occasions as evidenced by irregular stitches of blue, green, and purple used to repair it.

"You're a fan of Mickey Mouse?" I turned it over in my hands. "I can get you a new one if you would like."

"Papa has offered me this too many times, but this is the first toy Ma gave me and there is not one other like it."

Shalu took the toy out of my hand and placed it back into the cabinet. Then she took out a bottle of lavender nail polish and handed it to me.

"How come you are not polishing the nails?" she asked with innocent curiosity.

"Not really my thing, I guess." I turned the bottle in my hands. "Back home, I get a manicure when my friend Claire makes me. Looks like you haven't opened this before."

"Sometimes I am wanting to see what it looks like on me, but Papa says this thing is waste of the time."

"Will you get in trouble if you put it on?"

"With Papa? *Arré*, no! He is only getting angry if my marks at school are not the perfect or if I do not finish my work at Auntyji's place. He thinks this thing is silly."

"He's probably right. You know what though? We should paint your nails."

"Really?"

Shalu smiled again, handed me the bottle, sat down on the cot, and held her fingers out.

After the nail polish had dried, Shalu set *chai* on the burner. It was strange seeing her tend to the pot while sitting on the floor beside the portable stove. She peered down at her fingers from time to time, her nails now pale lavender, as if someone else's hands were doing the work.

Shalu walked back to the green cabinet and pulled out a tin. She opened it and pulled out a little plastic bag. She handed me the bag.

"Is this a lock of hair?"

"That is piece of my ma's hair."

"Your mom?" The neighbor next door turned off the Hindi language newscast that had been blaring. The room suddenly seemed very quiet. I had the sense I was being thrust into a dark part of Shalu's past.

"Yes, yes. She died when I was very little. I was not even two years old." She paused for an instant and continued, "I do not remember her. But Papa tells me stories about her all the time. He describes the sound of her laughter and the coconut smell of her skin. He always reminds me of her kindness and stubbornness. When she died, Papa cut this hair from her and kept it for me. So, I would be having some part of her to hold on to, no?" Though

223

Shalu's voice was matter of fact, the very act of her showing me the lock of her mother's hair revealed the burden of her mostly motherless childhood.

"It is like he is sharing his memories so they can be yours."

"This thing is true."

Shalu didn't say anything for a while. Then she shrugged. "What to do? Papa does everything he can be doing to make my life all right."

I turned to her. "That's true Shalu. I see it." I thought back to the days when Shalu was sick with typhoid fever in the hospital and how Rajesh's angst had subsumed the room.

Shalu took the plastic bag with her mother's hair and reverently placed it back in the tin.

Finally, she pulled a small blanket from inside the green cabinet. It was crocheted from yellow and green yarn with white fringe around the edges. The pastel hues and plump yarn were entirely out of place in the tin-roofed shanty in the middle of sweltering Mumbai. As Shalu unfolded it, though, I realized it was familiar. The blanket was exactly like the one that my mother had crocheted for me, the one that I slept with every day until I was twelve, the one that my mother had carefully boxed away many years before, or so I had thought. It was the baby blanket in the photo that had fallen out of my father's copy of *The Good Earth*.

"Shalu, where did you get that blanket?" I was startled to realize my childhood heirloom was in another child's possession.

"From Pramila auntyji."

I was struck by the way Shalu referred to my mother as "Auntyji"—there was, at once, a formality and a familiarity to the word. I wondered why.

"Are you talking about my mother?"

"Yes, of course, Didi. Mostly it is too hot in Bombay to use it, *na*? But it is very soft and it is coming from America, so I am loving it. This blanket she gave to me long time back, I was just a baby. I meet Auntyji whenever she comes to India. Even now, when she comes, she brings the gifts. Papa tells her no, but still she is bringing them." Shalu ran her hands over the blanket.

"Did she tell you that she made it?" My head was spinning. I touched the familiar fabric without mentioning its provenance.

"Yes, she told me this."

Despite myself, I smiled at Shalu in that annoying, empty way that adults sometimes smile at children. I was only half-listening, half-engaged. Another part of me was rummaging around in my mind, trying to figure out how a part of my childhood, something my mother had made for me, had wound up in Shalu's house so many years later. It had taken an unlikely trip to Shalu's slum to uncover this particular slice of my mother's life.

Young women have a certain conceit when we think of older women, as if intrigue and mystery belong to the young. It's a silly notion. My mother and her sister were surrounded by little mysteries. Late-night rendezvous, secret phone calls, unspoken family connections—and those were just the things I knew about. In some ways, I thought, the women of my family were as much a mystery to me as Shalu's mother was to her. However long or short our time together on Earth, perhaps the real conceit is that we truly know anyone, even our own mothers.

I kept thinking back to the day when Shalu had woken up in the hospital. Rajesh had said something cryptic to me. *This is not the first time you people have helped me and my Shalu.* In whatever way that might have been true, as I thought back to Shalu's green cabinet and the blanket my mother had once crocheted for me sitting inside it, I had the distinct feeling that there was more to the story.

When I finally took my leave and found my way out of the slum, I was struck by its bustle. Here a group of women stood outside and washed clothes using a few buckets of water, their saris hiked to mid-calf to avoid getting them wet. There a man with a makeshift ladder repaired his corrugated tin wall. Here a man sorted trash from recycling. There a woman was tending to a large group of children. A man was getting a shave in an open-air barber shop. In an alleyway, children played ping-pong without a table. A teenager sat beside a pile of old shoes separating the soles from the leather. A girl sat outside her tiny home, books spread before her, doing her homework. From outside the shanty town, I could never have imagined the industry inside.

All those years my parents had spoken to me about the power of fate. Growing up in upscale Suburbia, USA, a place where anything seemed possible and the exceptional was expectation, I never really understood what they meant. Encompassed by this makeshift city, Shalu's neighborhood, I finally got it. Circumstance—fate—does define us. Poverty was Shalu's birthright, her mother's death a defining moment. Her story was one among thousands in this single slum which was one among thousands scattered through India which was one country among hundreds in which such places existed. I felt a familiar uneasiness. It was as if I were looking at the night sky, my eyes preoccupied by one star, only to find that as I grew accustomed to the dark, hundreds of other stars, previously unseen, appeared in my view. Innumerable stars, untold stories.

"You seem very quiet today, no?" Maasi asked as she served dinner that evening. "How was Shalu's place?"

The discoveries at Shalu's place had rattled me for reasons I was still trying to understand. Try as I might, I couldn't escape thoughts about family and fate, about what separates us and what binds us.

There was no simple way to describe what I had seen. "Have you ever been there?" My tone carried a hint of accusation in it.

"No," she said simply.

Lost in my thoughts, I watched her dole out the food without lifting a finger to help.

"It's hard to imagine a child being born into such a place, isn't it?"

I used to bristle when my American friends asked me about the caste system in India. There was always something judgmental about the question—something that bore the stench of Orientalism. But now, I was asking the same essential question.

Vini nodded. "I wish I had a magic wand to fix the problem but it's complicated." Vini served herself and seemed to settle in, preparing for an inquisition.

"Maasi, Shalu also mentioned that you are paying her school fees."

"I haven't been paying her school fees. Your mother has."

"Mom? Since when?" When Shalu had stated that Auntyji had been paying her tuition, I imagined she had meant Vini. I couldn't believe she had been referring to my mother all along.

"Since Shalu first started KG." Vini looked directly at me.

"Kindergarten? She has been paying Shalu's fees for over a decade?" I asked, wondering if I knew my mother at all. I tried to wrap my mind around the whole scenario.

"Yes." Vini peered at her food as if she wondered if she was ever going to eat it.

"Mom has known them for a long time then."

"She has."

"Did you know that Mom gave her a blanket that she had stitched for me—something I treasured? It was troubling, seeing something of mine at her place." It was ridiculous. I had so much and Shalu so little and yet I felt betrayed and there was no hiding it.

"I know she always brings her gifts, but I didn't realize she gave your old things to her. Is it a problem?"

"Of course not! It's just that—it's just that I've always felt that there was this barrier between me and Mom. The harder I've fought to break it, the more entrenched it gets. I don't know why exactly. Then I come here and Rajesh says something about our family helping his. I find my baby blanket at Shalu's house. Now you're telling me that my mother is putting her through school? Why wouldn't she just tell me about all of this? Did she think I would be jealous?"

I wasn't truly jealous, not about the blanket, or gifts, or the schooling. What bothered me was that my mother had chosen to share a part of her life with Shalu and Rajesh, a part of her life which she had not chosen to share with me.

"Shyama, as I said before, it is not my story to tell. You must speak to your mother about this one."

I stared down at my plate and forcefully bit my tongue so I could avoid saying what I was thinking. *Maybe you could tell me about what is going on with you and Rajesh then? Is that your story to tell?*

Chapter 24

Bombay, 1970

By the time *Diwali* approached, Dev had been gone for three months. The vigor that suffused the hallways and rooms when Dev was present was gone in his absence. The affection that filled her evenings with Dev was replaced by a void. In that place lurked shadows and intrigues, doubts and dismay. And inevitably, Pramila felt herself being reclaimed by the past, by recollections of those final seconds with her father and of choices she had once made.

Preparations for the New Year were already in full swing. Red boxes full of sweets—*burfis* and *laddoos* and *halwas* and *pendas* and *googras*—were scattered all over the house ready to deliver to neighbors, family, and business associates. The hissing and popping of firecrackers could be heard all over the city. *Rangolis* made of grains of rice dyed every imaginable color were arranged in intricate patterns at the thresholds of the flats in her building. Light from clay *diyas* danced on the images. Each ritual of celebration only made Pramila miss Dev more acutely.

When Dev called to wish her a happy New Year, Pramila could scarcely hear the sound of his voice over the surge of blood in her vessels. The long gaps in static that punctuated their conversations—as their words were transmitted along thousands of miles of lines—only accentuated the vast distance between them.

The cracking of fireworks continued late into the night, long after her in-laws had retired. Sitting in the kitchen, Pramila saw it, an envelope with a typed address. She tore it open, breathing an immense sigh of relief. Her visa had arrived. She would soon be on her way to join Dev in America.

The entire family saw Pramila off the day she departed. Dev's brother and cousins crowded around with good wishes and packages to take to him. Placing the packages aside, Pramila bent over to touch the feet of Bapuji as she bid him goodbye. He patted her head as one might pet a cat and then began chatting with his nephew. After Pramila touched Ma's feet, the older woman grasped her by the shoulders for an instant. *Khushi ma rejo.* Live in happiness, she said. Ma averted her face, trying to hide her grief.

Pramila embraced Ma knowing that Bapuji would certainly disapprove.

"Ma, I want you to know that your kindness has been a gift and you will always have my respect," Pramila said, making sure her voice pierced the din of the airport. "And there is one more thing I must mention—you are a top-notch cook! One of the best!"

Out of the corner of her eye, she was certain she could see Bapuji recoil at her comment. Ma gave Pramila a subtle smile, loath to draw too much attention to herself.

When Pramila finally turned to Vini and Ba, everything else in the airport seemed to fall away from her: the crowds of unknown faces, the friends and cousins who had come to bid her farewell, even the walls of the airport. Only they existed for her.

Together they sat for some moments, mother and her daughters, Pramila in the middle holding Ba's right hand and Vini's left. Ba struggled to remain composed, conversing with Vini in a cursory, preoccupied way. Her eyes were glazed over from the tears that had already been shed. As the boarding announcement was made, Pramila was overcome by a sense of dread.

Reading Pramila's expression, Vini reached over her sister's shoulder and tilted her head toward her.

"*Nani-ben, absoss nai kar thi.* Little sister, you must not have regrets. What has happened has happened. You have a new life waiting for you with Dev."

Pramila opened her mouth to speak but the words were held up in her throat. All she could do was nod.

"You must not worry. I will take care of Ba. You go on, make a home, build a life, give me some nieces and nephews." Vini's smile quivered. "You must do this."

Though Pramila knew her sister had felt both emotions over their fates before, there was no suggestion of bitterness or envy in her sister's voice today. Still seated, they embraced.

Pramila rose and turned to her mother. She bent down to touch Ba's feet but mother pulled daughter up into an embrace. Ba took a deep breath in before she began to speak.

"*Jo, beta.* Look, my dear. Your father is not here so I must be speaking for him first. He wished for you to see the world, *na*? And here you are moving to America!" Ba's voice faltered and she took a while to gather herself. "He would be pleased to know that a child of his, a daughter of his, had seen more of the world than he."

"Ba, I never intended any of this," Pramila mustered.

"You must not be thinking that I am of different mind from your father. I too am proud, my girl. Every bit as much as your father."

Obscured by tears, the airport took on a liquid quality. Pramila grabbed her mother and sister with a shaking desperation. She wept, burying her face in her mother's shoulder without letting go of her sister. The women held on to one another until the final boarding call was made. Ba tightened her grip around her girls one last time. Then they parted, with arms and hearts empty. Each step Pramila took toward the gate felt as though it lasted an eternity. It was as if time itself sought to hinder the separation. And yet it moved on, nevertheless. Soon Pramila was at the exit and Vini and Ba were far behind her, waving and trying to smile for each other.

◆ ◆ ◆

Pramila's flight landed in Buffalo, New York at night. Even through the walls of the jetway, the cold January air would not be denied. She rushed into the terminal finding her sweater inadequate to stave off the cold.

As she set foot in the terminal, it occurred to her that she had just left behind everyone she had ever known to come to a place where she knew not a single soul except for Dev. Save Dev, nobody who knew her in the past would share in this new American future and nobody in this future would know her Indian past. She was starting anew.

Even though the gate was bustling with people, the airport was orderly. People stood in line at the gates. There were so many types of people. People with black hair, brown hair, red hair, and even yellow hair. People with different skin colors: pale pink, *chai* brown, and black. She forgot herself briefly, fascinated by the variety of humanity surrounding her, when she saw a young man, waving from several yards away, trying to get her attention. At first, she did not recognize him, for Dev had left for America a mustachioed man.

"Dev?" she asked the clean-shaven version of her husband.

"*Su vat che?* What's the matter?" he asked, rushing toward her.

"You just look so different!"

"I thought I would try a new look for our new home! What do you think?" Dev asked as he grabbed her by her left hand. They embraced awkwardly, as if their bodies needed reintroduction.

"You do not like it?" he asked, touching his upper lip.

"No, it is quite . . . nice. I suppose it will just take me a few days to get used to it."

After a mind-numbingly frigid walk to the parking lot, they sat down in a mind-numbingly frigid car.

"You must be hungry. I have made you a proper *desi* meal." Dev turned to Pramila and grinned at her. "I am so happy you are here now."

He turned the ignition and the car started reluctantly.

Pramila's heart lurched as Dev pulled on to the wrong side of the road. She reminded herself that this was the way Americans drove. Even then, she grasped the handle of the car door to steady herself for an unexpected impact. As they entered the city proper, she gazed at the landscape. Tall buildings surrounded her in every direction. Beneath them, patches of blackened snow lay on either side of the road. Districts of skyscrapers transformed into neighborhoods of brick buildings with wrought-iron fire escapes. There was something forlorn about those brick buildings, more so now that a cold rain had begun to fall. Everything in the American city seemed built around keeping the elements out—closed off to the outside world—so different from the open terraces and balconies of Bombay. And whereas in Bombay people could be seen sprawling in every direction, here there was hardly a soul in sight.

She glanced at Dev. He looked so different without his mustache. Not like the man she had married. Here she was, sitting in a car with a strange-looking man in a strange city with no idea where she was going. Did she really even know him? What would happen if suddenly he pulled over and left her on the side of the road?

As he navigated through the streets of Buffalo in his beaten-up old Chevrolet Impala, Dev narrated. *The city is so different now that it has become fall, it was much nicer when I arrived as it was summer*—arré *but the snow, it is something to see—what you see is just the remaining snow which gets too dirty with the traffic and all.*

Marveling at this new world, Pramila was speechless.

"You are so quiet! What is this?" Dev asked.

"It is all just—just so different."

"I felt the same way at first. Like I was lost. I was missing home so much. I have never spent so much time by myself in the whole of my life. *Diwali* was hopeless without you."

"Mine, also."

"Not to worry. This place, we will make it our home." Dev placed his hand on hers.

Pramila stared through the rain-splattered window and wondered how. How could they possibly make this strange place home?

The car had finally grown comfortable by the time they pulled on to their street. Dev parked the car next to a snowbank.

They made their way to apartment #371. Dev had placed a garland of artificial flowers over the door. Pramila was touched by the tiny reminder of home.

"This is not a tip-top kind of place but for now, I am thinking it will do. Someday we will move to something nicer."

They entered a tiny living room with a couch and old recliner. The kitchen was adjoining. With the few decorations he had, Dev had done his best to enliven the dreary little flat. He had created a small shrine at one corner of the kitchen counter with tiny marble figurines of the Goddess Lakshmi and the Lord Mahavir and an incense holder. The dining table was in the center of the kitchen. Dev had set the table for two with mismatched plates and silverware.

"*Aav, bes.* Come sit." Dev pulled a chair out for her at the table. He went to the kitchen and began to warm dinner.

"No, no, you sit. I will warm everything." She was not used to having a man wait on her.

"I have been doing this food-making business for quite some while now. You have had a long trip. Sit. Sit," Dev insisted. Exhausted by the travel, she didn't argue.

Pramila fidgeted for a few moments as she watched Dev bustle around the kitchen. What would her father-in-law say if he saw Dev warming dinner?

"What would Bapuji say to this?" Dev said, reading her mind. Pramila smiled.

Dev brought out one item at a time, first the curried green beans and short-grain rice. Then came a salad composed of cucumbers and a yellow-orange tomato. Finally came a pot of split pea soup that Pramila presumed was to take the place of *dal*. Dev looked so proud as he sat down in the chair across from her.

"*Arré*, I forgot the bread," Dev said as he walked back to get the plate.

"Bread?"

"Yes, I should have learned how to make *rotis* before leaving India. This is the one thing I cannot make yet, so we will eat the bread instead."

Pramila stared at the meal and wanted to cry. She wanted to cry because Dev had put so much effort into making the meal. She wanted to cry because the thought of eating split pea soup, day-old bread, and the sad yellow-orange tomato was dreadful.

She quickly ironed out the grimace that she was certain had appeared on her face. She allowed Dev to put substantial portions of food upon her plate. She dubiously broke off a piece of bread, dipped it in the pea soup and grabbed some of the green beans with it and put it in her mouth. Dev had doused the soup and green beans with enough *masala* to make it actually seem tolerable. And she was hungry.

Over dinner they talked about family in India and listened as the rain pelted the living room window harder and harder as if competing for Dev's attention. Pramila ate every crumb on her plate, all the while missing home in the pit of her stomach with each bite.

The sound of the rain subsided suddenly. Dev motioned to the window.

She walked over to see delicate white flakes dropping from the sky.

"Snow?" she asked.

"Yes, that is snow," he said, as if he were accustomed to seeing snow all his life.

Pramila watched the gentle flurries as they floated by, light and unhurried. Dev placed his hand on her shoulder. She leaned toward him, softening into the welcome familiarity of his touch.

"*Bahut achcha hai.* It is very fine," she said.

Chapter 25

After the *Janmashtami* downpour, the sky became listless once again. I, on the other hand, felt quite the opposite of listless. I was troubled by the secrets that surrounded my mother and Shalu. I was energized and anxious, wanting to see Arjun again. Days after our kiss on the landing, he'd been asked for a second interview in New Delhi and planned to stay on for a few extra days to visit a cousin who lived nearby.

The weekend lasted just shy of eternity. I was thankful for the weekdays, at least then I was busy at work. In the evenings, I occupied myself with the newspaper or read *The Good Earth*. Early in my travels, scooped up by the whirlwind of India and obsessed with the old photograph, I hadn't made much progress with the book. After my trip to Shalu's house, however, I found myself reading it at every spare moment. Somehow a farmer's experiences with poverty during the upheaval of early twentieth-century China felt particularly compelling after seeing Shalu's house in a modern *jhopadpatti*. As I did with other books that I loved, as I neared the end I slowed the pace of my reading, much like someone enjoying late-night company might nurse a drink.

One night, reading in bed, I found myself obsessed with a particular chapter. After living in a state of destitution, the fortunes of the farmer and his family had changed. In his wealth, the farmer had taken a concubine, spending the family's hard-earned gold lavishly upon the woman, even as the farmer's wife toiled away doing chores and grew gaunt from illness. I read and re-read the chapter, struck by the wife's profound sense of betrayal.

Then, as had become an unconscious habit when I read the book, I pulled out the photo of my mother and me. Creases left behind long ago had begun to feel familiar to my touch. The reasons for my fascination with the picture were becoming clearer. It was as if the photo, taken decades ago, encapsulated some fundamental truth about our relationship. There I was holding my crocheted yellow and green blanket, an infant oblivious to the complexities of the world around me. My mother stood statuesque, hovering over me in her deep purple sari. But her face betrayed a remoteness, a sense of alienation from the moment, perhaps from me.

The distance between us had remained through the years. We bridged two different generations and two vastly different civilizations. It was precisely because of those differences that I craved a glimpse into my mother's past, something I was denied. In the vacuum, I created my own story. But stories we tell ourselves to fill such voids are meager substitutes for the truth. I tucked the photo back into the book and closed it, my eyes settling on the dust jacket. All I knew was that Pearl Buck's novel was about much more than the plowed fields that graced its cover.

There was a gentle knock at the door.

"Shyama, are you in there?"

Irritated with my aunt for not leveling with me about my mother's relationship with Shalu, I had been avoiding her for a few days.

"Yes."

"*Sa Re Ga Ma Pa* will be on TV soon. Come join me."

"You can come in, Maasi." I swung my legs over the side of the bed.

Vini cracked the door open.

She glanced at my hands. "Where did you get that?" Vini's eyes fixed on my hands as she pushed the door fully open.

"The book? Oh, I borrowed it from Dad."

"Can I see it?" She sat down on the bed beside me.

I handed her the book.

She thumbed through it. She opened the cover and studied the copyright page.

"This is not your father's. This is your grandfather's book."

"What do you mean?" My grandfather passed away long before I was born. How had the book managed to make it all the way to my father's bookcase in America?

"This book belonged to my father. I was there the afternoon he bought it. He found it in New and Secondhand Bookstore. He was so excited he found a first-edition copy."

"The shop in Kalbadevi?" I had been in that very same store the night I went to Edward Theatre with Daniel and Natasha. I imagined my grandfather wandering the narrow passages between the tall piles of books with the same sense of wonder I experienced.

"Your father must have given it to Mom then."

Vini sighed. "No, he didn't give it to her. She took it."

"She took it?"

"I mean to say she kept it. My father had just started reading it. But he never finished . . ." She took a breath in before continuing. "He died before he could. Died of a heart attack. Your mother insisted on keeping it as a memory of him. I can't even remember when I last saw it, too many years ago to count. I always wondered what happened to it. I never realized she took it to America with her."

"Mom never talks about your father. She never talks about how your dad died. All I know is that he was in his fifties."

I wondered for a moment if Vini would suggest that I speak to my mother about the issue. But this time she must have figured it was also her story to tell.

"Beyond his family, my father cared about two things. Books and *bidis*." Vini laughed at the thought. "I've told you how we didn't have electric lights at our old flat and how he used to read by the light of the bulb in the common passageway of our *chawl*."

The rhythm of Vini's story telling was halting, like a rock skipping through the water, jumping through the decades and swerving past long-spent emotions.

"I was engaged to be married once you know. There was none of this 'love marriage' business back then. My mother wouldn't have it. Mine was to be arranged only. After meeting so many boys, finally one had said yes. Everything was fixed. Papa was so happy, so relieved. Hardly a few days later, the boy's family called back. They had changed their minds. Just like that. We all knew it was probably my last chance. I was getting too old, nobody would want to marry me. I was completely, how do you say it? Devastated. And Papa, he was even worse. The stress was too much.

"Back then nobody knew that all those *bidis* were so bad for the health. Papa had a massive heart attack. The doctor came but it was too late. Papa knew it was the end. I suppose we all did. He died right there in our own home."

Both of us fell silent, any thoughts of *Sa Re Ga Ma Pa* abandoned.

"Your mother was with him moments before he died. She would not leave his side and when they took his body away, she stayed there in the room for days and days. We could not convince her to come out."

Vini seemed to recall something and flipped toward the front of the book. She landed upon one specific page which had been dog-eared so that the folded section covered nearly half of it.

"This was the page Papa was on the day he died. Your mother folded it so the crease couldn't be mistaken for another."

I wondered what my grandfather thought of Pearl Buck's prose, so spare and moving. Why did he stop reading at that particular scene? When he laid the book down that last time, could he have known he would never pick it up again? I ran my hands across my face, feeling grief for the loss of a man I'd never met, feeling grief for Vini's circumstances and my mother's.

"Your mother and Papa were very close. To this day, I do not think that she has ever recovered from his death."

Vini ran her fingers gently along the creased page. She averted her eyes as she handed me the book, still open.

"I need to check on something in my room." Her was voice thick. She rose abruptly to escape without shedding a tear. "I'll meet you in a few minutes to watch the show."

"Maasi," I stood up. "I'm sorry about your father. I'm so sorry."

Vini paused at the door but did not look back. "Not to worry, it was long ago."

I cradled the book in my hands and sat back down on the bed.

It felt heavier than before. I closed it and admired the cover. My grandfather's hands had once grazed that same cover, his eyes had once skimmed the same words. I ran my fingers down the spine, as if through the binding I could touch his fingers. I was surprised by what I felt. Gratitude, of all things. I was grateful for just a snapshot of my family's past.

I opened the book again to the creased page and read the words. It was early in the story before the farmer was corrupted by his newfound wealth, when his change of fortune allowed him to move through the world with a certain contentment. I folded the page along the groove and straightened it again, a deep and some-how welcome sorrow coalescing in my chest.

A few moments later, I walked into the living room where Maasi sat waiting for me. I sat down beside her, placing my hand upon hers. She grasped it and gave a deep sigh. Then, she picked up the remote, turned on the TV and flipped the channel to *Sa Re Ga Ma Pa*.

Shortly after the show finished, there was a knock on the door.

"Vini, it is Attaji here," came the muffled voice from the other side.

Vini hurried to the door and opened it. "*Arré?* Come in, come in. *Attaji, aap kayse hain?* How are you?"

"Oh fine, I am fine. Your surprise to see me is well placed, I am usually quite tucked into bed at this hour. At my age, one does not go looking for trouble, particularly at night, no? Hello Shyama." He stepped inside without leaning on his cane in the slightest.

"Please sit. Will you take some *sakar-badam* milk? I just put some on the stove," Vini said. The milk, sweetened with sugar, had slivered almonds and a hint of cardamom added in.

"I don't care to trouble you."

"*Arré?* What kind of talk is this? Come, come. Sit." Vini was off to the kitchen.

Attaji took a seat on the couch, his cane held to the floor by his right hand. He looked at me intently.

"So Shyamala. Have you found what you are looking for in this country of ours?" His eyes glimmered in the lamp light.

"I suppose. I still have a job," I said sweetly, deliberately avoid-ing what he really meant.

"Perhaps it is wise to keep certain things private, no? It seems the walls have ears these days." He nodded at the door. The way he twisted his cane against the floor lent a certain gravity to his words.

Vini maasi returned with the *sakar-badam* milk and a tray full of savories.

"I am not sure how to say this exactly. People have been talking again." Attaji, usually playful in his speech, sounded different.

"*Arré?* About Shalu? Not again," Vini said.

"No, not about Shalu. This is about you." Attaji focused on Vini.

"Me?" Vini was amused. "An old lady like me?"

"Yes. I have not heard the rumors directly from the source. Although I am sure we both know who she is."

"What is that woman saying about me now?"

"This thing about Rajesh."

Vini tilted her head and looked squarely at Attaji. Her eyebrows furrowed, then suddenly relaxed as if she now understood what he was implying. Then she laughed. It was one of those hearty, resonating belly laughs and it continued for some time. By the time she had stopped laughing, I was laughing myself.

"Next thing you know, Champa is going to accuse *me* of being pregnant! Can you imagine?" Vini's eyes began tearing. "The Pope might give me the sainthood, *na?* People would bow at my feet like Mother Mary. It would be a modern-day miracle!"

Attaji sipped his cup and analyzed Vini. "As preposterous as the notion may be to you, people are talking. I just wanted you to know."

"Let them talk. What can they do to a woman of my age? Ruin my reputation? Hurt my chance of marriage? Get me in trouble with my parents?" Vini took a sip from her cup, grinning over its rim.

I sipped the *sakar-badam* milk. Coupled with Vini's nonchalance, the warm-sweet spiciness was reassuring.

"Listen Viniben, one might think that with all the water troubles, people would have something more important to talk about. But people never change. When it comes to these things, once the rumors start, they are hard to stop." He stopped and measured his words. "Whether this is true or not is no business of mine. I just don't want anyone to get hurt."

I contemplated who it was that stood to get hurt. Vini because other residents would look down upon her for carrying on with Rajesh? Or Shalu and Rajesh because the rumors might threaten their employment with Vini and others in the building? Champa was meddling again, I was sure, and I wondered how much Arjun had divulged to his mother about us.

"Enough talk about me and my nonsense! How have you been Attaji?" And with that, Vini decidedly changed the subject.

Attaji stayed for over an hour, discussing the drought and complaining, in his immensely well-mannered way, about how his grandchildren rarely stopped by for a visit.

I enjoyed the late evening conversation. For a moment or two, I even nodded off. As I opened my eyes, still half asleep, I had the notion that the *kurta*-pajama-wearing form at the other end of the couch was my grandfather. There was a particular comfort I felt in Attaji's presence, one that I had never experienced before.

"Why don't you turn in, Shyama," he suggested, his deep, soothing voice emerging through my haze of drowsiness.

"I should." Though I felt quite satisfied where I was.

"Enjoy a proper sleep while you are young, *beta*. When you are old like me, you will find that sleep can be most elusive."

He offered his right hand. I took it in mine and sat upright.

After wishing Attaji and Vini goodnight, I grudgingly picked my body off the couch, and headed to bed. I re-read the page in *The Good Earth* that my mother had creased down the middle long ago. Just as I drifted off to sleep, still clutching the book, I realized that though Vini had laughed incredulously about the rumors, she had never actually denied them.

◆ ◆ ◆

I was worried about Natasha. Since Daniel's going-away party, she'd missed several days of work. I had called her many times worried about how she was faring, but she hadn't called back. When she finally returned to work, she avoided me. Only after everyone had headed home did Natasha appear.

"Sorry I didn't come to the party." She slumped over the wall of my cubicle.

"I am too. It would've been good for both of you to say good-bye at least."

"How was he?"

I bit my lip, wanting to spare Natasha more hurt but unable to tell her anything other than the truth. "He was heartbroken."

Her expression was beyond forlorn. "I imagine he must have been. I know he made it clear to you how he felt. It isn't like me to talk about such things, but I loved him too." The word "love" formed awkwardly in her mouth as if she had never said it aloud before.

"I know Natasha, it can't be easy."

"You know, these past few weeks I kept thinking about how I make *chai*."

I wasn't following Natasha's line of thought, but I didn't interrupt.

"I cannot recall the last time I made *chai* for only me, you see. There is always somebody in the house who drinks it with me. We live in a joint family so I might be having *chai* with my grandfather, my grandmother, my father, or my mother. Perhaps all of them together. I never have tea alone."

I thought of all those mornings spent drinking coffee alone at my kitchen table in LA.

"My grandfather likes *chai* with more sugar, my grandmother likes it creamy, my father favors a hint of ginger, and my mother loves the flavor of green tea. I know exactly how to make *chai* so that everyone will drink it. With just a little extra sugar and milk, a dash of grated ginger and a few leaves of green tea. For me the joy of making tea is that I can satisfy everyone's taste. I don't make it to suit my own. I think of the whole family. And so it is with every decision I make. Large or small, it is with the thoughts of what is best for our family."

"And the same is true for deciding whom you marry?" In a way, Natasha's situation was not so different from mine—in part, we were both trying to live up to someone else's expectations.

"How can it be any different with such a decision? Imagine what my parents would think, not to mention my grandparents? What would our friends say? They would see me as rebellious and selfish. I can't even begin to imagine what would happen to our kids." She raised her eyebrows as if to request some sort of answer.

I had none.

"If I chose Daniel, I might very well lose all of them. Family, friends, neighbors. What would I do without them? How could he replace them all? Would I make *chai* for only Daniel and me for the rest of my life? It was too much to ask of me and of him, *na*?"

I felt for her; she had faced an agonizing decision where what she desired most might alienate her from everyone and everything she knew.

"It was also too much to ask of them. Even if they did come around, how could I live with myself knowing that I had only thought of my needs and nobody else's?" Natasha pushed back her hair which fell in wavy layers that framed her face. If Daniel were present to witness her expression, I could only imagine that he would have fallen for her even more.

◆ ◆ ◆

With the air between us finally cleared, later that week, Natasha and I went out to lunch between meetings. Gayatri tagged along. Even though I should have known better by now, I suggested we eat at the *pav bhaji* stand near the office. Nothing sounded more delectable than the mix of finely chopped onions, garlic, potatoes, carrots, peas, and tomatoes, spiced and sautéed in a massive wok right at the side of the road and served with toasted bread. Even to my mind's nose, the imagined scent of turmeric, *garam masala*, and cumin was irresistible. Like an addict, I was out for a third time that week to get my fix.

I was finishing my last few morsels when my mobile rang.

"Hullo Arjun," I said, my mouth full.

"Hi Shyamala! Did I catch you eating?"

"Yes, *pav bhaji* with Natasha and Gayatri."

"Ah—I hope you are not eating that on the street." I scanned the crowd near the stand. Could he see me?

"Maybe?" I said sheepishly. "Vini will kill me if she knows I am eating this stuff on the street! She is so afraid I'll get sick again!"

"I am absolutely going to deny knowing anything about it!"

"Did you get the job?" I braced myself in case they had offered him the job on the spot.

"Not sure. I hope so." He grew thoughtful. "Listen, can you talk?"

I took in the hive of people around me. At least Natasha and Gayatri were out of earshot. "Yes."

Arjun took a deep breath in. "I, I can't stop thinking about *Janmashtami*—about you."

I stood by the *pav bhaji* vendor, the noisy swarm surrounding me, hoping I hadn't imagined the words. He waited patiently for me to respond.

I paused for a moment, my thoughts scattershot. Before *Janmashtami*, when I thought about Arjun a sense of caution would overcome me. We were from opposite sides of the Earth for one. His mother was an absolute nightmare. But mostly, I just wasn't sure that I was done with the heartbreak from Neil. But since *Janmashtami*, more and more, the thoughts of Arjun came unimpeded by any such caution.

"Me too."

"Well then, when I get back, join me for dinner at my place."

Just then Gayatri walked over, her eyes like saucers. "Arjun?"

I tried to shoo her away, wanting to focus on him.

"I'd love to. Just text me the time and your address. Shall I bring anything?"

"Just you will do."

My face grew warm as we hung up.

"Is he offering to make you dinner?" Gayatri surveyed me intensely.

"Yes! He just invited me to dinner," I admitted, hoping that would satisfy her curiosity.

"*Shabash!*" she said, voice full of innuendo. "You know, I've had a couple of guys make me dinner—on the subcontinent that is not so common. Is it Hakka noodles out of a package though? Because that doesn't count. The last time a guy made me Hakka noodles, he started talking about maths."

"Math?"

"Yes, Hakka noodles—maths. They are bloody red flags."

"Talking about math is a red flag?" I furrowed my brow.

"It's the whole bit. You see, first, they start by talking about religion or metaphysics—which is bad enough on the first date—then next thing you know they are trying to convince you that some bit of Hindu cosmology is true science that can be mathematically proven. I can't tell you how many times a guy has brought this kind of thing up to me, like it is some type of thinking-man's come on, but every one of them has been a *pukka* creep!"

My face warmed again. As far as I was concerned, Arjun could cook me Hakka noodles out of a package and talk to me about math, I didn't care. I just wanted to see him again.

Chapter 26

Pramila waited to feel it. *Pyaar*. Love. She thought she would fall in love with Dev the way one descends a staircase to get to the bottom, step by step but inevitably. Instead, *pyaar* came in fits and starts. She felt twinges of it during the least consequential of moments, the ones that occurred between wedding anniversaries and *Diwalis* spent together, times that were captured neither in photographs nor in journal entries, whose influence lived on after the exact memory had long since faded. But there were days when *pyaar* seemed remote and foreign to her. Times when her old aspirations beckoned and she wondered if she could ever truly love him.

It was the April before Shyamala's birth when she and Dev packed the car and headed to Washington DC. They spent the night at the least expensive motel they could find. Waking early, the couple raced from one white-washed landmark to the next, pointing to the White House and the Capitol Building as if they were surprised to find that the structures existed beyond picture postcards and the history books Pramila was so fond of reading. As impressive as those buildings were, nothing was as breathtaking as the spring. The year's renewal was far more extraordinary when one had lived through a Buffalo winter. The air was balmy, forgiving. "*Jo,* look," Pramila said, pointing up the path ahead. Soon, the couple was walking beneath rows of cherry trees in full blossom as tiny pink petals came drifting down, swept along by a breeze. Sunlight flitted in and out between the branches. They stood beneath them, Dev facing skyward, as petals rained down upon them like velvet confetti. He laughed with absolute abandon. He reached his hand toward her, his face suddenly becoming serious. Dev swept his index finger against the angle of her chin. It was on that day Pramila had felt it for the first time, fleeting though it was; the fullness and the depth and the contour of love.

◆ ◆ ◆

Shyamala was born on the bleakest and most frigid of Buffalo days in 1973. The snow had fallen in heavy drifts that collected outside windows and thickly frosted tree trunks. Much of the city had been rendered inaccessible. The day felt like perpetual dusk.

In the months prior to her daughter's birth, Pramila had watched her lean belly become more rotund, her body more alien as the baby grew within it. Her hips hurt unpredictably and midstep. She never grew accustomed to Shyamala's hiccups. They had a strength that seized her adult body. On the other hand, when Dev was away at work for so many weeks leading up to this cold Buffalo day, Pramila took comfort in having another being beside her, albeit inside her, those oft lonely nights.

When Dev was out of town for work, the hours of daylight went by quickly. She had filled her mornings with volunteering at the library, working to reshelve books and teaching people to read, leaving each shift with armfuls of books to occupy her time. At the library, she overheard a group of women chatting about the

Equal Rights Amendment, and before long had committed her afternoons to lobbying with them. The days were fulfilling to her. But as the sun went down, Pramila's anxiety bubbled to the surface. The anxiety only grew as the due date approached. How would she raise the child in this foreign land so far from everyone she knew and everything she knew? She was convinced that Dev would be hundreds of miles away when the baby finally came. *Chinta nai kar,* he would say. Not to worry. I will be here.

And Dev had been home that blustery week that Shyamala entered their lives. On the last night of December, as the nurses wheeled her into the delivery room, Dev held her hand tightly. Pramila desperately wished that he could have been with her during the birth. His presence might have made things much less frightening. Instead, a vice tightened around her belly in wave after excruciating wave. It was as if her body had allegiance only to the child within her.

Pramila recited her prayers, imagining the meditative expression of Lord Mahavira as the nurses pushed her through a set of double doors. The walls of the delivery room were as stark white as the snow that blew outside that night. The only other color in the room was the sky blue of the towels and covers, unless one counted the reflective silver of the stainless-steel instruments nearby which, incidentally, could have been on retainer from a torture chamber.

Before she knew it, Pramila lay flat on her back, her legs splayed open on the table. The nurses in the delivery room spoke kind words to her as they adjusted her body. Their cheerfulness was entirely at odds with the crushing agony in her belly. Then, the doctor entered the room. She dreaded to look down for Dr. Snyder stood there, evaluating her, considering her most private body parts as if he were considering his next move in a chess game. Suddenly, she felt a warm gush of fluid between her legs. Her belly deflated before her eyes and soon, tears welled up within them.

"Well, it seems as though your waater has broken," Dr. Snyder said as if all were routine. "And judging from your contraactions, the baby should be coming soon." His long Chicago "a"s were even longer today.

Her mind raced toward Ba and Vini, half a world away. Then, it settled into thoughts about her father—about the day he died— about what she had wanted to tell him. She thought about the person she had once been and the person she had become. How could this be her life? She who never wanted to be wife or mother. She had been so wise once. She had recognized the price of wife- hood, of motherhood. She had sought a life free from exactly this burden. Yet here she was, exposed, her body no longer her own and her mind unable to focus on anything other than the past and this pain. And now the truth, once so obvious to her, was apparent once again as the next contraction seized her. This had all been a great mistake.

But there was no turning back.

The delivery was neither exalted nor miraculous. When they held the little girl up to Pramila, she breathed a deep sigh of relief upon hearing the baby's cries. There was even a moment of elation, brief as it was. A moment in which she felt intense affection for the child who had grown within her, as if in this act of giving birth she was connected to all those who had come before her. Her mother and her mother's mother and her mother's mother's mother back in time until the beginning. But then she felt a void, aware she'd left behind something treasured and dear and nothing, not even the child, could quite take its place.

Then, after being at the center of attention for the better part of three hours, Pramila found herself alone as the doctor and the nurses tended to the baby. After a long while, Dev brought the child to her. He cradled the baby tenderly, his eyes bright. When he placed the child within her arms, Pramila expected to feel the connection again. Instead, she felt something else—a stifled sort of panic.

As if sensing her apprehension, the child began to whimper. Pramila held the baby away from her. She was entirely unequipped to take care of another human being. There were so many things that would need to be done. How did one feed a child correctly? How did one stop her from crying? There was nobody nearby to ask. How would Pramila ever be able to predict her needs? And when it came to schooling, how did one guide her? How would she find a boy for the child to marry someday? The questions shot through her mind in a barrage and then dispersed, unanswered, leaving behind a thick haze of uncertainty. The haze had not dissipated by the time they had left the hospital and headed home.

Dev, for his part, was captivated by the child. He tended to every one of the child's needs. And when it came to swaddling— this task he did with the precision of an origami master. In accordance with the *rashi*, the Hindu moon sign, they named the child Shyamala. The Dark One—because she was born during the waning moon, the dark fortnight that was believed to be the time of Lord Krishna's birth.

Pramila resented her husband for the ease with which he had become a father. Dev's body had not been battered by Shyamala's entrance into the world. Dev did not have to suffer the discomforts of feeding her at the breast. Dev did not worry himself about the child's well-being in some theoretical future. To him, all was certain when everything in Pramila's life was uncertain. When her library friends asked to visit, she rarely accepted, there was simply too much to do at home. Early parenthood was an endless cavalcade of duties. One day flowed into the next and all days ended in sheer physical exhaustion. But in this blur of days, there was one day in particular that Pramila could not forget.

Dev had awoken with the baby. Pramila followed his soft, lyrical murmurs into the living room. He had just managed to get Shyamala back to sleep. The couple had eaten breakfast in peace, Dev admiring the still white landscape outside the kitchen window. The sun was lit like a pale orb behind a thin veil of cloud cover. Dev commented on how the dim rays still caused the snow beneath to shimmer if one stood just so. Pramila struggled to find the correct angle. She gave up, choosing instead to enjoy the peace. She thought back to the last breakfast that she and Dev had eaten simultaneously at the table—it was the day Shyamala was born. Was that a mere three weeks ago?

Dev left for work after breakfast, leaving Pramila at the door watching as his car puttered away, the exhaust visible in the frigid air. It was just past eight o'clock. If she was lucky, Dev might return by 6 p.m. That left her with the baby for ten hours. Ten hours. Pramila made her way inside and headed to the bassinet. For a while she hovered over the child, adjusting the blankets repeatedly to be sure that the baby could breathe. Pramila tried to take a nap herself but she was restless and found herself by the bassinet again.

It was then that the child awoke. And she awoke in a rage. Pramila tried, dutifully and despite her own discomfort with the sensation, to place the baby at her breast. It was pointless, Shyamala would not feed. Pramila hastily prepared a bottle of formula only to have that rejected. Despite the child's cries and writhing, Pramila changed her diaper. But Shyamala continued to cry. Pramila adjusted the swaddling blanket and rocked the baby in her arms but the fold of the blanket came undone as the baby thrashed about. Desperate to make the child stop crying, she bundled the baby up, placed her in the stroller and decided to take her for a walk in the frigid January weather.

At first, the pace of the child's screams slowed. But just as the two rounded the corner, Shyamala began to cry again. In seconds, her cries went from mildly grating to blood-curdling. Between cries, the child held her breath.

Pramila sang the Indian lullaby that Dev used to soothe Shyamala.

"*Me ek a beeladi pali che.*"

But the child had no interest in the adventures of pretty, prowling cats. She screamed. The cries pierced her mother's ears. They reverberated in her mother's mind. Pramila could not think straight. She was exhausted.

"*Maherbani kar.* Do me a favor . I beg you. Please stop crying," she pleaded, her voice guttural.

But Shyamala simply would not stop shrieking. Pramila was revolted by the sound. She felt her knees give way. They crashed hard on the icy ground. Warm tears fell down Pramila's cheeks in plump drops. They landed in the snow beneath her, melting the flakes for an instant before turning into ice themselves. Voices bounced about in her head, some barely recognizable, others frighteningly unknown to her, each seemingly with its own admonition. Even through the litany of voices, Pramila could hear Shyamala's shrill cries.

Then, like a thunderclap, with her knees still buried in the snow, a voice rose above the rest. *Leave the child.*

Slowing her breath, she focused on the voice. *Leave the child.*

She considered. She could step away just to have a little peace. Just for a moment.

Maybe longer.

Now the voice made suggestions in rapid succession, drowning out the other voices. *Leave the child at a neighbor's door. Then you can get away. Just ring the bell. Somebody will discover her. They will know how to take care of Shyamala. Then you can have a sliver of peace. You just need a little peace. Maybe you can go back to the way things were before the child entered the world.*

Then, the voices quieted. She thumbed through her options coolly. *Leave her at this building. Leave her at the next building.*

With her choices laid out before her, Pramila's panic subsided. She adjusted the baby's blankets and eyed the apartment building just across the street. She crossed gingerly, walked judiciously along the pavement to a pathway that led to a neatly groomed front porch. There, she parked the stroller in the doorway, rang the doorbell and lingered for a moment before backing away. Then, she retraced her steps back to the street.

Suddenly it was calm. She could not hear crying. Perhaps the child had finally fallen asleep, too exhausted to cry anymore, Pramila thought. Just then, a loud crack arose as a heavy accumulation of snow slid off the roof behind her and plummeted to the ground. Jolted by the sound, Pramila's heart leapt. She blinked several times, as if coming to, suddenly conscious of the scene, the now deserted street, the harshness of the day, and the tiny being behind her, whom she had just abandoned.

What had she done?

She stopped in her tracks, did an about-face, rushed along the sidewalk and ran back to the apartment building where Shyamala lay whimpering in her stroller. Thank God she was unharmed! The accumulation of snow had crashed down just a few yards away. Grasping the handle, Pramila succumbed to a wave of despair so deep she could not give it voice. She let out a prolonged sigh, her warm breath visible in the cold air. *What have I done?* How could it be that she had forsaken her own flesh and blood? The child might have perished, alone and cold, on this unforgiving January day. What kind of mother could do such a thing? How could she have explained herself to Dev, to her sister, to her mother, to *herself*?

Shyamala remained still save the occasional residual sob that shook her tiny body. Pramila thanked the heavens for that final snowflake, the one that caused the entire drift to crash. That was what had saved her baby.

That evening, when Pramila heard Dev's briefcase being set upon the front porch, she mechanically patted Shyamala's tiny head. She donned her coat, hat, gloves, and scarf. She gave Dev a cursory greeting and before he had even entered the apartment, walked out of the door. Solitude was her only solace. Finally, she could escape it all. The desperation to feel what a mother should feel for a child. The sheer terror of trying to understand what the baby's cries meant. The million menial tasks—the washing, the cleaning, the planning of meals, the slow steady rhythm of her aspirations escaping her.

Pramila watched as the sun's rays dropped from the horizon. Whenever she approached a neighbor's house, she turned her head slightly. Through open curtains, she caught sight of domestic scenes: a husband and wife seated at a table talking over the last morsels of dinner or a father building a tower of blocks for his young daughter. She tried to picture herself in each scene, tried to imagine the warmth and comfort that lay within. Why had she felt neither within the walls of her house? Why did she feel nothing but this deep, primordial sadness?

She recognized the distance growing between her small family and herself. Resigned, she sought comfort within the chasm. She embraced it. For in her melancholy, she was somehow immune—inaccessible—undaunted.

◆ ◆ ◆

The idea came to him after a trip to the doctor in March. While describing the baby's sleep habits, Pramila had suddenly burst into tears. When Dev had asked the doctor why Pramila had such strong swings in emotions, he had said something vague about baby blues and patted Dev on the shoulder on his way out of the office. On the way home, Dev suggested that Pramila should go to visit Ba and Vini in India. He insisted that he could manage for a few weeks while Pramila was away.

In the days before her departure, she regained some of her industriousness. She managed to cook nearly two weeks' worth of dinners and stash them in the freezer for Dev to eat. She stocked the house with baby formula and rice cereal. She folded loads and loads of laundry, feeling a slight twinge of satisfaction from the tidy stacks of onesies and washcloths.

Pramila had left the arrangements for Shyamala's care to Dev. Kishoriben, an Indian aunty from the next building, had jumped at the chance to watch Shyamala when Dev was at work. She was a kind, rotund woman in her fifties who yearned for a grandchild. She would surely wonder why a mother would leave a newborn child to go gallivanting back to India. Pramila did not feel up to providing any explanations.

On her departure day in early spring, Pramila was ready an hour before it was time to leave the house. She sat with Shyamala on the floor. While the baby cooed and vied for her attention, Pramila was busy imagining what it would be like to step into the old flat in Mumbai.

"Shyamala is calling you," Dev said.

"Calling me?"

"Those sounds she is making? She is calling you."

"Yes, of course," Pramila said defensively.

"*Vath kar*. Talk to her. She will not be seeing you for quite some time."

"You think I do not know this?"

Dev had taken to interpreting Shyamala's noises for Pramila. These reminders had begun to grate on her nerves. If he had something to tell her, he should just speak directly. He was always so cautious, so accommodating. And the way he looked at her! She knew that Dev saw her as a failure. Perhaps he should just say so. Then she could tell him that the situation was untenable, that they should just part ways.

"Listen, why don't we go to the park? We will take some photos so I have pictures to show Shyamala when you are gone."

"Fine."

Dev dressed Shyamala in a red tunic and gently combed her rather untamable hair.

It was an unusually warm afternoon in April. A warm breeze kicked up while they were at the park. Shyamala, who had thus far only worn winter clothes that rendered her inaccessible to the elements, turned her face toward the wind and laughed a wholehearted belly laugh. Dev joined in as if it was the most joyous sound he had ever heard. He propped Shyamala up on a park bench, tucked the baby blanket Pramila had crocheted under her, and asked Pramila to come into the frame. She stood behind the giggling child and looked down upon her as a breeze swept up. Shyamala laughed again and Dev snapped a photo.

Several days later, Dev had the pictures developed. He searched for the photo, flipping eagerly through the stack until he found the one from the park. He was pleased that he had captured Shyamala's laughter. But as he glanced at Pramila's image, he could not help but feel that she belonged in a different scene all together. Pramila's face was vacant, joyless. Dev could not recognize his wife in the snapshot. He separated the photo from the rest, tucking it away into an old book of Pramila's that he was reading.

He reminisced about home often those days. Home, where mothers and sisters and uncles converged upon a young mother, their comings and goings a safety net that he hoped would be Pramila's salvation. Dev was convinced that sending Pramila away was the only way to get her back.

The photograph was never far from his mind back then. Some nights, he glanced at it before reciting his prayers and others, he simply left it undisturbed in *The Good Earth,* unable to endure the sight of his wife so alone and adrift in the world.

Chapter 27

Mumbai, September 2006

Just beyond my closed bedroom door, one morning, I heard an urgent knock.

"Coming," I announced, wondering what was so pressing at this early hour.

I threw the front door open to find Kaushik uncle. He seemed preoccupied. Sweat beaded on his upper lip. As the water situation at our building grew dire, the role of secretary of the building society cooperative was taking a toll on him. He'd only been in office a few months. Vini had held it before him.

"Shyamala—I am stopping by all the flats just now to tell the neighbors there is a chance the waterrrr will run dry today. If it comes, make sure you stock up, no?"

"No water at all? What about the tanker, the one that delivers the extra water?"

"I called tankerrr company but there was no answer, probably too many people are inquiring at once. I mean to see if we are getting what we were promised. Problem is, the supplies are low everywhere, even the tanker companies, *na*? At this point, we may not be able to count on them either."

"That doesn't sound good."

"Not good at all." Kaushik uncle shook his head.

"Let Viniben know please. I still have many more flats to go." He wiped his brow and headed off to Champa's flat.

Poor guy, I thought, breaking the news to Champa wasn't going to be pleasant.

I felt a sort of dread bubble up. What were we going to do without any water? We had already been rationing. Even if the water lasted this week, what would happen next? We could live without bathing every day, as miserable as that sounded in 95°F weather with 95 percent humidity. We could pass laundering our clothes less frequently. But what happened when we ran out of water for cooking? For drinking?

I envisioned Bombay, a city of seventeen million people surrounded by millions more living in suburbs, without water. There had been a time for a discussion about wastage and infrastructure and the impact of a warming Earth, but the window of opportunity to address those issues to prevent this particular drought had long since passed. Now the residents of the megacity, myself included, were almost entirely at the mercy of forces of nature to which we had rarely given thought. Trade winds and oscillations, temperature differentials and troughs. The ancients prayed for the proper convergence of these forces, calling them the god of this or that. But in 2006, for all our knowledge of the origin of these meteorological effects, we still could do little more than pray as the ancients did for rain to come. Without rain, the city could not go on. Arjun had said just that the night we went to the Gateway of India.

I went to see if Vini was in her bedroom. The door was partly open. She stood beside the Godrej *cabat*, the long metal doors wide open, with her new portable phone in her hand. She was silently reading from the ledger I had seen before. She lifted the phone as if she were about to dial and then abruptly threw it on the bed.

I knocked softly on the door. "Vini maasi?"

She reacted with a jolt and nearly dropped the ledger from her hands. "*Arré bhagvan!* Oh my God! You frightened me!"

"Sorry!" I entered the room gingerly. "Kaushik uncle just dropped by."

"Oh? What did he have to say?" she asked with cursory interest. She closed the ledger and set it in her *cabat*. Then she closed the door with a metallic shudder and turned the lock with a loud clank. She gave the *cabat* a slight pull to assure it was latched.

"He says that the water supply today will be very low. It may not come at all!" I said with alarm.

Maasi turned to me, the interest returning to her voice. "Is that right? The tanker may not come even?"

"That is right. No water at all."

She digested the information with little emotional reaction. "No rain, no water, isn't it? All this time, people like us were protected. Now we must live like other Mumbaikars that have struggled to get water all these years."

It was an oddly philosophical thing to say considering that we might be cooking and drinking from yesterday's supply.

"You don't seem surprised."

"Shyamala, one good night of rain is not enough. One week of solid rain is not enough. It is no surprise that the water has nearly run out. Come though, with Champa in this building—the municipality will have the water running in no time, just so they don't have to listen to her *bakwas!*"

I glanced at my aunt with confusion. Her initial sense of panic when I walked into the room had transformed into an unexpected glibness.

"Listen, I must go out for a little while. Not to worry, I will pick up some extra water bottles while I am out."

"You haven't even had your *chai* or breakfast yet."

"I am not hungry. I'll come back and have it." With that, Vini grabbed her clothes and headed into the bathroom.

I went back into the kitchen, scratching my head. Who was Vini about to call on the phone? Why had she been so spooked when I walked in on her? What was in that ledger? It took every bit of self-control I had to avoid rummaging through Maasi's belongings for a spare key to open the *cabat*'s metal doors for a peek. Her lack of surprise when I mentioned that we might not have water at all made me certain that she knew more than she was letting on. But perhaps the strangest thing of all was that she was starting her day without her newspaper and her breakfast.

◆ ◆ ◆

Arjun asked me to meet him for dinner at his flat in Santa Cruz East at half past seven.

The rickshaw driver dropped me off at the complex and I made my way to the elevator. There was a white-haired elevator operator sitting on a stool behind the criss-crossing wrought-iron cage door. He pulled it open and allowed me in. He looked at me expectantly.

"Oh, sorry. Seventh floor." I grabbed on to the waist-level railing as we lurched upwards.

The elevator slowly made its way up.

"Madam," the operator said as he opened the door again.

My pulse quickened as I continued to the end of the hall where I finally found #718. I knocked on the door.

Hardly a second or two elapsed before it opened.

"Hello Shyamala. I hope you had no trouble finding my place!" Arjun declared, welcoming me into his flat. The scent of *garam masala* and sautéed onions spilled out of his door.

"None at all. Something smells good! *Pav bhaji?*"

"Wow, you have a discerning nose! Thought I'd treat you to your favorite."

I smiled. No Hakka noodles out of a package here.

Arjun guided me from the tiny foyer, past a small dining table to a large living room. Off to the right was the kitchen, its boundary demarcated by a counter.

He wore a traditional Indian woven shirt with a Nehru collar and sleeves folded to the elbow along with a pair of faded dark-blue jeans. The outfit gave him an unassumingly chic East-West vibe, with his wild hair and several-days-unshaven beard.

Arjun had quite the taste for interior design too. His decor was Indian-mod, with teak furniture marked by sleek edges and simple lines. A picture window was opposite the front door. Bookcases lined the wall to the right of it. His couch, thickly cushioned and adorned with oversized red pillows, overlooked the window. On the wall opposite the bookcases was a large wooden desk. I immediately felt at home in his surroundings.

"And you have a discerning eye, Arjun."

"Thanks Shyama. I have collected these pieces one by one. That desk is my favorite—found it in an old antique shop—must be a hundred years old if I had to guess. But I don't want to bore you talking about furniture." He strode into the kitchen and offered me a drink. He held my gaze for a moment before he resumed chopping cilantro.

I sipped from my glass, suddenly aware of the heat.

"Ask me something, anything," Arjun requested as he added vegetables to the pot. I smiled; I'd made the same request at our dinner on *Janmashtami*.

"Why aren't you married?" I might as well ask exactly what I wanted to know.

"Direct. *Achcha*, I like that." Arjun nodded. "Well, it is not for my parents' lack of trying. In fact, over the years I have met quite a few girls recommended to the family. But it didn't take me long to figure out the match-making thing wasn't going to work for me. I wanted to pursue this ridiculous journalism thing—it isn't exactly a great selling point. Most parents want doctors and engineers for their daughters, something stable. I had no idea where my next paycheck would be coming from. And my habit of forgetting to shave didn't much help either."

"I can't imagine that." I laughed. His five o'clock shadow held quite a sway over me. Arjun glanced at me, knowing full well that he was teasing me.

"Even though I have told my mother that I am not suited for the match-making thing, still she tries. Although, she has been distracted as of late. The water situation has her quite worried. She thinks your building is not receiving the correct allocation of water."

"But everyone is getting shorted."

"Ah, but when Champaben and the well-to-do get shorted that is another thing altogether, no?" He stirred the large pot on the stove. "This week the city evacuated a slum not far from here and entirely razed it. It was a scourge on the neighborhood, people said. But it was also siphoning water from the municipality. That must have had something to do with it. Barbed wire fencing has been cropping up near water mains all around the city to prevent people from accessing."

Arjun dipped a spoon in the pot of the mixed vegetable *bhaji* on the stove and tasted the contents. He dropped in a dollop of garlic paste, and then added the cilantro. He stirred the pot, turned down the heat, covered it and then walked to the picture window.

"Come here for a second." He drew the sheer curtain and pointed into the distance. "See that?"

I walked over and stood beside Arjun. "The slum?"

He nodded.

"I visited Shalu's home in the *jhopadpatti*."

Arjun turned to me. "You did? Vini let you go?"

"Shalu invited me and there was no way I could refuse. I couldn't have imagined the way people lived in the slum but the more I looked around, the more I was struck by how much industry and resilience surrounded me—how Shalu saw it as home."

Arjun considered me before speaking. "Without the slum, the middle class of Mumbai would cease to function. The people who live there—we utilize their services, depend on them for cooking, cleaning, and childrearing. But when times get tough, we bloody raze their homes and take their water." His tone grew reflective and bitter.

"It reminds me of home. Growing up in LA, you hear people complain about immigrants—taking jobs and using services—but the same people who complain eat the fruit those immigrants harvest and hire them off the street for cheap labor. People are completely blind to their own hypocrisy."

Arjun's expression softened. "Imagine me ranting about this to some unsuspecting girl at one of those matchmaking sessions? 'Hi, I am Arjun, I think people like you are completely blind to your own hypocrisy.'"

"Sounds perfectly reasonable. Who could resist you?" I joked.

"Like—let me count—about ten women." Arjun laughed. "Shit *yaar*, should have gone to medical school, I guess."

"It took you ten rejections to realize you weren't cut out for the arranged marriage thing?"

"Actually, it only took me two. But it took eight more rejections to convince my mother." Arjun grinned as if that were some sort of achievement. "Needless to say, since then I've found it better to keep my love life to myself."

He walked back into the kitchen where he pulled dishes out of the cabinet.

Relieved to hear that Arjun had managed to insulate his private life from Champa's meddling, I followed him and took the plates from his hands. I could at least set the table.

When our hands met on the dishes, he stilled. "Tell me who this chap is—this guy you loved before." His eyes searched mine as if both demanding and fearing the answer.

"His name is Neil," I said grudgingly, hoping not to ruin the direction of the evening. I didn't want to dredge up old memories.

"What happened between the two of you?" Arjun prodded.

I hesitated. "I guess—I guess he didn't love me the way I loved him. Actually, he never loved me at all."

Arjun was silent. We still stood in the kitchen, me still holding the dishes and Arjun standing empty handed. He seemed to absorb my words before he spoke, his expression intense, his fingers now glancing mine.

"Loving the wrong person, I know about that."

This was the first time Arjun had mentioned anyone in his past. I froze. Did he think that by revealing his heartbreak, I would feel more comfortable revealing mine?

"Really? Who?" It was my turn to push.

"Her name was Avani. She was rich. Her husband was absolutely despicable."

"Husband?"

"Well, she said they were in the middle of a divorce. He was a bloody cheat. She had moved out of his family's place. She needed saving and I needed someone to save."

Every alarm bell in my brain was ringing.

Suddenly, Arjun rushed to the stove. "*Hai, hai*, I forgot about the *pav bhaji*! I hope it didn't burn."

Standing beside the empty table with plates still in my hands, I watched as he stirred, feeling like the *bhaji* stuck to the side of the pot.

"All's well. Caught it just in time. We'll be eating in a minute."

But I wasn't sure I felt like eating anymore.

Silently, I began to set the table. The ceramic dishes made an assured "clank" as they hit the wood. Arjun brought the *pav bhaji* over. After plating the food, he seemed to reassess the evening.

"About Avani—I told you because, like you, I know how it feels to love the wrong person. But there is something about *pyaar*—about love—I think sometimes the memory of it holds more power than the love itself did. As it recedes into the past, it becomes *maya*—illusion. Don't you think?"

I couldn't deny that he had a point; how long had I held on to the memory of my love for Neil before I realized the whole thing had been an illusion?

"So, what remains between you and Avani is just memory?"

"Now just *maya*." His eyes met mine and I could feel him searching again. He reached over and touched my left hand. "What I had with Avani is over. I want something real, Shyama." He hesitated and then seemed to brace himself for a plunge. "With you. I felt it that first day we met on the stairwell—at the Gateway and Chowpatty—I feel it now."

My heart thudded against my ribcage. I knew there were one hundred reasons why Arjun and I would not work. There was my baggage with Neil and, it seemed, his baggage with Avani. There was Champa. Most of all, there was the fact that the places we each called home couldn't be farther apart and still be on planet Earth. But I didn't let those thoughts settle in. Instead, I turned my hand and grasped his gently.

Arjun's eyes glinted in the light and he continued as if he'd been waiting to share something that had weighed heavily on him.

"From that first day we met, you've said exactly what you think in this, this slightly frazzled but somehow magnetic way. The way you care about Shalu and Vini, it's so refreshingly genuine,

Shyamala. Sometimes I listen to others, my mother included, talking about what they want to buy, how they plan to spend their weekend, what they ate for dinner and I just, I don't get it. It's like the kitchen is on fire and everyone is in the living room bloody admiring the furniture. But you *do* get it—and it matters to me in a way that I didn't realize until I met you." He took a deep breath in. "Please tell me it is over with Neil."

I thought about when Neil first left me and all the nights that I cried alone afterwards. For so long I had been reeling, for so long I had been adrift and afraid, for so long I had been hiding in my little ranch house. Now, I sat on the edge of my chair in the unescapable Mumbai heat and looked at Arjun. *Janmashtami* was the first night I had been able to let it all go.

"Yes, it is. It has been for a long time. It just took me a while to figure it all out." As we ate, I replayed his words in mind. *What I had with Avani is over.*

Closets open and skeletons revealed, the evening felt limitless.

After dinner, Arjun's attention turned to a large stack of vinyl in the living room. Before long Ella Fitzgerald's voice filled his suburban Mumbai apartment. He stepped into the kitchen and retrieved a small bundle wrapped in newspaper.

"Come over here, I have something for you," he said. Soon his hand was at my hip, pulling me away from the table and toward him. "I couldn't resist buying one of these for you. I went all the way to Juhu Beach to pick it up."

He unwrapped the bundle with care, revealing a garland of jasmine just like the one he had bought me that night on the beach at Chowpatty. He stepped behind me, so close that I allowed myself to fall into him, feeling his thighs, abdomen, and chest against the back of my body. He pulled away slightly as he leaned to our right.

"I liked what these did to you last time," he said softly. Gently, he fastened the flowers to my hair. Their sweet scent overcame that of the spices still lingering in the air. I took a greedy breath. I could sense the damp coolness of the flowers through the strands of my hair. My breath quickened.

Arjun turned to face me. He seemed as though he was going to say something. I waited for him for an instant. But soon his right hand was at the small of my back. He pulled me in toward him, his left hand tenderly caressing my neck and his thumb against my lower lip. His eyes seemed almost to gaze beyond me. I felt the last layer of my armor give way and it seemed like there might be no way for me to go back. I leaned forward and kissed him.

The first piano notes of 'Summertime' rang through the room carrying with them, as if on a whiff of a breeze, Ella Fitzgerald's voice. Drop by drop, I felt the tension melt away. I leaned into Arjun's touch.

I had been in love once before. With Neil, the first realization came to me at one singular moment. I never could have imagined sensing that instant with anyone else. But as Arjun leaned in, the expression that came over him suggested that this was his moment.

For me, desire had always been clouded by doubt, by the million reasons to deny it. Not on this night. Arjun, in his questions, sought truth and returned truth in kind. Truth. Simple, unadulterated, like the clank of ceramic on wood. My body was steady underneath me as my lips met his yet again. My hands landed at his waist and I pulled him into me.

Slowly, he swept my hair over my left shoulder, capturing each errant strand. It seemed as if every fiber, every sinuous dendrite of my nerves might rise to meet his touch. His lips glanced my neck just above my collar, once, twice. He traced his fingers along my upper spine. My eyelids closed, sealing out any sensation that sought to compete with his touch. I took a deep breath in, greeted again by the scent of jasmine.

Arjun was taking my tunic off me before I could even finish unbuttoning it. My head got stuck in the neck of the tunic as he rolled it off me and we fell into an explosion of laughter.

"Shit *yaar*, I am totally out of practice!" he whispered.

I took my time as I unbuttoned his collared shirt. Each time I successfully unfastened a button, I looked at him triumphantly.

Arjun raised his brow in jest and grasped me by the small of my back. With his other hand, he caressed my face, making his way to the notch between my collar bones, in between my breasts and on to my waist. His touch was insistent and soon his fingers were at my waist.

From his hair, my hands made their way to the nape of his neck. I grasped him with both hands, fingers intertwined, and pulled him to me. He yielded; his mouth against mine, his chest against mine, his hips against mine. His body's intent was clear.

"Shyama," Arjun whispered through his next kiss.

Caught up in a current that I didn't wish to fight, I didn't hear him.

"Oh God Shyama." His hips pressed deeper into mine. "I want this too—more than I can tell you. Shyama, you see I am all in."

Suddenly, Arjun pulled away. I tried to decipher his body language and words which seemed to be working at cross-purposes. "Arjun, what's wrong?"

His breathing was fast paced and halting. His eyes desperately searched mine. "I didn't want to ruin this night—but I have to tell you. I got the job in New Delhi. I found out just before you got here."

My blood ran cold. I had always known it was a possibility, but perhaps selfishly I had bought into Arjun's notion that the job was a long shot. I had been so busy telling myself that Arjun was just an appealing distraction, that I hadn't really thought through what would happen if he actually got the position. But after the sentiments he had expressed tonight, the implications of the job in Delhi were more than I had bargained for.

"I—I don't know what to say."

"Just tell me what I mean to you. Tonight, I've told you everything—about Avani—about why I am so drawn to you, about the job. But I don't know how you feel. I know you were hurt and that is hard to get through. But you haven't spoken to me about what is in your heart—not once. You haven't told me how you feel about *us*—about what you want from me. I sense this hesitation in you, Shyama. I've wanted to tell you about the job all night but I didn't. I didn't because I was afraid if I told you, you would bolt."

"Hesitation? Arjun, I think I've made it clear what I want."

But I couldn't deny it: I hadn't once said how I felt for him, even as Arjun had confided the same. I was only thinking about our next moment together, nothing beyond that.

"Maybe it's because you were hurt last time. Maybe it's because you've lost faith. But I think you might be closing yourself off from the future you deserve, settling for something less than I am willing to give you. We can be more than a passing summer fling. But you have to open yourself to the possibility."

Arjun's words had struck my core with the shudder of an arrow striking a bull's-eye.

Shaken, I considered him before making my way to where my tunic lay on the ground. With my shoulders slumped, I picked it up.

Arjun walked toward me.

"Shyama?" He reached for my hand. His touch was plaintive. I turned to him. His eyes held mine, waiting for my response. "I don't have all the answers, Shyama. I have nothing but my word to offer you—nothing more than the truth. This thing between us, the New Delhi job, I think we can figure it all out, together, if you'll just give us a try." His voice wasn't hurried, strident, or defensive. He searched my face trying to read whether I believed him.

I knew he was speaking the truth—just as he had done from the first day I met him. In the moment though, the implications, like so many dominoes, collapsed in front of me. What would it mean to be with Arjun? Would I give up my life in the States? What would that mean for all of those whom I loved in America? What would living in India for the long haul mean for all my plans for the future? This wasn't how my story was supposed to go.

Arjun was asking more of me than I was ready for.

I pulled my hand away. "Arjun, I know—I know what you are saying to me. But I—I don't think this is going to work." I felt myself in a hasty retreat. "This is not my world. I don't belong here."

"Come on, Shyamala, we both know that is not what is going on!" He appeared as though physically wounded.

"Well, pray tell, what *is* going on here?"

"I think that you have some concrete notion that your life has to go a certain way and this whole experience with me, with India, with taking risks, losing control, and letting go of expectation—it scares the hell out of you."

All this time, I had been so guarded with my sentiments, so careful not to get carried away but here I was, walking right into another heartbreak. Anger was rising within me, at first reticent and bubbling and then uncontained as if from a geyser, anger at myself for letting my guard down. I lashed out at him with an accusation that, even as I said it, I knew was blatantly unfair.

"How did this become about me? You got a job in New Delhi. That's great. But I can't just commit to pulling up stakes."

"I am not asking for you to be the one to give everything up. I am just asking for us to talk this out."

A silence arose between us. Even in this *gulley*, away from the main street, I could hear the meep-meep of the rickshaws on the road. They sounded exactly like the Road Runner as he stymied the stupid coyote in those cartoons I watched as a kid on Saturday mornings.

"I think you want this as much as I do but you are afraid that your life is going off script."

I glowered at Arjun, my tone frigid. "Well, sounds like you have me all figured out. This was a mistake. I shouldn't have come here."

Without looking back, I made my way to the front door.

"Wait, Shyama, it's bloody late, let me take you home," Arjun pleaded.

"I don't need to be saved Arjun, not now and not by you." I stepped into the corridor and slammed the door behind me.

For a while, I stood outside Arjun's flat, stung and furious. Over time, I became conscious of my surroundings. I was standing alone in an apartment building in Bombay and night had fallen. The honking of car horns, a measure of the city's wakefulness, had dissipated. I felt the reticence of any woman traveling in an unknown city after dark. Bombay, London, LA, Athens, or Saigon. It is a world full of countless, intangible threats. Threats that, despite all my independence, capability, and authority in the light of day, were undeniably real in the night. Furious about Arjun's accusations and the realities of our modern world, I was unable to decide what to do next.

Finally, I flipped my phone open. It was well past midnight. I had told Vini that Arjun would drop me off by 11:30 p.m. She had called four times, undoubtedly worried that I wasn't home. I was about to ring her when the phone buzzed.

"Hallo?"

"Subhash?" I was utterly relieved to hear a familiar voice.

"Yes, yes. I am calling from my new mobile!" Subhash said, his excitement uncontained.

"Hey, congrats!" I tried to sound excited for him.

"Listen, where you are? Your auntyji made hundred calls trying to find you and finally she has reached me after getting my number from Natashaji."

"I am in Santa Cruz. Just left my friend's place, I was just on my way home."

Subhash didn't say anything for a second and the phone connection filled with a series of unasked questions. I blessed the dear man for leaving them unsaid.

"You do not move from your place, I am coming to bring you to the home," he instructed. "I'll let your auntyji know."

I was beyond grateful. I gave him Arjun's address.

I sat in the corridor outside Arjun's flat, exhausted. In the span of a few hours, I had gone from pleasantly musing about Arjun and the evening we'd have together to realizing that I was still alone—that I might always be alone. Maybe my father had a point. For all our planning and posturing, our sense of control over the future was delusion.

When Subhash arrived downstairs, I was so relieved to see him that I nearly embraced him.

Seemingly sensing my state of mind, Subhash was quiet on the way home. Without a word, he took me the long way.

"This is not a shortcut, just thinking you might be liking to see the sea before heading to the home."

He cruised along Chowpatty Seaface. A quarter moon hovered above the city. Hardly a soul was out that night and, in short measure, we found ourselves at Marine Drive where the coastal road made a graceful arch as it embraced Back Bay. Illuminated, as it was on this evening, the semi-circular coastline was transformed into the fabled Queen's Necklace, each streetlamp along the curved road a glinting jewel, shimmering in the waters of the bay. Had it been any other night, my eyes would have settled upon the elegant pattern of lights studding the coast. But on this night, I found my eyes drawn beyond—to the sandy shore and the foamy waves battering it and then to the vast obsidian expanse of the Arabian Sea that extended seamlessly into the cosmos. It was a breathtaking blackness—unfathomable and consuming.

"Subhash, why did you come to pick me up?" I asked as we veered back toward Walkeshwar, suddenly feeling ashamed of the way I was indulging in self-pity.

Subhash glanced at me through the rear-view mirror before speaking, seemingly perplexed by the question.

"Are you not a guest in my country? If it is so, then it is my duty to watch after you. Are you not another man's child? Then should I not look after you the way I hope your father would look after my child?" He peeked at the mirror again. "Ms. Mehta, whatever has happened, it is done. Not to worry, tomorrow is another day. And there is another one after that, no? Who is to know what will happen?"

"Shyamala, please call me Shyamala. Subhash, you are a true friend and I thank you." The last few words were soundless, unable to escape the surge of emotion in my chest.

When we finally arrived at Vini's, Subhash and I got out of the car. I pulled out my wallet to pay him for his time. He placed his hand on mine and shook his head sternly, his expression admonishing.

"Not to worry, Shyamalaji, I was driving the company car with the company petrol only!"

He smiled as he watched me enter Vini's building before getting back into the car. I waved to him until the Honda disappeared from my sight. It occurred to me, as I shuffled home, that Subhash would've come to get me whether he had a company car full of company petrol or not.

And, no matter the hour, I was sure he would've made his good deed seem like no great effort at all.

Chapter 28

Mumbai, September 2006

Vini was at the dining table waiting for me when I arrived at the flat. She was nursing a teacup, sipping pensively. She slid a second cup of the *sakar-badam* milk across the table, inviting me to take a seat. She sized me up for a second.

"Arjun?"

I nodded, holding the cup without sipping from it.

"Let's go stand on the balcony a bit," Vini suggested.

We slid outside into the tepid night. It was quiet, save the errant flapping of bird wings from a tree nearby and the pulsating "frrrr-frrrr" sound of a person pedaling a bicycle. It was the closest thing to silence I had heard since arriving in India. Funny, I thought, how one could hear silence—how one could sense a thing in its negative. I suddenly missed the serenity of my garden in LA, and the silence of home.

Vini didn't ask questions, apparently content to stand next to me, her shoulder just glancing mine.

After about fifteen minutes, she spoke. "Seems hard to believe, Shyamala, but I still remember it—what it's like to feel alone. But I think sometimes that our expectations cloud our perceptions. The hard thing is to free ourselves from those expectations so we can see the truth that surrounds us. Look at me, things didn't work out the way I wanted. But alone is not a word I would use to describe myself and the life I have had. From reading my morning newspaper, to my chats with Attaji, to watching Shalu grow up, to this time I've had with you—my life is full."

I nodded, understanding the truth in her words but grappling with how exactly they applied to me.

Vini tried to suppress a yawn.

"Thank you Maasi. It's late, if you need to call it a day that is okay with me. I'll head to bed in a bit."

She squeezed my shoulder slightly and left me.

I thought about Vini's past and took solace in being understood without the need for explanation.

When I finally retired, I found myself unable to sleep. The oppressive humidity quickly grew unbearable. After a restless twenty minutes of tossing about in bed, I got up, turned on my light and opened *The Good Earth*.

I was nearing the end of the book, had already mourned the death of the farmer's wife and taken more than a bit of pleasure as each of her sons refused to work on their greedy father's land. But that night, try as I might, I couldn't seem to get through more than a paragraph. I began aimlessly flipping through the book. Suddenly the pages fell open. But this time I hadn't stumbled on the photograph, but rather the light-blue paper of an aerogram.

I hadn't seen an aerogram in years. When I was a child, my parents frequently sent them to family in India. But modern methods of communication had rendered the aerogram—a letter that folded to create its own envelope with cut-rate prepaid postage stamped on to an exterior fold—obsolete. Why would one take the time organizing one's thoughts and then penning words on to paper, when one could simply pick up the phone and ring someone half a world away for pennies on the minute? Aerograms were a relic of the past, like typewriters and patience.

The aerogram had yellowed at the edges. I held the brittle paper, turning it so I could see the address written on its front. The words were in my mother's hand. She had addressed the letter to my father in Buffalo from India. From the postmark, I could see that it had reached its destination. Interesting, I thought, that the aerogram and the old photograph should have made it into the same book. Before I realized, I found myself delicately unfolding the trifold paper, noting that it had been opened before. The script was small and slanted and it covered every square inch of paper. I was surprised to see it was written in English. On some lines, the last letter was cut off, as if my mother was writing more than the page could contain.

The letter was dated April 22, 1973, nearly four months after I was born.

> Dear Dev,
> I realize that this letter is long overdue. I hope you and Shyamala are well. I am sure Shyamala is thriving under your watchful eyes.
>
> Ba and Vini have welcomed me here. Ba has grown much older and Vini far sterner since we left. Bombay has changed, even in the two years that we have lived away from it. I am sure you would adjust well. But I feel a stranger to the place.
>
> Something has changed in me as well since Shyamala's birth. For you, the world simply carried on the day she was born. For me, the world stopped and the ground beneath me shifted. I

have tried and tried to regain my footing but the harder I try, the faster I fall. Time and time again, I have failed to write these words down. But I realize, I must. I owe you that much.

One day, not long before I came to India, I made a grave mistake. It was a horrible day, a day in which I could not console our girl. Out of an inexplicable desperation, I abandoned her in the cold. It wasn't for long, but it was long enough. Once her screams quieted, my mind became clear. I knew I had made a dreadful mistake. But it was reason that brought me back to her side, not feeling. And that was what disturbed me the most. Why didn't I feel anything for her? Why didn't I feel anything at all?

Now that you know, you must be thinking many things. You must be disgusted at who I am. What kind of person walks away from their child in the miserable cold of winter? What kind of mother? I have been asking myself since the day it happened. I will not excuse the inexcusable just as I would not ask you to forgive the unforgivable. But motherhood is not so natural to some of us. It asks too much.

Dev, I was not honest with you when we met. I did not tell you what I had known all along. I had never wished for this life. Long ago I knew that being a wife—being a mother—was not for me. It is just that things happen—things one does not intend—sometimes circumstances are set into motion and take us in unexpected directions. You must remember these things when you feel angry.

You are a good man—kind and funny. That is why I married you. You made it possible for me to shut out the past—at least for a while. But the past can cast its long shadow upon us, and I have been caught up in its darkness.

I have made a decision. It is a decision I am making because, in the end, it is best for you and Shyamala. I am not coming back to America. Please forgive me, dearest Dev, but I cannot.

Sincerely,
Pramila

My eyes hung on the last two sentences for several minutes. I folded the aerogram back up, placing it unceremoniously back in the book where I had found it.

I sat bolt upright in bed and slowly put the book on my night-stand. My mother had abandoned me, not once, but *twice*. Was this the secret that had kept us apart—the unspoken burden that had weighed our relationship down for all these years? It was as if the entire foundation of my life, my understanding of my beginnings, had been based on artifice. I suppose I should have felt as though my life had been upended by the content of the letter. But I didn't *feel* upended. If anything, I felt a sense of clarity. In fragments, I was coming to know parts of my mother's past. I was beginning to understand how those struggles explained our present—why she never spoke of her life in India, why she could never seem to share those memories with me. Hardly in her mid-twenties, she had lost my grandfather, the person in life to whom she was closest. When she finally regained her footing from losing him and started a new life with my father, she found herself in this deep unexplained melancholy. She must have been suffering from post-partum depression. Did that term even exist back then? Without a name to give her affliction of the mind, did she merely see it as a defect in her character?

Of all the revelations though, it was the one that Vini had mentioned that I obsessed over. My mother had aspirations that didn't include marriage and motherhood, aspirations that actually precluded motherhood. My mother, the woman who seemed to be in such a hurry to marry me off before my biological clock ran out, hadn't wanted to be a mother herself.

I turned off the light, flopped on my back, and stared at the ceiling.

An old book can tell more than one story, I thought to myself. There was the story written on the pages and the story of those who had once pored over its words. From a secondhand bookshop to my grandfather's hands in the days before his death, to my mother's in the months after, to my father's hands while she was in the midst of her crisis, and now, to mine as I puzzled over her past, *The Good Earth* had borne witness to almost forty years of my family's history. Was it coincidence that each of us turned to the book during hard times? Probably.

Still, I couldn't help but feel that the book's binding held together much more than simply its pages.

And there was another story, one I already knew. Despite all the struggles, despite the despair that was penned on to my mother's aerogram, she *had* come back to me. Looking back, she had always been there—every soccer game, every award assembly, every graduation, every milestone of any importance in my life. Even during my teen angst-riddled years, when I thought I would rather have been left alone. Even after Neil. She had devoted herself completely to our family. What prompted her to do that when she knew her calling lay elsewhere? What kind of love allowed for such a sacrifice?

◆ ◆ ◆

After a sleepless night, I awoke to another sweltering day. Trying to keep busy, I put on my jogging shoes and hit the pavement. As I emerged from the landing and out into the sun, I thought about how, after months of living in it, I was running out of adjectives to describe the misery of the heat. Maybe this is how people learn to acclimatize, maybe they just run out of ways to complain.

As I ran out of the front gate of Vini's complex, a man stood by, watching me. I took my usual route, making my way up Ridge Road toward the Hanging Gardens. Usually, I continued my jog in the gardens, but today I slowed to a walk and eventually sat down under the protective branches of a pipal tree. I wiped the sweat off my brow and basked in the slight ocean breeze. After a morning of running from them, it was here that my thoughts caught up with me.

I remembered my mother's words inscribed in the letter. *Long ago I knew that being a wife—being a mother—was not for me.* How ignorant I had been about my mother's past! About my own! Though I hadn't exactly been prescient about my imaginings for my future either. For all intents and purposes, Arjun and I were done. It was just as well. I'd been delirious for the past few months, perhaps it was time for a slug of reality. How the hell would we have made it work anyway? It was madness to think that either one of us would move half a world away to be with the other. It was insanity that I could ever consider this place home. No, it was better this way. End of story.

I continued along the footpath to the vista point where I could view Chowpatty Beach and Back Bay. I stood in the sun, taking in the city below. I couldn't imagine it had room for me.

I had to face the truth. Marriage just might not happen for me. Thirty years later, my situation was not very different from Vini maasi's. One generation later and half a world away, why had the accepted recipe for a woman's domestic fulfillment remained the same? Find a man. Fall in love. Get married. Have children. Live happily ever after. The end.

On my way home, I stopped at a little corner shop and treated myself to a bottle of almost cold Limca soda. I was about to take a sip when someone touched my shoulder to get my attention.

"Miss?"

I turned with a start. It was the same man that stood beside the front gate at Maasi's house as I had left for my run earlier that morning.

"Yes?" I felt uneasy and hoped that others were within earshot.

"I have been waiting for your aunt for some time but she has not been home."

I took a good look at the guy. He couldn't have been over fifty. He was thickly built and stood about six feet in height. He had a square jaw, a sharpish nose, and no mustache. I racked my mind trying to figure out if I might have met him before. He wore a starched, collared shirt and tailored dress slacks. A new round of sweat rolled down the side of my face.

"Could you kindly deliver a message?" Though the sentence was asked as a question, the man was not offering an option.

The clerk behind the counter watched warily.

"Your aunt owes us some money. Not a big sum. But she will need to pay it soon." He spoke slowly and clearly, making sure his point was not mistaken. And though his voice wasn't overtly threatening, an "or else" seemed to be implied.

Blood pulsated behind my eardrums. What had Vini gotten herself into? I did my best to restrain an overwhelming sense of panic. I was the sheltered product of immigrant parents in suburban America. I paid my taxes, obeyed crosswalks, and turned my library books in two days early. I was patently unwise to the ways of *goondas*, thugs, hoodlums, or blackmailers no matter how well dressed they were or what country they came from.

"I don't know who you are or what you're talking about. I think you should leave us alone," I said, as loudly as I could muster. My breath was fast and my mind was spinning. I put the Limca back on the counter not having taken a sip and walked out of the store, trying my best to seem casual.

Once I was on the street, I immediately turned toward Vini's place. As far as I could tell, the man hadn't followed me. I walked with haste until I had turned the corner. Then, I ran.

Behind the gates of Vini's complex, breathing heavily, I finally allowed myself to think. After months of suspecting something, this interaction was my first confirmation. But confirmation of what exactly? Sure, there were Vini's furtive phone calls and the odd late-night communications with Rajesh, but those didn't add up to much.

Heart still thudding against my breastbone, I wiped my brow as I entered Vini's building. I had hardly climbed two steps before I noticed something was wrong. Neighbors had assembled along the stairwell going up to Vini's landing. Panic gripped me again. Had something happened to her?

I wove in and out of the congregation and found my way to the top of the stairwell, standing on my toes and craning my neck to find Vini. I caught her standing near the door, holding a bag of groceries, unperturbed. It appeared as though she had just arrived and had been drawn into conversation before she had a chance to enter the house.

"Nothing, absolutely noth-ing is coming out of those taps," an old woman next to me said, raising her hand to her forehead and flicking it forward in typical Indian fashion.

"I turned and turned the faucet but there is not a drop of water, *yaar*. Not a drop since two days back!" said Pankajbhai standing a few steps above our landing.

"*Hai-la!* I mean we are storing the water in the buckets but even this can last only so much time. How is one to make *chai* or cook without even a bit of water?" I couldn't make out who was speaking, but her frustration resonated. Heads nodded in agreement.

"All this money we are paying to the tanker company. Year in and year out we have paid them. Where is that water now?" asked Jagdishbhai.

Kaushik uncle emerged on to the landing from the stairwell above, slowly making his way past fellow residents to a spot where he could get everyone's attention. He was frazzled, clearly shouldering the burden of being the secretary of the building association.

"Listen everybody," he said. "I warned you all yesterday that the water might run out—"

"That is not the question. We knew the municipality water would run out. We are asking *why* we are not getting anything from the tankers!" Jagdishbhai interrupted.

"*Arré bhai*, let me finish. I just spoke to the tankerrr company. They are not able to fulfill the demand—"

"Fulfill the demand?" Champa stepped into view. "What kind of bloody *dholia* talk is this? The British left this country more than fifty years ago—save us the fancy bullshit, *yaar*—we need to know when we will be getting our water!" Most of the neighbors seemed to agree.

"Champaben is right. With all the extra money we are paying, when will they see fit to give us what is rightfully ours, what we have already paid for?" asked Jagdishbhai.

"Don't forget that I have paid also," Kaushik uncle said defensively. "Just like you, I have no water in my taps, no water for cooking, no water for washing. The company has told me to inquire again this afternoon. For now, I suggest for you all to buy some bottled water for at least the cooking."

"After we have spent so much money to pay for this bloody tanker, we have to pay even more?" Champa's tone was admonishing.

Vini, who had been silent, finally broke in.

"Under the circumstances, I think Kaushikbhai is doing the best he can. What is he to do? Last time I checked, the apartment association cannot make it rain. Prime Minister Manmohan Singh doesn't have this power, even you do not have this power, Champa."

From the steps, I could see that Champa had a direct line of sight to Vini. Unhappy with the way she had been addressed, she glowered at my aunt.

"Ahhh, Vini speaks *yaar*. And when she speaks, everybody must listen, isn't it?" Her head bobbed back and forth and her eyebrows rose. "Even when she cannot keep her own affairs in order!"

"Champa, look at me, I am an old woman. Until Shyamala came for a visit, I lived alone with my books. I doubt anyone cares about my affairs, especially when there is no water to drink."

Champa grinned ruefully. She had a score to settle. I did not like the direction the conversation was taking.

"I am sure many would be interested to know how you have been carrying on. You act as if you care more about that maid and her father than your neighbors," Champa said.

"I certainly shouldn't care for them any less."

The stairwell was silent, nobody so much as shuffled a foot. Water or not, the confrontation between these two women had been a long time in the making and the crowd had been waiting for it.

"I wonder if there is a reason. Don't think we haven't noticed those late nights when the girl's father stops by. What is his name again?"

Jagdishbhai, who was standing on the landing not far from Champa, smirked. It seemed that Attaji uncle was right, some of the neighbors had been talking.

"Rajesh. His name is Rajesh. And Champa, if you have something to say, just say it already. I need to go make dinner." If Vini was annoyed by Champa's accusations, she didn't show it. In fact, she almost seemed to be goading her.

Champa seemed to relish this moment of attention. She wasn't going to play her hand quite yet.

"Why don't you tell us why it is that man, Rajesh, stops by so late at night? Surely, he can't be fixing your car in the dark?"

Champa's innuendo didn't bother Vini, but it certainly bothered me. How dare she make accusations in this setting! What business was it of hers? Angry, I pushed my way up the final few steps to the landing.

"What the hell is going on here? People here are concerned about their water and you bring up this nonsense! It's none of your business what my aunt is doing and with whom in the evening."

The gaggle on the staircase above me took a collective breath.

I glanced over at Champa, provoked by her smug expression. She had overstepped one too many times. As if she were better than the rest of her neighbors! Champa, the woman whose son had an affair with a married woman. The woman whose son would rather live in a flat in the suburbs than live under her roof. The same son who detested the avarice of those with means—people just like his mother, who didn't bother to consider those with much less. What would happen if she only knew the truth about her perfect son?

Thus far, my disdain had been just for Champa, but now I could feel my fury at Arjun creeping in. Just a night ago he had accused me of being fearful of going off script—afraid to take risks. Yet all this time he had been hiding in his Santa Cruz flat, keeping his love life a secret from his mother, never telling her how he felt about her gossip and greed. What would happen if I told her right here and right now?

"Before you go and criticize others, maybe you should take a good, hard look at yourself and your own family!" Though I couldn't see the people who'd gathered on the stairwell above, I realized that the hush in the crowd meant everyone was waiting for my next words. Was I going to follow up with some accusation of my own?

Vini shook her head, her eyes imploring me to stop.

In the stillness of the moment, everyone on the stairwell heard the footsteps as someone made their way up the stairs. Neighbors on the landing turned their heads toward the sound while the neighbors below parted ways as the person made her way through the throng.

It was Shalu.

She walked self-consciously through the crush of people, clearly wondering why so many eyes were now fixed on her. The landing was overloaded, but the neighbors made room for Shalu. Then, two by two, every set of eyes settled back upon me.

I was incensed about Champa's accusations of Vini and furious with Arjun. Consumed by that anger, I wanted to lash out. But as I considered Shalu and Vini, I realized something. If I divulged the truth about Arjun in this moment, if I told Champa about his disdain for the hard, thoughtless avarice that seemed to cloud her opinions, it would be for the worst possible reason. There would be no going back. Not for Vini and Champa. Not for Vini and me.

And never for Arjun. I'd never be able to forgive myself.

Shalu raised her eyebrows and spoke barely above a whisper. "What is happening?"

I glared at Champa. "Nothing important. We're just demonstrating that in times of crisis, adults love their petty little distractions." I shook off my indignation, feeling a burst of tenderness for the girl.

Vini caught my eye. She nodded her head slightly in approval. The crowd still held its breath.

"These fine people were complaining about how little water there is because of the drought and all. I am sure they realize that there are parts of the city that hardly get water even when there is no drought," Vini said.

At this statement, the crowd, which had suppressed its opinion thus far, suddenly erupted.

"*Arré yaar*, this is no time for lectures about the slums, Viniben!" someone yelled.

Jagdishbhai and Pankajbhai started yelling to each other across the stairwell. Other side conversations competed to be heard. Voices boomed through the building.

"If everything is so perfect there, why don't you go live with your sister in America!" someone shouted from the stairwell above.

Champa sneered and began speaking conspiratorially to a group of women who surrounded her, taking an opportunity to scowl at us. Kaushik uncle had been swarmed by the neighbors who now peppered him with questions. The people on the stairwell below tried to join the fray.

Vini, Shalu, and I looked at each other. Rather unexpectedly, Shalu smiled.

"You two really know how to start a big *dhamaal*."

"A ruckus?" I asked.

Shalu shook her head, not understanding.

"Like, a commotion?" I could barely hear myself speak over the uproar behind me.

Shalu nodded, turning to Vini who shrugged her shoulders without disagreeing.

"What should we do now?" I asked Vini.

"I'm hungry, aren't you?" she inquired as she raised her grocery bags and ushered us into the flat.

Chapter 29

Bombay, April 1973

Pramila set foot on the airplane for Bombay with no intention of returning to America or her family. Once she reached India, she would write Dev a letter explaining herself. It was clear in her mind: Dev and Shyamala would be better off without her. Dev was young and could remarry and Shyamala would have a mother worthy of her.

Pramila felt driven, an intense anticipation growing stronger as the distance between her and her family in India grew shorter. She imagined her father, her mother and Vini standing outside the airport waiting to greet her. She had to remind herself that Papa was no longer there.

There would be much to explain.

Time had rendered her mother and sister strangers to her. In the two years and four months since Pramila had moved to the US, Ba seemed to have aged at least five. Her white sari hung loosely on her thin frame, revealing the angle of her collarbones. Her corneas had developed an opaque green ring around their circumference. Vini seemed far sterner than she remembered. Vague though it was, Pramila was conscious of a sense of disappointment brewing within her.

"*Dikra. America jaine patni thai gai, ma thai gai.* My dear, you have gone to America and become a wife and mother. Now you have returned to India and returned to me," Ba said as she held Pramila in her arms, her eyes misty. She continued to hold Pramila's hand after releasing her from the embrace.

In the presence of her sister and mother, here in Bombay, Pramila expected to feel relief. Everything was as it should have been. She was home. Nothing else should have mattered.

Vini continued to stand behind their mother with her hands at her sides.

"Vini, have you nothing to say?" Ba prodded her elder daughter.

"Why have you not brought Shyamala?" Vini considered Pramila with the conditional affection of a sister.

"*Chal* Vini. Come on Vini, Pramila can explain all later," Ba said.

"Why to wait? I am just hoping to understand."

Ba looked sternly at Vini.

If she sensed Ba's glare, Vini did not flinch. "I just cannot understand. *Shyamala ketli nani che.* Shyamala is so young. How can you leave such a small child behind? She needs her mother. How is Dev to care for her alone?"

"It was Dev's idea—"

"But he cannot take care of baby when he is at work."

"There is a lady in the building, she is just a few doors down from us."

"So, you have left her with an *ajaani*, someone you do not even know?"

"*Arré Vini! Shanti rakh.* Take it easy. Let your sister at least settle herself before you start asking and asking questions. What kind of welcome home is this?"

On the way to the flat, Ba peppered her with news from India. The India-Pakistan war and crop failures had led to crippling inflation. The Indian government had launched Project Tiger, a conservation program to save the endangered animal. But Pramila only half-listened. She was busy gazing out of the window at the cityscape, taking note of all that had changed. Her body anticipated every turn on the route home. In a while, they would be veering left and away from the ocean. Not long, and they would be home.

She opened her eyes with a start when the taxi continued straight. She nearly shouted out, wondering why the driver was leading them astray. Pramila kicked herself. As per Papa's wishes, Jayant uncle had indeed sold several of their properties allowing Ba and Vini to move from the tiny old flat in Sikkanagar to a larger apartment in Chowpatty. They had written to her about their move in much detail last year. Pramila had backed the idea at the time but now, confronted by the inconstancy of life, she bristled at the changes. Her past, who she was, it was all slipping away. Papa was gone and with him the chance for the life she had wanted—and now the flat in Sikkanagar, the perpetual landmark of her childhood, was gone as well. She felt as though she was walking on a suspension bridge with missing wooden slats. Each time she stepped on the slats that appeared intact, these too gave way under her feet. With each step she tried to regain her footing but only found herself even more off balance. She was not sure how much longer she could hang on.

The new flat in Chowpatty was a stone's throw from the sea. By all measures, it was an improvement from the one in Sikkanagar. It had its own bathroom, a more spacious kitchen, and guest room. At high tide, the apartment filled with the sounds of the ebb and flow of the sea. During low tide, however, Pramila was overwhelmed by a salty, fishy odor that seemed to saturate the apartment. It was so pervasive that it followed her into each room, even finding its way to Pramila's nose and taste buds. Sometimes it tasted like her meals had been harvested from a fishnet. How her mother and Vini could stand the odor, Pramila could not fathom. Not only did they seem unperturbed by the odor, it was like they didn't notice it at all. When the sea waters receded, Pramila often found herself drifting into the guest room as it was farthest from the sea, unconsciously trying to escape the malodorous wake. And, more than once, her nose led her out of the building and into the streets of Bombay.

One April morning at low tide, shortly after her arrival in India, Pramila headed out of the front door before Vini and Ba had awakened. With all haste, she moved away from the seafront, walking toward Opera House. This was a part of the city she had walked innumerable times in the past. But as a child, anticipating the open sea and the hours of play that lay at land's end, she paid no attention to what was above or around her. Today, she was careful to note every detail of her route.

She continued along past her favorite Parsi cafe. The savory smell of boiling pulses and onions blended into *dhansak* alternated with the sweet smell of *nankhatai*. *Nankhatai*. She could practically taste the sweetness and feel of the flaky biscuits as if they were melting in her mouth. She and Vini used to save their *paise* and *annas* so they could buy little pink boxes of the delectable treats to eat on the way to Chowpatty Beach. No matter how much they tried, by the time they reached the shore, the box was empty save for a few crumbs. She took in a breath of air, hoping for just another whiff of the *nankhatai*. But mixed in with the delightful sweetness was a trace of the fishy odor that she had tried to escape.

Pramila continued inland. She veered past a *chaiwala* peddling *masala* tea. She cleared his cart, barely avoiding a large heap of trash. It was interesting, she thought, how conscious one had to be when walking along the streets of Bombay. A misplaced step here or there, and one could find one's foot in a pile of refuse or something far worse. This street wariness was a skill that native Bombayites developed without even noticing. It was a habit recognized as such only after it was broken, as in Pramila's case, by time spent in her hamlet outside Buffalo. There heaps of trash did not line the street. This was true of nearly everywhere she had traveled in the United States. Americans, she reflected, set their feet on the ground without a second thought about what they might be stepping in.

Pramila crossed Warerkar Bridge over the train tracks. She took the footpath to the Royal Opera House building. How many times had she passed its immense baroque facade without giving it another thought? Here it was, with its European-inspired, elaborately sculpted marble frieze and romantic old wrought-iron balconies that hovered above the city—and she was just noticing it as if for the first time. She thought of Papa again.

Deeper and deeper into the city she went, toward Girgaon through Khetwadi, farther and farther from the sea, but she still could not shake the smell. At Nanubhai Desai Road, Pramila veered toward Sikkanagar.

Soon Pramila was standing across the street from her old flat, gazing at the home where her father had breathed his last breath. The paint on the building had faded since she had last visited, exposing the concrete undersurface. The clothesline outside her old flat had been lowered, its position droopy and awkward. Inside, electric lights illuminated the flat. She should have had no expectation that life would have remained constant in the time since she had left. And yet the changes troubled her.

When she returned to the flat in Chowpatty, she found Vini sitting on the kitchen floor, sifting flour. Ba was nowhere to be seen.

"*Kyan gai ti?* Where did you go?" Vini turned to Pramila but did not meet her sister's gaze.

"*Chakkar mate.* Just for a walk."

Pramila stood in the living room studying a tiny brass figurine of Ganesh that sat upon the teak table just outside the kitchen, waiting for her sister to speak. She grabbed the figurine and felt the cool metal against her skin. She turned back to Vini.

Vini remained silent. She placed the sifted flour into a large jar. She placed the dishes noisily into the sink. She walked from the kitchen into the bedroom and from the bedroom into the bathroom and then back into the kitchen. She moved from room to room with great purpose. Pramila knew what this meant. Vini had something on her mind and didn't know how to say it.

For days now Pramila had tried to make small talk with her sister but Vini was cool, disinterested. For days Pramila had felt the prickly sensation of her sister's judgment against her skin. As she watched Vini move to and fro, Pramila suddenly felt anger bubble up within her. She was struck by the ferocity of the emotion. For days, she had done everything to avoid this moment but now, she could not restrain herself.

"*Maherbani kar*, Vini. Do me a favor, Vini. If you have something to say, just say it!" She turned the heavy brass Ganesh over and over in her hand.

Vini scowled. "You want to know? I will tell you! How does a mother of a baby leave her alone and come halfway across the world by herself? I just cannot understand it."

"I have hardly left her alone. Dev is there and the aunty—"

"*Hai, hai!* God forbid that I forget about the aunty! Come on Pramila! How could some stranger possibly replace a mother?"

"What do you know of it? It is all so easy for you! Sitting back and judging. You know nothing of being a mother."

Vini winced. "You are right. I don't know anything of being a mother, other than that I always wanted to be one. It was not meant to be. But I will tell you one thing, if I had been so lucky as you," she said, pointing with her index finger, "I would not have abandoned my child."

"Lucky? Who decides this? You think I asked for this? Did you ever think that I might not have wanted to be a wife or a mother? That day Papa died—"

"*Arré bhagvan.* Listen to yourself! You are still living in the past. You're not even denying that you have abandoned Shyamala! You are so focused upon what it is that you want—what of Shyamala? Did she have a choice? What of Dev? You wanted to be a *shramaniji*. I wanted to have a family. We both wanted different lives. Tough! We have only one *life*. We have been given what we have been given and there is no running or hiding from it."

"You are having all the answers no? Did it ever occur to you why I left Shyamala?"

"There is no excuse for abandoning your child." Vini spoke coldly.

"So that is it? There is nothing more to say—full stop?" Pramila was pulsating with rage, the heaves of her breath stifled by the fishy stench. "Is this because you are jealous?"

Vini laughed joylessly. "You know what Pramila? There was a time that I *was* jealous. But you see, I have stopped dreaming of the past, stopped expecting a change in the story. Papa died. I never married. You married Dev and went to America. I am alone. That is the way it will always be. What purpose does it serve to be jealous?"

"None, I suppose. Just as there is no purpose in my trying to explain what happened. You have made up your mind and nothing is going to change it." With that, Pramila stormed out of the flat, slamming the door behind her. She was down the stairs and back on the street again. She listened for Vini's footsteps behind her but heard nothing.

In her hand she still held the brass Ganesh, only now with such force that her fingers had become white.

◆ ◆ ◆

Pramila boarded the first bus neither knowing nor caring where it took her. Luckily, she had stashed money in her sari blouse that morning. She took a seat behind the driver, listening for the click of the conductor's ticket puncher.

She opened her hand to reveal the object within.

As a girl, Pramila had marveled over Ganesh's S-shaped trunk, wavy ears, and rotund body. Like the other children, Pramila had developed an affection for the plump and lovable god before she was old enough to understand the story of how he got the head of an elephant. When she was five or six, Papa told her one version of the story.

You see, he had said, *Parvati was a goddess with immense powers. Ganesha was her son. But not just any son. Parvati created Ganesha by breathing life into a likeness she had drawn in turmeric paste. Ganesha was the most loyal of sons. When Parvati bathed, she asked him to keep guard at the front door. One day, Parvati's husband Shiva came home to find this unknown boy blocking his entrance into his own house. Enraged, Shiva demanded the boy move out of his way. When Ganesha refused, Shiva ordered his army to remove the boy. The entire army failed to defeat and remove Ganesha so Shiva himself had to fight the boy. Shiva was a god as well, you see, and he defeated Ganesha, cutting off his head with his trident and killing Ganesha instantly.*

At first, Pramila did not hear Papa's last sentence. She was busy wondering how Ganesha could fight an entire army without his mother taking notice. *That was a very long bath Parvati took,* she thought. Then, suddenly, the last part of the tale sunk in. *Shiva, the Lord Shiva, cut off Ganesha's head?* Pramila asked. She began to cry.

Poor Papa. He never had a chance to tell the rest of the story—the part where the devastated Parvati threatened to destroy the Earth unless Shiva met two demands. One: that her son be brought back to life. Two: that her son become God among gods. Shiva immediately regretted his actions and acquiesced to Parvati's demands. He asked Lord Brahma to bring to him the head of the first creature to cross his path. Brahma returned with the head of an elephant. Shiva placed it atop Ganesha's body and brought him back to life.

As the bus made it through Bombay, Pramila imagined Parvati, shattered by the sight of her slain son, willing to destroy creation itself unless Ganesha was made to live again. This was what a mother did for her child. Pramila peered out of the window again, conscious of the fishy odor. *I am no Parvati,* she thought.

She got off the bus near Zaveri Bazaar. The streets teemed with people, taxi*walas, chaiwalas,* garland sellers, costume-jewelry hawkers, wedding shoppers, children in uniform headed home from school, and just plain loiterers. The alleys and lanes seemed much narrower than she remembered, jammed with storefronts on either side. Pramila meandered around, any concept of the hour forgotten in this timeworn part of Bombay. Around dusk, the mass of people around her rose like a groundswell, gathering her up and propelling her along Mumbadevi Road. She was ushered along a short distance. In front of her lay the Mumbadevi Temple, its elaborate steeple rising skyward, the sound of bells announcing the time for evening prayer. And soon another flood of people swept her along, this time into the temple. She did not fight the surge, almost relishing her surrender to its will.

She entered the modestly lit temple just as the *aarti* was about to start. The smell of incense emanating from its walls was as much a permanent fixture as the idols around her. For the first time that day, the fishy odor was nearly imperceptible. The surge of people now pushed her into the deepest recesses of the building, where behind pounded silver doors stood the statue of the fierce-eyed, bejeweled Mumbadevi. The goddess shimmered, consumed by the golden light of the *diya* that the priests held before her. In twos and threes and fours, people placed their hands on a silver dish upon which a lit *diya* sat. They placed an offering on the dish and then reverently swayed the dish, making the flame dance in homage to the goddess. Pramila hummed the prayer, allowing the devotees around her to fill in the words. She closed her eyes to immerse herself completely into the rhythm, still sensing the amber glow of the flame as it moved. Her mind emptied. Her body felt weightless. Everyone around her disappeared. Only the golden light and the music remained.

Through closed eyelids, she sensed the light flicker rapidly and then grow intense. She thought something may have caught fire. With a jolt, she opened her eyes. But the flame burned softly, reflecting vaguely upon the silver doors.

The sound of gongs now filled the temple, tinny and resonant. Pramila feared that the voices of temple-goers might be lost among its notes. But they prevailed until the end, even as the prayer came to its final crescendo. *Mata-ki Jai*. Victory to the feminine divine. The final words reverberated through her with unforeseen force even as the gongs fell silent. Devotees dropped their heads in unison.

Pramila did not bow her head as the others did. Nor did she join her hands in front of her chest. Abruptly, she began moving toward the exit.

"*Prasad nahin lena hai*? You don't want the offering? Come, you must take," said a man.

Pramila heard him but did not respond. She moved briskly, the way a thief might abscond with his loot without drawing attention to himself. She too had come into possession of something she had been seeking. She had traveled half a world away to find it. She too feared that at any instant it might be lost to her again.

Pramila stepped out of the temple and started for Mumbadevi Road. The indigo of the sky plunged into a hundred shades of purple and pink and orange and yellow. She took long strides, fleeing the desperation that she had shed in that temple. But it was in pursuit and catching up quickly.

"What you are running away from?" said a person from behind.

There was something familiar in the voice, something that compelled Pramila to turn back. Under the hastily darkening night stood a figure in a crimson sari. Framed by stark white hair was a face that Pramila could have sworn she had seen before.

"In our own ways we are all running from something, no? The way you are rushing-rushing, you must be running from something very bad indeed."

"I just don't want to miss the bus." Pramila made no motion, still staring at the figure.

"You think you know me, isn't it? Maybe you are trying to place me. I was once a much younger woman." The old woman's tone was light even as her expression remained serious.

"You resemble someone else I have met in the past only," Pramila answered.

"Oh, I suppose you have seen others like me before? Have you laughed at us? We know that you speak about us with scorn."

In the fading light, the woman's hair glowed indigo-white. Her features were aged, stunning. Pramila knew her to be *hijra*, but there was something else about her.

"No—your voice—it is familiar."

"How can that be? In a city as large as this?" the woman said coyly. "Most people look upon us and avert their eyes. They mock us, harass us. Only when they want us to confer blessings do they seek us out. But if you tilt the mirror a bit, you will find that we are only a reflection of what is around us. We are as ancient as the *Ramayana*. We are here, we have always been, we will always be."

Pramila turned back toward the temple to get her bearings. The night was nearly complete. The desperation was catching up fast.

"Children are different, much more curious . . ." The woman smiled. And now, Pramila was certain that she had met this woman before.

"Ah, you are remembering, no? So long ago it must have been. You were merely a girl—"

"You remember me also?" Pramila asked. She tried to dust off obscured memories long since past, holding on to one recollection in particular. It was from long ago—a vague memory of a wedding procession and a group of women who had held it up demanding a ransom.

"I never forget a face. I never forget the conversation. Every wedding or birth that I have attended. I remember the families upon whom I bestowed the blessings. You were but a girl when we met. Do you remember?"

As Pramila racked her mind, a young man approached.

"Madam, is this one bothering you?" He sneered at the woman in the rumpled sari with revulsion.

"Bothering me? No, she and I are speaking only. You are the one that is bothering me. *Arré,* get out of here and don't create trouble where there is none," Pramila scolded, irate at the man for deriding the old woman.

They watched as the man walked away.

"Do you remember what I said to you?" the woman persisted.

"No. Please tell me."

"From so many years ago you remember me? But you have forgotten my words? Come now!" She laughed.

"I was but a girl, you said so yourself. I have long since forgotten."

"Forgotten? I doubt it is so." With that, the old woman smiled a lovely, perceptive smile, walked in a small circle around Pramila, and waded into the darkness of the night.

"Wait," Pramila begged as she reached for her remaining rupees, but the woman had disappeared around a street corner. Pramila followed her, but she was gone.

Pramila scanned the street, crowds of unknown people milling about. She needed to get home. Slowly she made her way to the bus stop, with each step trying to prod open that tiny fold in her mind in which the memory of the woman resided.

Maybe she was merely some sort of apparition, a creation of a faltering mind. But the music at the temple had been real. Her walk through Zaveri Bazaar felt like a delusion but her argument with her sister earlier that morning was real. Her first few days in India had felt like a dream. But leaving America, that was real. Trying to escape her despair, that was real. Leaving her husband, that was real. Leaving her newborn daughter, that was real.

She opened her eyes widely as if seeing things clearly for the first time in months.

"*Me su karyu?* What have I done?" Here she was waiting for a bus, in the middle of the night, on some strange street corner, thousands of miles and oceans separating her from the child who would someday wonder what had become of her mother. Could she live with that?

◆ ◆ ◆

When she finally arrived back to the flat that night, the lights were on and Ba had fallen asleep on the small sofa. As Pramila entered the room, Ba sprung up.

"*Pramila, kyan hati?* Where were you? You have made us worry so much. Are you okay?" Ba placed an arm around her younger daughter.

"Ba, I have made a terrible mistake." Pramila's speech faltered. She thought about the letter she had penned; no doubt it had already made its way to Dev in America. And there was nothing she could do about it now.

Ba was silent for a moment then glanced Pramila's cheek with her finger. "Yes. I know."

"Ba—"

"Go rest, my child," Ba said softly, "you have come a long way."

Pramila took her mother's slight frame in her arms and embraced her.

Afterwards, Pramila laid upon the mattress and tried to sleep. She thought about the old woman in the crimson sari. What had the *hijra* said to her? Like liquid, Pramila's memories began to run together. And soon she was a girl, aged six or seven, back in the courtyard of Sikkanagar, her feet in chappals that her sister had outgrown. She watched a youthful incarnation of the elegant old woman speak to her uncle and then turn in her direction. Pramila could not take her eyes off the woman. Just then the fabric of her aunt's sari fell in front of her—momentarily turning the world magenta. Pramila had pushed the fabric out of her way. The woman approached her and smiled. It was a perceptive, lovely smile. And then she leaned toward Pramila and whispered in her ear. This time the *hijra*'s voice was unmistakable.

There are many, my child, who believe that fate befalls us regardless of how we choose to act. But long ago, a guru born in these lands taught that fate befalls us <u>unless</u> we choose to act.

◆ ◆ ◆

The sun had scarcely risen when Pramila awoke the next morning. Traces of the scent of night jasmine spilled through her open window from the street below. She piled her night clothes, tunic sets, saris, and blouses beside her and folded each one the way Ba had taught her. She had the *chai* on the table when her mother and sister emerged from their rooms. Ba glanced at her and nodded. At 10 a.m. she called the travel agent to find out when he could book the next ticket back to Buffalo.

Chapter 30

Tucked away in Vini's apartment, having escaped the mayhem outside, the three of us surveyed each other and then, in unison, burst into laughter. Shalu, not having been privy to the exact nature of Champa's accusations, must have been laughing at the absurdity of the adults. Vini and I were laughing mostly out of relief, I even more than she, given my run-in at the shop earlier that day. I was also more than a bit giddy from my twenty-four-hour emotional roller-coaster—running out on Arjun, threatened by some unnamed man on the street, stumbling upon my mother's secret. It was all too much to process and laughter seemed a sensible response.

Vini and Shalu began putting the groceries away, Shalu noisily recapping her surprise at the number of people on the landing as she had made her way up the stairs earlier.

"*Arré*, Shyamala didi was looking so much furious when I finally saw her."

"I know, isn't it? I have never seen her so angry." Vini dropped her voice. "I can't remember the last time somebody stood up for me in that way! Champa's expression was too good!"

"I am so much sorry I missed it," Shalu said, conspiratorially.

"*Na re na*. No, no. It is better you didn't hear any of the nonsense. Enough of that talk. Tell me how your lessons went today."

Shalu began recounting what she had learned in her history class earlier that day. She was washing long beans in the sink. Vini was putting away groceries.

"We learned about Bay of Pigs."

"Did you get marks on your maths exam?" Vini asked.

"Ninety-nine percent. I beat Amish by ten points!" Shalu said with pride.

"Why not a hundred percent?" Vini inquired, her intonation reminding me of my mother.

"I did not show all of my work and Miss took off one point."

"She is a tough Miss. But I've heard your papa tell you exactly that!"

"I know," Shalu said, seemingly more disappointed that she was being lectured at than actually having missed a point.

In watching the two, I was struck by the rhythm of their movements around the tiny kitchen. They prepared dinner without any need to consult each other, anticipating what needed to be done, not once colliding or working at cross-purposes.

Their manner of speaking also had a rhythm. Vini spoke with the informed curiosity of a family elder. Shalu responded in the tones of a child cared for, a child held to account. My heart flooded with affection for my aunt and the way she had created a second home for Shalu. It occurred to me how often I had taken the efforts of my own parents for granted.

"Shyama, what is going on over there? You look lost in your own world! Come set the table." Vini handed me a pile of plates, bowls, and silverware.

I took them from her, content to play a role in their domestic scene.

Before long, the scent of *rotis* cooking on an open flame met that of popped mustard seeds, cumin and turmeric and wafted out of the kitchen. We brought out the steaming dishes one by one, the conversation warm and familiar. We ate heartily, Vini and I choosing not to mention the controversy on the landing. Perhaps Vini felt it too, the particular alchemy of the evening, a fusion of setting, mood, and tacit solidarity, and had no desire to bring reality into the mix.

After dinner, as we cleared the table, I suggested that Vini and I go walk the Seaface at Nariman Point to give Shalu a couple of hours to study without distraction.

When we finally emerged from the building, the atmosphere outside was muggy. Dark clouds lurked overhead. Seeing this, Vini rushed back to the apartment, emerging with an umbrella.

"You're an optimist," I said when she returned.

She took a whiff of air. "It is going to rain tonight."

I glanced at the sky. It had appeared just as threatening many times before and had not relinquished its moisture.

Down the gentle slopes of Walkeshwar we went in the taxi, headed for Chowpatty Beach. This route, along the shore on Marine Drive, was now steeped in memories.

"Are you quite all right, Shyama?" Vini observed me. "You never did say what happened last night, with Arjun."

"Not sure I'm ready to talk about it."

"No need then. When you are ready, no?"

I nodded, glancing at the bay through my open window. My hair blew in the breeze the entire way to the Seaface.

We stepped on to the walkway, among a throng of people who had seen an opportunity to bask in the relative coolness of a cloud-covered sky and had flocked to land's end. The pungent scent of the sea overwhelmed me. Then a wind whipped from the shoreline, whisking away the smell. *Dupattas* and saris were blown about,

312

hairstyles were ravaged. If anyone felt inconvenienced though, it was impossible to tell.

We veered toward the wall that paralleled the water's edge. The sea beyond it was restless, gray-brown and murky; it swirled and seethed, sending off huge swells that crashed into the coastal barrier wall and sent off a cool sea mist that delighted the people on the walkway. I marveled at the massive concrete breakwater just beyond it that looked like a tangle of oversized jacks strewn about by some leviathan playing a game with his friends. Just then, a wave broke against the wall, and a thin veil of water rose high into the air, bathing us in the mist as well. Maasi laughed like a child. I couldn't help but do the same.

We walked along the sea wall for some time, our heads turned to the water's edge. I sensed my opportunity and dipped my toe into the controversy.

"Maasi, why did Champaben say those things on the stairwell today?"

She turned to me and answered somewhat flippantly. "Boredom, I suppose. Since Arjun doesn't live in her house, she can't run his life any longer. What has she left to do?"

My heart lurched at the sound of Arjun's name.

"No other reason?"

Maasi scrutinized me. She took her time before speaking.

"Shyama, if you mean to ask whether the rumors are true, I am not sure what to tell you," she answered, impatiently.

"It's just that today after my run, this guy I've never seen before came up to me and started saying things. He was making vague threats."

"What? Are you okay?" Vini gave me a quick once-over to confirm for herself.

"I'm a little rattled. But he wasn't threatening me, Maasi, he was threatening you. He said you owed him money." I swallowed hard and braced myself for my next words. "Are you being blackmailed, Maasi?" As it left my mouth, the sentence sounded ridiculous.

"Why would anyone blackmail me?" my aunt asked with amusement, her initial alarm dissipated.

I felt myself falter. Perhaps I had misconstrued what the well-dressed man had said at the shop. I thought back to his remarks.

No, I was certain. He had made threats against my aunt.

I took the plunge.

"Because of—maybe because of your relationship with Rajesh?"

Maasi sighed impatiently and shook her head. "I tell you, one spoiled grain of rice rots the whole jar! No, Shyama, no—I am not having an affair with Rajesh. People are so bloody predictable, isn't it? First with Shalu, now with me—they just love to jump to the conclusion they find most vulgar. Shalu is a teenager without a mother, she falls sick and needs the medical attention. Well, obviously, she must be pregnant! Vini speaks to Rajesh late into the night and cares about his daughter. Well, obviously, she must be having an affair with him! How does any of this bloody affect Champa and the rest of the neighbors? The only vulgar thing, in actuality, is their way of thinking. Forget about the truth! Meanwhile, the whole of the complex, all of Mumbai has no water to drink! I tell you it is absolute bullshit!"

I nodded sheepishly. She was right. It was absolute nonsense and I had fallen for it. Still, that didn't explain why the man had threatened me in the shop in Walkeshwar. A huge swell rose against the breakwater but receded without sending forth a gush of water.

"So, then you're not being blackmailed?" I asked with reticence.

"I wouldn't call it blackmailed exactly."

I knew it! I wasn't imagining the furtive nature of those phone calls, something unseemly had been going on. I decided to take a different approach.

"Do you know this man who was threatening you?"

She nodded. "Where exactly should I start? We weren't supposed to run out of water so quickly but water supplies in the city depleted much faster than anyone was expecting. Has Shalu ever told you how much difficulty she had to get the water at their house? Listen, India is no different from anywhere else, if you have enough money, you can make the system work for you."

Maasi glanced at me, seemingly expecting that I would grasp her train of thought. Seeing that this was not the case, she forged on. "Several months back, before you came to India, I made an arrangement with a man at the water tanker company. To increase water supplies elsewhere."

"Elsewhere?" My mind whirred as it tried to piece together what Vini was saying. "You mean Rajesh and Shalu's neighborhood—her home?"

Vini nodded.

"But where did the water come from?"

"Well, that is a long story." Vini looked down as she spoke. "As you might imagine, water can be difficult to acquire during a drought."

I felt as though I was pulling a stray thread from a sweater and as I pulled, more and more of the sweater was coming undone. I thought back to the landing from earlier in the day. And then it occurred to me.

Without warning, I stopped walking. "You aren't stealing water from your own building, are you?"

Vini stopped as well. A couple walking behind us collided with us, grumbling at our carelessness.

"Are you pilfering water from your own building?" I whispered, suddenly conscious that others might be listening.

Vini turned to me and I knew the answer to the question before she had uttered the answer. "Yes."

"And this arrangement is based on some sort of baksheesh? A bribe to reallocate water to the slum? Water that you and your neighbors paid for—water that you have been stealing from your neighbors and—yourself?" I could hardly believe what I was hearing. Maasi must have been keeping an account in that ledger that she stashed in her metal *cabat*.

"Listen, our building gets more than our fair share of water. The water I am helping to redistribute—it's not much, I know. It probably makes no difference in the big picture. But I couldn't go along pretending like things were so bad for me when I know that things are much worse for others. I am just not able to do it."

I glared at Maasi incredulously. "If you have been paying a baksheesh this whole time, why is that man threatening you now?"

"The law of supply and demand, isn't it? Demand has gone up and now he wants me to pay a higher price."

After accidentally rerouting the traffic behind us, Vini began to walk again, though her pace was much slower. I trailed a step behind, trying to put the pieces of her story together.

"Are you going to pay?"

"Eventually," my aunt said, unfazed. "He has come around making threats like this before. But he wants his money more than anything else, so he'll stay quiet."

It was hardly a bona fide strategy. If Maasi didn't pay, would he reveal her deception to her neighbors? I faced the horizon where the gray of the sea met the gray of the sky and the barely perceptible line in between. In that instant, I felt it, the rain that was coming.

I turned to my aunt, though she spoke first.

"Shyama, you are looking at me like I have lost my mind." Maasi paused in consideration. "Okay, I admit it only, I am a bit crazy. But there is more to the story. I know you have been struggling with this thing between our families, Rajesh's and ours. Maybe if I explain it, you will understand better."

"Go on." I could taste the salty sea air on my tongue. I was having difficulty imagining an explanation that would make the situation clear.

"A long time ago we made a promise," she said, as a gust of wind snapped my *dupatta* over her shoulder.

"We?" I pulled the fabric back.

"Your mother and I."

"What kind of promise?"

"The kind one makes as *tapas*—how do you say it in English?" Vini thought for a second. "Penance. At least, I think that was how Pramila saw it."

"Penance? For what?" I asked, suddenly knowing exactly for what. My mother had penned it on to the old aerogram tucked into the pages of *The Good Earth* that sat on my nightstand.

"I didn't realize what was happening at the time. But things become clearer as the years go by, no? You see, your mother felt that she had made an unforgivable mistake long ago. This is why she sought penance. But after all this time, I am still not sure she has forgiven herself for it, not to this day even."

"Please tell me more." My words were barely a whisper.

We walked on, my aunt retelling the story with each step, while wind whipped from the sea.

Chapter 31

Bombay, 1993

On her first evening in Bombay, Pramila sat on Vini's sofa, contemplating how many hours it had been since she had sat on her own sofa in LA. How many miles had she traveled going back and forth between India and the United States over the years? How many countries had she flown over making the voyages? Even one such journey would have been unimaginable to her own grandmother. As many times as she had made the trip over the years, she was surprised at how each time, it elicited the same feeling. She felt it now. It could only be described as a sense of fracture, a reminder of a certain twoness, a being neither completely here nor there. The Bombay that she still called home existed only in the past, the cadence of life in America now more familiar.

Pramila was relieved she had come to Bombay to be with her sister at this time. Just the week before, Vini's maid, Chandrika, had died in a car accident. Vini was devastated. With Pramila in the US, Vini had lived alone since the death of their mother. Chandrika and her husband Rajesh had become a sort of surrogate family. Rajesh had recently begun working for Vini as well, doing odd jobs and occasionally serving as driver and mechanic. And now there was the matter of their daughter, Shalu.

A few hours after Rajesh had left for the day, he returned, with an inconsolable Shalu in his arms. The baby must have been about eighteen months old.

Vini answered the door. "What happened?" she asked in Gujarati, concern in her voice.

Rajesh was frenzied. "I am sorry for coming so late in the evening—this is the only place I could think to come."

"Come in, come." Vini swung the door wide open and smoothed the child's hair to soothe her.

Pramila shifted into the corner of the sofa to allow space for everyone. She glanced at Rajesh. He appeared exhausted; his eyes had heavy bags underneath them. Instead of relaxing against the back of the couch, he perched on the edge. Sitting in her father's lap, Shalu peered, wide-eyed, around the room. Her sobbing slowly settled. With an unknown setting to explore, she soon got bored of crying and before long, toddled about the couch.

The adults in the room watched the child.

"How am I going to raise Shalu without her—without my Chandrika?" Overcome with sorrow, he swallowed. "I don't have anyone in Bombay."

Pramila considered Rajesh's sentence, allowing the gravity of the words to sink in.

"Could you send for someone from back home?" Vini inquired.

"I wish I could. Who would I send for? I have two younger brothers. Neither one is married. They are not able to take care of a child. And my mother and father are old now, I cannot bring them to Bombay at their age."

As Vini and Rajesh spoke, his attention was glued upon the child, tracking every move she made. Shalu made her way to the bookcase and grabbed a sandalwood box off a shelf. She turned to her father, seeking his approval.

Rajesh tilted his head slightly, as if to say no.

Shalu put the box back on the shelf but did not remove her hand; she turned to her father again.

Vini stood up and walked to the shelf. She picked up the box, opened it, and handed it back to Shalu. With this, the little girl dropped heavily on to the floor, bottom first, and began opening and closing the box. Vini walked to the kitchen and returned with a few small spoons. She handed them to Shalu who began arranging them in the box, first putting all the spoons in the box and closing it, then opening it and taking all the spoons out. Each time she closed it, she turned to her father and smiled.

Pramila smiled too.

Distraught, Rajesh did not seem to notice. "All I can think is to send her away to live with my parents."

"Where do they live?" Pramila asked.

"In Kosamba, Gujarat, five hours' train ride from here."

Pramila's stomach dropped. The idea of Rajesh being that far from his only daughter bothered her immensely. The many reasons why slipped into her consciousness even as she tried to push them away.

"What choice do I have but to send Shalu away?" Rajesh shrugged his shoulders in desperation.

Shalu heard her name and walked to the couch, her plump little hand carrying several spoons. Pramila held her hand open and Shalu gingerly placed two spoons in her palm and looked up at her. As she closed her hand around the spoons Pramila smiled down at her. Then she opened her hand and gave one spoon back and then the other. Shalu accepted them and went to retrieve the box. Sensing she had found a playmate, the little girl leaned her little body against Pramila's legs, preparing for a serious game of hand-the-spoon-back-and-forth-and-put-it-in-the-box.

Pramila was surprised that she had earned Shalu's trust so quickly. While they arranged and rearranged the spoons, Pramila's ears remained trained on the conversation between Vini and Rajesh.

"There must be something that can be done." Vini rubbed her chin.

"It is best for her anyway, *na*? Look at me, I can hardly keep going!"

"I don't think this is a good time to judge. You have hardly had a chance to even mourn Chandrika, isn't it? You must not make a hasty decision."

Pramila desperately wanted to express her agreement, but hesitated. In the drama that was unfolding, she was a character with a bit part.

Shalu raised her arms at Pramila.

"*Tane uppar aavu che?* Do you want up?" Pramila loved the sweet, sing-songy quality of Gujarati baby talk.

Gently, Pramila placed Shalu on her lap facing forward. It was a strange feeling, one that she rarely experienced anymore—the feeling of holding a young child. She found the warm presence pleasing despite the heat of Bombay. Shalu opened the box and began removing the spoons again. She craned around and looked at Pramila for approval. Pramila smiled and kissed the baby's head, taking in a deep breath of that long-forgotten baby smell.

"There is no time only. Every day I do not work, is a day that I cannot pay my expenses. I must send the money back home. My youngest brother still has school fees to pay, my mother has to pay to see the doctor."

"Rajesh, as I told you before, I can help with those expenses. Let me pay for those days you haven't worked yet. If you must, you can consider it advanced payment," Vini said.

"You have increased my pay once already, I am not taking handouts," Rajesh answered sternly.

It seemed inconceivable to Pramila that an employer was demanding to pay her servant more and the servant was refusing the raise.

Pramila heard the muffled thud of the spoons hitting the couch. She glanced down at Shalu. The baby was still except for the quiet motion of her chest rising and falling. Her head was in the crook under Pramila's shoulder and she was fast asleep. Poor thing was probably exhausted from the week, Pramila thought, a week that the girl was too young to know had changed her life forever. She brushed the baby's hair with her fingertips and settled into the rhythm of her breath. It was a remarkable sensation, the heavy carelessness of a baby slumbering in her arms. She tried to remember how it had felt to hold Shyamala so many years ago.

Rajesh hesitated. "You must think I have come begging for help. This is not my intention. My father and grandfather and great-grandfather before him, we have always worked, we have never asked for—I just—I just didn't know where else to go."

Though she hardly knew Rajesh, the desperation in his voice was too much for Pramila to bear. Sitting on the couch, she took Vini's hand in hers. Vini's eyes met Pramila's. An understanding seemed to flow between them, the sister who had always wanted a child and the sister who had nearly given hers up.

Vini nodded slightly.

Pramila spoke deliberately, her eyes fixed upon Shalu. "Let us help you, Rajesh—we will arrange for Shalu's care so you can work. Shalu has lost one parent, we must do everything we can to make sure she doesn't lose the other."

How many years had it been since she had left Shyama on the neighbor's front porch? Somehow, the words still felt like redemption.

"What this child needs, you tell us, but you must not send her away. You must never send her away. She needs her father. And you need her," Vini said as if the debate was settled.

"But I cannot accept—"

"Not to worry. This is no favor to you, Rajesh. This is between me and Chandrika," Vini said simply. She squeezed Pramila's hand.

Rajesh opened his mouth to speak but was overcome. He inhaled, swallowing once before speaking.

"This thing—this thing that you are doing—I can never . . ." He raised his hands as if in prayer and bowed his head slightly.

"It will work, *na*? Then we are set! No more needs to be spoken! Shalu can stay," Vini resolved.

"*Shuk—*"

"*Arré?* None of this *shukria-bukria* business. Thank yous are for Americans. Not family. This is family business!"

"And before you know it, she will be old enough to start school. She must get admission into a good one, no?" Pramila knew full well the price tag to get admission to such a school. "I have an idea that will work."

"Look at this, Rajesh, one might think Pramila is the elder sister, isn't it? I had better understand what I am agreeing to, *na*?" Vini said with amusement.

Pramila elbowed Vini, careful not to wake the baby. "For years, I wore Viniben's hand-me-downs—frocks and chappals. Don't think I have forgotten who is the younger sister!"

The two women laughed, causing Shalu to stir slightly.

Vini shushed her younger sister. "*Arré*, you'll wake the baby!"

Pramila settled the child for a moment, tucking Shalu's hair away from her face and straightening her dress where it had gotten caught beneath her. Vini studied her sister, wearing a slightly furrowed brow and conciliatory half-smile. They had just made a promise to Chandrika's daughter, a promise each sister knew was about more than childcare and schooling. Though they would never speak of motives afterwards, Vini knew just how much the promise meant to Pramila. And she knew the reasons why.

"These things you are doing for Shalu—for us—even in our dreams we could not have imagined such kindness. Once Shalu is old enough to know, she must know the truth of our agreement. A man can sacrifice his pride for his daughter, but only his daughter. I am begging, no more talk of paying me extra. Me and Shalu must live as we do now. In the home Chandrika made for us."

Vini looked at Rajesh admonishingly but did not scold him for thanking her.

Though she could have held the sleeping child all night, Pramila realized it was time to give her back. Cradling Shalu's head in her hand, she gently handed the baby to Rajesh. For the first time that evening, Rajesh smiled, if only slightly.

Before Rajesh and Shalu left for the evening, Pramila went to her luggage seeking a particular item. She had packed it after she heard about Chandrika. It was a yellow and green blanket that she had crocheted for Shyamala years ago. Now in college, Shyamala had long since forgotten the old thing and Pramila thought it might bring some small comfort to Shalu. She pulled the blanket out of her suitcase and placed it around the toddler for her bus ride home.

After Rajesh and Shalu left, the two women sat on the couch in the living room. Vini read the paper, flicking it from time to time and commenting on the stories as she read. Pramila gazed at the room which was bathed in warm light and listened to the soundscape created by Vini's voice and the occasional snap of the newspaper. She imagined the scene from the outside and smiled to herself. She thought that, perhaps, an onlooker might see contentment in it.

For more than a decade, she had carried this burden with her, this shame. Heavy, unwieldy, its weight had taken a toll. She had wanted so much to be liberated from it, to jettison the guilt she felt over her abandonment and alienation from Shyamala. But she could not let it go. Even when she heard that doctors had a name for that period after Shyamala's birth—post-partum depression, they called it—she still could not forgive herself for what had happened. So many years later, she still felt it weigh on her relationship with her daughter. Until tonight. Until tonight, when she felt that weight give, if ever so slightly.

In the darkness of the night, where the seen and unseen become one and truths often reveal themselves, Pramila realized something. Perhaps she hadn't simply been seeking liberation from her past mistakes. It was more than atonement that she had desired. She had wanted redemption. Not in her next life or any lives that her soul might embody in another incarnation. She wanted redemption in this life. Now she had the chance.

Chapter 32

Despite the ominous appearance of the clouds to the west, people continued to gather at the Seaface, undeterred. The sea was turbulent, bubbling and swirling as though sitting over a flame, ready to boil over. Vini and I continued to meander along with the masses as she recounted her story.

"You know, your mother and I have never spoken about that promise we made to Rajesh."

"Why not?"

"I understood, in part at least, why it needed to happen this way. She needed a chance to forgive herself and I needed a chance for her to forgive me. What more was there to say?"

"I don't understand why she would need to forgive you." I was still unraveling the mysteries that defined the relationship between sisters.

"When she came to India in that dark period after you were born, I could have done better. I was not the sister Pramila needed me to be. I was not sympathetic or understanding. Maybe it came from jealousy. I had been the one who wanted a family and there she was, given the greatest of gifts, and she was throwing it all away." As Vini spoke, she pulled her *dupatta* over her shoulders to shield her arms from the wind.

"I can't imagine she blamed you."

Vini considered me. "Do you know that prayer we Jains recite during the *Paryushana* holiday?"

"*Pratikraman*?" I knew it as the Jain prayer of atonement.

Like Jains throughout the world, my mother recited the *Pratikraman* prayer every year during *Samvatsari*, the last day of *Paryushana*. In an intricate process, the prayer enumerated the harms an observer might have committed against other living things, from simple one-celled creatures to fellow human beings. Through the words of the prayer, transgression by transgression, we sought forgiveness for harmful action, thought, or intent. There was immense power in the act. Even as I thought about it wandering along the Seaface, the hair on my arms stood on end.

"You see, just because she didn't blame me doesn't mean that I was blameless. I was resentful and cold when Pramila needed me most and I have never forgiven myself for it." She averted her eyes, overcome by emotion. "When we made that promise to Rajesh—it was for me as much as for Pramila. I was trying to redeem myself too. Who knew, at the time, that I would grow so close to Shalu? Whatever gift we thought we were giving that night, we—I—have received far more in return, isn't it?"

I thought back to dinner earlier that evening and the unassumingly tender mood that pervaded Vini's apartment. How quiet her life would have been without Shalu's presence.

"When I heard about the water problems at the slum, what was I to do? I couldn't just pretend nothing was happening. I had to *do* something, isn't it? Even if the water I stole was not enough, it felt like the right thing—the only thing—I could think to do. Pramila is family, yes. But she is so far away—that girl and her father are all that I have here in Bombay."

"Does Rajesh know about the water?"

"He knows I was working to help the slum acquire water—he might know I twisted a few arms to get what I wanted. He does not know that the water—um—happens to be redistributed from our building—without the knowledge of the other residents—or that I am paying a baksheesh to get it to the slum." She cleared her throat and regrouped for an instant. "*Bilkul* no! Are you kidding? He won't even let me pay him one rupee more, won't even keep the change if I give him money to buy a part for the car."

"But Maasi, I still don't understand one thing. Why all this talk about some kind of—um—relationship between you and Rajesh?"

"To some people, it seems unimaginable that someone like me could become friends with someone like Rajesh—that I could care for him without some sort of funny business." Maasi hesitated, that Victorian sensibility revealing itself again. "But if that kind of nonsense keeps people from realizing I have been stealing water from right under their noses, then the bloody fools deserve it! Growing up with Pramila has taught me to appreciate a good prank!"

I nodded and laughed.

A low grumbling sound came from the west. We turned our attention to it. The band of clouds off the coast was a foreboding shade of gray save for a single silver-gold ray that pierced the sky.

"So, does it make sense now how I got involved in all of the water"—Maasi cleared her throat—"the water redistribution business?"

"I think so."

In the farthest periphery of my vision, I saw a flash of light and then heard a deafening crash. I jerked my head toward the clatter and watched, in awe, as the sky unleashed one continuous torrent of water into the raging sea beneath it. We stood less than a quarter of a mile from the downpour.

Maasi instinctively reached for her umbrella and opened it. Within seconds, the cataclysm consumed us. A jubilant whoop arose from the crowd as Mumbaikars finally got what they had been waiting for. I found myself cheering as well as water edged in on us from every direction. Despite the rain, the air was still warm.

We ran to the road swept along by the mass of people trying to escape the deluge. People scattered at the edge of the road, everyone trying to hail a taxi.

Maasi peered at me under the umbrella that covered us.

"Well, Maasi, you said it would rain!" I yelled over the downpour, holding my hands out in the torrent.

She motioned at the street. "Look at how everyone is behaving, it is like they have never seen rain before!"

While the rain fell on us from above, a wave broke against the sea wall and sprayed us from the side with salt water. Following on the heels of the giant wave, a gust of wind nearly tore the umbrella from Maasi's hand.

"Might as well fold up this bloody thing before it takes out someone's eye," she said. At least, I thought that was what she said; without the scant protection of the umbrella, the rain pounded deafeningly on my head.

As we proceeded along Marine Drive, the sky was fraught and dusky. Save for us and a few other unfortunate souls who still hadn't found a cab, the walkway was now abandoned. Street traffic had come to a crawl as drivers contended with a sudden abundance of water. Curtains of rain fell without pause. The water seemed to have no point of origin and no destination, as if the earth itself had been submerged in an enormous pool. This was no Californian shower, I thought to myself. This was something else entirely—this was the monsoon.

◆ ◆ ◆

For two weeks it rained and rained and rained. The city that had been consumed by drought for many months and had prayed for relief from the skies now discovered water to be leaking from every imaginable space. During downpours, people living in low-lying areas could find themselves wading through waist-deep waters. Worli, one of the coastal enclaves of the city, received nearly twenty inches of rain during a single twelve-hour-long cloudburst. Traffic was often at a standstill, trains intermittently stopped running, and rickshaws were seen being carried off by streams that once were roads. Everyone from the shopkeeper in the suburbs, to the venture capitalist on Malabar Hill, to the slum dweller in Dharavi, experienced the relentless, destructive power of dripping water as they counted the leaks in their shops and homes.

In years past, the city had seen its fair share of inconveniences due to torrential rain and flooding. But this was different. The monsoon season had begun months later than usual. In Bombay, the average yearly rainfall, most of which comes during the monsoon, was usually seventy inches. This year it had capped a hundred inches with no end in sight. The city was paralyzed. Nobody had seen a monsoon season like this in living memory, Vini said. Really.

Each day, I watched TV and read the paper to find out the latest. Just as it was during the drought, the city's obsession was with water. When would there be a break in the downpours? What was the city doing to alleviate the flooding? When would the trains run consistently again? Would the flooding lead to outbreaks of the mosquito-borne dengue virus? And still, it seemed, few would wish to go back to that driest of dry spells. One could deny or despair at it, but the world around us was changing. In the future, there would be a day when the rains that quenched the thirst of our ever-wanting species would not come.

Given the city's water-logged condition, Vini urged Rajesh and Shalu to stay with us until things settled down. Shalu could stay with us, he said, but he would remain behind to tend to their home. I could only imagine how their tin-roofed house was faring in the deluge.

My office was mostly shuttered during this time. It simply took too long for people to come into work and, when they did, the availability of power was spotty. When the power and phone lines were down and I couldn't work, I read *The Good Earth*, often by candlelight. I was grateful to have uninterrupted time to dig into it. I had finished the book but was gripped by the end of the story, reading it over again and again.

The farmer's saga grew ever more tragic with each re-reading, the drama more evocative under the flickering candlelight. I bore witness as he lost his wife to illness and each of his six children to marriage or war or alienation or death. Throughout the story though, through drought and famine and war, he had held on to his land. Until now, the last scene. As if I were in the corner of the room, I watched as the now decrepit farmer listened to his two sons scheming about selling his land. I watched as he begged them not to sell it. To do so, he pleaded, would spell the end of their family. Lost within the scene, I couldn't help but feel sorry for him. But then I thumbed through the pages of the book, rife with displays of his avarice and selfishness, his betrayal of his wife. Maybe he had it coming all along. Over and over again, I went back to that final scene, opting for candlelight even when we had power. I couldn't decide whether the farmer deserved his bad fortune.

During the hours that phones were operational, I reached out to friends and co-workers to find out how they were faring. Arjun called twice on my mobile. Both times, as the device rang and his number flashed on the screen, I willed every molecule of my body to resist picking up the phone. I refused to listen to the messages he left.

Thoughts of Arjun aside, there is a limit to how much a human being can tolerate being confined to four walls. On day fifteen, noticing a brief break in the rain, I double-knotted my sneakers and hit the wet pavement. The air was so sodden that I felt as though I was inhaling the billowy center of a cumulus cloud. The narrow road was relatively quiet save for the occasional chirping of a songbird. The pipals and the gulmohars and the palms swayed gently in the slight breeze, renewed by the water that now flowed readily to their roots. I slowed to a walk. For one blissful moment in Mumbai, it seemed I was alone.

I thought of the farmer and his wife, of my mother and Vini, of Arjun and Neil, of Natasha and Daniel, of things past and things present, of the mistakes we make and how we come to terms with them. I thought about the simultaneous reality and illusion of control and what we know and what we don't know about those we love. As I walked under the fern-like leaves of a gulmohar tree, a heavy raindrop spilled down and splattered upon my cheek where Arjun had once kissed it. I did not wipe it away.

All this time, I had carefully constructed this picture of what the perfect life was—the perfect house in LA, the perfect husband in Neil, the perfect relationship with my parents—but fate didn't conform to the outlines of that picture. The more I was bound by expectation, the more shaken my faith in the future became.

That night at Arjun's apartment, he had picked up on a subtlety that even I had not. Truth was, I had longed for Arjun, yearned to feel his touch since Chowpatty. Still, I had never admitted why I wanted him, not to him and not to myself, even as his wild-haired worldliness grew to occupy more and more of my idle thoughts, even as he unfurled the truth of his past, even as I thought I was being forthcoming. Perhaps I was holding back to protect myself from being hurt again. Perhaps I was using his busybody mother and his job in New Delhi as excuses, an escape hatch to avoid taking the plunge again.

Back at the flat, I dialed my parents. It was the first time I had called since I read my mother's aerogram.

"Hi Mom."

"Hi *beta*." She sounded upbeat. "How are you? I was just about to call to check in again with all that rain in Mumbai."

"I'm fine. It's insane over here though—one minute everyone is praying for the rain and the next, everyone is praying for the rain to stop. I've never seen it pour like this."

"If Mumbai is anything, it is a place of extremes, no?"

"That's an understatement. Anyway, we've been managing. I've been working from home. Shalu has been staying with us."

"Vini was telling me. She must have grown so big since I last saw her." My mother spoke with affection.

I hesitated for a moment, trying to figure out exactly how to bring up what I had learned. "Mom, I heard what you and Maasi are doing for Shalu and Rajesh."

"Vini told you?"

"She did. She told me—quite a lot." I wanted to tell her that, in so many fragments, I had come to know her story. I had sought understanding of my mother's past and gotten a glimpse of it, in all its mortal complexity. But I couldn't explain what I knew, not now, not over the phone, perhaps never. Vini had been right; it was only my mother's story to tell.

There was silence on the other end of the line. Eventually, my mother spoke. Her words were halting, as if she were tailoring them to fit what she thought I must now know.

"There are many things that I have regretted, Shyamala. Life doesn't always go the way you plan." Her voice was laden with emotion. "But I have learned over time that there is a—a *mithaas*—a

333

certain sweetness to imperfection. Every now and then, in some unexpected way, you might even get a chance to make things right."

For the first time in a long time, I understood exactly what she meant.

"Mom, I am sorry for those things I said before I left." I was relieved to offer the apology, realizing just how much the exchange from months ago had bothered me.

"You mean, when you told me that you did not want the type of life I had?"

I felt a searing pang of guilt as she spoke. She had not forgotten.

"Listen *dikra*," she said, using the Gujarati term of endearment my father usually used. "Mothers and daughters, we don't always see the big picture when we relate to each other, we misunderstand sometimes, we argue sometimes. We are like parts of a braid. At times we are pulled away from each other, going in opposite directions. At times we are pushed together. We go back and forth, back and forth. In the end, though, we are eternally intertwined. We are bound as one."

I breathed heavily into the phone, overcome by my mother's grace. "I know, Mom, but it still bothers me—what I said."

"Let it be, now."

Through my window, I saw the rain start up again. It came in wild droves. Everything beyond the glass pane was obscured.

"Is that the rain?" my mother asked from 8,500 miles away.

"You can hear it?"

"Oh yes. I know that sound well," she said wistfully. "It is the sound of home."

"I guess it is, Mom. I guess it is." I held the phone away from my face so my mother could hear the rainfall. We both listened until she had to go. Gently, I hung up, walked to the window, and watched the rain fall.

After twenty minutes or so, Shalu poked her head into my room. I was happy to see her.

"I am just making the cold coffee. Would you care for a cup?" she asked.

I laughed.

"Why are you laughing?"

"That last bit you said, you sounded just like me!"

"Shouldn't I learn English from an American?" she asked innocently.

"Of course! Unfortunately for me, though, while your English gets better and better, my Hindi has hardly improved at all!"

Shalu grinned and didn't contradict me. She went to the kitchen and brought two delightfully frothy cups of the brew out to the table.

I sat across from Shalu and sipped the sweet-bitter-creamy-cold concoction.

"Didi?"

"Yes?" I looked up from my cup.

"Do you miss the America?"

"I guess I did for a while. But lately, with everything going on over here, I haven't thought much about it."

Shalu ran her finger around the rim of her cup.

"Are the things more fair over there?" she asked. She had her long hair in a bun. Wisps of it escaped the arrangement making her appear even younger than her fifteen years. She waited intently for an answer.

"More fair?"

"I have heard that, you know, things are more fair in the America. That there are no poor people like me. That everyone has equal chance and it doesn't matter which is the family you are coming from."

I sipped from my cup deliberately, thinking about how to respond.

"I'm not sure any country is as fair as it should be. There are poor people in America. Some people get more opportunities, some see more discrimination. People achieve success, even those who come from tougher situations. But it isn't easy and it isn't always fair."

"I think about fairness all of the times. Every time I leave my place and come here, I think of it only. All these posh flats in Walkeshwar. But Papa says it is too much time-pass, that I must concentrate on my studies."

"I think about fairness too, Shalu."

"Papa says we cannot control what others do. Why then to waste the time? We must just do our part to make the life better for ourselves."

"Your father is a wise man." Even then, I couldn't help but think about those who lived in gilded towers, presiding over the world below. If fate was responsible for any part of their success, should that not invoke some desire to make the world a fairer place?

"Do you think I will succeed?" Shalu gulped her coffee. Her gaze was intense, just shy of piercing.

I felt the immense weight of her inquiry and answered with care. "Shalu, I'm as certain of that as any one of us can be certain of anything in this world."

"But somebody had to give me a chance, no? Vini aunty and Pramila aunty, they are giving me a chance," she persisted.

"Maybe you would have succeeded without help, Shalu." I tried to sound hopeful for the both of us. But then I considered the odds of a poor, low-caste girl moving away from the slum.

"I don't think so." Shalu gave voice to my own doubts.

"I don't have the answers, Shalu. What I know is that everyone deserves a chance and all of us need help along the way. Birth and timing and luck, they all play a role in how we will fare in life. Maybe those things matter more than anything else. But I think skill and capability and effort matter too. And none of us knows the exact recipe."

Shalu sighed, her expression pensive. "That is what Papa thinks also."

"But destiny is also made of opportunities taken, don't you think?" I said.

Shalu nodded and smiled. "Didi?"

"What, Shalu?"

"If you have forgotten all about the America, maybe you should just stay here. I will too much miss you when you go." Her sincerity would have crushed the doubt of the fiercest of cynics.

"I will miss you too." I reached across the table, taking her delicate hands in mine.

As Shalu sipped her coffee, my heart ached for her. I wondered how many children through time must have asked the same questions, only to receive the same inadequate answers.

After a handful of days of additional rain, the forecast predicted a two-day break over a weekend. The sun, finally having cast off its vaporous cloak, shone brilliantly from the sky, mirrored a million times over in every puddle and pond in Bombay. I decided to take the bus to the suburbs to see Natasha. She announced plans to take me shopping. Apparently, she had seen enough of my baggy tunics and mismatched leggings.

From my moving perch on the bus, I could see that unintended urban lakes had formed on streets all over the city. But road conditions only deter the driving of those who are faint of heart. Our bus driver apparently was of a more steadfast ilk. Undaunted by the flooding, he grinned as the bus careened through the streets, sending arcs of water from its wheel wells high into the air. Three times I gritted my teeth, fearing that the bus would spin out of control or lose traction and simply float away. But like some whip-wielding circus master, he managed to tame the beast into submission and the bus sped from one stop to the next, grinding to a stomach-turning halt on arrival. My stomach had barely reoriented itself by the time I reached Natasha's flat.

After the hi's and hellos were exchanged and the customary tea was drunk and the snacks were eaten, we hailed a rickshaw to Santa Cruz bazaar. The rickshaw*wala* dropped us off several blocks from the market. Once our feet hit the pavement, we were caught in a gush of human traffic. There was no choice but to move forward. I joined their ranks, not once losing track of my conversation with Natasha despite the obstacle course around me.

The bazaar was a series of cramped permanent and semi-permanent edifices along a narrow walkway in which the shopper could find anything from bangles to bras to hair clips to decorative knick-knacks to stainless-steel dishes. Sitting under white fluorescent lights, shopkeepers hawked deals to passers-by.

When we entered clothing stores, shopkeepers pulled out tunic after tunic, sari after sari from the shelves, unfolding them and displaying them for our approval. The fabrics came in a mind-numbing profusion of colors and designs. Some fabrics had gold borders, others had detailed beadwork and embroidery. There were more choices than I could wrap my head around and after a while I merely nodded in approval or shook my head in rejection.

Thanks to Natasha's ever apparent competence, I left the bazaar with two overflowing shopping bags full of the latest Indian fashions (fitted and tailored on-site), gifts for friends and family both local and abroad, and a handful of accessories that Natasha concluded, in distinctly South Asian fashion, that I needed. Natasha hadn't mentioned Daniel once the whole afternoon. Nor did I bring up my breakup with Arjun, though he was not far from my thoughts. All in all, the afternoon was a success.

The bus home was standing room only by the time I entered. I gripped the railing overhead with one hand and my shopping bags with the other. I observed the swarm of brown faces around me and smiled. Nobody around me knew I was an American. In their ignorance, for just an instant, I could shed my hyphenated state of being. People are the lifeblood of a city, and I was just one of many residents coursing through its veins.

All at once, the scent of something familiar drifted in the tepid air. I took it in again. It was a fragrance—sweet and delicate. *Floral*, I thought. It was floral. Tightening my grip on the railing to steady myself, I closed my eyes and took another long, deep breath, determined to identify the scent.

At first, I couldn't place it. But with each successive breath, I grew closer—laden as it was with recent memories and redolent of sea air, sun-soaked sand, and formless possibility.

I opened my eyes.

Jasmine.

The scent came from somewhere toward the front of the bus. I craned my head forward and saw a young woman with a lei of white flowers bound to her hair. I let the essence of the flowers fill me, conscious that something within me was shifting. I felt as if the weight of all that had happened in the past months rested on some unseen fulcrum. And now, the slightest of forces applied at just the right moment—the scent of jasmine of all things—had tipped the balance. Without thinking, I adjusted my shopping bags and my tunic and found myself inching my way to the bus exit well before my intended stop. The conductor shot me a puzzled expression as I passed him.

Like everyone else disembarking, I jumped off the bus while it was still moving. Still in Santa Cruz, I walked along the busy street through an abundance of car and rickshaw horns, knowing I was close to where I needed to go. I walked at a vigorous pace despite the heat. When I was unsure of where to turn, I asked for directions in broken Hindi.

Finally, I turned into a familiar alley. Where the alley ended, I entered the apartment complex and boarded the elevator, greeted by its white-haired operator.

"Seventh floor only?"

"Yes," I said, the fragrance of the jasmine still lingering in my mind.

The elevator slowly clambered up the shaft. I felt each turn of its pulley. My shopping bags felt inordinately heavy. My mind was spinning.

When the elevator crawled to a stop, the operator pulled back the wrought-iron gate and regarded me apathetically. I exited and turned right.

The hallway seemed far longer than I recalled it. With each step, I felt my assuredness falter. Perhaps I should turn around. There were so many ways this could go wrong. There were so many reasons why it wouldn't work. I thought about my conversation with Shalu and about how destiny is made of opportunities taken, rolled my shoulders and shrugged off the doubts. I felt possessed by something I could not name. Was it merely fate—the scent of those flowers tied into a stranger's hair that brought me here? Or was it free will that took hold of my feet and propelled me forward?

Apartment 718 drew closer. My footsteps slowed. I reached the door and stood there, unable to decide what to do. Finally, I dropped my bags on either side of the door and tucked a lock of hair behind my ear. I could have adjusted my tunic or re-braided my hair, but I didn't.

When I had gathered the courage, I rapped my knuckles against the door. I could hardly hear my knock over the buzzing in my ears.

I waited, my chest rising and falling as if I were engaged in some momentous effort.

Perhaps he was home.

Perhaps he wasn't.

I pressed my right hand flat against the door. My heart thudded at twice the speed of the second hand of a clock. For an instant, I thought about running, about sprinting down the hall and into the stairwell. But I stood still.

The door slowly receded from my touch. I raised my head.

He stood at the threshold, unshaven and wild-haired as ever, his expression like none I had seen before.

Arjun.

"Shyama?" he asked, as though discerning reality from hallucination.

I looked at him, my clothes rumpled, my errant lock of hair loose again, my will entirely sapped. In making my way to his threshold, I had revealed all I felt and there was nothing left to say.

He reached toward me. An eon passed before he finally cupped my cheek in his right hand. With his left, he gently tucked the lock back behind my ear again.

I put my hand over Arjun's and sighed. We stood that way for a while, his hand on my cheek, my hand on his hand.

"I don't know what will happen." My voice was unexpectedly steady.

"I don't either," Arjun said. Then, he withdrew his hand, stepped into his flat and swung the door open wide.

I glanced at him.

Without looking back, I picked up my bags and stepped inside.

AUTHOR'S NOTE

The places and events in Mumbai, including the drought that features so prominently in this story, are used fictitiously. It is notable that in 2005, Mumbai did experience an extreme monsoon season and in 2006 the season arrived early.

While I have tried to maintain accurate translations of Hindi and Gujarati as much as possible, in some cases I have taken the liberty of paraphrasing to convey a sentiment in a way that might be more recognizable to the English reader.

GLOSSARY

I have put together a list of words and phrases that my characters use in the book:

South Asian words

aarti—Hindu prayer ceremony

achcha—used to express agreement or emotion

agraha—polite insistence to a guest to accept hospitality

ahimsa—non-violence

ajaani—a stranger

anna—unit of currency

arré—hey, come on, are you kidding me, what?

aujo—goodbye

avvo—come in

ba—mother (capitalized when an address)

baap re—father (typically used as *arre baap re*—'oh my father', similar to 'oh my god')

bandhani—a technique that uses small knots or bindings in fabric to achieve a specific pattern when dyeing clothing

bapu—father

bakwas—nonsense

ben or bhai—a suffix to convey 'sister' or 'brother' among close acquaintances

beta—dear

bhagvan—god

bidi—hand-rolled cigarette

bilkul—absolutely

bindas—no worries

brahmin—the highest caste

cabat—cabinet

chaal—come on

chaali—central walkway in tenement housing

chalo—ok or let's go

chawl—type of tenement housing with a central walkway (*chaali*)

chup—shut up

desi—native/from the homeland

dava khanu—pharmacy

dholia—white person

dhamaal—a commotion

didi—older sister

dikra—term of endearment

Diwali—festival of lights, symbolizing the triumph of good over evil

diya—an oil lamp usually made of clay

dupatta—scarf worn over a *salwar kameez*

durbar—court

gilli danda—game played with a bat

goonda—hired criminal

gora—a white man

gulley—alleyway

hai hai—oh no or oh my goodness

hai-la—oh no

han—yes

handi—earthen pot

Harijans—the lowest caste

hijra— "the third gender"

kanya-daan—giving away the bride

Janmashtami—celebration commemorating the birth of Lord Krishna

jhopadpatti—slum

ji—a suffix conferring respect

jo—look

kem—why

kurta—tunic top

limbu—lemon

maasi—maternal aunt (capitalized when an address)

mandap—temporary platform often adorned with decorations

masti—fun or mischief

maya—illusion

mithaas—sweetness

mithai—sweets

na/nai—no

namaste—I bow to you or greetings to you

paisa—unit of currency

phataphat—quickly or hurry up

Paryushana—the most important annual Jain religious observance of the year

Pratikraman—Jain prayer ritual

puja—prayer

pyaar—love/affection

rangoli—Diwali decoration made from colored grains of sand

sabji—vegetables

sadhvi—a nun or religious ascetic who has renounced worldly possessions

sakar-badam—sugar and almond

salwar kameez—tunic and matching pants

samjho—understand this

sasuma—mother-in-law

seedha—straight ahead

shabash—excellent or wonderful; an exclamation that denotes approval

shramaniji—a Jain teacher

shukriya—thanks

tapas—penance

Tirthankaras—Jain religious leaders who have conquered the cycle of birth and death

walas—sellers (a suffix)

yaar—friend

zapat—shoes

South Asian dishes and foods

bhelpuri

burfis

chai

dahi

dal

dhansak

garam masala

gathia

ghee

Gobi Manchurian

gola

googras

halwa

idli

jalebi

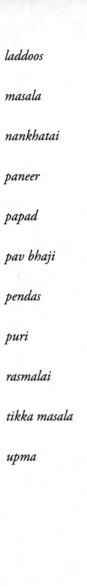

laddoos

masala

nankhatai

paneer

papad

pav bhaji

pendas

puri

rasmalai

tikka masala

upma

Phrases not translated in the novel

Main dhone ke liye aapke kapde le ja sakti hun—Can I take your clothes for washing

Aap ni Shalu kaisu hee?—not translatable because Shyamala's Hindi is off

Kem cho—How are you?

Govinda ala re ala—part of a song that commemorates Lord Krishna and the Dahi Handi

Me ek a beeladi pali che—line from an Indian lullaby

ACKNOWLEDGEMENTS

My journey writing *Dry Spells* has been filled with believers who have propelled me forward even as life and career often seemed to pull me in different directions. My deepest appreciation to Liv Maidment and the wonderful team at Madeleine Milburn Literary, TV and Film Agency who took a risk with my manuscript and shared in its sprawling vision. To Victoria Oundjian and the team at Lake Union for their passion and ambition for *Dry Spells*, including Victoria Millar, Sadie Mayne, and Swati Gamble. To Julie Woodside, Em Cooksey, James Skow, and Sharon Logan—my trusted workshopping group—who patiently provided feedback year after year, never settling for anything less than good, old-fashioned storytelling. Julie Woodside introduced me to my first beta readers from Bound by Books who had the patience to read *Dry Spells* out of thick three-ring binders and gave me the confidence to share the story beyond a few trusted friends. The Coffee and Ink group awed me with a breadth of wonderfully rich writing styles and provided me with endless encouragement and inspiration. To Phyllis Molloff, my tenth grade English teacher, who taught me to love the artistry of constructing a sentence, a process that has been a never-ending consolation in what can otherwise be a lonely endeavor. It was in her classroom that I first had the notion of writing a novel. *Dry Spells* also owes an immense debt to the keen observations of Octavio Paz in his lyrical essays from *In Light of India*. I am indebted to Pearl S. Buck, whose spare prose and profound social commentary in *The Good Earth* is featured in *Dry Spells*. Her work remains timeless and ever so relevant today.

For their quiet but unflagging encouragement, I owe much gratitude to my in-laws, Regina and Robert. To my family in Mumbai and Gujarat, whose boundless warmth will always make India home and to my family abroad who manage to capture the essence of India in even the most far-flung places. Special thanks go to Vandanbhai, who drove us all over modern Mumbai to visit the locales that became the heart of *Dry Spells*.

To Biju the cat, who cares neither for books nor acknowledgments, but whose quiet presence was the simplest of pleasures when I was writing.

To Kavita and Sanjay, whose little pattering feet were a welcome greeting on weekend mornings when I was typing away on my laptop trying to liberate the words that I had carried through my workweek. Over the years, they became my beloved second critique group (not always book-related!) and my most dedicated cheerleaders. To Brian, whose faith in me and this process was unwavering even as my doubts crept in. Without him, *Dry Spells* would never have made it into the world. To my grandparents, Kamalaben, Dalichandbhai, Leelavatiben, and Girdharlalbhai who came from small villages in India with an awareness of the immense importance of education. Finally, to Bakula and Harshad, for taking a voyage to a far-away place but never, ever letting me forget who I am and where I come from.

Archana

ABOUT THE AUTHOR

Photo © B. Thornton 2022

Born near Chicago to immigrants from India, Archana Maniar relocated with her parents to Mumbai at age four. After the culture shock abated, she fell in love with her homeland until chance brought the family to California. During vacations and family occasions, Mumbai was a frequent destination. She attended college at UCLA, where she studied political theory and biology before attending medical school at the University of California, Davis. As a professor of medicine and practicing infectious disease physician, she was a frontline healthcare worker from the start of the Covid-19 pandemic and was deeply involved in health system pandemic preparedness. Always a writer in the margins of her day, storytelling became an obsession during her medical career, a way to process her observations about human nature during health, stress, and sickness. With a stubborn case of wanderlust, when she is not working or writing, she is usually traveling somewhere with her family.

Follow the Author on Amazon

If you enjoyed this book, follow Archana Maniar on Amazon to be notified when the author releases a new book!

To do this, please follow these instructions:

Desktop:

1) Search for the author's name on Amazon or in the Amazon App.
2) Click on the author's name to arrive on their Amazon page.
3) Click the "Follow" button.

Mobile and Tablet:

1) Search for the author's name on Amazon or in the Amazon App.
2) Click on one of the author's books.
3) Click on the author's name to arrive on their Amazon page.
4) Click the "Follow" button.

Kindle eReader and Kindle App:

If you enjoyed this book on a Kindle eReader or in the Kindle App, you will find the author "Follow" button after the last page.